Non-Combatants and Others

Also published by Handheld Press

Non-Combatants and Others

Writings Against War, 1916–1945

by Rose Macaulay

with an Introduction by Jessica Gildersleeve

Handheld Classic 15

This edition published in 2020 by Handheld Press
72 Warminster Road, Bath BA2 6RU, United Kingdom.
www.handheldpress.co.uk

ISBN 978-1-912766-30-7

1 2 3 4 5 6 7 8 9 0

Series design by Nadja Guggi and typeset in Adobe Caslon Pro and Open Sans.

Printed and bound in Great Britain by Short Run Press, Exeter.

Contents

Jessica Gildersleeve is Associate Professor of English Literature at the University of Southern Queensland. Her research concerns the relationships between narrative, culture and affect, and has addressed a range of women writers of the twentieth and twenty-first centuries, including Elizabeth Bowen, Rosamond Lehmann, Katherine Mansfield, Sarah Waters, and Pat Barker. Her most recent books include *Elizabeth Bowen: Theory, Thought and Things* (ed., with Patricia Juliana Smith, 2019) and *Don't Look Now* (2017), a study of the cinematic adaptation of Daphne du Maurier's story.

Introduction

BY JESSICA GILDERSLEEVE

'Leave it at that'

Rose Macaulay's short story, 'Miss Anstruther's Letters' (1942), published in the middle of the Second World War, describes the aftermath of the bombing of the eponymous character's home in London during the Blitz. The entire block of flats, and almost all contained within them, are destroyed. Miss Anstruther has only moments to save what she can: a pile of books, 'a china cow, a tiny walnut shell with tiny Mexicans behind glass, a box with a mechanical bird that jumped out and sang, and a fountain pen' (277). In her panic she forgets her most treasured possession: a bundle of letters written by her lover over the course of two decades. Miss Anstruther herself is safe, but without these letters she is bereft. The sheaf of notes constituted her memories of the life they – for unexplained reasons – secretly and illegitimately shared. With the letters destroyed, her private relationship and private identity are similarly consigned to the flames. She is now only the anonymous, unloved, forgotten Miss Anstruther.

'Miss Anstruther's Letters' is frequently cited for its apparently autobiographical representation of Macaulay's sense of loss following the death of her married lover, Gerald O'Donovan, in that same year, and the destruction of her home in the bombing shortly after. Her cousin and biographer Constance Babington Smith, for example, includes this story in full in her 1972 biography of Macaulay, because, she says, it is 'a testimony of her love for Gerald ... which she wrote under the conventional veil of fiction' (Smith 1972, 161). Yet in its depiction of loss and trauma, the story also constitutes one of Macaulay's most haunting and evocative arguments against war.

At the story's end, Miss Anstruther stands perpetually accused of failure. In the floating ashes, she finds one remaining fragment of the bundle of letters. The scrap reads: 'leave it at that. I know now that you don't care twopence; if you did you would' (281). It is a devastating final blow: Miss Anstruther had failed to remember, failed to save, failed to care. Too late she 'remembered the thing she wanted most, the thing she had forgotten while she gathered up things she wanted less' (278). She had failed to care in the past and failed again to care now, such that the accusation stands; '[y]ou don't care twopence, he seemed to say still … the twenty years between were a drift of grey ashes that once were fire, and she a drifting ghost too. She had to leave it at that' (282). 'One must live how one can,' Elizabeth Bowen wrote in various refrains throughout her writing of the Second World War (Gildersleeve 2014, 9–11). Bowen expressed a determination to repair, to heal, to survive. But Macaulay's Miss Anstruther is, like her letters, like her home, like her life before the war, damaged beyond saving.

These mounting instances of failure form the core of Macaulay's writings against war, for they fail to effectively resist war's instigation and continuation. That is, it is precisely in our failure to remember, save, and care for and about love, community and connection, that we allow or approve of war. Like the useless but beautiful 'china cow,' 'tiny walnut shell,' and box with its singing bird, these are markers of civilisation which must be preserved. This is why Miss Anstruther is a ghost after the destruction of her home, merely 'a revenant … [who] still haunted her ruins' (275) – she is no longer human without the signifiers of civilisation.

By permitting war, by abandoning civilisation, we are savage or inhuman, Macaulay repeatedly asserts in the writings against war collected in this volume. 'War and more war, stupid and cruel destruction, the savage dancing his tribal dance, whooping in his feathers, tomahawk and war-paint, until the jungle swallows him up and the world as we know it crashes in ruins' (235). In 'Apeing the Barbarians' (1937), which uses now problematic racist and colonial terms, Macaulay compares war to 'heretic-burning and ordeal by torture, one of the primitive, age-old barbaric pests', noting that '[a]ll civilised people today admit that it is a childish and outmoded barbarity … But the snag is that large numbers of people in all countries are very little civilised' (229). Those who are civilised and see the arguments against war can find themselves intimidated by the 'savages' who are for it: 'Faced with savages who declare continually and publicly that they are proud to be militarist and that prolonged peace is an ideal for cowards and decadents, and that there can only be peace after their own domination of the world by conquest, the civilised lose their nerve and follow a bad example, not in words but in deeds' (231). The comparison continues in 'Consolations of the War' (1941): here, war is 'a grotesquely barbarous, uncivilised, inhumane and crazy way of life to have had forced on us by a set of gangsters who are making us use their own weapons and practise their own horrid incivilities – as if we were jungle savages like themselves instead of twentieth-century men and women who had hoped war to be for ever outlawed' (243).

In calling up and rejecting this association of civilisation with war, Macaulay is aligned with the attitudes of, for example, the Bloomsbury Group – Clive Bell wrote in 1928 that '[c]omplete human equality … is compatible only with complete savagery' (quoted in Hargreaves 1997, 138). Indeed, in an expression of the popular conviction of war's necessity, not only were the people of Europe determined to assert the barbarity of enemy nations – 'the Germans said that we gouged out the eyes of prisoners of war; we said that they made a habit of cutting off the arms of Belgian children and of crucifying Canadians' (222) – but, too, 'the 1919 campaign medals bore the inscription "The Great War Fought for Civilisation"' (Hargreaves 1997, 138). Thus, Macaulay concludes in 'Apeing the Barbarians', pacifism is necessary precisely because it represents the behaviour of 'reasonable beings'. In order to achieve this, 'all those who feel strongly on the matter should continue to protest against the present intemperate and nerve-ridden unreason which impels civilised and humane persons to ape the distasteful ferocity of the barbarians that we shall all, if we go on like this, extremely soon become' (235).

'Miss Anstruther's Letters' was written during the Second World War. This story, and the other essays collected here, written between 1936 and 1945, were the product of Macaulay's attitudes twenty years after she wrote her great anti-war novel, *Non-Combatants and Others* (1916). British history is so often dominated by discourses of victory and courage, as in the 'myth of the Blitz'. However, the history of pacifism and conscientious objection in a range of forms regularly disrupted such dominant public narratives. The works collected in this volume are part of an evolving history of pacifism and attitudes to the First World War in Britain, from the early years of the Great War until the closing years of the Second.

Pacifism and changing attitudes to the Great War in Britain

In late 1916, Siegfried Sassoon was home on convalescent leave. But by July 1917, when he was commanded to return to the front, he refused. His open letter, 'Finished with the War: A Soldier's Declaration,' was published in several newspapers and read aloud in parliament.

> I am making this statement as an act of wilful defiance of military authority because I believe that the war is being deliberately prolonged by those who have the power to end it. I am a soldier, convinced that I am acting on behalf of soldiers. …

> On behalf of those who are suffering now, I make this protest against the deception which is being practised upon them; also I believe it may help to destroy the

callous complacency with which the majority of those at home regard the continuance of agonies which they do not share and which they have not enough imagination to realise. (Sassoon 1917)

His protest would be a significant turning point in British responses to the war, since for a serving officer to make such a potentially treasonous statement had hitherto been unthinkable. He was saved from a court-martial only by the actions of his friend, fellow soldier and poet, Robert Graves, who persuaded the authorities that Sassoon was mentally ill, suffering from shell shock (what we now recognise as Post-Traumatic Stress Disorder).

Sassoon stresses the suffering of soldiers in battle in his Declaration. This theme is famously common in the poetry of most of the British 'war poets', and represents the turn in poetic treatment of war from the neo-Georgian writing of, for example, Rupert Brooke. His poetry describes a far more innocent and painless belief in the mother country and war's aims than those of his successors, making clear the profound transition in attitudes to the war that took place in poetry between 1914 and 1918. His 1914 poem 'The Soldier' appears to suggest a unity between nation and soldier, men and women, and also implies the support of the non-combatant – my sacrifice for you means that you must 'think only this of me' (Brooke 2010, 139). The Brookes were family friends of the Macaulays, and Rose and Rupert were themselves great friends. Indeed, Smith asserts that Basil Doye in *Non-Combatants and Others* is based on Rupert and, too, that the description of Paul Sandomir's death in that novel is a way of mourning for him (Smith 1972, 70–71). It is certain that Macaulay would have read 'The Soldier' – it is equally likely that its cultivated innocence is the target of much of her anti-war writing.

Brooke's sentiments were rejected by the new wave of aggressively anti-war poetry by, among others, Isaac Rosenberg, Ivor Gurney, Wilfrid Owen and Sassoon. The cumulative effect of such works presents an ideological conflict, not only between Britain and its enemies, but between and among those on the war front and those on the home front, between combatants and non-combatants, chiefly between men and 'non-men' – women, and those men who cannot or will not fight. This conflict propelled for many years a widespread privileging of the combatant voices of wartime, rather than the perspectives of the non-combatants. Paul Fussell's *The Great War and Modern Memory* (1975), with its focus on the shell-shocked soldier and with little attention paid to women or the home front, is a case in point (Light 1991, 8). As Carol Acton points out, '[t]he male combatant has seen war, when war is defined as combat, and speaks of war from a privileged position. Seeing and its attendant knowledge give him the right to speak and by definition deny the woman who has not seen a voice' (Acton 2004, 55). This militarist discourse actively worked to oppress women and suppress their voices. Indeed, as one critic observed in 1914:

> The military state is the state in which woman has no place; the military mind is the mind that sees in woman only a drudge or a toy, and gives her the one right only to existence – the possibility of bearing sons who will in time become soldiers. Women may ... prove in a thousand ways their fitness to take part in public life – but it will avail them little so long as one vestige of the tradition and the point of view born of militarism remains in the world. The military point of view is that of contempt for woman, of a denial to her of any other usefulness than that of bearing children. It is this spirit of militarism, the glorification of brute force, and this alone, that has kept woman in political, legal and economic bondage throughout the ages. (Colbron, quoted in Costin 305)

Trudi Tate and Suzanne Raitt note that, even though a '[l]ack of knowledge was not gender-specific, nor even specific to civilians', during the First World War 'ignorance was often figured as feminine: a woman indifferently beautifying herself while soldiers die' (Tate and Raitt 1997, 2). Macaulay's novel is one of a few – such as Mary Agnes Hamilton's *Dead Yesterday* (1916) or Rose Allatini's *Despised and Rejected* (1918) – which depict, instead, what Acton calls 'a specifically female gaze' and way of 'see[ing] and know[ing] war'. In such works, 'the male combatant can become the object of the woman's gaze' (Acton 2004, 56), or, as in *Non-Combatants and Others*, the focus might instead be on the experience of wartime on the home front and the desire to abolish war altogether. Indeed, for all one must sympathise with the ordeal of the soldiers at the front, attitudes like Sassoon's must also be recognised as unfair, since patriotism was sharply distinguished on gender lines: 'a person who acts in a way consistent with her/his nationally endorsed gender script is also a patriotic person; one who does not is deliberately dividing oneself from national norms' (Albrinck 1998, 272).

This is critical for Macaulay, who recognised the way in which combatants and non-combatants alike were subject to the monstrous invasions and expectations of the war (see Tylee 1988, 208). The difference of experience is central to much women's writing of the period. Vera Brittain's memoir *Testament of Youth* (1933) shows how the tension between men's and women's wartime experience 'gives rise to a gap between the healing of the witness and the event witnessed' (Brittain 2009, 202). However, for Macaulay, as for Storm Jameson, the 'enemy is war itself – which robs them of their identity; and they cease to be clever, competent, intelligent, beautiful, in their own right, and become the nurses, the pretty joys, and at last the mourners of their men' (quoted in Tylee 1988, 206). From such 'borderline positions', Meg Albrinck makes clear, women wartime writers like Macaulay 'make the "uncomplaining" figure of the female volunteer speak the same horrors of war that soldiers do; in doing so, they affirm the soldier poets' arguments on war while balancing the soldier poets' depiction of wartime women' (Albrinck 1998, 280). In one sense, then, Macaulay's work suggests the importance of a sense of community and connection, not only among soldiers, or among civilians, but also between those fighting and those at home. Women's work at home was just as critical – if just as dull – as men's work on the front, Macaulay emphasises in her poem, 'Spreading Manure' (1916):

> I think no soldier is so cold as we,
> Sitting in the Flanders mud.
> I wish I was out there, for it might be
> A shell would burst to heat my blood ...
> I wish I was out there, and off the open land:
> A deep trench I could just endure.
> But, things being other, I needs must stand
> Frozen, and spread wet manure. (Macaulay 1916/2001, 168)

Indeed, at the beginning of the war, Macaulay's own youthful desire for romantic adventure on the high seas caused her to be envious of the men sent to battle when she too would have liked to participate. Later, however, this identification with the soldier's experience takes the form of a shared suffering – as in Alix's imagining of her brother's death – and a desire to prevent further unnecessary pain. Macaulay pays attention to the experience of women at home, and to that of non-combatants more broadly, thereby constructing a community of anti-war activists and sympathisers based on more than only on women's experience. That Alix is a largely androgynous figure, a non-combatant who limps, as if she is herself a returned soldier, breaks down those boundaries to drive the point home, while at the same time preventing her co-option as a symbol of 'Woman' for political use.

This is the fraught context in which Macaulay wrote, and in which *Non-Combatants and Others* appeared. The soldiers sent off to slaughter, returning shell-shocked, wounded, or not at all – they were voiceless, experienced beyond their years, and the novel is heartbroken by their senseless loss. The desperate attempted suicide of Alix's young soldier brother haunts the novel in this way.

Her friends instruct her, and the reader, 'not to *think*. Not *imagine*. Not to *remember*' his sadness, the fact that he 'was such a little boy' (112). As Acton and others assert, those at home were similarly silenced. All were victims of the great machine of war. This is the source of Macaulay's frustration, and the focus of her writing against war.

Sisters and brothers

Macaulay's life was, from the start, a strange mix of the conventional and the unconventional. She was the second of seven siblings, and her father, George Campbell Macaulay, was a scholar with radical political beliefs, who was rejected by a range of institutions until he eventually became Professor of English Language and Literature at the University of Wales in 1901. Her mother Grace (née Conybeare) was equally independent – even eccentric in her youth – though this had faded by the time her daughters were young women. Rose and the elder group of her siblings – 'The Five,' they called themselves – enjoyed a blissful childhood of freedom in the small village of Varazze in Italy, where the sisters and brothers played together without adhering to Victorian codes of gendered behaviour for boys and girls. The young Rose enjoyed swimming and boating with her brothers and read adventure tales which instilled in her a desire to one day become captain of a navy ship – what she described in 1944 as 'a heroical-romantic mood that craves adventure' (263). However, when Rose was ten years old, her toddler sister Gertrude contracted meningitis and died. It was an early trauma for the children. Shortly thereafter the family returned to England, where the idyll of her childhood was abruptly ended. Rose and her sisters were enrolled in the local school, and her aspirations of joining the navy were flattened. Perhaps the greatest sadness here for Rose was the disruption of her close bond with her siblings as she was divided from her brothers by gender and from her sisters by her independence. She did well at school and was sent to Somerville College at Oxford. But in 1909, her brother Aulay, who was working in India, was robbed for a pitiful sum of money and murdered by the side of the road. Rose was devastated.

Over and over in her writing we see the loss of babies, young children, and siblings, the trauma of death and of separation, and the disruption of equality and community. 'Many Sisters to Many Brothers' (1915), for instance, takes the form of a letter from a sister to a brother, recalling their egalitarian childhood now obliterated by a war which keeps him '[i]n a trench … while I am knitting': 'Oh, it's you that have the luck, out there in blood and muck: / You were born beneath a kindly star' (Macaulay 1915/2001, 72). This poem is typically read as evidence of Rose's lingering naval ambitions and her envy of her (literal and symbolic) brother's ability to fight, while she must hopelessly, uselessly remain at home. She worked as a 'land girl' and as a VAD nursing assistant, neither of which she performed with much success. After this early enthusiasm for the war, 'she rejected militarism for good' (Frayn 2014, 60). But in the context of her sibling losses, 'Many Sisters to Many Brothers' becomes more than evidence of her early romanticisation of the war: it manifests the fractured community of equality in which she had grown up.

Between these tragedies and the stress of her studies, Rose was unable to take her final university examinations (in the event she was awarded an *aegrotat* degree, signifying her qualifications). Like Woolf, it appears she suffered a number of psychological breakdowns throughout her life, although these were rarely acknowledged by her family and friends or, later, by critics. After leaving Oxford, she moved back to the family home and began to write. Her sixth novel, *The Lee Shore* (1912), won a Hodder & Stoughton prize, which made her financially independent for a number of years. She escaped her mother's constricting desire to keep her at home and moved to London to pursue her writing career – she would produce a book almost every year for the rest of her life. *Non-Combatants and Others* was her eighth novel, written in the midst of the First World War. It is, like most of her fiction, philosophy and thought shaped into narrative. Although her earlier works had enjoyed success, this latest novel did not. Its pacifism was confusing for a nation being asked to wholeheartedly support the war (Emery 1991, 155).

Pacifism and feminism during the wartime and interwar periods hold simultaneously complementary and antagonistic positions towards one another, and the question of what attitude suffragists should take to the war was a critical one (Byles 1985, 474). Emmeline Pankhurst, for instance, believed that militancy and militarism were critical to the role of the suffragist and moreover that patriotism superseded both: once war was underway, they devoted themselves to support for the war effort rather than the suffragist cause (Byles 1985, 474). On the other hand, in 1915, the International Congress of Women, in recognition of the association between militarism and oppression and therefore that 'suffrage was essential to peace,' signified a global effort by women to labour against the continuation of the war (Costin 1982, 305). Indeed, for many pacifist suffragists, 'war work was nothing more than capitulating to the argument for physical force; the whole point of democracy was that government no longer rested on brute strength but on the consent of the governed, and represented a higher stage of civilisation' (Byles 1985, 476). This attitude aligns with Alix's for much of *Non-Combatants and Others* – any work done in aid of the war is in support of its aggression.

By the 1930s, Macaulay's pacifism had become more formalised. She joined, with several other writers (including Bertrand Russell, Aldous Huxley, Storm Jameson, Vera Brittain and John Middleton Murry), as a member of the Peace Pledge Union (PPU), founded by Dick Sheppard in 1934 (Lukowitz 1974, 116–17). Although the works collected here signify Macaulay's pacifism, her biographers make clear that after Sheppard's death and as the Second World War wore on, Macaulay became less convinced by these arguments, even resigning from the PPU in 1938 (see Smith 1972, 140, 142). Yet in that same year Macaulay produced, with Daniel George, *All in a Maze*, an anthology of anti-war writing for the International Peace Campaign. Like *Non-Combatants and Others*, however, the book was not successful, coming again at a time when approaching war seemed to necessitate a patriotism with which she was at odds.

At its base, Cyrena Mazlin observes, Macaulay 'was repulsed by violence and battled with the prospect that on occasion it became necessary. Throughout her life, Macaulay suffered from constant concern about the means that nations used to achieve and maintain a kind of peace' (Mazlin 2011, 60). Thus, by 1940, when the terrors of what was really happening in Europe were starting to filter through to Britain, Macaulay admitted that there is now 'a choice of bestialities: let the foul scene proceed, or let it give place to one fouler, while we abandon Europe to a cruel and malignant enslavement, breaking faith with the conquered countries which look to us for freedom' (238). Rather conservatively, and perhaps in line with a reading of her life which refuses to see Macaulay at odds with the nation during the Second World War, Smith sees this as a 'superficial' and 'emotional' pacifism always in tension with 'the young hero-worshipper who had relished tales of daring, and had herself longed to be a man' (Smith 1972, 141). Ignoring the overt narrative of pacifism in *Non-Combatants and Others*, she claims that Macaulay's devotion to peace only appeared at the approach of the Spanish Civil War (139). The tension in Macaulay's pacifism is also articulated in her Second World War novel *And No Man's Wit* (1940):

> Oh, what does one mean by pacifist? I think war is horrible and cruel and grotesque, of course, and belongs to the dark ages as much as the rack and thumbscrew do. But if you ask me, is nothing worse, I thinks it's worse to let more and more people be tortured and enslaved without protest – I mean, effective protest. On the other hand, is war the only way to stop it, and have we tried all the others? Of course we haven't.

You see, I don't know what I think; one's altogether confused. It would be simpler if one could be wholly pacifist. But the pacifists don't seem to have alternative ways to suggest of stopping the Nazis. (Macaulay 1940, 315–16)

In a 1941 essay Macaulay argues that war should not be mistaken for 'a grand life': 'we think it is a perfectly beastly life, only to be endured because the things we are fighting against are still more beastly' (243). Ultimately, says Mazlin, Macaulay's pacifism can only be resolved by understanding it not simply as 'a protest against all forms of violence; rather, she believes that it is necessary to concentrate on an "active participation in peace-making" which, unfortunately, may involve violence in extreme situations' (Mazlin 2011, 61; see also Emery 1991, 251). These are what Sharon Ouditt calls 'the mental and moral dilemmas involved in making a transition from a position of indifference to the war to one which demands a positive commitment to opposing it and all future conflicts' (Ouditt 1993, 161). Those dilemmas are at the heart of *Non-Combatants and Others* and are being worked through in this novel and in Macaulay's later essays.

Non-Combatants and Others, War and the psychology of suffering

The writings collected here demonstrate the evolution of Macaulay's thought on war and pacifism. The development of her ideas between 1916, when *Non-Combatants* was published, and 1936, the first of the series of essays included here, and her writing of the Second World War, indicates a shifting subtlety of argument in the face of an increasingly difficult moral situation. '[M]orality is in a bad way,' she says in 1945 (269). But *Non-Combatants and Others* as well as these other writings against war demonstrate that Macaulay's overwhelming interest in the effects of war is their psychological impact. Indeed, in many ways it is thoughtfully engaged with the developments in psychoanalysis and trauma occurring around this time, particularly in relation to returning shell-shocked soldiers. This is what war does to us, she explains; this is how it damages us.

One of the ways in which this is made clear is, of course, in the representation of Alix's cousin John. Just returned from the war, he is at first shown to be suffering from physical injuries: he is 'home on a month's sick-leave ... with a red scar from his square jaw to his square forehead, stammering as he talked because the nerves of his tongue had been damaged' (9). He is the centre of the discussions at home, asked regularly for his opinion on the progress of the war. But at night, he sleepwalks. Traumatised, he stands 'barefooted, in pink pyjamas ... gripping with both hands on to the iron balustrade, his face turned up to the moon, crying, sobbing, moaning, like a little child, like a man on the rack' (23). Alix responds with horror, rejecting the experience as she is 'most suddenly and violently sick' (24), and aghast at her cousin Dorothy's suggestion that 'what they can bear to go through, we ought to be able to bear to hear about' (25). Macaulay is therefore quick to identify the profound effects of the war on the soldiers and on those at home, too. All are deeply damaged by its reach.

In these writings against war, a second way in which Macaulay records the psychological effects of trauma are in the structure of the narrative itself. *Non-Combatants and Others* as well as several of her poems of the period have a fragmented form. 'Picnic: July 1917' (1917), for instance, concludes:

> Oh we'll lie quite still, not listen nor look,
> While the earth's bounds reel and shake,
> Lest, battered too long, our walls and we
> Should break ... should break ... (Macaulay 1917/2001, 86)

The stanza might be seen to represent Alix's experience writ small, as she hunkers down, attempting to avoid the war until it invades and she and the poem both break. 'Miss Anstruther's Letters', too, formally articulates the damage of the traumatised mind as it moves back and forth in time, repeating particular moments and phrases as Miss Anstruther perpetually and unwillingly recalls the moment when her life was torn in two. This use of fragmentation and silence can be seen to represent the voicelessness of both combatants and non-combatants, as well as a structural confrontation of authorised wartime discourse (Albrinck 1998, 281). Alix's gender ambiguity and her lameness both perform a similar function – that is, while Jane Emery sees the latter as a 'sign of her emotional vulnerability' (Emery 1991, 150), Debra Rae Cohen observes that 'Macaulay uses Alix's lameness to unsettle the distinctions between soldier and civilian, wounded and unwounded, male and female war experience, and ultimately to deconstruct the very notion of noncombatancy itself' (Cohen 2002, 31). It is not so much that she is a woman out of place, but that her very presence articulates a line between the combatant and the non-combatant which destabilises wartime discourses of gender, strength, and morality. This challenge to authority is perhaps why Peter Childs argues that the novel 'express[es] a "female" Modernism' (Childs 2000, 133).

The suffering recorded in the novel is perhaps the more profound for the way in which it is a product of a series of overwhelming and universal lies about the war's justice and necessity, repeated and developed by the people themselves. Owen famously describes the Latin phrase 'dulce et decorum est, pro patria mori' (it is sweet and right to die for one's country) as 'that old lie' (Owen 1920/1994, 59), and Macaulay recalls this necessity for lies to continue war in the writing collected here. Dorothy's insistence that civilians should be able to bear to hear about what soldiers have experienced suggests that the soldiers have it worse than those at home, whereas Alix's suffering indicates otherwise. The theme recurs in one of Macaulay's essays published during the Blitz of 1940. Again, it is the non-combatants, those at home, who must be lied to if the war is to continue unabated. As an injured woman faintly calls for her baby, lost in the rubble of their ruined home, '[t]he rescue squad call back, "All right, my dear. We'll be with you in ten minutes now." They say it at intervals for ten hours' (236). Another mother, eventually rescued, calls for her own children as she is driven away in an ambulance: '"The children are safe," she is told. "They will be out quite soon. You'll see them soon." But she will not, for they are all dead, two boys of eleven and twelve, two babies of three and one. "If only," she moans, "they didn't suffer much ..."' (237). The lies told to these mourning mothers are the same as those told to the soldiers, the same as those told to the mothers of soldiers, and what is the difference, Macaulay asks. All *do* 'suffer much', all have lost their precious children to the monster of war. Dawn approaches. Still, the rescuers insist, 'All right, my dear, you'll be out in a jiffy.' But '[t]here are only two voices in answer now ... Not much hope now for the others' (237). 'Civilian war deaths are no worse than those of the young men in the fighting forces; all alike are sentient human beings, dying suddenly or in agony,' Macaulay tells us (238). All are suffering as the result of 'the blind, maniac, primitive, stupid bestiality of war' (238).

Alix is a softly spoken, gentle young woman. The noise and argument of and about the war is felt by her almost as physical blows, and she shrinks from the world, hiding from its awful knowledge. True, she is sensitive. But to a more nuanced and balanced view she might also be seen to enact Macaulay's observation that 'the voices of those with whom we disagree ... sound louder than those which utter our own views' (211). 'Truth comes treading soft-foot, murmuring like a dove or a noontide bee, scarce audible but to the instructed ear,' she says, 'while Error, harpy-like, rends the air with her shrieks' (212). Such is the effect of those by whom Alix is surrounded: merry and patriotic young people; thoughtless others; loud voices with no imagination. Yet when her mother returns, or she engages in conversation with her brother's pacifist roommate, their voices are soft, yet clear and powerful. To the pacifists only is reason and civilisation offered, while war and its proponents bang, crash, shriek.

In both *Non-Combatants and Others* and in her other writings against war, Macaulay repeatedly designates war in metaphorical terms as a monster and as a disease in order to describe its dominance: it is an 'encouraged and pampered monster ... growling on its maniac way' (233), while in 'Miss Anstruther's Letters,' the 'flames' of war destroy possessions 'like a ravaging mouse or an idiot child' (273). Similarly, '[n]o nation is immune, nor ever has been, from this unpleasant disease, the worst of which is that it is highly infectious. Once a state of war starts, all the combatant nations get it' (230). She quotes Max Plowman noting that fascism begins as 'an insidious infection' before developing into 'a full-grown disease' (233). The effect is a pervasive thoughtlessness in the wider populace, the mindlessness of the mass, so many modernists lament. 'Crowds have the half-ludicrous, half-sinister suggestibility of the pack, who may be sent by the huntsman's word after any quarry,' Macaulay wrote in 1936. 'Yet, taken singly, most of them [are] probably the ordinary, stupid, kindly Briton, who can be persuaded of anything' (216).

In *Non-Combatants and Others* as well as other essays here, the mass is often identified with those who mindlessly follow the teachings of the church: 'If by any chance Great Britain were to break several covenants, pledges and treaties, and invade, bomb and gas some weaker country in order to annex it, would that be unjust? It was unjust, we said, when Italy did it; but the Church to which the Italian State adheres said otherwise' (224). But Macaulay is careful to distinguish between different manifestations of 'the Church' in this novel, for it is not faith but religion with which she takes issue. At Mass with Kate, Alix struggles to make sense of the preacher's symbolic representation of 'the strong city' (121): 'what sort of strength had that city? Was it merely a refuge, well bulwarked, where one might hide from fear? Or had it strength to conquer the chaos? ... The city wasn't yet strong enough ... Would it be one day?' (122–23). There are only questions here – the novel, written midway through the war, cannot imagine its end. However, towards the end of the novel Alix admits to her brother that not only does she plan to join her mother's 'funny society', she 'shall very probably join the Church, too, before long ... it seems to me to stand for all the things she stands for and some more, of course' (197). It is a decision and a tension which might be seen to articulate those shared by Macaulay and O'Donovan, whose commitment to formalised religion wavered throughout their lives – a belief in the *caritas* and community offered by the Christian church, while holding strict reservations about the narrow-minded xenophobia which so often accompanied these behaviours.

So where are we left at the novel's end? A series of vignettes depict the various characters ringing in the new year – an act of hope for rebirth and renewal amid the devastation and death of the war. But the final sentence cannot achieve any resolution: 'The year of grace 1915 slipped away into darkness, like a broken ship drifting on bitter tides on to a waste shore. The next year began' (206). It foreshadows the language of T S Eliot's 'The Waste Land' (1922), a poem Macaulay would much admire. Eliot's poem, however, was written after the war, and can afford the hope it offers at its conclusion. Macaulay's novel cannot. If 1915 is a 'broken ship' cast adrift, its passengers are left stranded. Where shall we turn? Alix chooses pacifism and the church – active choices, if nothing else. Perhaps, in the end, it is thoughtless passivity which comes in for the harshest criticism: those who fail to feel, fail to care, and fail to act, in any sense.

Works cited

Acton, Carol. 'Diverting the Gaze: The Unseen Text in Women's War Writing', *College Literature* 31.2 (2004): 53–79.

Albrinck, Meg. 'Borderline Women: Gender Confusion in Vera Brittain's and Evadne Price's War Narratives', *Narrative* 6.3 (1998): 271–91.

Brittain, Vera, *Testament of Youth: An Autobiographical Study of the Years 1900–1925* (London 2009).

Brooke, Rupert, *Rupert Brooke: Collected Poems* (Cambridge 2010).

Byles, Joan Montgomery, 'Women's Experience of World War One: Suffragists, Pacifists and Poets', *Women's Studies International Forum* 8.5 (1985): 473–87.

Childs, Peter, *Modernism* (London 2000).

Cohen, Debra Rae, *Remapping the Home Front: Locating Citizenship in British Women's Great War Fiction* (Boston MA 2002).

Costin, Lela B, 'Feminism, Pacifism, Internationalism and the 1915 International Congress of Women', *Women's Studies International Forum* 5.3/4 (1982): 301–15.

Emery, Jane, *Rose Macaulay: A Writer's Life* (London 1991).

Frayn, Andrew, *Writing Disenchantment: British First World War Prose, 1914–30* (Manchester 2014).

Gildersleeve, Jessica, *Elizabeth Bowen and the Writing of Trauma: The Ethics of Survival* (Amsterdam 2014).

Hargreaves, Tracy, 'The Grotesque and the Great War in *To the Lighthouse.*' *Women's Fiction and the Great War*, eds, Suzanne Raitt and Trudi Tate (Oxford 1997), 132–50.

LeFanu, Sarah, *Rose Macaulay: A Biography* (London 2003).

Light, Alison, *Forever England: Femininity, Literature and Conservatism Between the Wars* (New York 1991).

Lukowitz, David C, 'British Pacifists and Appeasement: The Peace Pledge Union', *Journal of Contemporary History* 9.1 (1974): 115–27.

Macaulay, Rose, 'Many Sisters to Many Brothers' (1915), *Cambridge Poets of the Great War: An Anthology*, ed. Michael Copp (Madison NJ 2001) 72.

— 'Spreading Manure' (1916), in ed. Copp (Madison NJ 2001) 168.

— 'Picnic: July 1917' (1917), in Copp (Madison NJ 2001) 85–86.

— *And No Man's Wit* (London 1940).

Mazlin, Cyrena, 'Rose Macaulay's *And No Man's Wit*: The Forgotten Spanish Civil War Novel', *Hecate* 37.1 (2011): 56–69.

Ouditt, Sharon, *Fighting Forces, Writing Women: Identity and Ideology in the First World War* (London 1993).

Owen, Wilfrid, *The Poems of Wilfred Owen*, ed. Owen Knowles (Ware 1994).

Sassoon, Siegfried, 'Finished with the War: A Soldier's Declaration.' 1917. *Wikisource* accessed 20 April 2020. <https://en.wikisource.org/wiki/Finished_with_the_War:_A_Soldier%E2%80%99s_Declaration>.

Smith, Constance Babington, *Rose Macaulay* (London 1972).

Tate, Trudi, and Suzanne Raitt, 'Introduction', *Women's Fiction and the Great War*, eds Suzanne Raitt and Trudi Tate (Oxford 1997) 1–17.

Tylee, Claire M, '"Maleness Run Riot" – The Great War and Women's Resistance to Militarism', *Women's Studies International Forum* 11.3 (1988): 199–210.

Note on the text

The text of *Non-Combatants and Others* was non-destructively scanned from the 1986 Methuen edition, and checked for typographical errors. The texts of the sixteen essays and 'Miss Anstruther's Letters' were typed from copies of the originals.

Non-Combatants and Others

To my brother
And other combatants

Let the foul scene proceed:
There's laughter in the wings;
'Tis sawdust that they bleed,
But a box Death brings.

Gigantic dins uprise!
Even the gods must feel
A smarting of the eyes
As these fumes upsweal.

Strange, such a Piece is free,
While we Spectators sit
Aghast at its agony,
Yet absorbed in it.

Dark is the outer air,
Cold the night draughts blow,
Mutely we start, and stare
At the frenzied show.

Yet heaven has its quiet shroud
Of deep and starry blue –
We cry 'An end' we are bowed
By the dread ''Tis true!'

While the Shape who hoofs applause
Behind our deafened ear
Hoots – angel-wise – 'the Cause!'
And affrights even fear.

— Walter de la Mare, 'The Marionettes'

War is just the killing of things and the smashing of things. And when it is all over, then literature and civilisation will have to begin all over again. They will have to begin lower down and with a heavier load … The Wild Asses of the Devil are loose, and there is no restraining them. What is the good, Wilkins, of pretending that the Wild Asses are the instruments of Providence, kicking better than we know? It is all evil.

— Reginald Bliss, *Boon*

There is work for all who find themselves outside the battle.

— Romain Rolland, *Above the Battle*

Part I

Wood End

CHAPTER I

John comes home

1

In a green late April evening, among the dusky pine shadows, Alix drew Percival Briggs. Percival stood with his small cleft chin lifted truculently, small blue eyes deep under fair, frowning brows, one scratched brown leg bare to the knee, dirty hands thrust into torn pockets. He was the worst little boy in the wood, and had been till six months ago the worst little boy in the Sunday-school class of Alix's cousin Dorothy. He had not been converted six months ago, but Dorothy, like so many, had renounced Sunday-school to work in a VAD hospital.

Alix, who was drawing Percival, worked neither in a Sunday-school nor in a hospital. She only drew. She drew till the green light became green gloom, lit by a golden star that peered down between the pines. She had a pale, narrow, delicate, irregular sort of face, broad-browed, with a queer, cynical, ironic touch to it, and purple-blue eyes that sometimes opened very wide and sometimes narrowed into slits. When they narrowed she looked as from behind a visor, critical, defensive, or amused; when they opened wide she looked singularly unguarded, as if the bars were up and she, unprotected, might receive the enemy's point straight and clean. Behind her, on the wood path, was a small donkey between the shafts of a small cart. A rough yellow dog scratched and sniffed and explored among the roots of the trees.

Alix said to Percival, 'That will do, thank you. Here you are,' and fished out sixpence in coppers from her pocket, and he clutched and gripped them in a small retentive fist.

Alix, who was rather lame, put her stool and easel and charcoal into the cart, got in herself, beat the donkey, and ambled off along the path, followed by the yellow dog.

The evening was dim and green, and smelt of pines. The donkey trotted past cottage gardens, and they were sweet with wallflowers. More stars came out and peered down through the tree-tops. Alix whistled softly, a queer little Polish tune, indeterminate, sad and gay.

2

Two miles up the path a side-track led off from it, and this the donkey-cart took, till it fetched up in a little yard. Alix climbed out, unharnessed the donkey, put him to bed in a shed, collected her belongings, and limped out of the yard, leaning a little on the ivory-topped stick she carried. She had had a diseased hip-joint as a child, which had left her right leg slightly contracted.

She came round into a garden. It smelt of wallflowers and the other things which flower at the end of April; and, underneath all these, of pines. The pine-woods came close up to the garden's edge, crowding and humming like bees. Pine-needles strewed the lawn. The tennis-lawn, it was most summers; but this summer one didn't play tennis, one was too busy. So the lawn was set with croquet hoops, a wretched game, but one which wounded soldiers can play. Dorothy used to bring them over from the hospital to spend the afternoon. An oblong of light lay across the lawn. It came from the drawing-room window, which ought, of course, to have been blinded against hostile aircraft. Alix, standing in the garden, saw inside. She saw Dorothy, just in from the hospital, still in her VAD dress. The light shone on her fair wavy hair and fair pretty face. Not even a stiff linen collar could make Dorothy plain. Margot was there too, in the khaki uniform of the Women's Volunteer Reserve; she had just come in from drilling. She usually worked at the Woolwich canteen in the evening, but had this evening off, because of John. She was making sand-bags. Their mother, Alix's aunt Eleanor, was pinning tickets on clothes for Belgians. She was tall and handsome, and like Alix's mother, only so different, and she was secretary of the local Belgian Committee (as of many other committees, local and otherwise). She often wore a little worried frown, and was growing rather thin, on account of the habits of this unfortunate and scattered people. One of them had been their guest since November; she was in the drawing-room now, a plump, dark-eyed girl, knitting placidly and with the immense rapidity noticeable on the Continent, and not to be emulated by islanders without exhaustion.

Alix's uncle Gerald (a special constable, which was why he need not bother about his blinds much) stood by the small fire (they were wholesome people, and not frowsty) with an evening paper, but he was not reading it, he was talking to John.

For among them, the centre of the family, was John; John wounded and just out of hospital and home on a month's sick-leave; John with a red scar from his square jaw to his square forehead, stammering as he talked because the nerves of his tongue had been damaged. Alix, watching from the garden, saw the queer way his throat worked, struggling with some word.

They were asking John questions, of course. Sensible questions, too; they were sensible people. They knew that the conduct of this campaign was not in John's hands, and that he did not know so much more about it than they did.

The room, with its group of busy, attractive, efficient

people, seemed to the watcher in the dark piny garden full of intelligence and war and softly shaded electric light. Alix narrowed her eyes against it and thought it would be paintable.

3

The dark round eyes of the Belgian girl, looking out through the window, met hers. She laughed and waved her knitting. She took Alix always as a huge joke. Alix had from the first taken care that she should, since the moment when Mademoiselle Verstigel had arrived, fluent with tales from Antwerp. It is a safe axiom that those who play the clown do not get confidences. The others looked out at her too when Mademoiselle Verstigel waved. They called out, 'Hullo, Alix! How late you are. John's been here two hours. Come along.' Alix limped up the steps and in at the French window, where she stood and blinked, the light on her pale, pointed face and narrowed eyes. John rose to meet her, and she gave him her hand and her crooked smile. 'You're all right now, aren't you?' she said, and John, an accurate person, said, 'Very nearly,' while his mother returned, 'I'm afraid he's a long way from all right yet.'

'Isn't it funny, it makes him stammer,' said Dorothy, who was professionally interested in wounds. 'But he's getting quite nice and fat again.'

'N-not so fat as I was when I got hit,' said John. 'The trenches are the best flesh-producing ground known; high living and plain thinking and no exercise. The only people who are getting thin out there are the stretcher-bearers, who have to carry burdens, the Commander-in-chief who has to think, the newspaper men, who have to write when there's nothing to say, and the chaplains, who have to chaplain. I met old Lennard of Cats, walking about Armentières in February, and I thought he was the Bishop of Zanzibar, he'd gone so lean. When last I'd seen him he was rolling down King's Parade arm-in-arm with Chesterton and I couldn't get by. It was an awfully sad change … By the way, *you* all look thinner.'

'Well, we're not in the trenches,' said Margot. 'We're leading busy and useful lives, full of war activities. Besides, our food costs us more. But Dorothy and I are fairly hefty still. It's mother who's dwindling; and Alix, though she's such a lazy little beggar. Alix is hopeless; she does nothing but draw and paint. She could earn something on the stage as the Special Star Turn, the Girl who isn't doing her bit. She doesn't so much as knit a body-belt or draw the window-curtains against Zepps.'

Alix looked round from the window to stick out the tip of her tongue at Margot.

'Mais elle est boiteuse, la pauvre petite,' put in the Belgian girl, with the literalness that makes this people a little *difficile* in home life. 'What can she do?'

Alix giggled in her corner. Margot said, 'All right, Mademoiselle, we were only ragging. There's the post.' She went out to fetch it. Margot was a good girl, but, like so many others, tired of Belgians, though this Belgian was a nice one, as strangers in a foreign land go. Alix hated and feared her whole nation; they had been through altogether too much.

Margot came back with the letters.

'Betty and Terry,' she said, with satisfaction. 'Betty's is for me and Terry's for you, mother.' (Terry was in France, Betty driving an ambulance car in Flanders.) 'Two for you, Alix.'

Alix took hers, which were both marked 'On Active Service,' and put them in her pocket. Simultaneously her aunt Eleanor began to read Terry's aloud (it was about flies, and bread and jam, and birds, and some music he had made and was sending home to be kept safe) and Margot began to read extracts from Betty's (about nails, and bad roads, and different kinds of shells, and people) and Uncle Gerald read bits out of the paper (about Hill 60, and Hartmannsweilerkopf, and Sedd el Bahr, and the *Leon Gambetta*, and liquor, and Mr Lloyd George).

4

Alix slipped out at the window and limped round to the side door and into the house and upstairs to the schoolroom, which she was allowed to use as a studio. It was littered with things of hers: easels, chalks, paints, piles of finished and unfinished drawings and paintings. Some hung on the walls: some of hers and some by the writer of the letter she took out to read. He painted better than she did but drew worse – or had, in the long-ago days when persons of his age and sex were drawing and painting at all.

Alix read the letter. It was headed obscurely with an R, some little figures of men, and two weeping eyes, which was where the writer was for the moment stationed. Every now and then a phrase or sentence was erased. The writer, apparently a man of honour, had censored it himself. His honour had not carried him so quixotically far as to erase the hieroglyphics at the head of the paper.

It said:

'Dear Alix, Since I last wrote we've been moved some miles; I mustn't, of course, indicate where to. It is nice country – less flat than the other place, and jolly distant ridges, transparent blue and lavender coloured. I'll do a sketch when we get into billets at the end of the week. My company is in the trenches now; commodious trenches they are, the best in the line, but rather too near the people opposite for comfort – they're such noisy lunatics. It's eight o'clock now, and they've begun their evening hate; they do a bit every evening. The only creature they've strafed tonight yet is a brown rat, whom we none of us grudge them. It's interesting the different noises the shells make coming; you can nearly always tell what kind they are. If I was musical I'd make a symphony out of them. I should think your cousin Terry Orme could. Some of them scream thin and peevishly, like a baby fretting; some howl like a hyena, some mew like a kitten. Then there's Lloyd George's Special, which says "Lloyd-Lloyd-Lloyd-Lloyd", and then all the men shout "*George*".'

(A page of further discursion on shells, too technical for reproduction here. Then resumed next morning,)

'I'm fairly sleepy this morning; we have to stand to from two to six AM, expecting an attack which never came off. I wish it had, it would have been a way to get warm. We've had poor luck tonight; the Tommy who was sent over the top to look at the wire was made into a French landlord, and our sergeant-major stopped one with his head, silly ass, he was simply asking for it. It's my belief he was trying to get back to Blighty, but I hope they won't send him further than the base. You would like to see the dawn coming over this queer country, grey and cold and misty. I watched it through my peri for an hour. The Boches lay *perdu* in their trenches mostly, but sometimes you'd see one looming over his parapet through the mist. I want some tea now more than most things. You might write soon. You never answered my last, so it's generous of me to be writing again. How's everyone at the School, and how's life and work? Your enemies the Ruski seem to be in a tight place, don't they? – Yours, Basil Doye.'

Alix read this letter rather quickly. It bored her. It concerned the things she least preferred to hear about. That was, of course, the worst of letters from the front. Life at Wood End, as at other homes, was full of letters from the front. They seemed to Alix like bullets and bits of shrapnel crashing into her world, with their various tunes. She might, from her nervous frown, have been afraid of 'stopping one'. She twisted up the letter into a hard ball with her thin, double-jointed fingers, as she stared, frowning, at a painting on the wall. The painting was of a grey-green pond, floored with a thin, weedy scum. A hole-riddled, battered old tin rode in the middle of it; reeds stood very quietly round; a broken boot was half sunk in the mud among them. Over it all brooded and slept a heavy June noon. It was well painted; Alix thought it the best thing Basil Doye had ever done. They had spent an afternoon by the pond in June 1914; Alix remembered it vividly – the sleepy, brooding silence, the heavy fragrance of the hawthorn, the scum-green pond, the tin and the boot, the suggestion of haunting that they had talked of at the time and that Basil had got rather successfully into his picture afterwards. Those were curious days, those old days before August 1914; or rather it was the days ever since that were curious and like a nightmare. Before that life was of a reality, a sanity, an enduringness, a beauty. It still was, only it was choked and confused by the unspeakable things that everyone thought mattered so much, but which were really evil dreams, to be thrown off impatiently. Underneath them all the time the real things, the enduring things – green ponds, music, moonlight, loveliness – ran like a choked stream …

Alix read her other letter, which was from her young brother Paul, and also written in a trench. The chief thing she thought about this was that Paul's handwriting was even worse than usual. He wrote in pencil on a very small piece of paper, and scrawled up and down wildly. He might have been twelve instead of eighteen and a half. Paul was rather a brilliant boy. When the war broke out he had been a distinguished head of his school, and had just obtained a particularly satisfactory Oxford scholarship. His letters since he went to the front in March, had been increasingly poor in quality and quantity. It made Alix angry that he should be out there. She thought it no place for children and, as. Paul's elder by nearly seven years, she knew all about his nerves.

CHAPTER 2

John talks

1

'Alix, you'll be late for dinner,' Dorothy's voice called across the landing. Alix went to the big bedroom she shared with Dorothy and Margot. Margot was hooking up her frock; Dorothy was washing with vigour and as much completeness as her basin would allow, and complaining that John was occupying the bathroom.

'I hate not having a bath after hospital. But one can't grudge it to the dear lamb. How do *you* think he looks, Alix? Rather nervy, he is still. That's the worst of a head wound. You know Mahoney, Margot, that Munster Fusiliers man with a bit of shrapnel in his forehead? The other men in ward 5 say he still keeps jumping out of bed in his sleep and standing to. The only way they can get him back is to say "Jack Johnson overhead", and then he scuttles into bed and puts his head under the pillow; only sometimes he scuttles under the bed instead, and then the only way they can get him out is to say "Minnie's coming", and he nips out quick for fear of being buried alive. I believe he frightened one of the young ladies he walks out with into fits one day by thinking he saw snipers in the trees. Of course one never knows how much of it he's putting on for a joke, he's so silly, but he *is* badly wrecked too.'

Margot said, 'Isn't Mahoney having massage now? Nan Goddard said she thought she was going to have him to do. She has four every morning now. She likes Mahoney; she thinks he looks such an innocent little dear.'

Dorothy said, 'Innocent, did she? Mahoney! Oh well, she'll get to know him better if she has him for massage. Did you hear Mahoney and Macpherson's latest exploit?' This need not be here retailed. It is well known that a convalescent hospital containing forty soldiers is not without its episodes, and provides many fruitful topics of conversation.

They dressed meanwhile. Dorothy, in white muslin was fair-skinned and fresh, with shining light brown hair and honest grey eyes. Margot, in yellow tussore, had hair a shade darker and curlier, and her eyes were hazel. They were both very nice to look at, and had pleasant, clear, loud voices, with which they talked about soldiers. Alix put on an old green shantung frock and a string of amber beads; she looked thin, childish, elf-like; her eyes were rather narrowed under brooding brows.

2

They were at dinner. Alix sat opposite John, who wore a dinner jacket again, as if there were no war. He looked brown and square and cheerful. Between the daffodils Alix saw his eyes, nervous and watchful, with the look in them that was in so many young men's eyes in these days. Next to him was Mademoiselle Verstigel, stolid, placid, eating largely, saying little.

Mr Orme spoke of the big advance that they all believed was coming directly.

'Not yet,' said John. 'N-not enough shells.'

'Wish I could go and help make some,' said Margot.

They all discussed the munitions question. John had strong views on it, differing in some particulars from his father's. John related the inner history of several recent episodes of war, to support his view. He was very interesting. John was not naturally an anecdotal person, but his mind had been of late stored and fed with experiences. Some officers are reduced by trench life to an extreme reticence; the conversational faculty of others is stimulated. Nervous strain works in both of these ways, often in the same person. Anyhow John had to talk about the war tonight, because at Wood End they all did. He answered his father's questions about barbed wire, his mother's about dug-outs, his sisters' about things to eat. They asked him all the things they hadn't liked to ask him while he was in hospital for fear of setting his brain working and retarding his recovery. Dorothy wanted to know if it was true what the men said, that their bully beef often climbed out of its tin and walked down the trench. John said it was not, and that it was one of the erroneous statements he had most frequently to censor in the men's letters. Margot wanted to know what sort of meals he had in the trenches. John said mess in the dug-out usually consisted of six courses (preceded by vermouth), three drinks, and coffee. He proceeded to describe the courses in detail.

His mother wanted to know about the nights, whether he got any sleep. John said yes, quite a lot, when it didn't happen to be his watch. What about the noise? his mother asked. Had he got at all used to it yet? John said it wasn't nearly so noisy as the Royal Free Hospital, where he had spent the last month. His father asked what he thought of the German soldiers as clean fighters. John said they seemed much like anybody else, as far as he'd noticed. Mademoiselle Verstigel, understanding this, shook her head in protest. His mother asked, did he think it was true that our Tommies were learning to pray, or was the contrary statement truer, that they were losing such faith as they had? John said he had not himself noticed either of these phenomena in his platoon, but he might, of course, ask them. His father, who was interested, both as a person of intelligence and as a man of business, in the Balkans, got there, and they discussed the exhausting and exhaustive topic of those wild and erratic states, the relations of each to other, to the Central Powers, to the Allies, and to the war, at some length. It was the period when people were saying that Greece would come in for us, that Roumania might, and it was essential to collar Bulgaria. So they said these things duly.

3

In a pause John said to Alix across the table, 'What's Aunt Daphne doing now?'

There was a slight sense of jar. Margot, who was sympathetic, was ashamed for Alix, because of what her mother, Daphne Sandomir, was doing. For this always unusual lady, instead of being engaged in working for the Red Cross, Belgian refugees, or soldiers' and sailors' families, was attending a peace conference in New York. She had gone there from France, which she had been helping the Friends to reconstruct. She was not a Friend herself, not holding with institutional religion, but she admired their ready obedience to the constructive impulse. She was called by some a Pacificist, by more a Pacifist, by others a Pro-German, by most a member of the Union of Democratic Control, which she was not, for reasons which she was ready to explain, but which need not be here detailed.

Alix told John, in her clear, indifferent, rather melancholy little voice, about the peace conference. In common with many children of two intensely enthusiastic parents (her father had been a Polish liberationist, who had died in a Russian prison) she had a certain half-cynical detachment from and indifference to ardours and causes. Her mother was always up to some stirring enterprise, always pursuing some vividly seen star. She had been at Newnham in the days when girls went to college ardently, full of aims and ideals and self-realisations and great purposes (instead of as now, because it seems the natural thing to do after school for those with any leanings towards learning) and she had lived her life at the same high pitch ever since. Alix found her admirable, but discomposing. She found Alix engaging, even intriguing, but narrow-hearted, selfish and indolent; she accused her of shrinking from the world's griefs in a way unworthy of her revolutionary father, whom she closely resembled in face and brain.

John was rather interested in the peace conference. He had read something about it the other day in one of the periodicals which flourished in the University to which he belonged, and which wholly approved of the enterprise. Not that John, for his part, wholly approved of the periodical; he found it a trifle unbalanced, heady, partisan. John was a very fair-minded and level-headed young man, of conservative traditions. But independent, too. When the temporary second lieutenant with both legs blown off, who had occupied the next bed to his in the Royal Free, had said, perusing the comments on the peace conference in the periodical in question (under the heading, 'A Triumph of Pacifism'), 'What sickening piffle, isn't it?' John had said, after a little cogitation, 'Well, I don't know. They *mean* well.' The legless lieutenant (Trinity Hall) had snorted, 'They mean well to the Boche … After all our *trouble* … all the legs we've lost … to cave in now … Besides, what do *they* think they can do? A lot of people gassing … I wonder who they *are*?'

John had said he believed one of his aunts was keen on it.

'Sort of thing aunts *would* be keen on,' the other youth had vaguely, and, indeed, quite inaccurately commented.

On the whole John didn't much hold by such movements, but he took a more lenient view of them than the rest of his family did.

His father said, 'A little premature, discussing peace terms before we know we're going to be in a position to dictate them.'

His mother murmured, 'Peace, peace, where there is no peace,' and smiled kindly at Alix to comfort her for her mother.

Dorothy said, answering her father, 'Well, *of course* we know we are. But I don't see any use in discussing things beforehand, anyhow: we shall be able to think when the time comes.'

Mademoiselle looked with her round black eyes from one to another, like a robin. She might have been reflecting in her mind that Dorothy was very English, Mr Orme very depressing, Mrs Orme very kind, John very impartial, and Alix very indifferent. What she said, turning to John, was (and she would seem to have been preparing the remark for some time: she was very keen on improving her English), 'The war is trulee devileesh, yes? The Boches are not as humans, no? More is it not Monsieur as the devils from below?'

John grinned. Dorothy said, 'True for you Mademoiselle.' Margot said, 'You're really coming on. Only you must say "like," not "as". "As" only comes in books; it's too elegant. And devilish isn't elegant enough.'

'El-ee-gant, ' Mademoiselle repeated the word softly. She was perhaps wondering whether it was necessary to be elegant at all in one's references to the Boches.

4

After dinner they got out a map of the western front and spread it on a table and made John say, so far as he knew, in which parts of the line the various battalions at the moment were, and Dorothy wrote their names, very small, all down the line. Alix slipped away while they were doing this, to smell the garden. Soon they began to sing in the drawing-room. Margot sang, 'When we wind up the watch on the Rhine,' a song popular among soldiers just then. She was no doubt practising for canteen concerts. John joined in the chorus, in a baritone voice somewhat marred by trench life. Alix went indoors and up to bed. She was shivering, as if she was cold, or very tired, or frightened …

She undressed hastily, whistling shrilly, and got into bed and pulled the bedclothes up round her neck and read Mr Clive Bell's last book, with much of which she differed violently, so violently that she made marginal and unsympathetic notes on it in pencil as she lay.

'I'll send it to Basil and see what he thinks, ' she thought.

Then Dorothy and Margot came up, merry and talking.

'You *are* a lazy little unsociable slacker,' Margot told her. 'John was telling us such ripping stories, too. Make him tell you tomorrow about the sergeant-major and the pheasant and the barbed wire. It was awfully funny.'

Dorothy yawned. 'Oh, I'm sleepy. Thank goodness its Sunday to-morrow, so we can lie in. Margot, you've pinched my slippers … Oh no, all right.'

Alix lay and read. Her cousins undressed and said their prayers and got into bed.

'Ready, Alix?' asked Margot, her finger on the switch.

'Ready,' said Alix, putting Mr Clive Bell under her pillow, where, deeply as she differed from him, he seemed to lie as a protection against something.

The switch clicked, and the room was in darkness.

Margot and Dorothy murmured on drowsily, dropping remarks about the hospital, the canteen, things John had said … The remarks trailed away into sleep.

5

Alix lay awake. Her forehead was hot and her feet were cold. She was tense, and on the brink of shivering. Staring into the dark she saw things happening across the seas: dreadful things, ugly, jarring horrifying things. War – war – war. It pressed round her; there was no escape from it. Everyone talked it, breathed it, lived in it. Aunt Eleanor, with her committees, and her terrible refugees; Mademoiselle Verstigel, with her round robin's eyes that had looked horror in the face so near; Uncle Gerald, with his paper and his intelligent city rumours; Dorothy and Margot with their soldiers, who kept coming to tea, cheerful, charming and maimed; John, damaged and stammering, with his nervous eyes and his quiet, humorous trench talk; Basil, writing from his dug-out of Boche and shells … little Paul out there in the dark … they were all up against the monster, being strangled … it was like that beastly Laocoon …

There was a balcony running along outside the bedrooms at the front of the house. The moonlight lay palely on it; Alix watched it through the long open window. Through the window came a sound of quiet gasping, choked sobbing, as if a child were in despair. Alix sat up in bed and listened. Margot and Dorothy breathed softly, each a peace-drugged column of bedclothes.

Alix, pale and frowning, scrambled out of bed, shuddered, and pattered on thin, naked feet to the window and out on to the moon-bathed stone balcony floor.

Outside his own window, John, barefooted, in pink pyjamas, stood, gripping with both hands on to the iron balustrade, his face turned up to the moon, crying, sobbing, moaning, like a little child, like a man on the rack. He was saying things from time to time … muttering them … Alix heard. Things quite different from the things he had said at dinner. Only his eyes, as Alix had met them between the daffodils, had spoken at all like this; and even that had not been like this. His eyes were now wide and wet, and full of a horror beyond speech. They turned towards Alix and looked through her, beyond her, unseeing. John was fast asleep.

Alix, to hear no more, put her hands over her ears and turned and ran into the bedroom. She flung herself upon Dorothy and shook her by the shoulders, shook her till she sat up startled and awake.

Alix stammered, 'John – John. He's walking in his sleep … out there … He's crying – he's talking … go and stop him.'

Dorothy, efficient and professional in a moment, sprang out of bed into her two waiting slippers, and ran into the balcony. Alix heard her, gentle, quiet, firm, soothing John, leading him back to bed.

Alix was most suddenly and violently sick.

When Dorothy came back, twenty minutes later, she was huddled under the bedclothes, exhausted, shuddering and cold.

'He's quiet now,' said Dorothy, taking off her slippers. 'Poor old boy. They often do it, you know. It's the nervous shock. I must listen at nights … I say, don't tell him, Alix; he wouldn't like it. Specially to know he was crying. Poor old Johnny. Just the thing he'd never do, awake, however far gone he was. Nor talking like that; he was saying awful things … did you hear?'

'Yes,' said Alix, in a small, faint voice. Dorothy looked at her curiously, and saw her grey pallor and shut eyes.

'Why, you're ill too: I believe Johnny's upset you.' She spoke with a kindly pity and contempt. 'Is that it, kiddie?'

'Don't know,' said Alix. 'No. Should think it was too many walnuts at dinner. Let's go to sleep now.'

Dorothy, before she did this, turned her head on the pillow towards Alix's corner and said kindly, 'You'll never be any use if you don't forget *yourself*, Alix. You couldn't possibly nurse if you were always giving in to your own nerves. After all, what they can bear to go through, we ought to be able to bear to hear about. But of course you're not used to it, I know. You should come to the hospital sometimes. Good-night. If you feel rotten in the morning, don't get up.'

Dorothy went to sleep.

Alix lay and watched the shadows shifting slowly round on the balcony, and listened for sobbing, but heard only the quiet murmur of the pines.

'What they can bear to go through … But they can't, they can't, they can't … we can bear to hear about … but we can't, we can't, we can't ….'

It was like the intolerable ticking of a clock, and beat itself away at last into a sick dream.

On the other side of the wall, John started and sat bolt upright in bed, with wide staring eyes … John, like many thousand others, would perhaps never sleep quietly through a night again. Yet John had been a composed sleeper once.

CHAPTER 3

Alix goes

1

It was Sunday next day. Dorothy and Margot conducted a party of wounded soldiers to matins. Mrs Orme, who thought it time Mademoiselle Verstigel went to Mass again, sent her over to Wonford, where there was a church of her persuasion. She herself had to go up to town to the Sunday club where soldiers' and sailors' families were kept off the streets and given coffee, news, friendship, music, and the chance to read good books, a chance of which Mrs Orme, a sanguine person, hoped undiscouraged that they would one day avail themselves. (Hope, faith, and love were in her family. Her sister, Daphne Sandomir, when in England, held study circles of working women to instruct them in the principles which make for permanent peace and hoped with the same fervour that they would read the books and pamphlets she gave them.)

Mr Orme and John walked over to the links to play golf. Alix, not having either the church, club, or golf habit, and being unfitted for much walking, sat in the wood, tried to paint, and failed. She felt peevish, tired, cross and selfish, and her head ached, as one's head nearly always does after being sick in the night. The pines were no good: stupid trees, the wrong shape. What sort of pictures would one be painting out there? Mud-coloured levels, mud-coloured men, splashes of green here and there … and red … And blue sky, or mud-coloured, with shells winging through it like birds, singing, 'Lloyd-Lloyd-Lloyd-Lloyd.' … The sort of picture Basil would be painting and the way he would be painting it she knew exactly. Only probably he wasn't painting at all today. It was Sunday-hate day. Whizz-bangs, pom-poms, trench-mortars spinning along and bouncing off the wire trench roof …. Minnie coming along to blow the whole trench inside out … legs and arms and bits of men flying in the air … the rest of them buried deep in choking earth … perhaps to be dug out alive, perhaps dead … What was it John had said on the balcony – something about a leg … the leg of a friend … pulling it out of the chaos of earth and mud and stones which had been a trench … thinking it led on to the entire friend, finding it didn't, was a detached bit …. Had John cried at the time? Been sick? Probably not; John was a self-contained young man. He had waited till afterwards, when he was asleep.

Alix, seeing her friends in scattered bits, seeing worse than that, seeing what John had seen and mentioned with tears, turned the greenish pallor of pale, ageing cheese, and dropped her head in her hands. Painting was off for that morning. Painting and war don't go together.

2

Mrs Orme came home in the afternoon, tired but still energetic. Mr Orme and John came in to tea too, with Sunday papers and having seen telegrams about the German offensive being stopped at Ypres. Callers dropped in to tea. They worried John by their questions. They kindly drew out Mademoiselle Verstigel, in French worse than her English.

Directly after tea Margot had to hurry away up to town to the canteen. The callers dropped out again, one by one. John and his father went out to smoke in the garden, and to look at young trees. Dorothy went to make a cake for the hospital.

Mrs Orme sorted, filed, and pigeon-holed case-papers about Belgians.

Alix, sitting in the window seat, said, 'Aunt Eleanor, I think I'm too far away from the School. I think I'd better go and stay in London, to be nearer.'

Mrs Orme abstracted part of her attention from the Belgians, paused, paper in hand, and looked at her niece with her fine dark kind eyes, that were like her sister's only different.

'Very well, child. You may be right. I'm sorry, though …' She jabbed a paper on the file, and gave more of her attention still. 'Go and stay in London … But with whom, dear? And what does your mother think?'

'Oh, mother,' said Alix, and gave her small, crooked smile. 'Mother won't mind. She never does. I'll write to her about it, any time … Well, I might be in rooms – alone or with someone else.'

'Not alone,' Mrs Orme said promptly. 'You're not old enough. Twenty-five is it? You look less. Oh yes, I know girls do it, but I don't like it. I wouldn't let Dorothy or Margot. Who could you share them with? You've not thought of anyone especial? It would have to be someone sensible, who'd look after you, or you'd get ill … Nicholas lives with another man, doesn't he? … Wait: I've just thought of something …' She began rummaging in her desk. 'I've a letter somewhere; I kept it, I know.' She looked for it. Alix thought how like she was, as she searched, to her sister Daphne; both were so often looking for papers which they knew they had kept; and both had the same short-sighted frown and graceful bend of the neck.

'Here,' said Mrs Orme, and held up an envelope addressed in a flowing hand – the sort of hand once used by most ladies, but now chiefly by elderly and middle-aged persons of an unliterary habit.

'Emily Frampton,' said Mrs Orme. 'No, you wouldn't know her, but she's a cousin. That is, not a cousin but married to one. She's the widow of your cousin Laurence who died fifteen years ago. None of us could think why … well.' She checked herself. 'She's very nice and kind, Emily Frampton.' But so different, she meant, from their cousin Laurence. This was so. Laurence Frampton had been scholarly, humorous, keen-witted, dry-tongued, and a professor of Greek. Emily Frampton was not; which is sufficient description of her for the moment.

'She and her two girls (her own, you know; she was a widow even before she married Laurence) live at Clapton. Violette, Spring Hill, Upper Clapton, N. They're poor; they want some nice person to board with them. She's very kind; you'd be taken care of.' Mrs Orme puckered her wide, white forehead and looked at Alix as if she were a Belgian with a case-paper. 'Really, till your mother comes back and takes the responsibility, I can't let you go just anywhere.'

'Well–' Alex drawled a little, uncertainly. 'I don't like being taken care of, Aunt Eleanor. And they sound dull.'

'Well, dear, you must settle. I own I couldn't personally live at – what's the name of the house –Geranium – Pansy – no Violet – Violette, I mean. Those sort of people are so dreadfully out of the currents; probably know nothing about the war, except that there is one, and …'

'Well,' said Alix, more quickly, 'perhaps I'll go there, Aunt Eleanor. I think I will.'

'You'll be doing them a kindness,' said Mrs Orme. 'And of course it will be much more convenient for you than going up to town from here every day. If you like I'll write to Mrs Frampton today. We shall miss you, dear.' She screwed up her eyes affectionately at Alix, and added, 'You don't look well, child. I wish your mother would come home. You miss her.'

'It's fun when mother's home,' said Alix. 'But it's quieter when she isn't. Mother's so – so stimulating.'

'Oh, very, ' said Mrs Orme, who thought of Mrs Sandomir as a spoilt, clever, fascinating, but wrong-headed younger sister. She couldn't tell Alix how wrong-headed she found her mother, but she added kindly, 'You know, my dear, that I think she is mistaken in her present enterprise, and would be much better at home.'

'Most enterprises are mistaken. All, very likely,' said Alix, and her aunt was shocked, thinking she should not be cynical so young.

'The child's a funny outcome of Paul Sandomir and Daphne,' she reflected, and returned to her case-papers.

3

John came in. Alix noticed how cheerful and placid he looked, and how his hand, holding his pipe, shook. He sat down and began to talk about the advantages of not digging up one of the lawns, for potatoes, which Margot wanted to do. His memories lay behind his watchful eyes, safely guarded. But Alix knew.

'I must write to mother,' she said, and left the room.

As she went upstairs she met Mademoiselle Verstigel coming down. Her Sunday dress was bright scarlet, with canary-coloured ribbons. She had saved it out of the wreck at home, when all seemed lost, and fled in it, like so many Belgians. She looked at Alix with her round eyes, and they too held memories. Alix stumbled at a stair. Mademoiselle caught her thin arm in her own plump one and saved her from falling. Alix hated the touch; she said, 'Oh, *merci*,' and gripped her stick tight and hurried on upstairs with her uneven, limping steps. She got into the schoolroom and shut the door.

'I must get away,' she said, breathing hard. 'I will go to Violette.'

Part II

Violette

CHAPTER 4

Saturday morning at Violette

1

Alix rode from South Kensington to Clapton in the warm mid-June night on the last bus. She had been at a birthday party in Margaretta Terrace, SW. Bus 2 took her to the Strand end of Chancery Lane. Here she left her companion, who had rooms in Clifford's Inn, and walked up Chancery Lane to Holborn, and got the last Stamford Hill bus and rushed up Gray's Inn Road and then into the ugly, clamorous squalor of Theobald's Road, Clerkenwell and OId Street. The darkness hid the squalor and the dull sordidness of the long straight stretch of Kingsland Road. Through the night came only the flare of the street booths and the screaming of the very poor, who never seem too tired to scream.

At Stamford Hill Alix got off, and walked down Upper Clapton Road, which was quiet and dark, with lime-trees. Alix softly whistled a tune that someone had played on a violin to-night at Audrey Hillier's party. The party and the music, and the students' talk of art-school shop, and the childish, absurd jokes, and the chocolates and cigarettes (she had eaten eighteen and smoked five) were like a stimulating, soothing drug.

A policeman at the corner of Spring Hill flashed his light over her and lit her up for a moment, hatless, cloaked, whistling softly, limping on a stick, with her queer, narrow eyes and white face.

She turned down Spring Hill, which is an inclined road running along the northern end of Springfield Park down to the river Lea. It is a civilised and polite road, though its dwellings have not the dignified opulence of the houses round the common.

Alix stopped at Violette, and let herself softly in with her latchkey. Violette was silent and warm; the gas in the tiny hall was turned low. The door ajar on the right showed a room also dimly lit, with a saucepan of milk ready to heat on the gas-ring, and a plate of Albert biscuits and a sense of recent occupation. It is very clear in an empty room by night what sort of people have sat and talked and occupied themselves in it by day. Their thoughts and words lie about, with their books and sewing.

There were also in this room crochet doylies on the chairs and tables, a large photograph of a stout and heavily moustached gentleman above the piano (Mr Tucker), small photograph of a thin and shaven and scholarly gentleman over the writing-table (Professor Frampton), some Marcus Stones, Landseers, and other reproductions round the walls, two bright blue vases on the chimneypiece containing some yellow flowers of the kind that age cannot wither, dry, rustling, and immortal, 'Thou seest me' illuminated in pink and gold letters, circling the picture of a monstrous eye (an indubitably true remark, for no inhabitant of the room could fail to see it), and the *Evening Thrill* and *The Lovers' Heritage* (Mrs Blankley's latest novel) lying on the table. Alix sat on the table and smoked another cigarette. She always smoked far too many. She was pale, with heavy, sleep-shadowed eyes. She had talked and smoked and been funny all the evening.

One o'clock struck. Alix turned out the gas and went up to bed, quietly, lest she should disturb the family. She crept into the bedroom she shared with Evie, and undressed by the light that came in through the half-curtained window from the darkened lamps in the street.

The faint light showed Evie, asleep in her lovely grace, the grace as of some lithe young wild animal. Alix never tired of absorbing the various aspects of this lovely grace. She got into bed and curled herself up. Between the half-drawn window curtains she could see the tops of the Park trees, waving and fluttering their boughs in a dark sky, where clouds drove across the waning moon. Footsteps beat in the road outside, came near, passed, and died. The policeman trod and retrod his allotted sphere, guarding Violette while it drifted drowsily into the summer dawn, which broke through light, whispering rain. Alix dreamed.

In Flanders, the rain sloped down on to men standing to in slippery trenches, yawning, shivering, listening …

2

Evie pulled back the curtain, and the yellow day broke into Alix's dreams and opened her sleepy eyes. She yawned, her thin arms, like a child's arms, stretched above her head.

'Oh, Evie,' said Alix. 'Can't be morning, is it?'

'Not half, ' said Evie, collecting her sponges and towels for her bath. 'It's last night still … Whatever time did you get back, child?' (Evie was a year younger than Alix, but more experienced. In her pink kimono dressing-gown, with her long brown plait down her back, and her face softly flushed from the pillow, she looked like the blossom a hazel-nut might have had, had it been so arranged.)

'Twelve – one – two – don't know,' Alix yawned, and pulled the bedclothes tight under her chin. 'Think I was too tipsy to notice.'

Evie, coming back from the bathroom, woke her again. She lay and watched, between sleepy lids, Evie dressing. Drowsily she thought how awfully, awfully pretty Evie was.

Evie was lithe and long-limbed, with sudden, swift grace of movement like a kitten's or a young panther's. She had a face pink and brown, fine in contour, and prettily squared at the jaw, eyes wide and dark and set far apart under level brows, and dimples. Of the Violette household, Evie alone had charm. Except on Saturdays and Sundays she trimmed hats at a very superior and artistic establishment in Bond Street. There was a certain adequacy about Evie; she did but little here below, but did that little well.

Alix sat up in bed, one dark plait hanging on either side of her small pale face, her sharp chin resting on her knees.

'I must do it sometime, mustn't I?' she said, and did it forthwith, tumbling out of bed and staggering across to the washstand for her sponge and towel. She dropped and drowned her dreams in her cold bath, and came back cool and indifferent. Through the open window the summer morning blew upon her merrily; it was windy, careless, friendly, full of light and laughter.

3

In the dining-room, when Alix came down, were Mrs Frampton, who was small, trim, fifty-three, and reading a four-page letter; Kate, who was inconspicuous, neat, twenty-nine, and making tea; and Evie, who has already been described and was perusing two apparently amusing letters. Mrs Frampton looked up from her letter to say, 'Good morning, dear. You came home with the milk this morning, I can see by those dark saucers. You ought to have stayed in bed and had some breakfast there.'

Mrs Frampton was very kind. She also was very early in going to bed: anything after midnight was to her with the milk.

Kate said, having made the tea and turned out the gasring, 'We're all late this morning. If we don't commence breakfast quick I shall never get through my day.'

They stood round the table; Mrs Frampton said, 'For what we are about to receive,' and Kate said, 'Some bacon, mother?'

'A small helping only, love … Such a nice long letter from Aunt Nellie. Fred and Maudie have been staying with her for the weekend, and the baby's tooth begins to get through. Aunt Nellie's rheumatism is no better, though, and she thinks of Harrogate next month. Do you hear that, Kate?'

Kate was critically examining a plate.

'Egg left on it *again*. If I've spoken to Florence once I've done so fifty times, about egg on plates. I'd better ring for her and speak at once, hadn't I, mother? She'll never learn otherwise.'

'Do, love.'

Kate rang. Florence came and Kate said, 'Florence, there's egg on this plate again. Take it away and bring another, and recollect what I told you about soda.'

'Oh dear me, dear me,' said Mrs Frampton, who had opened the paper. 'Just listen to this. One of those Zeppelins came again last night and dropped bombs on the East Coast, killing sixteen and injuring forty. Now, isn't that wicked! Babies in the cradle formed a large proportion of the fatalities, as usual. Poor little loves. You'd think those men would be ashamed, with all the civilised world calling them baby-killers last time.'

'They're just inhuman murderers,' said Kate absently. 'I expect they're dead to shame by now … This bacon is somewhat less streaky than the last. We must speak to Edwards about it again. I shall tell him we shall really have to deal with Perkins if he can't do better for us. Another slice, Evie?'

'Some more toast, love,' Mrs Frampton suggested to Alix. 'And a little preserve. You don't eat properly, Alix. You'll never grow strong and big and rosy … Kate, this tea isn't so nice as the last. A touch raspier, it seems. What do you think?'

'I prefer it, mother. It has somewhat more taste. But if you think it's too strong …'

'No, love, I expect you're right. Is it the one-and-ninepenny?'

'One-and-eight.'

Evie giggled over her correspondence.

'And who have *you* heard from, Evie?' asked her mother, looking indulgently at her pretty younger daughter.

'Floss Vinney, for one. She's got some more blouse patterns, and wants me to go round again and help her choose. There's one a perfect treat she was thinking of last week; she thinks it'll make up to suit her, but it won't a bit; it's fussy, and she's too fussy already, with that frizzy hair. It would suit me nicely, or you, Alix, but it'll smother Floss. I told her so, but she wouldn't believe me. She thinks Vin will like her in it, but I bet he doesn't. Though, of course, you never can say *what* a man will like, they're so funny. Oh, dear they are comic!' Evie gurgled over some private experiences of her own: she did not lack them.

'Floss usually looks very nice in her clothes,' said Kate with delicate heroism, because, for reasons, she disliked to think so. Alix, hearing her, passed her the jam (preserve, Violette called it) impulsively, without being asked; and as a matter of fact, Kate, eating bacon, did not want it. Mrs Frampton, moved doubtless by some sequence of thought known to herself, said, 'They say those Belgians in the corner house eat ten pounds of cheese each week. Edwards' boy told Florence. Just fancy that. Not that one grudges them anything, poor things.'

Kate said, 'Mr Alison' (the vicar of the church she attended) 'says those corner Belgians have been very troublesome indeed lately. They've all quarrelled among themselves, and all but the wounded young man and his mother think the wounded young man is well enough to go to the front now, and he will slam the doors so, and two new ones have come, so they're packed as tight as herrings (but they say Belgians always *will* overcrowd), and the one that lost her baby on the journey has found it again, and the others aren't pleased because it cries at nights, and they all say they don't get enough to eat. The vicar's had no end of bother with them. And now two of them say they won't stay here, they'll go off to Hull, where Belgians aren't allowed. The vicar reasoned with them ever so long, but they will go. They say they have uncles there. I'm sure it's very wrong if they have. It does seem mad, doesn't it?' The lack of discipline among this unhappy people, she meant, rather than the uncles at Hull.

Mrs Frampton said, 'To think of them behaving like that, after all they've been through!' She scanned the paper again, having finished her small breakfast.

'Here's a German in Tottenham Court Road strangled himself with his window cord. Ashamed of his country. Well, who can blame him? We must leave that to his Maker. Now listen to this: Lord Harewood says Harrogate is a nest of spies. Quite full of German wives, it is. Fancy, and Aunt Nellie going to take the baths there next month. Lowestoft too, and Clacton-on-Sea. I'm sure I shall never want to visit any of those East Coast places again; you'd never know whom to trust; not to mention all these airships coming, and being put into gaol if you forget to pull the blinds, and having your dog confiscated if he runs out by night … Girl robbed her grandmother; she spent it all on dress, too. Fancy, with all the distress there is just now. Home Hints: Don't throw away a favourite hat because you think its day is over. Wash it in a solution of water and gum and lay it flat on the kitchen dresser. Stuff the crown with soft paper and stand four flat-irons on the brim. But clean the irons well first with brick-dust and ammonia. The hat will then be a very nice new shape … Here's a recipe for apple shortcake, Kate: I shall cut that out for Florence … Dear me, how late it gets! We must all get to our day's work … Have you heard news from your mother, Alix dear?'

'Yes.' Alix had two letters before her. 'Mother writes from Athens. She's been interviewing Tino (don't know how she managed it); trying to get him to sit on a council for Continuous Mediation without Armistice. I gather Tino thinks it a jolly sound plan in theory, but isn't having any in practice. That's the position of most of the neutral governments, apparently.'

As none of the family knew what Continuous Mediation without Armistice meant, the only comment forthcoming was, from Mrs Frampton, 'Your mother is a very wonderful person. I only hope she isn't getting over-tired, going about as much as she does … You've had some news from the front, too, haven't you?'

'Yes,' said Alix. 'A friend of mine has just got wounded. He's being sent home.'

'Oh, my dear, how unfortunate! Not seriously, I trust?'

'No, I shouldn't think so. A nice blighty one in the hand, he says. He seems quite cheery about it. He tried to return a bomb to the senders, and it went off just before its proper time. It happens often, he says. It must be difficult to calculate about these time-bombs.'

'A dreadful risk to take, indeed! It's his left, I suppose, as he writes?'

'He dictated it. No, not his left.'

'The right? Dear me, now, how sad that is. It so hampers a man. What used he to work at, love?'

'He paints.'

'Well now, isn't that a pity! He must learn to paint lefthanded when the war's over, mustn't he? But I hope his hand will be quite well again long before then. It's given you quite a shock, dearie, I can see. You've gone quite pale. Would you like a little sal volatile?'

'No thank you, Cousin Emily. It's not given me a shock a bit … Do you want me to do the lamps, Kate?'

'Well – I don't know why you should. Evie's nothing to do this morning …' Kate looked doubtfully at her sister, who said promptly, 'Oh, hasn't she? That's all you know. I'm for a cutting-out morning. Thanks muchly, Alix; I'll do the dusting if you'll do the lamps.'

4

Kate retired to domestic duties in the back regions.

Evie, before doing the dusting, took up the *Daily Message* and glanced through the feuilleton. It had been the same feuilleton for many weeks. It was always headed by a synopsis and a list of characters: 'John Hargreave, a strong quiet man of deep feeling, to whom anything underhand is abhorrent. Valerie Lascelles, a beautiful girl of nineteen, who loves John. Sylvia, her sister, exactly like Valerie in face, but not in character, for she is shallow and hard and lives abroad, the widow of a foreign count. Cyril Arbuthnot, a smart man about town, unscrupulous in his methods, who sticks at nothing. ' No wonder Evie found it interesting.

Then she flicked competently round the drawing-room with a duster, calling to Florence to clear away quick, because she wanted the table for cutting out.

Alix did the lamps in the pantry.

Mrs Frampton did accounts and wrote to Aunt Nellie, in the dining-room.

Florence cleared away, also in the dining-room.

Kate looked in in her hat and coat, with the little red books that come from shops on a Saturday morning. 'I'd better get in a new tongue, I suppose, mother. The one we have will scarcely be sufficient for Sunday.'

'Yes, dear. Get one of the large ones.'

Kate went bill-paying.

Evie extracted incomprehensively-shaped pieces of brown paper from the pages of *Home Chat*, a weekly periodical which she took in, and began her cutting-out morning.

Alix returned from the lamps and said, 'I'm going out for the day with some people. I may go on to Nicholas in the evening, very likely.' (It may or may not have been before mentioned that Alix had a brother of that name.)

'Very well, dear. Bring your brother or some of your friends back with you afterwards, if you like. I'm sure it would be very nice if they stopped to supper. Our supper's simple, but there's always plenty for all. And the Vinneys are coming round afterwards, so we shall be a nice party. I asked them because they've got that cousin, Miss Simon, staying with them, and I thought they'd be glad of an evening's change for her. '

'That fatty in a sailor blouse,' Evie, who observed clothes, commented. 'I should think they'd be glad of a change *from* her. She's a suffragette, and talks the weirdest stuff; she's as good as a play to listen to … I shouldn't think your brother'd get on with the Vinneys a bit, Alix.'

'Probably not, ' said Alix. 'He doesn't with most people.'

Evie looked as if she shouldn't think he did.

'What's the name of that new floor-polish, to tell Aunt Nellie?' said Mrs Frampton, pausing in her letter.

But, as Kate was out, and as it was neither Ronuk nor Cherry Blossom (suggestions of unequal levels of intelligence from Evie and Alix), she had to leave a space for it.

CHAPTER 5

Afternoon out

1

Alix sat on the bus and rushed through the shining summer morning down Upper Clapton Road, Lower Clapton Road, Mare Street, Hackney Road, Shoreditch, Bishopsgate, and so into the city. The noon war news leaped from placards, in black and red and green. A mile of trenches taken near Festubert – a mile of trenches lost again. Alix did not care and would not look. Anyhow it wasn't Paul's part of the line. London was damp and shining under a windy blue sky. They had cleared away the bodies of those struck down last night by motor buses in the dark. What a sacrifice of life! Was it worthwhile?

The traffic was held up every now and then by companies of recruits swinging along, in khaki and mufti, jolly, absorbed, resolute, self-conscious, or amused. There went down Threadneedle Street the Artists' Rifles. Some looked like studio artists, pale, intelligent, sometimes spectacled, others more like pavement artists, others again suggested sign-painters. But this last was probably an illusion, as sign-painters since last August had been mostly too busy painting out and repainting names on signs to have time for soldiering. Many classes have lost heavily by this war, such as publicans, milliners, writers, Belgians, domestic servants, university lecturers, publishers, artists, actors, and newspapers. But some have gained; among these are sheep-growers, house-agents, sugar-merchants, munitionmakers, colliers, coal-owners, and sign-painters. An unequal world.

The bus waited, held up opposite a recruiting station. Alix, looking down, met the hypnotic stare of the Great Man pictured on the walls, and turned away, checking a startled giggle. Anyhow she was lame, and not the sex which goes either, worse luck. (On that desperate root of bitterness she never dwelt: that way madness lay.) Her swerving eyes fell next on one of the pictures of domestic life designed and executed (so common report had it) by the same Great Man; the picture in which an innocent and reproachful infant inquires of a desperately embarrassed but apparently not irate parent, 'Daddy, what did *you* do to help when Britain fought for freedom in 1915?' Alix giggled again, and looked up at the white clouds racing across the summer sky, where there was no war nor rumours of war.

2

At Bond Street she left the bus and went to Grafton Street, where there was a small exhibition of pictures by two young artists known to Alix. Here she met by appointment three friends, her fellow-students at the art school. Their names were Nonie Maclure, Oliver Banister, and Thomas Ashe. Miss Maclure and Mr Banister were there before her. They greeted her with 'What cheer, Joanna?' – Joanna, because in a play composed and produced recently by their combined talent, Alix had taken this part. Alix went to speak to the exhibitors, who were standing about and failing to look detached, and began to look round, murmuring to her friends, 'What's the show like? … Oh, she's got that yellow thing in …' and so forth. Presently Mr Thomas Ashe joined them. (It may here be mentioned, lest readers should be unfairly prejudiced against Mr Ashe and Mr Banister, that one of them had a frozen lung and the other a distended aorta. They were quite good young men really, and would have preferred to go.)

They criticised and appreciated the pictures for an hour, with the interested criticism and over-appreciation usually poured forth by young persons on the works of their fellow-students and contemporaries, often at the expense of the older and staler and less in the only movement that really matters.

'That's like some of Doye's things,' said one of the young men, and the other said, 'Doye's wounded, isn't he? I saw it in the paper today. I hope it's not much.'

Alix said it wasn't. 'He's on his way home. I hope they send him to a hospital in town, so we can all go and see him.'

Nonie Maclure shot her a curious glance. She had never known quite how deep the intimacy between these two had gone. She sometimes wondered. She had thought just before the war that it went very deep indeed. But in these present days Alix seemed prepared to play round at large with so many young men, and to flirt, when that was the game, with a light-handed recklessness only exceeded by Nonie herself; and Nonie, of course, was notorious.

3

They went out to lunch. The world is divided into those who have lunch in their own homes, those who have lunch in someone else's, those who have lunch in hotel restaurants, those who have lunch in nice eating-shops, those who have lunch in less nice eating-shops, such as **ABC**'s, those who have lunch in eating-shops very far from nice, those who have lunch in handkerchiefs, and those who do not have lunch at all. The classes are, of course, not rigid; many people alternate from day to day between one and another of them. Alix and her friends were, most days, either in class four or class five. Today they were in class four, being out for a happy day, and they had lunch in a little place in Soho, full of orange-trees in green tubs, and sunshine, and maccaroni. They found one another interesting, entertaining, and attractive. Nonie Maclure was dark and good-looking, a fitfully brilliant worker, and a consistently lively companion. Oliver Banister was gentle and fair and delicate, and indifferent to most things, only not to art or to Nonie Maclure. He had tried to get passed for the army, but, as he was rejected, he settled down tranquilly and without the bitterness that eats the souls of so many of the medically and sexually unfit. He recognised the compensations of his lot. Tommy Ashe, on the other hand, was bitter and angry like Alix; like her he would have hated the war anyhow, even if he had been fighting, being a sensitive and intelligent youth, but as it was he loathed it so much that he would never mention it unless he had to, and then only with a sneer. It was partly this that drew him to Alix and her to him. They were in the same case. So they found they could trust one another not to talk of the indecent monster. Also he admired her unusual, delicate, ironic type. Anyhow it was the fashion to have some special friend among the girls at the school, and it helped one to forget. So he and Alix plunged into a flirtation not normally natural to either.

The four of them flirted and ragged and joked and were funny all the afternoon, which they spent in Richmond Park. Alix and Tommy Ashe went off together and lost the other two, and lay on the grass, and became rather more intimate than they had ever been before. When soldiers strolled by they looked the other way and pretended not to see, and talked very fast about anything that came into their heads. Sometimes the soldiers were wounded; once a party of them, in hospital blues, sat down quite near them, with two girls in VAD uniform, who called the soldiers by their surnames and chaffed them. They were all being merry and funny and having a good time. One was a boy of eighteen, pink-cheeked and hilarious, with his right leg cut short just below the thigh.

'Look here, it's time we found those two people,' said Alix, sitting up. 'We must really set about it in earnest.'

So they went away, but presently they felt more like tea than finding the others, so they had some. When finally the party joined itself together, it went to Earl's Court and had a hilarious hour flip-flapping, wiggle-waggling, and joy-wheeling. It desisted at half-past six, dishevelled, battered and bruised, and separated to fulfil its respective evening engagements.

4

Alix went to see her brother Nicholas. Nicholas was a journalist, on the staff of a weekly paper which cost sixpence and with whose politics he was not in agreement. As there was no paper, weekly, sixpenny or otherwise, with whose politics he was in agreement, this was not strange. It may further be premised of Nicholas that he was twenty-seven years old, of good abilities, thought war too ridiculous a business for him to take part or lot in, was probably medically unfit to do so but would not for the world have had it proved, was completely lacking in any sense of veneration for anything, negligently put aside as absurd all forms of supernatural religion, shared rooms with a curate friend in Clifford's Inn, and had from an infant reacted so violently against the hereditary enthusiasm which nevertheless looked irrepressibly out of his eyes that he had landed himself with an unintelligent degree of cynicism in all matters.

Hither Alix went, when the evening sunshine lay mellow on Chancery Lane. Alix had a curious and quite unaccountable feeling for Chancery Lane. It seemed to her romantic beyond all reason. Just now it was as some wild lane on the battle front, or like a trench which has been shelled, for the most recent airship raid had ploughed it up. A week ago it had been the scene of that wild terror and shrieking confusion which is characterised by a euphemistic press as 'no panic'.

Alix limped past the chaos quickly. An old man tried to sell her a paper. '*Star*, lady? *Globe, Pall Mall, Evening News?* British fail to hold conquered trenches …' Alix hurried by; the newsvendor turned his attention to someone else. Evening papers, of course, are interesting, and should not really be missed; they often contain so much news that is ephemeral and fades away before the morning into the light of common day; they are as perishable and never-to-be-repeated as some frail and lovely flower.

But Alix, ignoring them, reached Clifford's Inn, and climbed the narrow oak stairway to the rooms inscribed:

MR N I SANDOMIR

REV C M V WEST

Both these gentlemen were in their sitting-room. The Rev C M V West reposed on a wicker couch, reading alternately two weekly church papers and the *Cambridge Magazine*. One of these papers was High Church, another Broad Church, the third did not hold with churches. The Rev C M V West was a refined-looking young man, very neatly cassocked, with a nice face and a sense of humour. In justice to him we must say that he worked very hard as a rule, but had been enjoying a deserved rest before evensong. To Alix he stood for a queer force that was at work in the world and which she had been brought up to consider retrograde.

Nicholas Sandomir lay in an easy-chair, surrounded by review copies of books. He was too broad-shouldered for his height; he was pale and prominent-jawed, with something of the Slav cast of feature; his mouth, like Alix's, was the mouth of a cynic; his eyes, small, overhung, and deep blue, were the eyes of an idealist. This paradox of his face was only one among many paradoxes in him; he was unreliable; he disbelieved in all churches, and lived, unaccountably, with a High Church curate (this, probably, was because he liked him personally and also liked to have an intelligent person constantly at hand to disagree with; also he came, on his father's side, of a race of devout and mystic Catholics). He despised war, and looked with contempt on peace societies (this was perhaps because, so far as he worshipped anything, he worshipped efficiency, and found both peace societies and war singularly lacking in this quality). He detested Germany as a power, and loathed Russia who was combating her (this, doubtless, was because he was half a Pole).

Anyhow, this evening, when Alix came in, he was sulkily, even viciously, turning the pages of a little book he had to review, called (it was one of a series) *The Effects of the War on Literature*. He waved his disengaged hand at Alix, and left it to West, who had much better manners, to get up and put a chair for her and pass and light her a cigarette.

'Did you meet Belgians on the stairs?' inquired West. 'They've put some in the rooms above us – the rooms that used to be Hans Bauer's. Five of them, isn't it, Sandomir?'

'Five to rise,' Nicholas replied. 'A baby due next week, I'm told.' (Unarrived babies were among the things not alluded to at Violette in mixed company: no wonder Violette found Nicholas peculiar.)

'It's awkward,' West added, lowering his voice and glancing at one of the shut bedroom doors, 'because we keep a German, and they can't meet.'

'What do you do that for?' asked Alix unsympathetically.

'Awkward, isn't it?' said West. 'Because they keep coming to see us – the Belgians, I mean (they like us rather), and he' – he nodded at the bedroom – 'has to scoot in there till they're gone. It's like dogs and cats; they simply can't be let to meet.'

'Well, I don't know what you want with a German, anyhow.'

'He's a friend of ours,' explained Nicholas. 'He was living in the Golders Green Garden City, and it became so disagreeable for him (they're all so exposed there, you know – nothing hid) that we asked him here instead. If they find him he's afraid they may put him in a concentration camp, and of course if the Belgians sighted him they'd complain. He means no harm, but unfortunately he had a concrete lawn in his garden, about ten feet square, where he used to bounce a ball for exercise. Also he had made a level place on his roof, among Mr Raymond Unwin's sloping tiles, where he used to sit and admire the distant view through a spyglass. It's all very black against him, but he's a studious and innocent little person really, and he'd hate to be concentrated.' ('It would make one feel so like essence of beef, wouldn't it?' West murmured absently.) 'He's not a true patriot, ' went on Nicholas. 'He wants the Hohenzollerns to be guillotined and a disruptive country of small warring states to be re-established. He writes articles on German internal reform for the monthly reviews. He calls them "Kill or Cure," or, "A short way with Imperialism", or some such bloody title. I don't care for his English literary style, but his intentions are excellent ... Well, and how's life?' Nicholas turned his small keen blue eyes on his sister. 'You look as if you'd been out for a joy-day. You want some more hairpins, but we don't keep any here.'

'I've been wiggle-woggling,' Alix admitted, and added frankly, 'I feel jolly sick after it.'

'Our family constitution,' said her brother, 'is quite unfit for the strains we habitually subject it to. Mine is. I feel jolly sick too. But my indisposition is incurred in the path of duty. I've got to review the things, so I have to read them – a little here and there, anyhow. And then, just as one feels one has reached one's limit, one gets a handbook of wisdom like this, to finish one off. '

He read a page at random from *The Effects of the War on Literature*. "'The war is putting an end to sordidness and littleness, in literature as in other spheres of human life. The second-rate, the unheroic, the earthy, the petty, the trivial – how does it look now, seen in the light of the guns that blaze over Flanders? The guns, shattering so much, have at least shattered falsity in art. We were degenerate, a little, in our literature and in our lives: we have been made great. We are come, surely, to the heroic, the epic pitch of living; if we cannot express it with a voice worthy of it, then indeed it has failed in its deepest lesson to us. We may expect a renascence of beauty worthy to rank with the Romantic Revival born of the French wars …'"

'Who is the liar?' asked Alix.

Nicholas named him. 'I am thinking,' he added, 'of starting an Effects of the War series of my own. I shall call it *Some Further Effects*. It will be designed to damp the spirits of the sanguine. I shall do the one on Literature myself. I shall take revenge in it for all the mush I've had to review lately. It's extraordinary, the stream of – of the heroic and the epic, isn't that it – that pours forth daily. The war seems to have given an unhealthy stimulus to hundreds of minds and thousands of pens. One knew it would, of course. No doubt it was the same during the siege of Troy, and all the great wars. Though, thank heaven, we shall never know, as that sort of froth is blown away pretty quick and lost to posterity. It's only the unhappy and contemporaries who get it splashed all over them. And this war is beastlier than any other, so the rubbish is less counteracted by the decent writers. The first-rate people, both the combatants and non-combatants, are too much disgusted, too upset, to do first-rate work. The war's going on, and means to go on, too long. Wells or someone said months ago that people don't so much think about it as get mentally scarred. It's quite true. Lots of people have got to the stage when they can only feel, not think. And the best people hate the whole business much too much to get any "renascence of beauty" out of it. Who was it who said the other day that the writers to whom war is glamorous aren't as a rule the ones who produce anything fit to call literature. War's an insanity; and insane things, purely destructive, wasteful, hideous, brutal, ridiculous things, aren't what makes art. The war's produced a little fine poetry, among a sea of tosh – a thing here and there; but mostly – oh, good Lord! The flood of cheap heroics and commonplace patriotic claptrap – it's swept slobbering all over us; there seems no stemming it. Literary revival be hanged. All we had before – and precious little it was – of decent work, clear and alive and sane and close to reality, is being trampled to bits by this – this imbecile brute. And when the time comes to collect the bits and try to begin again, we shan't be able to; they'll be no more spirit in us; we shall be too battered and beaten ...' Nicholas, wound up to excitement, was talking too long at a stretch, He often did, being an egoist, and having in his veins the blood of many eloquent and excited revolutionary Poles, who had stood in marketplaces and talked and talked. gesticulating, pouring forth blood and fire. Nicholas, reacting against this fervour, repudiating gesticulation, blood and fire, still talked ... But on 'battered and beaten' he paused, in disgusted emphasis, and West came in, half absently, still turning the pages of the *Challenge*, talking in his high, clear voice, monotonous and fast (Nicholas was guttural and harsh). 'You underrate the power of human recovery· You always do. It's immense, as a matter of fact. Give us fifty years – twenty – ten ... Besides, look at the compensations. If the good are battered and beaten, the bad are too. It's a well-known fact that many of the futurist poets, in all the nations, have gone mad, through trying to get too many battle noises into their heads at once.

So they, at least, are silenced. I suppose they still write, in their asylums – in fact I've heard they do (my uncle is an asylum doctor) – but it gets no further …' He subsided into the *Cambridge Magazine*.

'Well, I'd rather have the futurists than the slops poured out by the people who unfortunately haven't brain enough even to go mad,' Nicholas grumbled. ('And anyhow, I don't believe in any of your uncles – you've too many.) The futurists at least were trying to keep close to facts, even if they couldn't digest them but brought them up with strident noises. But these imbeciles – the war seems to be a sort of tonic to their syrupy little souls; it's filled them up with vim and banal joy. Not that the rot that has always been rot particularly matters; it merely means that the people who used to express themselves in one inane way now choose another, no worse; but it's the silencing or the unmanning of the good people that matters. Here's Cathcart's new book. I've just read it. It's the work of a shaken, broken man. It's weak, irrational, drifting, with no constructive purpose, no coherence. You can almost hear the guns crashing into it as he tried to write, and the atrocity reports shrieking in his ears, and the poison gas stifling him, and the militarists and pacificists raving round him. His whole world's run off its rails and upset and broken to bits, and he can't put it right side up again; he's lost his faith in it. He can only fumble and stammer at it helplessly, weak and maundering and incoherent. He ought to be helping to build it up again, but he's lost his constructive power. Hundreds of people have. Constructive force will be the one thing needed when the war is over; anyone with a programme, and the brain and will to carry it out; but where's it to come from? Those who aren't killed or cut to bits will be too adrift and demoralised and dazed to do anything intelligent. We're fast losing even such mental coherence and concentration as we had. Look, for instance, at the two, while I'm talking (quite interestingly, too); are you listening? Certainly not. West is reading a Church newspaper, and Alix drawing cats on the margins of my proofs … I'm not blaming you; you can't help it; you are mentally, and probably, morally, shattered. I am too. People are more than ever like segregated imbeciles, each absorbed in his or her own ploy. Effects of the War on Human Intelligence: that shall be one of my series. I've spent an idiotic day. So have both of you, I should guess. Yet we all three have natural glimmerings of intelligence.'

'I've not spent an idiotic day,' said West placidly.

Nicholas looked at him sardonically. 'Well, let's hear about it.'

'By all means.' West drew a long breath and began, even faster than usual. 'I'll skip my before-breakfast proceedings, which you wouldn't understand. But they weren't in the least idiotic. After breakfast I spent an hour talking to a friend of mine on leave from France. The conversation was very interesting and instructive; for me, anyhow. We talked about how rotten the grub in the trenches is, how shameless the ASC are, how unreliable time-fuse bombs, and so on. Then, since I am a parson, he kindly talked my shop for a change, and naturally very soon Jonah pushed his head in, and Noah, and a few more of the gentlemen who seem to keep the church doors shut against the British workingman. I kicked them outside the Church on to the dust-heap and left them there, I hope to his satisfaction, and came home and wrote a sermon advocating the disuse of the custom of perusing early Hebrew history or reading it in churches. It's quite a good sermon, as my sermons go. (By the way, that may, I'm hoping, be one of the Effects of the War on the Church. We've all of us become so anxious to bring the working-man into it – and it's very certain he won't come in with the Old Testament legends barring the way. I'll write that one of your series for you, if I may.) Well, then I had lunch with a lady who's interested in factory-girls' trade unions, and we discussed the ways and means of them. That was jolly useful. '

'He's one of the clergymen, you know,' Nicholas explained aside to Alix, 'who have been said by an eminent Dean to be tumbling over one another in their anxiety to become court chaplains to King Demos. He's hopelessly behind the times, of course, because Demos is in fetters now. West's an Edwardian churchman, though he fancies he is Neo-Post-Georgian.'

'Oh, I'm as early as you like,' West said amiably. 'Pre-Edwardian – Victorian – or even Pauline; *I* don't mind … Well, then I attended a meeting of my parish branch of the UDC. The meeting was broken up by rioters. So I addressed them from a window on freedom of speech. My vicar came along as I was doing so, and came in and lectured me on taking part in political movements. So I stopped, and did some parish visiting instead, and had a good deal of interesting conversation, and incidentally was given very strong tea at three different houses. Then I came home and read the *Church Times*, the *Challenge*, and the *Cambridge Magazine*. All interesting in their way, and quite different. No, I know you don't like any of them. People write to the *Challenge* every week asking "Are Christianity and War compatible?" and come to the conclusion that they are not, but that Christians may often have to fight. People write to the *Church Times* saying that they have found a clergyman who won't wear a chasuble, and what shall they do to him? People write to the *Cambridge Magazine* saying that everyone over forty should be disenfranchised and interned, if not shot. Jolly good papers, all the same. How can they help being written to? None of us can. I get written to myself … Well, next I'm going to church to read evensong, and for an hour after evensong – but you wouldn't understand about that. Anyhow, eventually I have supper with the vicar.' He ran down with a jerk, and turned to Alix, who had been following him with some interest. 'That's not an idiotic day; not from my point of view,' he informed her.

'Sounds all right,' she said. 'But it's not the sort of day Nicholas and I were brought up to understand, you know. We know nothing about the Church. From not going, I suppose.'

'You should go,' he assured her. 'You'd find it interesting ... Of course it's been largely a failure so far, and dull in lots of ways, because we've not yet fulfilled its original intention; it hasn't so far succeeded in preventing (though it's fought them and largely lessened them) any of the things it's out to prevent – commercialism and cant and cruelty and classes and lies and hate and war. It's got to break the world to bits and put it together again, and before it can do that it's got to break itself to bits and put itself together. It's got to become like dynamite, and blow up the rubbish – its own rubbish first, then the world's ...' He consulted his wrist-watch, said, 'I must go', shook hands with Alix, and went quickly, trim and alert and neat, to blow up the world.

'He talks too much, ' said Nicholas, in his hearing. 'Who doesn't, in these days? I do myself. It's better than to talk too little. If we say a great deal, we may say a word of sense sometimes. If we say very little, the odds are that all we do say is rubbish, from lack of practice.' He yawned. 'You'd better stay to dinner. I've got Andreiovitch Romevsky coming, to meet Adolf Kopfer, our German friend, so talk on the European situation will be hampered and constrained.'

'Funny thing he stands for,' Alix commented, still thinking of Mr West. 'The Church ... I suppose it really is out to stop war.'

'Presumably. But, as its representatives say, its endeavours so far have been a frost. It's been as unsuccessful as the peace conferences mother attends. But apparently the members of both are obliged, by their faith, to be incurable optimists. West's always full of life and hope; nothing daunts him.'

'Funny,' Alix mused still. The thought glanced through her, 'Clergymen can't fight either, they're like me. Perhaps religion helps them to forget; takes their minds off. Like painting. Like Richmond Park and Tommy Ashe. Like wiggle-waggling. I wonder.'

On that wonder she left the Church, and said, 'Cousin Emily asked me to bring you back to supper with me. You'd meet the Vinneys, from the Nutshell, who are coming in afterwards, so we should be a nice party, she says. But Evie says you and the Vinneys wouldn't get on. I don't think Evie thinks you're fit for respectable society at all. So you'd better not come.'

'Shouldn't dream of it,' Nicholas grunted. 'Even if I hadn't got Russians and Germans coming here. You and your Violettes and your Nutshells! It beats me what you think you're up to there.'

Alix gave her faint, enigmatic smile. 'It's nice and peaceful,' she said. 'Like cottonwool … Well, good-night, Nicky. No, I won't stay to dinner, thanks. You can tackle your own awkward social situations for yourself. I'm for Violette.'

5

She limped down the wooden stairs, and the court was golden in the evening light, a haven beyond which the wild river of Fleet Street surged.

'Special. War Extra. British driven back …' The cries, the placards, were like lost ships tossed lightly on the top of wild waters. They would soon sink, if one did not listen or look …

CHAPTER 6

Evening at Violette

1

After supper Kate got out the good coffee cups, and they waited for the Vinneys. Kate was rather pink, and wore a severe blouse, in which she looked plain; it was a mortification she thought she ought to practise when the Vinneys came. Evie was skilfully altering a hat. Alix made a pen-and-ink sketch of her as she bent over it.

Mrs Frampton knitted a sock. *The Evening Thrill* came in, and Kate opened it, for Mrs Frampton liked to hear titbits of news while she worked.

'Stories impossible to doubt,' read Kate, in her prim precise voice, 'reach us continually of atrocities practised by the enemy …' She read several, unsuitable for these pages. Mrs Frampton clicked horror with her tongue. The papers she took in were rich in such stories. As it was impossible to doubt them, she did not try. Possibly they gave life a certain dreadful savour.

'To think of the march of civilisation, and this still going on,' Mrs Frampton commented. 'I'm sure anyone would think they'd be ashamed.'

Kate said, with playful acidity (Kate had reached what with many is a playful age), 'Thank you, Alix. Thank you ever so much, Alix, for getting between me and the lamp.'

Alix moved, her attempt foiled.

Kate read next the letter of a private soldier at the front. 'The Boches are all cowards. They can't stand against our boys. They fly like rabbits when we charge with the bayonet. You should hear them squeal, like so many pigs, There's not a

German private in the army that wants to fight. The officers have to keep flogging them on the whole time.'

'Poor things, I'm sure one can't but be sorry for them,' said Mrs Frampton. 'Knit two and make one, purl two, slip one, pass the slipped one over, drop four and knit six.' (Or anyhow, something of that sort, for she had got to the heel, as one unfortunately at last must.)

'It's wonderful how long the war goes on, since all the Germans are like that,' said Kate, without conscious irony, as she took up her own knitting. Hers was a body-belt. 'I believe this new wool is different from the last. Somewhat stringier, it seems. Brown will have to take it back, if it is.'

'I say, just fancy,' said Evie, 'those sequin tunics at B & H's have come down to seven and eleven three. I think I could rise to that, even in war time.'

The war mainly affected Evie by reducing the demand for hats, and consequently lowering the salary she received at the exclusive and ladylike milliner's where she worked.

As she spoke she caught sight of her three-quarter likeness as etched by Alix.

'Goodness gracious,' she commented. 'You've made me look anything on earth! I mayn't be much, but I hope I'm not that sort of freak.'

'It's very good,' said Alix complacently. 'Rather particularly good. I shall take it to the School on Monday and show it to Mr Bendish.'

'It may be good,' said Evie, 'since you say so. All I say is, it isn't me. It's more like some wild woman out of a caravan. Don't you go telling people it's me, or they'll be coming to shut me up. There's the bell; that's them.'

The Vinney party arrived. It consisted of Mr Vincent Vinney, a bright young solicitor of twenty-eight; his lately acquired wife, a pretty girl who laughed when he was witty, which was often; his young brother Sidney, a stout, merry youth of nineteen, a bank clerk; and their cousin Miss Simon, the fat girl in the sailor blouse, which was, it seemed, her evening toilette also. (In case some should blame the Vinney brothers for not taking an active part in the war, it may be remarked that the elder supported a wife and the younger a mother, that they represented a class which, for several good reasons, produces fewer soldiers than any other, and that they both belonged to the Clerks' Drill Corps, and wore several flags on their bicycles. And young Mrs Vinney belonged to a Voluntary Aid Detachment, not at present in working.)

They came in with the latest news. The British had been driven back out of a thousand yards of trench they had taken. They hadn't enough ammunition.

'Well,' said Mrs Frampton, knitting, and really more interested in her heel than in the fortunes of war, 'it's all very dreadful to think of. But I suppose we must leave it in the hands of the Almighty, who always moves in a mysterious way.'

(Mrs Frampton had been brought up evangelically, and so mentioned the Almighty more casually than Kate, who was High, thought fit.)

'Well, what I say is,' said young Mrs Vinney, who was of a cheerful habit, 'it's not a bit of use being depressed by the news, because no one can ever tell if it's true or not. It's all from that Bureau, and we all know what they are. Why, they said there weren't any Russians in England, when everyone knew there were crowds, and they always say the Zepp raids don't do any damage to factories and arsenals, and everyone knows they do. They don't seem to mind what they say.'

'Well, for my part,' Evie said, 'I don't see why we shouldn't all be as chirpy as we can. We can't help by being glum, can we?'

'That's just it,' said Mrs Vinney. 'Now, there's the theatre. Of course, you know, Vin and I wouldn't go to anything really festive just now, like the *Girl on the Garden Wall*, but I'm not ashamed to say we did go to the *Man Who Stayed Behind*.'

'Why wouldn't you go to anything really festive?' Alix asked, curious as to the psychology of this position.

Mrs Vinney looked round for sympathy.

'Why, what a question! It's not the moment, of course. One wouldn't *like* to. *You* wouldn't, would you?'

'Oh, me. I'd go to anything I thought would amuse me.'

'Well,' Mrs Vinney decided, 'I suppose you and I aren't a bit alike. I just couldn't, and there it is. I dare say it's all my silliness. But with the men out there in such danger, and laying down their lives the way they're doing … well, I *couldn't* sit and look at the *Girl on the Garden Wall*, not if I had a stall free. The way I see it is, the men are fighting for us women, and where should we be but for them, and the least we can do is not to forget all about them, seeing gay musical plays. The way I'm made, I suppose, and I don't pretend to judge for others.'

'It's all a question of taste and feeling,' Kate pronounced absently, more interested in a new stitch she was introducing into her body-belt.

The fat dark girl, Miss Simon, came in on the mention of women. It was her subject. 'Women's work in war time is every bit as important as men's, that's what I say; only they don't get the glory.'

Mrs Vinney giggled and looked at the others.

'Now Rachel's off again. She's a caution when she gets on the woman question. She spent most of her time in Holloway in the old days, didn't you, dear?'

'She thinks she ought to have the vote,' Sid Vinney explained to Alix in a whisper. Alix, who had hitherto moved in circles where everyone thought, as a matter of course, that they ought to have the vote, disappointed him by her lack of spontaneous mirth.

Miss Simon was inquiring, undeterred by these comments, 'Who keeps the country at home going while the men are at the war? Who brings up the families? Who nurses the soldiers? What do women get out of a war, ever?'

'The salvation of their country, Miss Simon,' said Mrs Frampton 'won for them by brave men.'

'After all,' said Sid, 'the women can't *fight*, you know. They can't *fight* for their country.'

Miss Simon regarded him with scorn.

'How much are you fighting for your country, I'd like to know?'

'One for you, Sid, ' said Evie cheerily, ignoring Sid's aggrieved, 'Well, you know I can't leave mother.'

'And fighting isn't everything,' Miss Simon went on, 'and war time isn't everything. There's women's work in peace time. What about Octavia Wills that did so much for housing? Wasn't she helping her country? And, for war work, what price Florence Nightingale? What would the country have done without *her*, and what did she get out of all she did?'

Mrs Frampton, who had not read the life of that strong-minded person, but cherished a mid-Victorian vision of lady with a lamp, sounder in the heart than in the head, said, 'She kept her place as a woman, Miss Simon.'

Evie, who was not listening much, finding the subject tedious, put in vaguely, 'After all, when it comes to fighting, we *are* left in the lurch, aren't we?'

Sid said, 'Oh dear no, Miss Evie. What price Christabel and Co.? They ought to have had the iron cross all round the militants ought. They did more to earn it than the Huns ever did.'

'Cheap sarcasm, ' said Miss Simon, 'is no argument. And I don't blame any woman for using what means she's got. There are times when a woman's *got* to forget herself.'

Kate said, 'I don't think a woman's *ever* got to forget herself,' and there was a murmur of applause. Alix giggled She wondered if social evenings at Violette were often like this.

'You don't understand,' said the round-faced girl helplessly. 'You may be all right, in your station of life, but you've got to look at other women's – the poor. We've got to do something about the poor. The vote would help us.'

'There have always,' said Mrs Frampton, 'been the poor, and there always will be.'

'That's just why,' suggested Alix, momentarily joining in, 'it might be worthwhile to do something about them. ' Miss Simon looked at her in sudden gratitude; she had a misplaced and soon-quenched hope that this seemingly indifferent and amused girl might prove an ally.

Kate said, placidly, 'Well, they say that if you were to take a lot of men and women and give them all the same money, they'd all be quite different again to-morrow …'

Mrs Frampton added that she went by the Bible. 'The poor ye shall have always with you.'

'Mrs Frampton, it doesn't say that. And even if it did – well, it's as Miss Sandomir says, it's all the more reason for thinking about them. Anyhow, you can't take the Bible that way; it's nothing to do with it.'

'It's the plain word of God, and that's sufficient for me, ' said Mrs Frampton repressively.

Vincent Vinney, tired of the poor, who are indeed exhausting, regarded in the mass as a subject for contemplation, brought the discussion back to women.

'What I'd like to know is, where is a woman to get her knowledge from, if she's to help in public affairs? A man can pick up things at his work and his club, but a woman working in the house all day has no time even to read the papers. And if she did, her husband wouldn't like her to start having opinions, perhaps different to his. There are far too many divorces and separations already because husbands and wives go different ways, and it would be worse than ever. Eh, Flossie?'

Mrs Frampton said, 'We heard of a woman only last month who went out to a public meeting –something about foreign politics, I think it was – and her baby fell on to the fire and was burnt to a cinder, poor little love.'

'Well, she might just as likely have been going out shopping.'

'But she wasn't, ' said Kate conclusively.

'I don't think, ' said Mrs Frampton, 'that a woman desires any more than her home and her husband and children, if she's a proper woman.'

Evie's contribution was, 'Well, I must say I do prefer men to girls, and I don't mind saying so.'

Sid's was, 'I heard of a man whose wife took to talking about politics, and he hung his coat to one peg in her wardrobe and his trousers to another, and he said, "Now, Eliza, which will you wear?" '

It was apparently the combination of this anecdote and Evie's remark before it that broke Miss Simon down. She suddenly collapsed into indignant tears. Everyone was uncomfortable. Mrs Frampton said kindly, 'Come, come, my dear, it's only talk. It isn't worth crying about, I'm sure, with so many real troubles in the world just now.'

'You won't see,' sobbed Miss Simon, who looked particularly plain when crying. 'You none of you see. Except her' – she indicated Alix – 'and she won't talk; she only smiles to herself at all of us. You tell silly tales, and you say silly things, and you think you've scored – but you haven't. It isn't *argument*, that you like men more than women or women more than men. And that man married to Eliza was an idiot, and not a bit funny or clever, and you all think he scored over her.'

'Well, really, ' said Sid, and grinned sheepishly at the others.

Kate had fetched a glass of water. 'Drink some,' she said kindly. 'It'll make you feel better.' But Miss Simon pushed, it aside and mopped her eyes and blew her nose and pulled herself together.

2

'Fancy crying before everyone,' thought Evie. 'And just from being in a passion about getting the worst of it in talk. She is a specimen.'

'The boys shouldn't draw Rachel on to make such a silly of herself,' thought young Mrs Vinney.

'Poor girl, she must have been working too hard, she's quite hysterical, ' thought Mrs Frampton.

'Having her staying with them must draw Vin and Floss very close together,' thought Kate, who had loved Vin long before Floss met him.

'We shan't have any more fun out of this evening; we'll go home,' thought Vincent, and glanced at his wife.

'What a difference between one girl and another,' thought Sid, and gazed at Evie.

'I wonder if many people are like these,' thought Alix, speculating. Were discussions at Violette, discussions in all the thousands of Violettes, always like this? Not argument, not ideas, not facts. Merely statements, quotations rather, of hackneyed and outworn sentiments, prejudices secondhand, yet indomitable, unassailable, undying, and the relation of stories, without relevance or force, and (but this much more rarely, surely) a burst of bitterness and emotion to wind it all up. Curious. Rachel Simon, like the rest, was stupid and ignorant, her brain a chaos of half-assimilated, inaccurate facts (she said Wills when she meant Hill) and crude sentiments. She seemed to belong, oddly, to an outworn age (the late eighties, was it? Alix wasn't old enough to know). But Alix was sorry for her, remembering the look in her face when they had each in turn dealt her a finishing blow. Alix rather wished Evie hadn't made that idiotic remark about men and girls; wished Mrs Frampton hadn't talked of proper women; wished Kate hadn't said 'But she wasn't'; even wished she herself had joined in a little. Only it was all too inane …

3

To change the subject Vincent Vinney said they had collared another German baker spy down in Camberwell.

'These bakers,' said Mrs Frampton, 'do seem to be dreadful people. We've left off taking our Hovis loaf, since they found that wireless in Camberwell the other day.'

'You can't be too careful, can you?' said Mrs Vinney.

'For my part I'd like to see every German in England shut up in gaol for a life-sentence. But we must be trotting, Mr Frampton, or we shall miss our beauty-sleep. Good-night; we've enjoyed the evening awfully. Oh, Evie, I've got those blouse patterns from Harrods; can you come round to-morrow afternoon and help me choose? Come early and stay to tea. You too, Kate, won't you? You *are* a girl; you never come when I ask you.'

Kate looked uncomfortable, and helped Miss Simon (now composed, but looking plainer than ever with her red eyes and nose) into her coat. To see the Vinneys together by their own fireside was rather more than Kate could bear, though she had a good deal of stolid outward endurance. Her hands shook as she handled the ugly green coat. She wanted to avoid shaking hands with the Vinneys, but she could not. The familiar physical thrill ran through her at Vincent's hearty clasp, and left her limp.

'I'm afraid it's commencing to rain,' said Kate.

'Good-night all,' said Mrs Frampton. 'We've had quite a little discussion, haven't we? I'm sure one ought to talk things out sometimes, it improves the mind. Now I do hope you won't all get wet. You must take our umbrellas.'

CHAPTER 7

Hospital

1

About a week later, Alix and Nonie Maclure went to see Basil Doye in hospital.

'Hate hospitals, don't you?' Nonie remarked, as they entered its precincts. 'I've a sister VADing here – Peggy, you know her, she's having a three-months' course – but I've not been to see her yet. I can't remember her ward; it's a men's surgical, I think. We'll go and find her afterwards. I don't think she'll be able to stick her three months, because of her feet. They swell up so; they make the nurses stand all the time, you know, even when they're doing needlework and things. She says half the nurses in the hospital have foot and leg diseases. Silly, isn't it? The VADs *could* sit down sometimes, but they don't like to when the regulars mayn't. They're unpopular enough as it is. Peggy asked the staffnurse in her ward why all the nurses didn't combine and ask to have the standing-rule altered, but she only said you can't get hospital rules altered, they *are* like that. Nurses must be idiots …'

They crossed the court that led to the wing with the officers' wards. It was dotted with medical students.

'Rabbits,' Nonie considered them. 'All that are left of them, I suppose. Peggy says they're mostly rather rotters. They have a great time with the nurses. One of them tried to have a great time with Peggy the other day, but she wasn't having any … The Royal Family wing we want, don't we? Darwin, Lister … No, that must be men of science. I suppose that's ours, up those stairs.'

68

It was one of those hospitals in which the wards are named after persons socially or intellectually eminent. In the wing Nonie and Alix wanted the wards were entitled Victoria, Albert Edward, Alexandra, Princess Mary, George, and so forth. One, named doubtless in happier international times, was even called Wilhelm. Out of Wilhelm, as they passed its glass door, came four figures white-clad from head to foot, wheeling a stretcher on which lay a round-faced little girl of sixteen, trying to smile.

'Going down to the theatre,' Nonie whispered. 'Rather shuddery, isn't it?'

2

They entered Albert Edward, which was a small ward of twelve beds, used just now for officers. It smelt of iodo-form. Several of the beds had visitors round them. Some of the patients were in wheeled chairs, smoking. One, in bed, was singing, unintelligibly, in a high, shrill voice. At the table by the centre window two nurses stood, a probationer and a VAD, making swabs and talking. They looked tired, and were very young. The other two nurses, the staffnurse and the super, were talking to two of the patients. They had learnt not to look so tired. Also perhaps the pleasant excitement of being in Albert Edward bore them up.

The staff-nurse said, 'Mr Doye? That's his bed over there – nine. He's up in a chair this afternoon. He's in pretty bad pain most of the time. They may have to amputate, but the doctor hopes to manage without. '

Alix and Nonie went across the ward to nine, where Mr Doye, in a brown dressing-gown, sat in a wheeled chair, smoking a cigarette and talking to the super, who was rather nice-looking and had auburn hair. In the next bed lay the singer, with fixed blue eyes and flushed cheeks and a capeline bandage round his head, carolling German songs in a high, monotonous voice.

'Quite delirious, poor thing,' the super explained to the visitors. 'His nerves are all to bits. He was a prisoner, till he got exchanged. And would you believe it, they'd never taken the shrapnel out of his head; he went under operation for it here last week.' She moved away, whispering first to Nonie behind the patient's back, 'He has to be kept pretty quiet, please; the pain gets bad on and off.'

'Hullo,' said Basil Doye, smiling at them. 'This is great.'

He had a soft, rather quick way of speaking; today he was huskier than usual, perhaps because he was ill. He was long and slim; he had used, in pre-war days, to lounge and slouch, but possibly did that no more. Anyhow today he merely lay limply in a chair, so they could not judge. His long pale face and flexible mouth and dark eyebrows were always moving and changing; so were his rather bright eyes, that kept shading and glinting from green to hazel. His forehead and rumpled hair were damp just now, either from the heat or from some other cause. His bandaged right hand was raised in a sling.

'You do look an old wreck,' said Nonie frankly. 'What did you go and do it for? A silly way of getting wounded, I call it, playing ball with bombs. '

'Rotten, wasn't it? But it would have played ball with me if I hadn't. It was bound to go off in a moment, you see, and I naturally tried to house it with the foe first; one often can. My mistake, I know. These little things will happen … I say, you're the first people I've seen from the shop. How's it going? Who are the good people this year?'

They began to tell him. He listened, fidgeting, with restless eyes.

'Have a smoke?' he broke in. 'No, I suppose you mustn't here. Sorry; didn't mean to interrupt …'

They were talking about the exhibition in Grafton Street.

'I must get round there,' he said, 'when I'm not so tied by the leg.'

'How long will they keep you here, d'you imagine?'

'Haven't an earthly. They may be depriving me of a finger or two in a few days. Or not. They don't seem to know their own minds about it.'

'Good Lord!' murmured Nonie, taken aback. 'I say, don't let them. You – you'd miss them so.'

> 'Halli, hallo, halli, hallo!
> Bei uns geht's immer so!'

shrilled number eight.

Doye moved impatiently. 'He ought to be taken away, poor beggar … I loathe hospitals. People who are ill oughtn't to be with other people in the same miserable condition; it's too depressing. One wants the undamaged, as an antidote. That's why visitors are so jolly.' His restless eyes glanced at Nonie's dark, glowing brilliance in her yellow frock, and at Alix, pale and cool and thin in green.

'Above all,' he added, 'one wants sanity and normalness and cheeriness, not people with their nerves in rags, like that poor chap. '

Eight broke out again, half singing, half humming some students' chorus –

> 'Tra la la, in die Nacht Quartier!'

The auburn-haired nurse came and stood by him for a moment, quieting him.

'Come now, come now, you must be quiet, you know.'

'Rather a pleasant person, that nurse,' said Doye when she had gone. 'Jolly hair, hasn't she? … Alix,' he added, 'do you know, you don't look up to much. Is it overwork, or merely the air of London in June?'

'It's the air of hospitals, I expect, ' Nonie answered for her. 'She turned white directly we got into the ward.'

'Beastly places,' Basil agreed.

Alix began to talk, rather fast. She told stories of the other people at the art school; Nonie joined in, and they made Basil laugh. He talked too, also fast. His unhurt hand drummed on the arm of his chair; his forehead grew damper, his eyes shifted about under his black brows. He talked nonsense, absurdly; they all did. They all laughed, but Basil laughed most; he laughed too much. He said it was a horrible bore out there; funny, of course, in parts, but for the most part irredeemably tedious. And no reason to think it would ever end, except by both sides just getting too tired of it to go on … Idiotic business, chucking bombs over into trenches full of chaps you had no grudge against and who wished you no ill … and they chucking bombs at you, much more idiotic still. The whole thing hopelessly silly …

'Heil'ge Nacht, Heil'ge Nacht,' trilled Eight, with a nightmare of Christmas on him.

'Oh, damn,' muttered Basil, and got scarlet and then white.

The staff-nurse came to them. She was not auburnhaired, but efficient and good-looking and dark, with a clear, sharp voice.

'I think your visitors had better go now, Mr Doye. '

She made signs to them that he was in pain, which they knew before. They went; he joked as he said good-bye, and they joked back. As they left the ward, eight's wild voice rose, in a sad air they knew:

> 'Mein Bi-er und Wei-ein fri-isch und klar;
> Mein Töchterlein liegt auf der To-otenbahr …'

'Come now, come now,' admonished Staff.

3

On the stairs they met a tall woman with a long pale face and black hair, and eyes full of green light. She stopped and said to Alix, 'How do you do? Basil told me you were going to see him today, so I left you a little time. He mustn't have too many at once. He has a lot of pain, for so slight a thing … I shall be glad when I can get him away for a change.'

Her eyes, looking at Alix's pale face, were kind and friendly. She liked Alix, who was Basil's friend and had stayed with them last summer in the country. She thought her clever and attractive, if selfish. She hurried on through the glass door into Albert Edward.

'Mrs Doye, isn't it?' said Nonie. 'Must have been just like him twenty years ago … I say, how sickening, isn't it, people getting smashed up like that. Poor old Basil. All on edge, I thought, didn't you? What rot he talked … I say, if he loses those fingers it will be all UP with his career … I don't expect he will.' She shot a glance at Alix, whom she suspected of feeling faint. 'Let's come and find Peggy. I haven't an earthly where her ward is. It's called after some man of science.' But there are so many of these, and all so much alike.

'If it was painters,' said Nonie presently, 'I might have remembered. Who *are* the men of science?'

'Darwin, ' suggested Alix intelligently. 'Galileo. Sir Isaac Newton. Sir Oliver Lodge. Lots more.'

'Well, let's try this passage.'

They tried it. It led them on and on. It looked wrong, but might be right, in such a strange world as a hospital, where anything may be right or wrong and you never know till you try.

They saw at last ahead of them a closed door – not a glass door but a baize one. From behind it screaming came, wild, shrill, desperate, as if someone was being hurt to death.

'O Lord!' said Nonie, 'it's the theatre. Look, it's written on the door. Come away quick. There must be an operation on. Beyond the door there was a shuffling and scuffling; it was pushed open, and two figures muffled in white, like the stretcher-women, dragged out a Red Cross girl in a faint.

'Fetch her some water,' said one. 'Idiot, why didn't she come out before she went off? These Red Cross girls – All right, she's coming round … I *say*, you know, you mustn't do that again. People are supposed to come out of the theatre *before* they faint, not after. It's an awful crime … Is it your first operation? Well, it was silly of them to send you down to such a bad one. I expect the screaming upset you. She didn't *feel* anything, you know … Here, drink this. You're all right now, aren't you? I must get back. You'd better go up to your ward and ask your Sister if you can lie down for a bit. '

Alix and Nonie had retreated down the passage.

'What a place,' Alix was muttering savagely. 'Oh, *what* a place.'

They came out on a different staircase; fleeing down it they were in a corridor, long and unhappy and full of hurrying house-surgeons and nurses and patients' friends (for it was visiting-hour).

4

'Huxley,' said Nonie suddenly. 'That's the creature's name … I say,' she accosted a fat little nurse with strings, 'where's Huxley, please?'

Huxley was far away. They reached it through many labyrinthine and sad ways. Through the glass door they saw a keen-faced doctor going from bed to bed with an attendant group of satellites – medical students, who laughed at intervals because he was witty, either about the case in hand or about some other amusing cases this one recalled to his memory, or at the foolish answers elicited from some student in response to questions. They were a cheery set, and this doctor was a wit. Every few minutes he washed his hands. The ward-sister companioned him round, and by the window stood four nurses at attention – the staff-nurse, the probationer, and two VADs with red crosses on their aprons. It was a men's surgical ward. It was long and light, and had twenty-one beds, and Cot. Cot was in the middle of the ward. He was there and had peritonitis of the stomach, and he sat up on his pillow and wept, and wailed at intervals, 'Want to do 'ome. Want to do 'ome.'

'You're not the only one, sonny,' number three told him bitterly. 'We all want that.'

Twenty-one sad faces apathetically testified to his truthfulness. Twenty-one weary sick men, whose rest had been broken at dawn because the night-nurses had to wash them all before they went off duty, and that meant beginning at 3.30 or 4, stared with sad, hollow eyes, and wanted to go 'ome.

The doctor washed his hands for the last time and went, his satellites after him. The probationer respectfully opened, the door for them. Nonie and Alix stood back out of the way as they passed, then Nonie's Peggy, who had seen them long since, came and fetched them in.

'I am glad to see you,' she said.

Nonie said, 'You look dead, my child, ' and she returned, 'Oh, it's only the standing. We're all in the same box. She,' she indicated the probationer, 'fainted this morning. And the staff-nurse has the most awful varicose veins. I believe most nurses get them sooner or later. They *ought* to be let to sit down when they get a chance, for sewing and things, but hospital rules are made of wood and iron. The other Red Crosser and I do sometimes sit, when Sister's out of the ward, but it's rather bad form really, when the regulars mayn't.

Funny places, hospitals … I've been getting into rows this morning for not polishing the brights bright enough. Staff told me they had quite upset Sister. Sister's very easily upset, unfortunately. Staff's a jolly good sort, though … But look here, you must go. It's time for teatrays; I shall have to be busy. I'll come round to-night after I'm off, Nonie – if I can get so far. You've got to go now; Staff's looking at us.'

They went. Staff called wearily to Peggy, 'Go and help Nurse Baker with trays, will you, dear. And you might take Daddy Thirteen's basin away. He's done being sick for now, I dare say, and he's going to drop it on to the floor in a moment.'

Peggy hurried, but was too late. These things will happen sometimes …

5

'Hate hospitals, don't you?' said Nonie, as she had said when they entered. They were going out at the gates now. 'I suppose they have to be, though.'

'Suppose so,' Alix agreed listlessly.

Then with an effort she threw the hospital off.

'That's over, anyhow. I shan't go again. Let's come and do something awfully different now.' They did.

6

When Alix got back to Violette, she was met in the little linoleumed hall by distress and pity, and Mrs Frampton preparing to break something to her, with a kind, timid arm round her shoulders.

'Dearie, there was a telegram … You were out, so we opened it … Now you must be ever so brave.'

'No,' said Alix, rigid and leaning on her stick and whitely staring from narrowed eyes. 'No …'

'Oh, darling child, it's sad news … I don't know how to tell you … Dear, you must be brave …'

'Oh, do get on,' muttered Alix, rude and sick.

'Dearie,' Mrs Frampton was crying into her handkerchief. 'Poor Paul … your dear little brother … dreadfully, badly wounded …'

'Dead,' Alix stated flatly, pulling away and leaning against the wall.

Violette was hot and smelt of food. Florence stumbled up the kitchen stairs with supper. From a long way off Mrs Frampton sobbed, 'The Lord gave, and the Lord hath taken away … It's the Almighty's will … The poor dear boy has died doing his duty and serving his country … a noble end, dearie … not a wasted life …'

'Not a wasted …' Alix said it after her mechanically, as if it was a foreign language.

'He died a noble death,' said Mrs Frampton, 'serving his country in her need.' Alix was staring at her with blue eyes suddenly dark and distended. The horror rose and loomed over her, like a great wave towering, just going to break.

'But – but – but –' she stammered, and put out her hands, keeping it off – 'But he hadn't lived yet …'

Then the wave broke, like a storm crashing on a ship at sea.

'It's a lie,' she screamed. 'Give me the telegram … It's made up; it's a damnable lie. The War Office always tells them: everyone knows it does …'

They gave it her, pitifully. She read it three times, and it always said the same thing. She looked up for some way of escape from it, but found none, only Violette, hot and smelling of supper, and Mrs Frampton crying, and Kate with working face, and Evie sympathetic and moved in the background, and Florence compassionate with the supper tray, and a stuffed squirrel in a glass case on the hall table.

Alix shivered and shook as she stood, with passion and

sickness and loss. 'But – but –' she began to stammer again, helplessly, like a bewildered child – 'But he hadn't lived yet …'

Kate said gently, 'He has begun to live now, dear, for ever and ever.'

'World without end, amen,' added Mrs Frampton, mopping her eyes.

Alix looked past them, at the stuffed squirrel.

'It's just some silly lie of course,' she said, indifferent and quiet, but still shaking. 'It will be taken back to-morrow … I shall go to bed now.'

When Kate brought her up some supper on a tray, she found her lying on the floor, having abandoned the lie theory, having abandoned all theories and all words, except only, again and again, 'Paul … Paul … Paul …'

CHAPTER 8

Basil at Violette

1

June went by, and the war went on, and the Russians were driven back in Galicia, and the Germans took Lemberg, and trenches were lost and won in France, and there was fighting round Ypres, and Basil Doye had the middle finger of his right hand cut off, and there was some glorious weather, and Zeppelin raids in the eastern counties, and it was warm and stuffy in London, and Mrs Sandomir wrote to Alix from the United States that more than ever now, since their darling Paul was added to the toll of wasted lives, war must not occur again.

July went by, and the war went on, and trenches were lost and won, and there was fighting round Ypres, and a German success at Hooge, and the Russians were driven back in Galicia, and Basil Doye left hospital and went with his mother to Devonshire, and there were Zeppelin raids in the eastern counties, and the summer term at the art school ended, and Alix went away from Clapton to Wood End, and her mother wrote that American women were splendid to work with, and that it was supremely important that the States should remain neutral, and that there were many hitches in the way of arbitration, but some hope.

August went by, and the war went on, and Warsaw was taken, and the National Register, and trenches were lost and won, and there was fighting round Ypres, and a British success at Hooge and in Gallipoli, and Zeppelin raids on the eastern counties, and Nicholas and Alix went away together for a holiday to a village in Munster where the only newspaper which appeared with regularity was the *Ballydehob Weekly Despatch*, and Violette was shut up, and Mrs Frampton stayed with Aunt Nellie and Kate and Evie with friends, and Mrs Sandomir wrote from Sweden that the Swedes were promising but apathetic, and their government shy.

September went by, and the war went on, and the Russians rallied and retreated and rallied in Galicia, and a great allied advance in France began and ended, and the hospitals filled up, and there were Zeppelin raids on the eastern counties, and Mrs Frampton and Kate and Evie came back to Violette, and the art school opened, and Alix came back to Violette, and the Doyes came back to town, and Mrs Sandomir wrote from Sermaize-le-Bains, where she was staying a little while again with the Friends and helping to reconstruct, that it was striking how amenable to reason neutral and even belligerent governments were, if one talked to them reasonably. Even Ferdinand, though he had his faults …

October began, and the war went on, and Bulgaria massed on the Serbian frontier, and Russia sent her an ultimatum, and the Germans retook the Hohenzollern Redoubt, and the hospitals got fuller, and the curious affair of Salonika began, and Terry Orme came home on leave, and Basil Doye interviewed the Medical board, was told he could not rejoin yet, visited Cox's, and, coming out of it, met Alix going up to the Strand.

2

Alix saw him first; he looked listless and pale and bored and rather cross, as he had done last time she saw him, a week ago. Basil was finding life something of a bore just now, and small things jarred. It was a nuisance, since he was on this ridiculous fighting business, not to be allowed to go and fight. There might be something doing any moment out there, and he not in it. His hand was really nearly all right now. And anyhow, it wasn't much fun in town, as he couldn't paint, and nearly everyone was away.

His eyes followed a girl who passed with her officer brother. He would have liked a healthy, pretty, jolly sort of girl like that to go about with … some girl with poise, and tone, and sanity, and no nerves, who never bothered about the war or anything. A placid, indifferent, healthy sort of girl, with all her fingers on and nothing the matter anywhere. He was sick of hurt and damaged bodies and minds; his artistic instinct and his natural vitality craved, in reaction, for the beautiful and the whole and the healthy …

Looking up, he saw Alix standing at the corner of the Strand, leaning on her ivory-topped stick and looking at him. She looked pale and thin and frail and pretty in her blue coat and skirt and white collar. (The Sandomirs never wore mourning.) He went up to her, a smile lifting his brows.

'Good. I was just feeling bored. Let's come and have tea.'

Alix wasn't really altogether what he wanted. She was too nervy. Some nerve in him which had been badly jarred by the long ugliness of those months in France winced from contact with nervous people. Besides, he suspected her of feeling the same shrinking from him: she so hated the war and all its products. However, they had always amused each other; she was clever, and nice to look at; he remembered vaguely that he had been a little in love with her once, before the war. If the war hadn't come just then, he might have become a great deal in love with her. Before the war one had wanted a rather different sort of person, of course, from now; more of a companion, to discuss things with; more of a stimulant, perhaps, and less of a rest. He remembered that they had discussed painting a great deal; he didn't want to discuss painting now, since he had lost his finger. He didn't particularly want cleverness either, since trench life, with its battery on the brains of sounds and sights, had made him stupid …

However, he said, 'Let's come and have tea, ' and she answered, 'Very well, let's,' and they turned into something in the Strand called the Petrograd Tea Rooms.

'I suppose one mustn't take milk in it here,' said Alix vaguely. She looked him over-critically as they sat down, and said, 'You don't look much use yet.'

'So I am told. They say I shall probably have at least a month's more leave … Well, I don't much care … There's a rumour my battalion may be sent to Serbia soon. I met a man on leave today, and he says that's the latest canard. I rather hope it's true. It will be a change, anyhow, and there'll be something doing out there. Besides, we may as well see the world thoroughly on this show, while we are about it. We shall never have such a chance again, I suppose. It's like a Cook's tour gratis. France, Flanders, Egypt, Gallipoli, Serbia, Greece … I may see them all yet. This war has its humours, I'll say that for it. A bizarre war indeed, as some titled lunatic woman driving a motor ambulance round Ypres kept remarking to us all. "Dear, me, what a very bizarre war!" It sounded as if she had experienced so many, and as if they were mostly so normal and conventional and flat.'

'Bizarre.' Alix turned the word over. 'Yes, I suppose that is really what it is … It's the wrong shape; it fits in with nothing; it's mad … My cousin Emily says it's a righteous war, though of course war is very wicked. Righteous of us and wicked of the Germans, I suppose she means. And Kate says it was sent us, for getting drunk and not going to church enough. I don't know how she knows. Do you meet people who talk like that?'

'I chiefly meet people who ask me why I'm not taking part in it. There was one today, in Trafalgar Square. She told me I ought to be in khaki. I said I supposed I ought, properly speaking, but that I was waiting to be fetched. She said it was young fellows like me who disgraced Britain before the eyes of Europe, and that I wouldn't like being fetched, because then I should have to wear C for Coward on my tunic. I said I should rather enjoy that, and we parted pleasantly.'

'The wide ones are two and eleven three, and the narrow ones one and nine. I like B & H's better than Evans', myself.'

The voice was Evie's; she was entering the Petrograd Tearooms with young Mrs Vinney. She saw Alix, nodded, and said 'Hullo.' It was Basil who made room for them at the table with him and Alix (the tea shop was crowded). He had met Evie once before.

'Oh, thanks muchly. Don't you mind?' Evie was apologetic, thinking two was company. Mrs Vinney was introduced to Basil, settled herself in her dainty fluffiness, emphasised by her feather boa, and ordered crumpets for herself and Evie.

'Quite a nice little place, don't you think so, Miss Sandomir? More *recherché* than an ABC or one of those. I often come here … What's that boy shouting? The Germans take something or other redoubt … Fancy! How it does go on, doesn't it?'

Alix said it did.

'Quite makes one feel,' said Mrs Vinney, 'that one *oughtn't* to be sitting snug and comfortable having crumpets, doesn't it? You know what I mean; it's just a feeling one has, no sense in it. One oughtn't to give in to it, *I* don't think; Vin says so too. What's the use, he says, of brooding, when it helps nobody, and what we've got to do is to keep cheery at home and keep things going. I must say I

quite agree with him.'

'Rather, so do I,' said Basil.

'But of course it all makes one think, doesn't it?' she

resumed. 'Makes life seem more *solemn* – do you know what I mean? And all the poor young fellows who never come home again. I'm thankful none of my people or close friends are gone. Mother simply wouldn't let my brother go; she says we've always been a peace-loving family and she's not going to renounce her principles now. Percy doesn't really want to; it was only a passing fancy because some friends of his went. Vin says, leave war to those that want war; he doesn't, and he's not going to mix up in it, and I must say I think he's right.'

'Quite,' agreed Basil.

'All this waste of life and money just because the Germans want a war! Why should we *pander* to them, that's what he says. *Let* them want. He's no Prussian Junker, shouting out for blood. There's too many of them in this country, he says, and that's what makes war possible. He's all for disarmament, you know, and I must say I think he's right. If no one had any guns or ships, no one could fight, could they?'

Evie agreed that they couldn't, forgetting knives and fists and printed words and naked savages and all the gunless hosts of the ancient world. Violette thought always gaped with these omissions; it was like a loose piece of knitting, stretched to cover spaces too large for it and yawning into holes.

'Mr Doye's been fighting, you know,' Evie explained, since Mrs Vinney was obviously taking him for one who left war to those that wanted war. 'He's wounded.'

'Oh, is that so?' Mrs Vinney regarded Mr Doye with new interest. 'Well, I must say one can't help *admiring* the men that go and fight for their country, though one should allow liberty to all … I hope you're going on favourably, Mr Doye.'

'Very, thanks very much.'

'Well, we must be trotting, Evie, if we're going to Oxford Street before we go home … Check, if you please … They're always so slow, aren't they at these places. Good-bye, Miss

Sandomir; good-bye, Mr Doye, and I'm sure I hope you'll get quite all right soon. '

Basil stood aside to let them out, and looked after them for a moment as they went.

3

He sat down with a grin. 'Makes life more *solemn* – do you know what I mean? ... What a cheery little specimen ... I say, I'd like to draw Miss Tucker; such good face-lines. That clear chin, and the nice wide space between the eyes.' He drew it on the tablecloth with his left hand and the handle of his teaspoon.

'She's ripping to draw,' Alix agreed. 'I often do her. And the colour's gorgeous, too – that pink on brown. I've never got it right yet.'

'I should think she's fun to live with,' suggested Basil. 'She looks as if she enjoyed things so much.'

'Yes, she has a pretty good time as a rule.'

'You know,' said Basil, thinking it out, 'being out there, and seeing people smashed to bits all about the place, and getting smashed oneself, makes one long for people like that, sane and healthy and with nothing the matter with their bodies or minds. It gets to seem about the only thing that matters, after a time.'

'I suppose it would.'

'Now a person like that, who looks like some sort of wood goddess – (I'd awfully like to paint her as a dryad) – and looks as if she'd never had a day's illness or a bad night in her life, is so – so *restful*. So alive and yet so calm. No nerves anywhere, I should think ... Being out there plays the dickens with people's nerves, you know. Not everyone's, of course; there are plenty of cheery souls who come through unmoved; but you'd be surprised at the jolly, self-possessed sportsmen who go to pieces more or less – all degrees of it, of course. Some don't know it themselves; you can often only see it by the way their eyes look at you while they're talking, or the way their hand twitches when they light their cigarette …' Alix remembered John Orme's eyes and hands. 'They dream a bit, too,' Basil went on, and his own eyes were fixed and queer as he talked, and his brows twitched a little. 'Talk in their sleep, you know, or walk … It's funny … I've censored letters which end "Hope this finds you the same as it leaves me, ie in the pink," from chaps who have to be watched lest they put a bullet into themselves from sheer nerves. You'll see a man shouting and laughing at a sing-song, then sitting and crying by himself afterwards … Oh, those are extreme cases, of course, but lots are touched one way or another … I'm sorry for the next generation; they'll stand a chance of being a precious neurotic lot, the children of the fighting men … It's up to everyone at home to keep as sane and unnervy as they can manage, I fancy, or the whole world may become a lunatic asylum … I say, what are you going to do now?'

'Buy some chalks. Then go home.'

'Violette? I'll see you home, may I?'

4

They went to the chalk shop, then to the Clapton bus. The evening wind was like cool hands stroking their faces. It was half-past six. The streets were barbarically dark.

'One would think,' said Basil, peering through the darkness at the ugliness, 'that in Kingsland Road Zepps might be allowed to do their worst.'

'On Spring Hill too, perhaps,' Alix said. Slums and the screaming of the disreputable poor: villas and the precise speech and incomparably muddled thinking of the respectable genteel: which could best be spared?

But Basil said, 'Oh Spring Hill. Spring Hill is full of joy and dryads.'

'Kate is afraid a very common type of person is coming to live there. We're getting nervous about it at Violette. We're very particular, you know.'

Alix, with the instinct of a cad, was laughing at Violette, wanting him to laugh with her.

'Sure to be,' he returned; and Alix realised blankly that he might laugh at Violette to her heart's content and his attitude towards dryads and Evie Tucker's face-lines would remain unaltered by his mockery.

With a revulsion towards breeding, she said, 'They're most awfully kind … Here's where I get off.'

He got off too, and they walked down Upper Clapton Road.

5

Someone came behind them, walking quickly, came up with them, slowed, and looked. 'Here we are again,' said. Evie, in her clear gay voice. 'You're coming in to see us, Mr Doye, I hope?'

Basil glanced from Alix to Evie. They were passing under a dim lamp, which for a moment threw Evie's startling prettiness in lit relief against the night. Extreme prettiness is not such a common thing that one can afford to miss chances of beholding it.

Basil said, 'Well, may I?'

Evie returned, 'Rather. Stop to supper.'

'I can't do that, thanks very much. But I'll come in for a moment, if I may.'

As they entered Violette's tiny hall, the clock struck seven. They went into the drawing-room, where Mrs Frampton and Kate sat knitting. It was stiff and prim and tidy, and rather stuffy, and watched from the wall by the monstrous Eye.

'Here's Mr Doye, mother,' said Evie. 'He saw Alix home.'

Mr Doye was introduced to Kate. Mrs Frampton said how kind it was of him to see Alix home.

'Particularly with the streets black like they are now. Have we a *right* to expect to be preserved if we go against all common-sense like that?'

'I never do,' said Basil, meaning he never expected to be preserved, but Mrs Frampton took it that he never went against common-sense.

'Well, I'm sure I go out after dark as little as I can; but the girls have to, coming back from work, and it makes me worry for them … Now you sit in that easy-chair, Mr Doye, and make yourself comfortable, and rest your hand. It's going on well, I hope? You'll stop and have some supper. of course? We have it at half-past seven, so it won't keep you long.'

Basil said he wouldn't, because he was dining somewhere at eight.

They talked of the news. Mrs Frampton said it seemed to get worse each day. She had been reading in the paper that Bulgaria was just coming in. Was that really so? Mrs Frampton was of those who inquire of their male acquaintances and relatives on these and kindred subjects, and believe the answers, more particularly when the males are soldiers. Basil Doye, used to his mother, who told him things and never believed a word he said, because, as she remarked, he was so much younger, found this gratifying, and said it was really so. Mrs Frampton said dear me, it seemed as if all the world would have to come in in time, and what about poor Serbia, could she be saved? Basil, wanting to leave the state of Europe and ask Evie if she had seen any plays lately, said casually that Serbia certainly seemed to stand a pretty good chance of being done in.

'And then, I suppose,' said Mrs Frampton, 'we shall have the poor Serbian refugees fleeing to us for safety, like the Belgians. I'm sure we shall all welcome them, the poor mothers with their little children. But it will be awkward to know where to put them or what to do with them. They've got those two houses at the corner of the Common full of Belgians now. I wonder if the Belgians and the Serbs would get on well together in the same houses. They say the poor Serbs are very wild people indeed, with such strange habits. Do you think we shall all be asked to take them as servants?'

'Sure to be,' said Basil, his eyes on Evie. Evie sat doing nothing at all, healthy, lovely, amused, splendidly alive. The vigorous young bodily life of her called to Basil's own, reanimating it. Alix sat by her, all alive too, but weakbodied, lame, frail-nerved, with no balance. Kate knitted, and was different.

'It will be quite a problem, won't it?' said Mrs Frampton. 'My maid tells me girls can't get enough places now, people all take Belgians instead.'

'They say the Belgian girls make very rough servants. We know those who have them,' said Kate, who had the Violette knack of switching off from the general to the personal. To Violette there were no labour problems, only good servants and bad, no Belgian or Balkan problem, only individual Belgians and Serbs (poor things, with their little children and strange habits). They had the personal touch, which makes England what it is.

Mrs Frampton wanted to know next, 'And I suppose we shall be having conscription very soon now, Mr Doye, shall we?'

'Lord Northcliffe says so, doesn't he?' Basil returned absently.

Mrs Frampton accepted that.

'Well! I suppose it has to be. It seems hard on the poor mothers of only sons, and on the poor wives too. But if it will help us to win the war, we mustn't grudge them, must we? I suppose it will help us to victory, won't it?'

'Lord Northcliffe says that too, I understand ... What do you think, Miss Tucker?' He turned to Evie, to hear her speak.

She said, 'Oh, don't ask me. *I* don't know. Don't suppose it will make much difference. Things don't, do they?' ·

Basil chuckled. 'Precious little, as a rule ... So that settles that. ' He caught sight of the clock and got up.

'I say, I'm afraid I've got to go at once. I shall be awfully late and rude. I often am, since I joined the army. I was a punctual person once. The war is very bad for manners and morals, have you discovered, Mrs Frampton?'

'Oh well,' Mrs Frampton spoke condoningly, 'I'm sure we must all hope it won't last much longer. How long will it be, Mr Doye, can you tell us that?'

'Seven years,' said Mr Doye. 'Till October 1922, you know. Yes, awful, isn't it? I'm frightfully sorry I had to tell you. Good-bye, Mrs Frampton.' He shook hands with them all; his eyes lingered, bright and smiling, on Evie, as if they found her a pleasant sight. In Alix that look seemed to stab and twist, like a turning sword. Perhaps that was what men felt when a bayonet got them ... The odd thing in the psychology of it was that she had never known before that she was a jealous person; she had always, like so many others, assumed she wasn't. Certainly Evie's beauty had been to her till now pure joy.

As she went to the door with Basil, he said, 'I say, I wish you and your cousin would come into the country one Sunday. We might make up a small party. Your cousin looks as if she would rather like walking.'

'She's rather past it, I'm afraid,' said Alix, and added, in answer to his stare, 'Cousin Emily, you mean, don't you? The Tuckers aren't my cousins, you know. And she's only a dead cousin's wife. The Tuckers aren't even that. '

'No, hardly that, I suppose. Well, ask Miss Tucker if she'd

care to come, will you? I should think she'd be rather a good country person. We might go next Sunday, if it's fine.'

Alix did not remark that Kate was not a particularly good country person. She merely said, 'All right … Mind the step at the gate … Good-night,' and shut the door.

6

She stood for a moment listening to the tread of his feet along the asphalt pavement, then sat down on the umbrella stand thoughtfully.

For a moment it came to her that among the many things the war had taken from her (Paul, Basil, sleep at nights) were two that mattered just now particularly – good breeding, and self-control. She knew she might feel and behave like a cad, and also that she might cry. It was the second of these that she least wanted to do. She had to be very gay and bright … For a moment her fingers were pressed against her eyelids. When she took them away she saw balls of fire dancing all over the hall and up the stairs.

'I shall ask Kate,' she said.

Florence came up the kitchen stairs with food. Kate came out of the sitting-room to help her set the table. Alix said, 'Let me help, Kate,' and began to bustle about the dining-room.

'You're giving mother Evie's serviette,' said Kate, who probably thought this outburst of helpfulness more surprising than useful.

'By the way, Kate,' said Alix suddenly, giving Mrs Frampton Kate's serviette instead, 'I suppose you wouldn't care to come for a long walk in the country on Sunday? I'm going with Basil Doye and some other people, and he asked me to ask you.'

Kate looked repressive.

'Considering my class, and church, and that I never take train on Sunday, it's so likely, isn't it? … And I rather wonder you like to go these Sunday outings, Alix. Don't you think it's nice to keep one day quiet, not to speak of higher things, with all the rushing about you do during the week?'

Kate felt it her duty to say these things sometimes to Alix, who had not been well brought up.

'It might be nice,' returned Alix, absently juggling with napkins. 'But it's difficult, rather … I say, I believe I've got these wrong still … I must go and change now.'

She found Evie changing already, cool, clear-skinned, cheerful, humming a tune.

It was difficult to speak to Evie, but Alix did it. She even hooked her up behind. She saw Evie' s reflection in the glass, pretty and brown. She tried not to think that Evie was gayer than usual, and knew she was. She changed her own dress, and talked fast. She saw her face in the glass; it was flushed and feverish.

7

They went down to supper. There was cold brawn, and custard and stewed apple, and cheese, and what Violett called preserve. An excellent meal, but one in which Alix found no joy. She wanted something warming.

'It was a pity Mr Doye wasn't able to stay,' said Mrs Frampton. 'He's quite full of fun, isn't he?'

'Talks a lot of nonsense, I think,' said Evie.

'The brawn would hardly have been sufficient,' said Kate, meaning if Mr Doye had been able to stay.

'A little custard, love?' Mrs Frampton said to Alix 'Why, you don't look well, Alix. You look as if you had quite a temperature. I hope you've not a chill beginning. These east winds are so searching and your necks are so low. You'd better go to bed early, dear, and Florence shall make you some hot currant tea.'

'Florence says,' said Kate, reminded of that, 'that those people at Primmerose have lost their third girl this month. The girls simply won't stay, and Florence says she doesn't blame them. They're dreadfully common people, I'm afraid, those Primmerose people. There are some funny stories going round about them, only of course one can't encourage Florence to talk. I believe the amount of wine and spirits they take in is something dreadful. In wartime too. It does seem sad, doesn't it? You'd think people might restrain themselves just now, but some seem never to think of that. Mr Alison says all this luxury and intemperance is quite shameful. He preached on it on Sunday night. His idea is that the war was sent us as a judgment, for all our wicked luxury and vice, and it will never cease till we are converted. Lord Derby or no Lord Derby, conscription or no conscription. He says all that is just a question of detail and method but the only way to stop the war is a change of life. He was very forcible, I thought.'

'Perhaps,' said Mrs Frampton, 'that's what Mr Doye meant when he said, didn't he, how all these measures, conscription and so on, don't make much difference after all. No, it was Evie said it, wasn't it? and Mr Doye agreed, and seemed quite pleased with her, I thought. Perhaps he meant the same as Mr Alison, about a change of life. I expect he's very good himself, isn't he, Alix?' ·

Evie, to whom goodness meant dullness, said, 'I bet he isn't. Is he, Al?'

'I don't know,' said Alix. 'You'd better ask him.' She added after a moment, 'I'll ask him for you on Sunday, if you like. We're going out somewhere, if it's fine. '

'It was very kind of him to ask me too,' said Kate. 'You must explain to him how it is I can't, with its being Sunday.' Across the table Alix's eyes met Evie's, suddenly widened in guileless, surprised mirth, with a touch of chagrin.

Evie said, 'Why, whatever did he ask Kate for? He might have known she wouldn't ... Men are ...'

'You're not coming, you're not coming, you're *not* coming,' said Alix within herself, breathing fast and clenching her napkin tight in her two hands and staring across the table defensively out of narrowed eyes.

So they left it at that.

8

But in the night Evie won. One may begin these things, if sufficiently unhinged and demoralised by private emotions and public events, but one cannot always keep them up. The policeman paced up and down, up and down Spring Hill, the rain dripped, the gutters gurgled, Evie breathed softly, asleep, the dark night peered through waving curtains, Alix turned her pillow over and over and cursed.

'I suppose,' she said at last, at 2am, 'she's got to come ...'

At 2.30 she said, 'It will be a beastly day,' and sighed crossly and began to go to sleep.

9

At half-past seven, while Evie did her hair, Alix said, on a weary yawn, 'I say, you'd better come out with us on Sunday, as Kate won't.'

Evie, with hairpins in her mouth, said, 'Me? Oh, all right, I don't mind. Will it amuse me? What's the game?'

'Oh, nothing especial. Just a day in the country. No, I shouldn't think it would amuse you much, especially as you won't know hardly any of the people. But come if you like.'

'You're awfully encouraging.' Evie considered it, and pinned her hair up. 'Oh, I expect I may as well come. It will be cheerier than stopping at home. And I rather like meeting new people … All right, I'm on. Gracious, there's the bell. You'll be late, child. If they're half as particular at your shop as they are at mine, you must get into a lot of rows.'

So that was settled.

CHAPTER 9

Sunday in the Country

1

Sunday morning was quiet and misty, and Clapton was full of bells. At Violette on Sundays each person led a different life. Kate, who attended St Austin's church, went to early Mass at eight, sung Mass for children at 9.45, Sunday school at 10. 30, matins (said hastily) at 11, High Mass (sung slowly) at 11.30, children's catechising at 3, and evensong at 7.

Mrs Frampton went to a quite different church, at 11 o'clock matins, and once a month (the first Sunday) did what was called in that church 'staying on'. She often went again in the evening.

Evie often accompanied her mother, and found, as many have, that after church is a good time and place for gathering together with friends.

Alix did not attend church, not having been brought up to do so. She often went off somewhere on Sunday with friends, as today.

Mrs Frampton said at breakfast, 'Take warm coats, dears; it's quite a fog, and your cough sounds nasty, Alix love. And don't leave your umbrellas; it might very well turn to rain.'

'It's quite cold enough for furs, I think,' said Evie, pleased, because her furs became her.

Through a pale blurred morning Alix and Evie travelled by bus and metropolitan to Victoria. Evie, lithe and fawnlike in dark brown, with her wide, far-set, haunting eyes and sudden dimples, was a vivid note in the blurred world; anyone must be glad of her. Evie needed not to say words of salt or savour; her natural high spirits and young buoyancy were lifted from the commonplace to the charming by her face and smile. Alix by Evie's side was pale and elusive and dim; her only note of colour was the dark, shadowed blue of her black-lashed eyes. She coughed, and her throat was sore. She talked, and made Evie laugh.

2

They entered Victoria Station at 10.29. Waiting in the booking-hall were their friends: Basil Doye, a married young man and young woman of prepossessing exterior, two or three others of both sexes, and Terry Orme with a friend, both on a week's leave. Terry was spending the week-end in town, with another subaltern, and was joining in the expedition at Alix's suggestion. Alix was fond of Terry, who was John's younger brother, and a fair, serene, sweet-tempered, mathematical, very musical person of nineteen. He seemed one of those who, as Basil Doye had put it, come through the war unmoved. His smile was sweet and infectious, and he was restful and full of joy, and could consume more chocolates at a sitting than anyone else (of over fifteen) that he knew. His friend was a cheery, sunburnt youth called Ingram who had got the DCM.

Terry said, 'Hullo, Alix, how are you?' and had the gift of showing, without demonstration, that he knew thing were rotten for her, because of Paul. He was a sympathetic boy, and tender-hearted, and thought Alix looked in poor case; quite different from his own vigorous and cheerful and busy sisters at Wood End. But then of course he and John hadn't been killed, and Paul had. It was frightfully rough luck on Alix. Terry was inclined to think that people out there had much the best of it, on the whole, beastly as it often was, and interrupting to the things that really mattered, such as music, and Cambridge.

Evie was introduced to everyone, and they all had a friendly and pleased look at so much grace and vividness. In the train they filled a compartment. Alix sat between Terry and the married young man, who was something in a government office. Opposite were Evie and Basil and the married young woman, who had lovely furs and a spoilt, charming face, and was selfish about the foot-warmer.

In the train they read a newspaper. Evie got the impression from their manner of reading it that they all knew beforehand what the news was, and a good deal more than was in the paper too; perhaps this impression was produced merely by nobody's saying 'Fancy', as they did at Violette. From their style of comment Evie was inclined to gather that some of them had helped to write the paper and that others were acquainted with the unwritten facts behind and so different from the printed words; perhaps it was merely that they had studied last night's late editions, or perhaps some were journalists, others makers of history, others gifted with invention. Anyhow they seemed to think they knew as much as, or a good deal more than, the paper did. Even the married young woman stopped for a moment being sleepy and sulky about the cold to contribute something she had heard from a Foreign Office man at dinner.

'He was pulling your leg,' her husband said. 'Linsey always does; he thinks it's funny.'

Evie thought him and his high sweet voice conceited.

Alix, looking at Evie opposite, speculated amusedly for a moment where Evie came in: Evie, who knew and cared for no news and had heard nothing from people behind the scenes, and hadn't even had her leg pulled by Foreign Office men. Well, Evie, of course, came in on her face. It was jolly to have a face like that, to cover all vacancies within. Evie sat there, understanding little, yet people spoke to her merely to discover what, with that face, she would say. And what she said pleased and amused merely by reason of its grace of setting.

Evie shivered, and Basil asked if she would like the window up.

'Well, it *is* cold,' said Evie, and he leaned across and pulled it up, asking no one else.

'Thanks so much,' said Evie, taking it prettily to herself. Her face and eyes were brilliant above her furs. Basil, with an artist's pleasure, took in her beauty; Alix felt him doing it. Yes, Evie came in all right.

They got out at some station. The air was like damp blankets, thick and pale and chill. There was no joy in it; dead wet leaves floated earthwards, unhappy like tears. They started walking somewhere, Alix leaned on her stick. She could walk all right, but she limped. She might soon tire, but she wasn't going to say so. They walked uphill, on a forlorn, muddy road. They walked in groups of two or three, changing and mixing and dividing as they went.

They talked …

3

Basil for a minute was beside Alix. He said, 'I say, will this be too much for you? Do say if you get tired, and we'll stop and rest.'

Alix hated him because she was lame and he hated lameness and loved wholeness and strength.

She said, 'No thanks, I'm all right,' and had no more to say at the moment. His eyes were on Evie's back, where she walked ahead with Maynard, the married man. He thought she walked like Diana, straight and free, with a swing.

Alix turned to speak to Terry, who was just behind with his friend Ingram. He came abreast of her, answering. Basil caught up the two in front.

'You look pretty fit, Terry,' said Alix.

'Oh, I'm in the pink.' His fair, unbrowned face was serene and smiling. His far-set blue eyes were not nervous, only watchful, and seemed to see a long way. He hadn't got Basil's or John's quick, jerky, restless movements of the hands. He looked as if the war had more let him alone, left him detached, unconsumed. Perhaps it was because he was a musician; perhaps because he was naturally of a serene spirit; perhaps because he was so young.

'Have a choc,' said Terry, and produced a box of them from the pocket of his Burberry.

Alix had one.

'How are they all at Wood End?' she asked.

'They too appear to be in the pink. They haven't much time to spare for me, though, they're so marvellously busy. Mother always was, of course; but Margot and Dorothy are at it all day too now. I wonder what they'll do with it when the war's over, all this energy. Mother says the war has been good for them; made them more industrious, I suppose. It's a funny thought, that the war can have been *good* for anyone. I can't quite swallow it. I don't think a thing bad in itself can be good for people, do you? It's very bad for me; it's spoiling my ear; the noise, you know; guns and shells and gramophones and so on … By the way, I wish you'd come and hear Lovinski with me on Monday night, it's a jolly programme.'

'All right,' said Alix, who found Terry restful. She talked to Terry, and saw Evie and Basil walking in front, side by side, laughing, Evie's joyous, young smile answering that other quick, amused, friendly smile that she knew.

4

'You *are* all funny,' said Evie to Basil.

'No?'

'Oh, you are. You do talk so … About such mad things.'

'Do we? What do you talk about at home?'

Evie tried to consider.

'Don't know, I'm sure. Oh, just things that happen, I suppose; and mother and Kate talk about servants and household things, and we all talk about the people we know, and what they've done and said. But you … you all talk about …'

'About the people we don't know, and what they've done and said. Is that it?'

'Perhaps. And public things, out of the papers, and what's going to happen, and why, and pictures, and … nonsense … Oh, I don't know … And you find such queer things funny … Anyhow, you all *talk*, even if it's only nonsense most of the time … And the girls and the men talk just the same way. That's funny. Alix is the same, She's the queerest kid; makes me scream with laughter often. She's a pet, though.'

'She is,' said Basil. 'But what people say – the way they talk – makes extraordinarily little difference, you know. It's what they are … The funny thing is, I didn't know that, not so clearly, at least, till I'd been out at the war. A thing like a war seems to settle values, somehow – shows one what matters and what doesn't; shovels away the cant and leaves one with the essentials …' ('Oh, dear me ' said Evie.) 'Sorry; I'm talking rot. What I mean is, isn't it a jolly day and jolly country, and don't you love walking and getting warm? … I suppose you chose your hat to match your face, didn't you? – pink on brown. Don't apologise, I like it. Yes, the hat, too, of course, but I didn't mean that.'

'Well, really!' said Evie.

5

They stopped at an inn for lunch. They crowded round a fire and got warm. They had hot things to eat and drink. They laughed and talked. Outside the wet leaves blew about. Alix's leg ached. Maynard, who talked too much and about the wrong things, persisted in talking about the psychological and social effects of the war. An uncertain subject, and sad, too; but probably he was writing an article about it somewhere; it was the sort of thing Maynard did, in his spare time.

'It's an interesting intellectual phenomenon,' he was saying. 'So many of the intelligent people in all the nations reduced largely to emotional pulp – sunk in blithering jingoism, like a school treat or a mothers' meeting.'

His wife, who had been a bored vicar's daughter before her marriage, and knew, said sleepily, 'Mothers' meetings aren't a bit like that. You don't know anything about them. They mostly don't think anything about jingoism or the war, except that they hope their boys won't go, and that the Kaiser must be an 'ard-'earted man. That's not blithering jingoism, it's common sense.'

Ingram, the cheerful young subaltern, said boldly, 'I think jingoism is an under-rated virtue. There's a lot to be said for it. It makes recruits, anyhow. As long as people don't *talk* jingo, I think it's a jolly useful thing.'

'It's turning some of our best professional cynics into primitive sentimentalists, anyhow,' said Maynard, thinking out his article. 'It's making Europe simple, sensuous and passionate. As evidenced by the war-poetry that was poured forth in 1914. (That flood seems a little spent now; I suppose we're all getting too tired of the war even to write verse about it.) … As evidenced also by the Hymn of Hate and the Deptford riots and other exhibitions of primitive emotion.

The question is, is all this emotion going to last, and to be poured out on other things after the war, or shall we be too tired to feel anything at all, or will there be a reaction to dryness and cynicism? People, for instance, have learnt more or less to give their money away: will they go un giving it, or shall we afterwards be closer-fisted than before?'

'Oh Lord!' said Basil, 'we shall have nothing left to give. Not even munition-makers will, if it's true that the income-tax is going to be quadrupled next year. It's about five bob now, isn't it? Give, indeed!'

'People,' continued Maynard, still on his own train of thought, 'may be divided, as regards the ultimate effects on them of any movement, into two sections – those who respond to the movement and join in all its works and are propelled along in a certain direction by it and continue to be so; and those who, either early or late, react against it, and are propelled in the opposite direction. Every movement has got its reaction tucked away inside it; and the more violent the movement, the more violent the possible reaction. The reactionary forces that come into play during and after war are quite incalculable. Goodness only know where they'll land us … whether they'll prevail over the responding forces or not. For instance, shall we be left a socialistic, centralised, autocratically governed, pre-Magna-Carta state, bound hand and foot by the Defence of the Realm Act, with all businesses state-controlled and all persons subject to imprisonment and sudden death without trial by jury, or will there be a tremendous reaction towards liberal individualism and *laissez-faire*? Who knows? None of us … What do you think about it all, Miss Tucker?' He addressed Evie, to tease her, and make her say something in that fresh buoyant voice of hers.

She did. She said, 'I'm sure I don't know anything about

It. I can't see that the war makes such a lot of difference to ordinary people. One seems to go on much the same from day to day, doesn't one?'

'I'm not at all sure,' said Basil, suddenly interested, 'that Miss Tucker hasn't got hold of the crux of the whole matter. There aren't two sections of people, Maynard – there are three; the respondents, the reactors and the indifferents – ordinary people, that's to say. What difference does the war make, after all – to ordinary people? I believe the fact that it, so to speak, doesn't, is going to settle the destiny of this country. People like you talk of effects and tendencies; you're caught by influences and reactions and carried about; but then, perish the thought that you're an ordinary person. You're only an ordinary person of a certain order, the fairly civilised, not quite unthinking order, that sees and discusses and talks a lot too much. A thing like a war, when it comes along, upsets the whole outlook of your lot; it dissolves the fabric of your world and you have to build it up again – and whether you like it or not, it will be something new for you. But does it upset and dissolve, or even disturb very much, the world of all the people (the non-combatants, I mean, of course, not the fighters) who don't think, or only think from hand to mouth? There'll be no reaction for them, or any such foolishness, because there's been no force. Here's to Ordinary People!' He emptied his glass of beer, and if he seemed to do it to Evie Tucker, that might be taken merely as acknowledgment of her discerning remark.

'Oh, mercy,' said Evie, on a laugh and a yawn. 'You do all go on, don't you.'

Alix, black-browed and sulky, thought so too. Why talk about rotten things like these? Why not talk about the weather, or the countryside, or birds and leaves, or servants, as at Violette instead of these futile speculations on the effects of a war that should not be thought about, should not be mentioned, and would probably anyhow never never end? It was Maynard's fault; he was conceited, and a gasbag, and talked about the wrong things. Terry Orme agreed with her.

But young Ingram said, practically, 'Surely that's all rot, isn't it? I mean, there can be no indifferents, in your sense of the word. Everyone must be affected, even if they haven't people of their own in the show, by the general kick-up. I don't believe in your indifferents; they wouldn't be human beings. They'd be like the calm crowds in the papers, don't you know, who aren't flustered by Zepps. I simply don't believe they exist.

'The fundamentally untouched,' Maynard explained. 'Superficially, of course, they are, as you put it, flustered. They read the papers, of course, for the incidents; but the fundamental issues beneath don't touch them. They're impervious; they're of an immobility; they're sublimely stable. The war, for them, really isn't. The new world, however it shapes, simply won't be. What's the war doing to them? All the beastliness, and bravery, and ugliness, and brutality, and cold, and blood, and mud, and gaiety, and misery, and idiotic muddle, and splendour, and squalor, and general lunacy … you'd think it must overturn even the most stable … do something with them – harden them, or soften them, or send them mad, or teach them geography or foreign politics or knitting or self-denial or thrift or extravagance or international hatred or brotherhood. But has it? Does it? I believe often not. They haven't learnt geography, because they don't like using maps. They've not learnt to fight, because it's non-combatants I'm talking of. They've not even learnt to write to the papers – thank goodness. Nor even to knit, because I believe they mostly knew how already. Nor to preserve their lives in unlit streets, for they are nightly done in in their hundreds. Nor, I was told by a clergyman of my acquaintance the other day, to pray (but that is still hoped for them, I believe). The war, like everything else, will come and go and leave them where it found them – the solid backbone of the world. The rest of the world may go off its head with ideas, or progress, or despair, or war, or joy, or madness, or sanctity, or revolution – but they remain unstirred. I don't suppose a foreign invasion would affect them fundamentally. They couldn't take in invasion, only the invaders. They remain themselves, through every vicissitude. That's why the world after the war will be essentially the same as the world before it; it takes more than a war to move most of us … We all hope our own pet organisation or tendency is going to step in after the war and because of the war and take possession and transform society. Social workers hope for a new burst of philanthropic brotherhood; Christians hope for Christianity; artists and writers for a new art and literature; pacifists for a general disarmament; militarists for permanent conscription; democrats say there will be a levelling of class barriers; and I heard a subaltern the other day remark that the war would "put a stopper on all this beastly democracy." We all seem to think the world will emerge out of the melting-pot into some strange new shape; optimists hope and believe it will be the shape they prefer, pessimists are almost sure it will be the one they can least approve. Optimists say the world will have been brought to a state of mind in which war can never be again; pessimists say, on the contrary, we are in for a long succession of them, because we have revived a habit, and habit forms character, and character forms conduct. But really I believe the world will be left very much where it was before, because of that great immobile section which weighs it down.'

Mrs Maynard, who had been making a very good lunch, yawned at this point, and said, 'Roger, you're boring everyone to death. You don't know anything more about the future than we do. None of us know anything at all. You're not Old Moore.'

'Old Moore,' Evie contributed (she had not been attending to Maynard's discourse, but was caught by this), 'says something important in foreign courts is going to happen in November, connected with a sick-bed. I expect that means the Kaiser's going to be ill. Perhaps he'll die.'

'Sure to,' agreed Basil. 'He's done it so many times already this year, it's becoming a habit … I say, we ought to be getting on, don't you think?'

Mrs Maynard shivered, and said it was quite an unfit day to be out in, and she wasn't enjoying herself in the least, and was anybody else?

Basil said he was, immensely, and found the day picturesque in colour effects.

Evie said she thought it was jolly so long as they kept moving.

Maynard said it was jollier talking and eating, but he supposed that couldn't last.

Terry said it could, if one had chocolates in one's pocket and didn't hurry too much.

6

Basil walked beside Evie. Evie's beauty was whipped to brilliancy by the damp wind. Evie was life. She might not have the thousand vivid awarenesses to life, the thousand responses to its multitudinous calls, that the others had, the keen-witted young persons who had been bred up to live by their heads; but, in some more fundamental way, she was life itself: life which, like love and hate, is primitive, uncivilised, intellectually unprogressive, but basic and inevitable.

Basil had once resented the type. In old days he would have called it names, such as Woman, and Violette. Now he liked Woman, found her satisfactory to some deep need in him; the eternal masculine, roused from slumber by war, cried to its counterpart, ignoring the adulterations that filled the gulf between. Possibly he even liked Violette which produced Woman.

Ingram walked by Alix. The yellow leaves drifted suddenly on to the wet road. Alix's hands were as cold as fishes; her lame leg was tired. She talked and laughed. Ingram was talking about dogs – some foolish pug he knew.

Alix too talked of pugs, and chows, and goldfish, and guinea-pigs. Ingram said there had been a pug in his platoon; he told tales of its sagacity and intrepidity in the trenches.

'And then – it was a funny thing – he lost his nerve one day absolutely; simply went to pieces and whimpered in my dug-out, and stayed so till we got back into billets again. He wouldn't come into the trench again next go; he'd had enough. Funny, rather, because it was so sudden, and nothing special to account for it. But it's the way with some men, just the same. I've known chaps as cheery as crickets wriggling in frozen mud up to the waist, getting frost-bitten, watching shrapnel and whizz-bangs flying round them as calmly as if they were gnats, and seeing their friends slip up all round them ... and never turning a hair. And then one day, for no earthly reason, they'll go to pot – break up altogether. Funny things, nerves ...'

Alix suddenly perceived that he knew more about them than appeared in his jolly, sunburnt face; he was talking on rapidly, as if he had to, with inward-looking eyes.

'Of course there are some men out there who never ought to be out there at all; not strong enough in body or mind. There was a man in my company; he was quite young; he'd got his commission straight from school; and he simply went to pieces when he'd been in and out of trenches for a few weeks. He was a nervous, sensitive sort of chap, and delicate; he ought never to have come out, I should say. Anyhow he went all to bits and lost his pluck; he simply couldn't stand the noise and the horror and the wounds and the men getting smashed up round him: I believe he saw his best friend cut to pieces by a bit of shell before his eyes. He kept being sick after that; couldn't stop. And … it was awfully sad … he took to exposing himself, taking absurd risks, in order to get laid out; everyone noticed it. But he couldn't get hit; people sometimes can't when they go on like that, you know – it's a funny thing – and one night he let off his revolver into his own shoulder. I imagine he thought he wasn't seen, but he was, by several men, poor chap. No one ever knew whether he meant to do for himself, or only to hurt himself and get invalided back; anyhow things went badly and he died of it … I can tell you this, because you won't know who he was, of course …' (But really he was telling it because, like the Ancient Mariner, he had to talk and tell.) He went on quickly, looking vacantly ahead, 'I was there when he fired … Some of us went up to him, and he knew we'd seen … I shan't forget his face when we I spoke to him … I can see it now … his eyes …' He looked back into the past at them, then met Alix's, and it suddenly as if he was looking again at a boy's white, shamed face and great haunted blue eyes and crooked, sensitive mouth and brows … He stopped abruptly and stood still, and said sharply beneath his breath, 'Oh, good Lord!' Horror started to his face; it mounted and grew as he stared; it leaped from his eyes to the shadowed blue ones he looked into. He guessed what he had done, and, because he guessed, Alix guessed too. Suddenly paler, and very cold and sick, she said, 'Oh …' on a long shivering note; and that too was what the boy in the trenches had said: and how he had said it: Perspiration bedewed the young man's brow, though the air hung clammy and cold about them.

'I beg your pardon,' said Ingram, 'but I didn't hear your name. Do you mind …'

'Sandomir, ' she whispered, with cold lips. 'It's the same, isn't it?'

He could not now pretend it wasn't.,

'I – I'm sickeningly sorry,' he muttered. 'I'm an ass … a brute … telling you the whole story like that … Oh, I do wish I hadn't. If only you'd stopped me.'

Alix pulled her dazed faculties together. She was occupied in trying not to be sick. It was unfortunate: strong emotion often took her like that; in that too she was like Paul.

'I d-didn't know,' she stammered. 'I never knew, before how Paul died. They never said … just said shot …'

He could have bitten his tongue out now.

'You mustn't believe it, please … Sandomir wasn't the name … it was my mistake … Sandberg – that was it.'

'They never said, ' Alix repeated. She felt remote from him and his remorse, emptied of pity and drained of all emotions, only very sick, and her hands were as cold as fishes.

A little way in front Evie and Basil were laughing together. A robin sang on a swaying bough. Alix thought how sad he was. She had a sore throat and a headache. The mist clung round, clammy and cold, like her hands.

'I don't know what to say,' Ingram was muttering. 'There's nothing *to* say …'

Alix stopped walking. The sky went dark.

'Terry,' she said.

Terry was at her side.

'All right … Aren't you well?'

She held on to his arm.

'Terry, I'm going home.'

He looked at her face.

'All right, I'll come too … If you're going to faint, you'd better sit down first.'

'I shan't faint,' said Alix. 'But I think … I think I may be going to be sick.'

'Well,' said Terry, 'just wait till the others have gone on, or they'll fuss round … I say good-bye, all of you; Alix is rather done, and we're going to the nearest station for the next train. No thanks, don't bother to come; we shall be all right.'

Alix heard far-away offers of help; hear Evie's 'Shall come with you, Al?' and Basil's 'What bad luck,' and the others' sympathies and regrets, and Terry keeping them off.

7

Alix and Terry were alone together.

Then Alix was, as she had foretold, sick, crouching on damp heather by the roadside.

'Have you done?' inquired Terry presently.

'Yes. I hope so, at least. Let's go on to the station.

'I wonder, is it something beginning? Do you feel like flu? Or is it biliousness, or a chill? Or have you walked too far? I was afraid you had.'

'I'm all right. Only that man – Mr Ingram – told me things, and suddenly I felt sick … He told me things about Paul … He didn't know who I was, and then suddenly he knew, and I saw him know, and I knew too. Do you know, Terry?'

'No' said Terry, levelly. 'I know what some men who were out there thought, but it wasn't true.'

Terry was a good liar, but now no use at all. Alix twisted her cold hands together and whispered hoarsely, 'You've known all the time, then … Oh, Paul, Paul – to have minded as much as all that before you died … to have been hurt like that for weeks and weeks …'

She was crying now, and could not stop.

'Don't, ' said Terry gently. 'Don't think like that about it; it's not the way. Don't think of Paul, except that he got out of it quicker than most people, and is safe now from any more of it. One's got to keep on thinking of that, whenever any of them slip up … I hoped you'd none of you ever know … That bungling ass … Alix, don't: it was such a short time he had of it …'

Alix gasped, her hands pressed to her choked throat, 'It seemed hundreds of years, to him. Hundreds and hundreds of years, of being hurt like that, hurt more than he could bear, till he had to end it …. He was such a *little* boy, Terry … he minded things so much …'

'The thing is,' Terry repeated, frowning and prodding the mud in the road with his stick, 'not to *think*. Not *imagine*. Not to *remember* … It's *over*, don't you see, for Paul. He's clean out of it … It's a score for him really, as he was like that and did mind so much.'

'It would be easier, ' said Alix presently, husky and strangled, 'if he hadn't liked things so much too; if he hadn't been so awfully happy; if he hadn't loved being alive … It isn't a score for him to lose all the rest of his life, that he might have had afterwards.'

'No,' Terry agreed, sadly. 'It isn't. It's rotten luck, that is. Simply rotten. That's one of the most sickening things about this whole show, the way people are doing that … But there's one thing about Paul, Alix; if he'd come through it he'd have kept on remembering all the things one tries to forget. More than most people, I mean. He was that sort. Lots of people don't mind so much, and can get things out of their heads when they aren't actually seeing them. I can, pretty well, you know. I think about other things, and don't worry, and eat and sleep like a prize-fighter. A chap like Ingram's all right, too; lots of men are. (Though what I suppose Ingram would call his brain seems to have gone pretty well to pot today. My word, I shall let him hear about that this evening.) But Paul – Paul would have minded awfully always; it might have spoilt his life a bit, you know … And worse things might have happened to him, too; he might have been taken prisoner … Paul,' he added slowly – 'Paul is better off than lots of men.'

Alix was staring at him now with wide, frightened eyes.

'I say, Terry,' she said hoarsely, 'what – what on earth are we to *do* about it all? It – it's going on now – this moment … I've tried so hard not to let it come near … and now … now …'

She was cold and shaking with terror.

'Now you'd better go on trying,' Terry suggested, and looked at his watch. 'Thinking's no good, anyhow … We ought to hit off the 3.15 with any luck. Are you going to be sick any more, by the way?'

'I can never tell, till just beforehand,' said Alix gloomily. 'But I wouldn't be much surprised.'

That was a sad thing about the Sandomirs: when they began to be sick it often took them quite a long time to leave off. It was most unfortunate, and they got it from their father, who had sometimes been taken that way on public platforms.

'Well,' said Terry patiently.

8

The others walked, and had tea, and walked again, and took a train back. Londoners like this sort of day. They like to see hedges, and grass, and pick berries, and hear birds. It refreshes them for next week's work, even though they have been at the time cold, and tired, and perhaps bored.

CHAPTER 10

Evening in Church

1

Alix was huddled on her bed in a rug. She had taken two aspirin tablets because her head ached, and really one is enough. She felt cold and low. She was occupied in not thinking about Paul or the war; it was rather a difficult operation, and took her whole energies. Paul was insistent; she pressed her hands against her eyes and saw him on the darkness, her little brother, white-faced, with the nervous smile she knew; Paul in a trench, among the wounded and killed, seeing things, hearing things … taken suddenly sick … unable to leave off … putting his head above the parapet, trying to get hit, called sharply to order by superiors … Paul desperate, at the end of his tether, in the night full of flashes and smashes and laughter and grumbling and curses … Paul laughing too, and talking, as she and Paul always did when they were hiding things. Paul in his dug-out, alone … unseen, he supposed … with only one thought, to get out of it somehow … The shot, the pain, like flame … the men approaching. who knew … Paul's face, knowing they knew … white, frightened, staring, pain swallowed up in shame … the end … how soon? Ingram hadn't said that. Anyhow, the end, and Paul, out of It at last, slipping into the dark, alone … A noble end, Mrs Frampton had said, not a wasted life … Anyhow, all over for Paul, as Terry had said.

And then what? Ingram hadn't said that either; nor had Terry: no one could say, for no one knew. What, if anything, did come then? Darkness, nothingness, or something new?

'He has, begun to live now, dear, for ever and ever,' Kate had said. 'World without end, amen,' Mrs Frampton had rounded it off.

World without end! What a thought! Poor Paul, finding a desperate way out from the world, slipping away into another which had no way out at all. But Mrs Frampton's and Kate's world without end was a happy, jolly one, presumably, and the more of it the better. It would give Paul space for the life he hadn't lived here. Oh, could that be so? Was it possible, or was it, as so many people thought, only a dream? Who could know? No one, till they came to try. And then perhaps they would know nothing at all either way, not being there any more …

Yet people thought they knew, even here and now. Nicky's friend, Mr West; he, presumably, thought he knew; anyhow, if not going so far as that, he had taken a hypothesis and was, so to speak, acting, thinking, and talking on it. He was clever, too. Mrs Frampton and Kate thought they knew, too; but they weren't clever. They believed in God: but Alix could have no use for the Violette God. Mrs Frampton's God was the Almighty, an omnipotent Being who governed all things in gross and in detail, including the weather (though the connection here was mysteriously vague). A God of crops and sun and rain, who spoke in the thunder; a truly pagan God (though Mrs Frampton would not have cared for the word), of chastisements and arbitrary mercies, who was capable of wrecking ships and causing wars, in order to punish and improve people. The God of the 'act of God' in the shipping regulations. A God who could, and would, unless for wise purposes he chose otherwise, keep men and women physically safe, protect them from battle, murder, and sudden death. An anthropomorphic God, in the semblance, for some strange reason known only to the human race, of a man. A God who somehow was responsible for the war.

A God who ordered men's estates so that there should be a wholesome economic inequality among them.

Such was Mrs Frampton's God, in no material way altered from the conception of the primitive Jews or the modern South Sea Islanders, who make God in their image. He had no attractions for Alix, who could not feel that a God of weather was in any way concerned with the soul of the world.

Kate's God, on the other hand, was for Alix enshrined in the little books of devotion that Kate had lent her sometimes, and all of which she found revolting, even on the hypothesis that you believed that sort of thing. They propounded ingenuous personal questions for the reader to ask himself, such as 'Have I eaten or drunk too much? Have I used bad words? Have I read bad books?' (As if, though Alix, anyone would read a bad book on purpose, life being so much too short to get through the good ones; unless one had the misfortune to be a reviewer, like Nicky, or to have bad taste, like many others; and then wasn't it rather a misfortune than a fault?) 'Have I been unkind to animals? the inquiries went on. 'Have I obeyed those set over me? Have I kept a guard of my eyes?' (a mysterious phrase unexplained by any footnote, and leaving it an open question whether to have done so or to have omitted to do so would have been the sin. Alix inclined to the former view; it somehow sounded an unpleasant thing to do.)

These books adopted a tone too intimate and ejaculatory for Alix's taste; and they were, it must be admitted, about all she knew of Kate's God, and her distaste for Him merely meant that she disliked some of Kate's methods of approach.

Alix felt, vaguely, that West's God was different. There was no softness about Him, or about West's approach to Him; no sentimental sweetness, no dull piety, but energy, effort, adventure, revolt, life taken at a rush. Dynamite, West had said, to blow up the world. Poetry, too; harsh and grim poetry, often, but the real thing. Kate's religion might be sung in hymns by Faber; Mrs Frampton's in hymns by Dr Watts; West's had very little to do with any hymns sung in churches. And it was West's religion which thought it was going to break up the world in pieces and build it anew. Certainly neither Mrs Frampton's nor Kate's would be up to the task; they would not even want it. Mrs Frampton worshipped a God of Things as they Are, who has already done all things well, and Kate one who is little concerned with the ordering of the world at all, but only with individual souls.

One would like to know more about West's God.

'You should go to church,' West had told her. 'You'd find it interesting.'

She might find it so, of course; anyhow, she could try. Paul was driving her to find things out; his desperation and pain, her own, all the world's, must somehow break a way through, out and beyond, fling open a gate on to new worlds … Anyhow, it might take one's mind off, help one not to think. It occurred to Alix that she would go to church this evening. It seemed, at the moment, the simplest way of watching these odd mystical forces, if there were any such forces, at work. She would be able thus to see them concentrated, working through a few people gathered together for the purpose. Alix's acquaintance with Sunday evening services, it may be observed, was rudimentary.

2

Meanwhile there was tea. Alix went down to it. There were Mrs Frampton, Kate, a Mrs Buller from Anzac next door, and a toasted bun. Mrs Frampton said to Alix, 'You do look low, dear. I'm sure it's a good thing you came home. Biliousness isn't a thing to play with. Suppose you were to go to bed straight away, and let Kate bring you up a nice hot cup of tea there?'

Kate said, playfully, 'This is what Sunday outings lead to.'

They were both at a great distance, as if Alix were at the bottom of the sea. So was Mrs Buller, who talked to Mrs Frampton about girls. Girls are, of course, an inexhaustible and fruitful topic – there are so many of them coming and going, and nearly all so bad. Mrs Frampton and Mrs Buller and Kate all found them interesting, if a nuisance, Alix found them a safe subject.

Mrs Buller was saying, 'On one thing I have made up my mmd, Mrs Frampton; never again will I have a **GFS** girl in my house. Besides all the meetings and things at all hours, to have the girl's Associate coming into my kitchen and talking about prayer (it was prayer, for I overheard) and ending up with a kiss you could hear upstairs – it was more than I could be expected to stand. And the girl smashed three cups that same afternoon, and answered me back in a downright impertinent way. So I said, "If *that's* what your **GFS** teaches you for manners, the sooner you and I part company the better," and I gave her her month.'

'I'm sure you were right,' said Mrs Frampton. 'Though of course one mustn't put it all on the **GFS**.' She said this because of Kate, who was a church worker. But as it happened Kate did not care for the **GFS**, having fallen out with the local secretary, and also having been told by her vicar that it was a society which drew too rigid an ethical line and no denominational line at all. Kate also drew rigid ethical lines, when left to herself and her own natural respectability; the comic spirit must be largely responsible for driving people like Kate into the Christian church, body which, whatever opprobrium it may have at various times incurred, has never yet been justly accused of respectability. So Kate joined in about Girls and the **GFS**.

Mrs Buller said, 'However, we may be thankful we aren't in the country, for my sister at Stortford has had five soldiers billeted on her, and how is her girl to keep her head among them all? She won't, of course. Girls and a uniform – it goes to their heads like drink.'

'It does seem an upset for your sister,' said Mrs Frampton.

'And Bertie's started again wanting to enlist,' continued their visitor, who had many troubles. 'If I've told him once I've told him fifty times, "Not while *I* live you don't, Bertie." So I hope he'll settle down again. But he says he'll only be fetched later if he doesn't; such rubbish. He actually wants to go as a common soldier, not even a commission. Think of the class of *company* he'd be thrown into, not to speak of the risk. Fancy his thinking his father and I could let him do such a thing.'

Mrs Frampton made sympathetic sounds.

They had tea. They went on talking, of Belgians, Zeppelins, bulbs, and Girls. Belgians as a curiosity (in the corner house), Zeppelins as murder ('to call that war, you know'), bulbs as a duty (to be put in quite soon}, and Girls as a nuisance (to be changed as speedily as may be). Mrs Buller stayed till nearly six.

'It's always a treat to see Mrs Buller,' said Mrs Frampton. 'But fancy, it's nearly time to get ready for church.'

Mrs Frampton's church was at half-past six. Kate's was seven. It was to Kate's that Alix wanted to go. She did not think that Kate's church would be much use, but she was sure that Mrs Frampton's wouldn't. Mrs Frampton's was florid Gothic outside, with a mellifluous peal of bells. Kate's was of plain brick, with a single tinny bell. Mrs Frampton's looked comfortable. Kate's did not. The road into another world, if there was another world, surely would not be a comfortable one …

3

Kate was pleased when Alix said she was coming. She thought the little books had borne fruit.

'It'll be something to do,' said Alix cautiously.

'I hope Mr Alison will preach,' Kate said. 'He's so helpful always.'

Alix wondered if Mr Alison knew about another world, and if he would tell in his sermon. If he did not, he would not be helpful to her. Probably not even if he did.

They went diagonally across the little common, to the unpretentious brick church whose bell tinkled austerely, It was an austere church both within and without, and had a sacrificial beauty of outline and of ritual that did not belong to Mrs Frampton's church, which was full of cheery comfort and best hats and Hymns A and M. Kate's church had an oblative air of giving up. It gave up succulent completed tunes for the restrained rhythms of plain-song which, never completed, suggest an infinite going on; it gave up comfortable pews for chairs which slid when you knelt against them; its priests and congregation gave food before Mass and meat on fast-days. The chief luxury it seemed to allow itself was incense, of which Alix disliked the sell. Certainly the air of cheery, everyday respectability which characterises some churches was conspicuously absent: this church seemed to be perpetually approaching a mystery, trying to penetrate it, laying aside impedimenta in the quest … The quest for what? That seemed to be the question.

The candles on the far altar quivered and shone like stars. They sang hymns out of little green books. They began by singing, in procession, a long hymn about gardens and gallant walks and pleasant flowers and spiders' webs and dampish mists, and the flood of life flowing through the streets with silver sound, and many other pleasant things. Alix glanced at Kate, curiously. Kate, prim and proper, so essentially of Violette, seemed in herself to have no point of contact with such strange, delightful songs, such riot of attractive fancy. For this was poetry, and Kate and poetry were incongruous.

Poetry: having found the word, Alix felt it pervade and explain the whole service – the tuneless chants, the dim glooms and twinkling lights, the austerity. Kate interpreted this poetry for her own needs through the medium of little books of devotion for which prose was far too honourable a word; jargon, rather; pious, mushy, abominable ...

It was odd. Kate seemed to be caught in the toils of some strange, surprising force. Alix hadn't learnt yet that it is a force nowhere more surprising than in the unlikely people it does catch. The further question may then arise, how is it going to use them? Can it use them at all: or does the turning of its wheels turn them out and get rid of them, or does it retain them, unused? It is certainly all very odd. This essentially romantic and adventurous and mystical force seems to have a special hold on many timid, unromantic and unimaginative persons. This essentially corporate and catholic body lays its grasp as often as not on extreme individualists. Perhaps it is the unconscious need in them of the very thing they have not got, that makes the contact. Perhaps it reveals poetry and adventure to those who could find them in no other guise. Perhaps it links together in a body those who must otherwise creep through life unlinked, gives awareness of the community to the otherwise unaware. Perhaps, on the other hand, it doesn't. The powers in human beings of evading influences and escaping obvious inferences is unlimited.

The lights were suddenly dimmer. Someone got into the pulpit and preached. He preached on a question, 'Who will lead me into the strong city?' A very pertinent inquiry, Alix thought, and just what she wanted to know. Who would? Who could? Was there a strong city at all, or only chaos and drifting ways of terror and unrest? If so, where was it, and how to get there? The strong city, said the preacher, is the city of refuge for which we all crave, and more especially just now, in this day of tribulation. The kings of the earth are gathered and gone by together; but the hill of Sion is a fair place and the joy of the whole earth; upon the north side lieth the city of the great King; God is well known in her palaces as a sure refuge. Above the noise of battle, above the great water-floods, is the city of God that lieth four-square, unshaken by the tempests.

Jolly, thought Alix, and just where one would be: but how to get into it? One had tried, ever since the war began, to shut oneself away, unshaken and undisturbed by the tempests. One had come to Violette because it seemed more unshaken than Wood End; but Violette wasn't really, somehow, a strong city. The tempests rocked one till one felt sick … Where was this strong city, any strong city? Well, all about; everywhere, anywhere, said the preacher; one could hardly miss it.

> 'Tis only your estrangèd faces
> That miss the many-splendoured thing …'

and he quoted quite a lot of that poem. Then he went on to a special road of approach, quoting instead, 'I went into the sanctuary of God.' Church, Alix presumed. Well, here she was. No; it transpired that it wasn't evening service he meant; he went on to talk of the Mass. That, apparently, was the strong city. Well, it might be, if one was of that way of thinking. But if one wasn't? Did Kate find it so, and was that why she went out early several mornings in the week? And what sort of strength had that city? Was it merely a refuge, well bulwarked, where one might hide from fear? Or had it strength to conquer the chaos? West would say it had; that its work was to launch forces over the world like shells, to shatter the old materialism, the old comfortable selfishness, the old snobberies, cruelties, rivalries, cant, blind stupidities, lies. The old ways, thought Alix (which were the same ways carried further, West would say), of destruction and unhappiness and strife, that had led to the bitter hell where boys went out in anguish into the dark.

The city wasn't yet strong enough, apparently, to do that. Would it be one day?

'I will not cease from mental fight,' cried the preacher, who was fond, it seemed, of quoting poetry, 'nor let my sword sleep in my hand, till we have built Jerusalem in England's green and pleasant land.'

The next moment he was talking of another road of approach to the city on the hill, besides going to church, besides building Jerusalem in England. A road steep and sharp and black; we take it unawares, forced along it (many boys are taking it this moment, devoted. and unafraid. Unafraid, thought Alix); and suddenly we are at the city gates; they open and close behind us, and we are in the strong city, the drifting chaos of our lives behind us, to be redeemed by firm walking on whatever new roads may be shown us. God, who held us through all the drifting, unsteady paths, has led us now right out of them into a sure refuge … How do you know? thought Alix. Beyond the steep dark road there may be chaos still, endless, worse chaos: or, surely more natural to suppose, there may be nothing. How *did* people think they knew? Or didn't they? Did they only guess, and say what they thought was attractive? Did Kate know? And Mrs Frampton? How *could* they know, people like that? How could it be part of their equipment of knowledge, anything so extraordinary, so wild, so unlike their usual range as that? They knew about recipes, and servants, and dusting, and things like that – but surely not about weird and wonderful things that they couldn't see? Alix could rather better believe that this preacher knew, though he did sometimes use words she didn't like, such as tribulation and grace. (It would seem that preachers sometimes must: it is impossible, and not right, to judge them.)

When the sermon ended abruptly, and they sang a hymn of Bunyan's about a pilgrim (402 in the green books), one was left with a queer feeling that the Church had its hand on a door, and at any moment might turn a handle and lead the way through … Alix caught for a moment the forces at work; perhaps West was right about them, and they were adequate for the job of blowing up the debris of the world. If only the Church could collect them, focus them, use them … Kate, and church people of Kate's calibre, were surely like untaught children playing, ignorantly and placidly, with dynamite. They would be blown up if they weren't careful. They kept summoning forces to their aid which must surely, if they fully came, shatter and break to bits most of the things they clung to as necessary comforts and conveniences. But perhaps people knew this, and therefore prayed cautiously, with reservations; so the powers came in the same muffled, wrappered way, with reservations.

Such were Alix's speculations as the music ended and the congregation filed down the church and shook hands with the tired vicar at the door and went out into the dark evening. The fog came round them and choked the light that streamed from the church, and made Alix cough. They hurried home through the blurred, gas-lit roads.

'Did you enjoy the service?' asked Kate.

'I think so,' said Alix, wondering whether she had.

'It's queer,' she added, meaning the position of the Christian church in this world.

But Kate said, 'Queer! Whatever do you mean? It was just like the ordinary; like it always is … I wish Mr Alison had preached, though; I never feel Mr Daintree has the same *touch*. He preaches about things and people in general, and that's never so inspiring; he doesn't seem to get home the same way to each one. Now, Mr Alison this morning was beautiful. Mr Daintree, I always think, has almost too many *ideas*, and they run away with him a little. However.' Kate's principle (one of them) was not to criticise the clergy, so she stopped.

'1 wonder if Florence is in yet,' she said instead, 'and if she's left the larder open, as usual, and let that kitten get at the chicken? I shouldn't be a bit surprised. She *is* a girl.'

Alix felt another incongruity. If Kate really believed the extraordinary things she professed to believe about the interfusion of two worlds (at least two), how then did it matter so much about chickens and kittens and Florence? Yet why not? Why shouldn't it give all things an intenser, more vivid reality, a deeper significance? Perhaps it did, thought Alix, renouncing the problem of the Catholic church and its so complicated effects.

'You've got your cough worse,' said Kate, fitting the key into Violette's latch. 'You'd better go to bed straight, I think, and have a mustard leaf on after supper. You're the colour of a ghost, child. Evie's back, I can hear.'

So could Alix.

'I shall go to bed, ' she said. 'I don't want supper.'

While she was undressing, Evie came in, to wash her hands for supper. Evie was radiant and merry.

'Hard luck your having to go back, Al,' said Evie, splashing her face and hands. 'I'm stiff all over; I'm for a hot bath afterwards. We had a lovely time; simply screaming, it was. Mr Doye is rather a sport. They're all a jolly set, though. Even that Mr Ingram, the one you were talking to, brightened up later on, though when first you turned back he looked as if he was at his father's funeral. You must have made an impression. But he got over it all right and was quite chirpy.'

'Was he?' said Alix.

'I've promised Mr Doye to go out again with him, next Sat. He's quite determined. I don't know what Sid Vinney'll say, because I'd half promised him. But I don't care. Sid's an old silly, anyhow.'

Evie smothered herself in the towel, scrubbing her smooth skin that no scrubbing could hurt.

'*Dommage*, you being seedy,' said Evie, and pulled off her walking shoes. 'You'd have enjoyed the day no end. Still feeling sick? Oh, poor kid, bad luck … Well, there's the bell, I must run. I've heaps more to tell you. But you'd better go off straight to sleep after supper; I won't disturb you when I come up.'

She ran downstairs. Alix heard her voice in the dining-room below, through supper. Evie had had a good day. Evie was lovely, and jolly, and kind, and a good sort, but Alix did not want to see her, or to hear her talk.

4

It was Kate who came up after supper, with a mustard leaf, which she put on Alix's chest.

'Shall I read to you till I take it off?' Kate said; and what she selected to read was the current issue of the *Sign*, the parish magazine she took in. (Mrs Frampton took the *Peep of Day*, which was the magazine of the church she attended.)

The mustard leaf, an ancient and mild one, which needed keeping on for some time, allowed of reading the *Sign* almost straight through, apart from the parish news on the outer pages, which, though absorbing, is local and ephemeral, and should not be treated as literature. Kate began with an article on the Organs in our Churches, worked on through a serial called Account Rendered; a poem on the Women of the Empire; a page on Waifs and Strays; A Few Words to Parents and Teachers on the Christian Doctrine of the

Trinity; Thoughts to Rest Upon; Keeping Well, some Facts for our Families; The Pitman's Amen (a short story); Wholesome Food for Baby; and so at last to Our Query Corner, wherein the disturbed in mind were answered when they had during the month written to inquire, 'Why does my clergyman worship a cross? Is not this against the second commandment?' 'What amusements, if any, may be allowed on Sunday?' 'If I take the Communion, should I go to dancing-classes?' 'How can I turn from Low Church to High Church?' 'Should not churchwardens be Christians?' and about many other perplexing problems. The answers were intelligent and full, never a bald Yes, or No, or We do not know; they often included a recommendation to the inquirer to try and look at the matter from a wider, or higher, standpoint, and (usually) to read the little book by an eminent Canon that bore more particularly on his case.

Alix got it all, from the Organs in our Churches to the Christian Churchwardens, mixed up with the mustard leaf, so that it seemed a painful magazine, but, one hoped, profitable. She looked at Kate's small, prim head in the shadow under the gas, and thought how Kate had been through love and loss and jealousy and still survived. But Kate's love and loss and jealousy could not be so bad; it was like someone else's toothache.

'We do not quite understand your question,' read Kate. (This was on turning from Low to High.) 'You should try to detach yourself from these party names, which are often mischievous … We think you might be helped by the following books … Twenty-five minutes: I should think that must be enough, even for that old leaf. Does it smart much?'

'Dreadfully,' said Alix, who was tired of it.

'Well, two minutes more,' said Kate, and went on to the Churchwardens, who, it seemed, should be Christians, if possible.

'Now then,' said Kate, advancing with cotton wool.

'Oo,' said Alix. 'It's been on too long, Kate.'

'You do make a fuss,' said Kate, padding her chest with cotton wool and tucking the clothes round her. 'Now you go off to Sleepy Town quick.'

Alix thought how kind Kate was. When one had any physical ailment, Violette came out strong. It was soft-hearted. Women are.

5

When Kate had gone, Alix lay with her eyes tight shut and her head throbbing, and tried to go to sleep, so that she need no longer make her brain ache with keeping things out. But she could not go to sleep. And she could not, in the silence and dark, keep things out; not Paul; nor the war; nor Basil; nor Evie.

At last Evie came. Alix, feigning sleep, lay with tightshut eyes, face to the wall. Every movement of Evie, undressing in her frightful loveliness, was horribly clear. Alix was afraid Evie, in passing her bed, would brush against her, and that she would have to scream. If only Evie would get to bed and to sleep.

Evie, after her undressing and washing, knelt in prayer for thirty seconds (what was Evie's God, who should say? One cannot tell with people like Evie, or see into their minds), then took her loveliness to bed and fell sweetly asleep.

Alix knew from her breathing that she slept; then she unclenched her hands and relaxed her body and cried.

CHAPTER 11

Alix and Evie

1

Basil had Evie on the brain. He liked her enormously. He was glad he had a month's more leave. He took to meeting her after she came out from her hat shop and seeing her home. They spent Saturday afternoons together.

Alix saw them parting one Saturday evening, as she came home. Spring Hill was dim and quiet, and they stood by the door into the Park, on the opposite side of the road to Violette, chaffing and saying good-bye. Alix saw Basil suddenly kiss Evie. It might be the first time: in that case it would be an event for them both, and thrilling. Or it might be not the first time at all: in that case it would be a habit, and jolly.

Anyhow, Evie said, 'Oh, go along and don't be a silly … Are you coming in to-night?'

He said 'No' and laughed.

Then they saw Alix turning into Violette.

'There now,' said Evie. 'She must have seen you going on. Couldn't have missed it … Whatever will she think?'

'She won't think anything,' said Basil Doye. 'Alix is a nice person, and minds her own business.'

'I believe it's her you're in love with really,' said Evie, teasing him.

He kissed her again, and said, 'Oh, do you?'

After a little more of the like conversation, which will easily be imagined, they parted. Evie went into Violette. She ran upstairs and into her dark bedroom and flung off her outdoor things. Turning, she saw Alix sitting on the edge of her bed.

'Goodness, how you startled me, ' said Evie.

'Sorry,' said Alix. 'Got a toothache.' She was holding her face between her hands. Evie said, 'Oh, bad luck. Try some aspirin. Or suck a clove … I say, Al. '

'What?'

'Did you see me and Mr Doye just now, in the road? You did, didn't you?'

'No, ' said Alix.

'Oh,' said Evie, dubious, glancing at Alix's face, that was dimly wan in the faint light from the street lamps, and twisted a little with her toothache.

Pity seized Evie, who was kind.

'I say, kiddie, do go to bed. What's the use of coming down with a face-ache? You'd be much better tucked up snug, with a clove poultice.'

'No,' said Alix, uncertainly, and stood up. 'It's better now. I've put on cocaine … Where are my shoes? … Of course I saw you and Basil in the road … Did you have a jolly afternoon?'

Evie knew that way of Alix's, of going back upon her lies; that was where Alix as a liar differed from herself; you only had to wait.

'Yes, it was a lark,' said Evie carelessly. 'Mr Doye's priceless, isn't he? Doesn't mind *what* he says. Nor what he does, either. He makes me shriek, he's so comic. You should have heard him go on at tea. We went to the rink, you know, and had tea there. He's so *silly*.' Evie laughed her attractive, gurgling laugh.

They went down to supper.

2

Sometimes Basil and Evie lunched together. By habit they lunched in different shops and had different things to eat.

Evie liked pea-soup, or a poached egg, bread and honey, a large cup of coffee with milk, and what she and the tea-shop young ladies called fancies. Basil didn't. When they lunched together they both had the things Basil liked, except in coffee.

'Did you tell him two *noirs*?' Evie would say. 'Rubbish, you know I always have *lait*. '

'A corrupt taste. One *cafe au lait*, waiter. You like the most ridiculous things you know; you might be eight. You aren't grown-up enough yet for black coffee, or smoking, or liqueurs. You must meet my mother; you'd learn a lot from her.'

'Oh well, I'm happy in my own way … As for smoking, I think it's jolly bad for people's nerves, if you ask me. Alix smokes an awful lot, and her nerves are like fiddlestrings. I don't go so far,' Evie said judicially, 'as to say I don't think it's good form for girls. That's what mother thinks, only of course she's old-fashioned, very. So is Kate. But after all, there *is* a difference between men and girls, in the things they should do; *I* think there's a difference, don't you?'

'Oh, thank goodness, yes,' said Basil, fervently, not having always thought so.

'And I don't know, but I sometimes think if girls can't fight for their country, they shouldn't smoke.'

'Oh, I see. A reward for valour, you think it should be. That would be rather hard, since the red-tape rules of our army don't allow them to fight. If they might, I've no doubt plenty would.'

Evie laughed at him. 'A girl would hate it. She'd be hopeless.'

'Plenty of men hate it and are hopeless, if you come to that.'

'Oh, it's not the same,' asserted Evie. 'A girl couldn't.' She added, after a moment, sympathetically curious, 'Do you hate it much?'

'Oh, much,' Basil deprecated the adverb. 'It's quite interesting in some ways, you know,' he added. 'And at moments even exciting. Though mostly a bit of a bore, of course, and sometimes pretty vile. But, anyhow, seldom without its humours, which is the main thing. Oh, it's frightfully funny in parts.'

'Anyhow, ' Evie explained for him, 'of course you're glad to be doing your bit.'

He laughed at that. 'You've been reading magazine stories. That's what the gallant young fellows say, isn't it? … Look here, bother the war. I want to talk about better things. Will you meet me after you get off this evening? I want a good long time with you, and leisure. These scraps are idiotic.'

Evie looked doubtful.

'You and me by ourselves? Or shall we get anyone else?'

'Anyone else? What for? Spoil everything.'

'Oh, I don't mind either way. Only mother's rather particular in some ways, you know, and she … well, if you want to know, she thinks I go out with you alone rather a lot. It's all rubbish, of course; as if one mightn't go out with who one likes … but, well, you know what mother is. I told you, she's old-fashioned, a bit. And of course Kate's shocked, but I don't care a bit for Kate, she's too prim for anything.'

'We won't care a bit for anyone,' suggested Basil. 'I never do. I don't believe you do really, either. If people are so particular, we must just shock them and have done. Anyhow, you don't suppose I'm going to give up seeing you.'

The quickening of his tone made her draw back from the subject. Evie liked flirtation, but did not understand passion; it was not in her cool head and heart. It was the thing in Basil that made her at times, lately, shy of him in their intercourse; vaguely she realised that he might become unmanageable. She liked him to love her beauty, but she was occasionally startled by the way he loved it. She thought it was perhaps because he was an artist, or a soldier, or both.

'Well, perhaps I'll come,' she said, to soothe him. 'Where shall we go? Let's go *inside* something, I say, not walking in the dark like last time. Oh, it was very jolly, of course, but it's not so snug and comfy. We might do a play? … I say, it's nearly two. I must get back. I got into a row yesterday for being late – that was your fault.'

They walked together to the side door of the select hat shop. 'Not really a shop,' as Evie explained sometimes. 'More of a studio, it is. It's awfully artistic, our work.'

While she went upstairs, she was thinking, '*Dommage*, his getting so warm sometimes. It spoils the fun … He'll be wanting to tie me up if I'm not careful, and I'm not ready for that yet … There are plenty of others … I don't know.'

3

As it happened, she met one of the others when she left the shop at five, and he took her out to tea at the most expensive tea place in London, which was always his way with tea and other things. He was on leave from France, and had met Evie for the first time three days ago, when she was out with Doye, whom he knew. His name was Hugh Montgomery Gordon, and he was the son of Sir Victor Gordon of Ellaby Hall in Kent, Prince's Mansions in Park Lane, and Gordon's Jam Factory in Hackney Wick. He was handsome in person, graceful, clear-featured, an old lawn-tennis blue, and a young man with great possessions, who, having been told on good authority that he would find it hard to enter into the kingdom of heaven, had renounced any idea of this enterprise he might otherwise have had, and devoted himself whole-heartedly to appreciating this world. He was in a cavalry regiment, and had come through the war so far cool, unruffled, unscathed, and mentioned in despatches. He had a faculty for serenely expecting and acquiring the best, in most departments of life, though in some (such as art, literature, and social ethics) he failed through ignorance and indifference. Meeting Evie Tucker in Bond Street, and perceiving, as he had perceived before, that her beauty was in a high class of merit, he was stirred by a desire to acquire her as a companion for tea, and did so. Evie liked him; he was really more in her line than Basil Doye (artists were queer, there was no getting round that, even if they had given it up for soldiering and had lost interest in it and fingers), and she liked the place where they had tea, and liked the tea and the cakes and the music, and liked him to drive to Clapton with her in a taxi afterwards.

'You don't seem economical, do you?' she remarked, as they whirred swiftly eastward. 'I hope not,' said Hugh Montgomery Gordon, in his slow, level tones. 'I can't stand economical people.'

He left her at Violette and drove back to his club, feeling satisfied with himself and her. She was certainly a find, though it was a pity one had to go so far out into the wilderness to return her where she belonged. Her people were, no doubt, what his sister Myrtle would call quite imposs.

4

As Evie and Captain Gordon had taxied down Holborn, they had passed, and been held up for a minute near Alix, Nicholas, and West, who stood talking at the corner of Chancery Lane.

'Hugh Montgomery Gordon,' Nicholas murmured. 'Bright and beautiful as usual. Know him, Alix? Surely he doesn't visit at Violette? I can't picture it, somehow.'

'Oh, he might, for Evie's sake. Evie picks them up, you know; it's remarkable how she picks them up. They look very beautiful together, don't they? Is he nice?'

'Just as you saw. I scarcely know him more than that. He was a Hall man; my year. I believe he had a good time there. He looks as if he had a good time still. West's opinions about him are more pronounced than mine. Is he nice, West?'

'He's in the family jam,' West told Alix, as sufficient answer.

'Gordon's jam, if that means anything to you.'

'Wooden pips and sweated girls,' Alix assented, having picked up these things from her mother. 'It must be exciting; so many improvements to be made.'

'No doubt,' agreed West. 'But the Gordons won't make them. They make jam and they make money – any amount of it – but they don't make improvements that won't pay. A bad business. It will be more tolerable for Sodom and Gomorrah in the day of judgment, at least I hope it will. They've been badgered and bullied about it by social workers for years, but they don't mind … And at the same time, of course, they've no more ideas about what to do with their money than – than Solomon had. They put it into peacocks and ivory apes. These rich people – well, I should like to have the Gordons in a dungeon and pull out their teeth one by one, as if they were Jews, till they forked out their ill-gotten gains for worthy objects … If you ever meet Gordon, Miss Sandomir, you might tell him what I think about him. Tell him we have a meeting of the AntiSweating League in our parish room every Monday, and should be glad to see him there.'

Nicholas wondered, though he didn't ask Alix, whether Evie was still on with Basil Doye, or whether a breach there had made a gap by which Hugh Montgomery Gordon was entering in. One thought of Evie's friendships with men in these terms; whereas Alix might drive with a different man every day without suggesting to the onlooker that one was likely to oust another. The difference was less between Evie and Alix (for Evie was of a fine and wide companionableness) than in what men required of them respectively.

'Evie and he,' Alix commented, considering them. 'They might be good friends, I think. They might fit. The jam wouldn't get between them – nor the money … I rather like him too, I think. He's so beautiful, and looks as if he'd never been ill. That's so jolly.' She was giving the same reasons which Basil had given for liking Evie. It occurred to her to wonder whether, if she'd been to the war, these two things would take her further in her mild inclination towards Hugh Montgomery Gordon – much further. Perhaps they would …

Alix went to her bus at the corner of Gray's Inn Road. Nicholas went back to his rooms to finish an article. West went to a Sweated Bootmakers' protest meeting in his parish room. West attended too many meetings: that was certain. Meetings, a clumsy contrivance at best, cannot be worth so much attendance. But he went off to this one full of faith and hope, as always.

5

Evie was using the telephone in the hall. She was saying, in her clear, cheery tones, 'Hullo, is that you? Awfully sorry, don't expect me to-morrow evening. I can't come … Awfully sorry … Don't quite know. I'll write.'

Alix went up to her room.

Presently Evie came in.

'Did you hear me phoning?' she inquired superfluously. 'It was to Mr Doye. Fact is I think he and I'd both be better for a little rest from each other. It'll give him time to cool down a bit. He's got keener than I like, lately. Fun's all very well, but one doesn't want to be hustled, does one? I don't want him asking me anything for a long time.'

Alix, sitting on her bed with one shoe off, pulling at the other, said in a small voice, 'I don't think he will.'

Evie turned round and looked at her, questioningly.

'You don't? Why, whatever do you know about it?'

Alix was bent over her shoe; her voice was muffled.

'Basil is like that. He doesn't mean things …'

'Oh …' Evie turned to the glass, and drew four pins out of the roll of hair behind her head, and it fell in a heavy nutbrown mass, glinting in the yellow gaslight. She began to comb it out and roll it up again.

'Doesn't mean anything, doesn't he?' she said thoughtfully. 'You seem awfully sure about that.'

'Yes,' agreed Alix. She had pulled off both shoes now, and tucked her stockinged feet under her as she sat curled up on the bed. She drew a deep breath and spoke rather quickly.

'He's always the same, he was the same with me once, he doesn't really mean it …'

'The same with you –' Evie, without turning round, saw in the glass the blurred image of the huddled figure and small pale face in the shadows behind her.

She drove in two more hairpins, then turned sharply and looked at Alix.

'You don't mean to say he used to be in love with you.'

'Oh … in love …' Alix's voice was faint, attenuated, remote.

'Well – anything, then.' Evie was impatient. 'You needn't split hairs … He went on with you, I suppose … And you …'

She broke off, staring, uncomfortably, at a situation really beyond her powers. .

Her cogitations ended in, 'Well, I think you might have told me at first. I thought you and he were just good friends. I didn't want him. I wouldn't have let him come near me if I'd known it was like that. I never do that sort of thing. Now do I, Alix? You've never seen me mean to other girls like that, have you? I never have been and I never will be … I don't want him. You can have him back.'

Alix giggled suddenly, irrepressibly.

'What's the matter now?' said Evie.

'Nothing. Only the way you talk of Basil – handing him about as if he was a kitten. He's not, you know.'

Evie smiled grudgingly. 'Well, anyhow *I* don't want him. Particularly if he doesn't mean anything, as you say … It isn't everyone I'd believe if they told me that; they might be jealous or spiteful or something. But I don't believe you'd say it, Al, if you didn't think it was true' – (Alix said, 'Oh,' on a soft, indrawn breath) – 'and you know him, so I expect you're right. And I'm not going on playing round with a man who makes love like he does and doesn't mean anything. It isn't respectable.'

'Oh – respectable.' Alix laughed again, shakily; it was such a funny word in this connection, and so like Violette.

'Well, I don't see it's funny,' said Evie. 'It's awfully important to be respectable, and I always am. I'll be good pals with any number of men, but when they begin to get like Basil Doye I won't have it unless they *mean* something.'

Thus Evie enunciated her code, and washed her hands and face and put on her dress and went downstairs. At the door she paused for a moment and looked back at Alix.

'I say, Al – I'm awfully sorry. I didn't mean to be a sneak, you know; I *wouldn't* have, if I'd known.'

'Not a bit,' Alix absurdly and politely murmured.

'Well, do get a move on and come down. It's too cold for anything up here … I say' – Evie paused awkwardly – 'I say, kiddie, you didn't really *care*, did you?'

Alix shook her head. 'Oh no.' Still her voice was small, polite, and attenuated.

'Well then,' said Evie cheerfully, 'no harm's done to anyone. But still, it's not the style I like, a man that plays about first with one girl, then another … I'm going down.'

She went.

6

The cold made Alix shiver. She stiffly uncurled herself and got off the bed. She brushed her hair before the glass. Her face looked back at her, pointed and ghostly, in the gaslight and shadows.

'Cad,' whispered Alix, without emotion, to the pale image. 'Cad – and liar.'

'It's the war,' explained Alix presently, with detached, half-cynical analysis. 'I shouldn't have done that before the war. I suppose I might do anything now. Probably I shall. There seems no way out …'

Alix had heard and read plenty of views on the psychological effects of war; some of them were interesting, some were true; many were true for some people and false for others but she did not remember that even the most penetrating (or pessimistic) had laid enough emphasis on the mental and moral collapse that shook the foundations of life for some people. For her, anyhow, and for Paul; and they surely could not be the only ones. Observers seemed more apt to take the cases of those men and women who were improved; who were strengthened, steadied, made more unselfish and purposeful (that was the favourite word), with a finer sense of the issues and responsibilities of life; or of those young sportsmen at the front who kept their jollity, their sweetness, their equilibrium, through it all. Well, no doubt there were plenty of these. Look at Terry. Look at Dorothy and Margot at Wood End, in their new strenuousness and ardours. They weren't demoralised by horror, or eaten by jealousy like a canker. They could even minister to combatants without envying them …

There were such. There might be many. But Alix looked at them far off, herself a broken, nerve-wracked, frightened child, grabbing at other people's things to comfort herself, ashamed but outrageous.

'There seems no way out,' said Alix, and looked, as she changed her frock, down vistas of degradation.

Downstairs Florence rang the supper bell. The smell of Welsh rarebit drifted through Violette. That, anyhow, was something; Alix liked it.

Alix and Basil

1

Evie had a good time for the rest of the week of Captain Gordon's leave. Mrs Frampton began to wonder whether this enormously wealthy and overwhelmingly well-dressed young man really meant anything. If you could tell anything by the size of the chocolate boxes he sent, he certainly meant quite a lot. Kate looked repressive when they arrived.

'How Evie does go on,' she said to Mrs Frampton at breakfast, before Evie came down, referring to the immense box from Buszard's by Evie's plate. That was the morning after Hugh Montgomery Gordon had returned to his duties in France. Apparently whatever else he meant, he meant not to be forgotten.

'She's a naughty girl,' Mrs Frampton admitted indulgently. 'I shouldn't wonder if that's from this new friend of hers, Captain Gordon. He looks such an extravagant man. But very handsome … What does your brother think of Captain Gordon, Alix? Didn't you say he knew him?'

Mrs Frampton was of those ladies who believe that men, good judges in most matters, are especially good judges of each other.

Alix said she didn't believe Nicholas had thought about Captain Gordon at all. 'But his friend Mr West has, quite a lot,' she added.

'Well, love, what does Mr West think?' Mr West was even better than Nicholas as a source of knowledge, being not only a man but a clergyman.

'Mr West,' said Alix, 'thinks Captain Gordon too rich. It's a fad of Mr West's that people shouldn't be too rich. I think they should.'

'Well, we're told, aren't we, that it is hard for a rich man to enter into the kingdom of heaven … A little more ham, Alix?'

'It's all a question,' said Kate, 'of the use people make of their wealth. They say that some of the wealthiest families in the land make the best landlords and are the kindest to all. I can't say I hold with socialism. It seems to me most wrong-headed.'

'Well,' Mrs Frampton agreed, 'it certainly does seem like flying in the face of what Providence has ordained, doesn't it? Let me see now, Alix, your brother doesn't hold with socialism, does he?'

Alix's brother, being clever and queer, might hold with anything. Mrs Frampton appeared to feel a morbid interest in his opinions.

'Nicky? He doesn't hold with anything, Cousin Emily; he's a general disapprover. I believe he hates socialism; he thinks it makes for dullness and stagnation and order and all sorts of things he doesn't like.'

Mrs Frampton said, 'Why, I should have thought what socialists wanted was quite an uprooting and an upset,' and then Evie's entrance interrupted a discussion which might have been fruitful.

Evie kissed her mother. She said, 'Whatever in the world are you talking about? Socialism? What a subject for breakfast. Buttered egg for me, please … Oh, chocs –' She opened them, smiling, and looked at the card inside.

'He is extravagant,' she said. 'This is an awfully special box. He must have ordered it from Buszard's before he went.'

'I don't think you should permit it,' said Kate primly.

'Oh, it's all right. He likes it. He's simply rolling.'

Evie was absorbed in the pencilled inscription on the card.

Life was pleasant to Evie. Her mother smiled indulgently on her. Evie certainly did seem to have a lot of young men at once, but then how pretty the child was, and how she enjoyed it. And she had sense, too; Evie never lost her head.

Evie opened the letter by her plate. She read it and laid it aside carelessly, and looked up.

'Yes, some ham, please … Mr Doye writes he's seen the Board again and he's to join in a week. I suppose he's satisfied now.'

Mrs Frampton clicked deprecatingly with her tongue. She regarded it always as a matter for great regret that wounded young men should have to return to the wars.

'Well, I'm sorry for that. Anyone would think he'd done enough, having lost a finger for his country. I call it shameful, sending him out again.'

'Perhaps he'll go to Serbia this time,' said Evie. 'He said there was a chance of his battalion getting sent there from France soon.'

'Well, well.' That seemed, if anything, more unreasonable still. 'I'm sure one's dreadfully sorry for poor Serbia – she does seem to be having a bad time; but I'm not sure that our men ought to be sent out to those parts. They're all so wild out there; it seems as if, in a way, they rather *like* fighting each other; anyhow they've always been at it since I can remember, and I think they'd much better be left to fight it out among themselves, while we defend poor France. But who are we to judge? I suppose Lord Kitchener knows what's right.'

'They say,' put in Kate, 'that Joffre had a great to do before he would persuade Kitchener to send forces out there at all. They say he came to the War Office and broke his riding-whip right across.'

'Fancy that! He must be a very violent man. But the French are always excitable. Lord Kitchener's one of the quiet ones, I've heard. A regular Englishman … Well, I'm sure I hope they're taking the right course … Alix, you haven't had half a breakfast; I'm sure you could manage another bit of toast. Evie dear, you'll have to hurry with your breakfast or you'll be late.'

Evie hurried.

She spent the week, with partial success, in avoiding Basil Doye. Since she had done with him, what was the use of scenes? She certainly wasn't going to let him go away with the impression that he would find her waiting on his next return from the war to beguile his leave-time. Her natural generosity forbade her to take and keep Alix's young man; her natural prudence forbade her to philander too ardently (having a good time is different, of course) with a young man who probably didn't mean business. Rightly Evie condemned these practices as Not Respectable. So she went off at lunch time with other friends, with a little pang, indeed, but less acute than she would have felt a week ago, before her rapid friendship with Hugh Montgomery Gordon. Basil Doye was being relegated quickly to the circle of Evie's numerous have-beens, to be remembered with pleasant indifference.

On the Saturday before he left London, Basil obtained an interview with Evie, by means of going, at immense sacrifice of time, to Violette. It was a short interview, and not intimate, for Mrs Frampton and Kate were present at it.

After it Basil called at Clifford's Inn to say good-bye to Nicholas and Alix, who, they told him, was there.

2

He found Alix alone, waiting for Nicholas to come in. She had been having tea, and was reading *Peacock Pie*. She preferred this poetry to any written since August 1914, which had killed fairies.

Looking up from it, she saw Basil standing at the door. He

143

was flushed, and looked cross; she knew of old the sulky set of his brows and mouth, that made him look like a petulant boy. It hurt Alix so much that she couldn't muster any sort of smile, only look away from him and say, 'I'm sorry; Nicky's not in yet.'

He said 'No,' abstractedly, and sat down in the chair on the other side of the fire. He sat in the attitude she had seen him in a thousand times (it seemed to her) before; his elbow resting on his knee, his hand supporting his chin, the other hand, with its maimed third finger, hanging at his side. She had seen him sitting thus happy, intimately talking; she had seen him moody and brooding as now. There had been a time when she could always lighten these moods, tickle his sullenness to laughter; but that time was past.

He said presently, 'I'm off to-morrow, you know.'

'Yes,' said Alix, who did know.

In her another knowledge grew: the knowledge that if he did not speak of Evie she could get through this interview without disgrace, but that if he did speak of Evie she could not. She did not want him to speak of Evie and break down the wall between them; yet she did want it.

He did speak of Evie. He said he had been to Violette to say good-bye.

'I said it to the whole family together. Evie wouldn't see me alone … I suppose she doesn't really care a hang. In fact, she's made that very obvious for the last fortnight.'

'Yes,' said Alix again, clinging to that one small word as to a raft in a stormy sea, which might yet float her through. Basil pushed the tongs with his foot, so that they made a clattering noise in the grate.

'She doesn't care a hang,' he repeated. 'She's on with that jam fellow now. Well, everyone to his taste. Hugh Montgomery Gordon obviously appeals to hers.'

Alix's hands were clasped tight over her knee. Her knuckles were white. She kept her eyes on the fire. She would not look at him.

'Yes,' she said.

Then silence fell between them, and though she would not look she felt his nearness, knew how he sat, angry and sullen, brooding over his hurt.

A coal fell from the fire. Alix, as if someone was physically forcing her, raised her eyes from it and looked at Basil, and knew then that she was not going to get through this interview without disgrace. For she saw him sit as she had seen him sit (it seemed to her) a thousand times before, inert, bent forward a little, with the shadows leaping and flickering on his thin olive face and vivid eyes, with one hand supporting his sharp-cut chin, the other hanging maimed (and that alone was something new, belonging to the cruel present not the kindly past) at his side. It seemed that those lean, quick, brown artist's fingers were dragging her soul from her. The sharp sense of all those other times when she and he had thus sat stabbed her like a turningknife. A thousand intimacies rose to shatter her, and, so shattered, she spoke.

'She doesn't care a hang.' She repeated his phrase, mechanically, sitting very still. 'But I do.'

Then she leant towards him, putting out her hands, and a sob caught in her throat.

'Oh, Basil – I do.'

For a moment the silence was only broken by the leaping, stirring fire.

Basil looked swiftly at Alix, and Alix saw horror in his eyes before he veiled it. The next moment it was veiled: veiled by his quick friendly smile. He leant forward and took her outstretched hands in his, and spoke lightly, easily. He did it well; few people could have attained at once to such ease, such spontaneous naturalness of affection.

'Why, of course – I know. The way you and I care for each other is one of the best things I've got in my life. It lasts, too, when the other sorts of caring go phut …'

'Yes,' said Alix faintly. The raft of that small word drifted back to her, and she climbed on to it out of the engulfing sea. She' took her hands from his and lay back in her chair, impassive and still.

Basil rose, and stood by the chimney-piece, playing with the things on it. He talked, naturally, easily, of what he was going to do, the probabilities of his being sent out with a draft to France almost at once, the possibility of his battalion being sent to Serbia. He talked too of their common friends, even of painting, which he seldom mentioned now. Alix heard his voice as from a great distance off, and from time to time said 'Yes.'

There was a sharp crack, and Basil held the stem of one of Nicholas's pipes in one hand, the bowl in the other; he had broken it in two. His fluent tongue, his flexible face, were under his control; but it seemed that his hands were not; they had shown thus blatantly the uncontrollable strain he felt. Alix winced away from it. She couldn't bear any more: he must go, quickly, before either of them broke anything else.

He went, slipping as it were unnoticeably away, with 'Good-bye' unemphasised, half ashamed, sandwiched between fatuities about the pipe and comments on the future.

'It was an ugly pipe, wasn't it? Tell Sandomir I broke it for his sake, compelled by my artistic conscience; it'll be for his good in the end … I'm sorry I've not seen him but you'll say good-bye for me … And to any of them at the shop … Good-bye … If we do get out to the East, we shall have a funny time in some ways, I fancy. I hear Salonika's a great place; glorious riviera climate. But less so inland; too much snow on the hills. Well, it can't be worse than France in winter, anyhow. I believe the Bulgars are very good-natured people to fight against; they aren't really a bit keen on this show … Want to get back to till their fields …'

His voice came from beyond the door. Then it shut, and muffled his steps running down wooden stairs. Alix let go her raft, and was submerged by the cold, engulfing seas.

CHAPTER 13

Alix, Nicholas, and West

1

Nicholas, coming in ten minutes later, found Alix lying in his cane chair, limp and white and sick.

'My dear,' he said after a glance, 'you seem very ill. You prescribe, and I'll see if West has any in his medicine cupboard.'

'Sal volatile, perhaps,' Alix murmured, and he went to find some. When he came back, she was sitting up, with a more pulled-together air. She sipped the sal volatile, and gave him a dim, crooked smile.

'It's my feelings really, you know, not my body. It's only that I'm … shocked to death.'

Nicholas stood, short and square, with his back to the fire, looking down on her with his small, keen, observant eyes.

'What's shocked you?'

'Me myself,' said Alix, forcing an unconcerned grin. 'Alone I did it.'

'What on earth's the matter, Alix?' asked Nicholas after a pause. 'Or don't you want to talk about it?'

It wasn't his experience of his sister, who he had always known of a certain exterior and cynical hardness where the emotions were concerned, that she ever wanted to 'talk about it'. But this evening she seemed queer, unlike herself, unstrung.

'Talking doesn't matter now,' said Alix, still swung between flippancy and tears. 'All the talking that matters is done already … Basil has gone away, Nicky. He'll perhaps never come back.'

'Oh, he will. Basil does.' Nicholas looked away from her, down at the fire.

'Yes,' said Alix. 'I expect he's sure to … I told him I cared for him,' she went on, in her clear, thin, indifferent voice, emptied of emotion. 'He doesn't care for me, you know. He pretended he hadn't understood. He pretended so hard that he broke your pipe. I was to tell you he was sorry about it —no, that he was glad, I think …' Her voice changed suddenly; anguish shook it. 'Can you make it any less bad, Nicky?' There was a pause, while Nicholas, resting his arm on the chimney-piece, stared down into the fire. He and Alix, like many brothers and sisters, had always had a shyness about them about intimate things. They were both naturally reserved; both fought shy of emotion as far as they could. They were, in some ways, very like. Despair had broken down Alix's reserve; Nicholas put his aside and considered her case in his detached way, as if it were a mathematical problem.

'Bad?' he repeated, weighing the word. 'Well, the fact is bad, of course – that you care and he doesn't. There's no altering that. It's his fault, of course, for caring himself once and leaving off. Well, anyhow, there it is. He's the poorer by it, not you … But the other part – your telling him – isn't bad. It was merely the truth; and it's simpler and often more sensible to tell the truth about what one feels. I wouldn't mind that, if I were you. Don't bring absurdities of sex etiquette into it. They're mere conventions, after all; silly, petty, uncivilised conventions. Aren't they?'

'Perhaps,' said Alix dully. 'I don't know.'

'Well, I do. Telling the truth is all right. It oughtn't to make things worse.'

'No,' said Alix. 'It does, you know.'

Nicholas, giving the subject the attention of his careful mind, knew it did. He couldn't theorise that away.

'Well,' he said at last slowly, 'if it does, you might quite truly look at the whole thing as a mental case; a case of nervous breakdown. The war's playing the devil with your nerves – that's what it means. You do things and feel things and say things, I dare say, that you wouldn't have once, but that you can scarcely help now. You're only one of many, you know – one of thousands. The military hospitals are full of them; men who come through plucky and grinning but with their nerves shattered to bits. There are the people like Terry and plenty more, who come through mentally undamaged, their balance not apparently upset, and the people like John (at least I rather guessed so when I saw him) and thousands more, who – well, who don't … War's such an insane, devilish thing; its hoofs go stamping over the world, trampling and breaking … O Lord! I've seen so much of it; it meets one all over the place. It makes one simply sick. This affair of yours is nothing to some things I've come upon lately … West says the same, you know. Of course, as a parson, he sees much more of people, in that way, than I do. He says lots of the quite nice, decent women he visits have taken to getting drunk at the pubs; partly they're better off than they were, of course, but it's mostly just nerves. You don't drink at pubs, do you?'

'Not come to it yet, ' said Alix.

'Well, you're lucky. I consider you're jolly lucky, considering the state you've been in for some time, to have done nothing worse yet than to have told a man you've every right to care for that you care for him. '

Alix was crying now, quietly.

'And I have done worse things, too … I tried to get him back from Evie. I told her he didn't really care for her – that he had been just the same with me. Oh, I know he did care for me a little, of course, but –' she choked on a laugh, 'he didn't behave as he does with Evie, a bit …'

'Probably not, ' Nicholas admitted.

'Well, there you are; I behaved like a cad about it. That's worse than drinking at pubs – much worse. It's even worse than telling him I cared … What can I do about it, Nicky? Is that part of the war disease too?'

'Certainly,' said Nicholas promptly. 'Precisely the same thing, and bears out all I was saying. And, as you remark, much worse than drinking at pubs … Sorry, but it does prove my case, you know. You don't do that sort of thing in peace time, at least, do you?' he added with impartial curiosity.

'I've forgotten about peace time … No, I don't think I used to … Suppose I shall have to tell Evie,' Alix added morosely. 'Though she doesn't care for him, a bit … What a bore … All right, Nicky; I'll try to look at myself as a mental case … And what's left is that Basil has gone. I love him, you know, extraordinarily. I – Oh, Nicky, I love him, I love him, I love him.' She passionately sobbed for a time.

Nicholas stood silent, thinking, till she lay back exhausted and quiet.

'I'm sorry,' she said huskily. 'I won't cry any more. That's all.' Nicholas was looking at her consideringly.

'I wonder,' he murmured, 'what the best remedy for you is. Something that takes your whole thoughts, I fancy, you want. Of course there's the School. But it doesn't seem altogether to work. Some strong counter-interest to the war, you want.'

'To take me outside myself,' Alix amplified for him. 'Perhaps you'd like me to collect bus tickets or lost cats or something, to distract my mind, Nicky dear.'

'I think not. Your mind, I should say, is distracted enough already. You need to collect that, rather than bus tickets or cats … To me it seems a pity you should live at Violette. I think you should stop that.'

Alix said apathetically, 'I don't think it much matters where I live. I can't live at Wood End. It's all war and warwork there, and I should go mad – even madder than now. I might drink at pubs … I thought Violette would be a rest, because they none of them care about the war really, a bit; but it isn't a rest any more. Ever since Paul … I've known one can't really put the war away out of one's mind: it can't be done. It's hurting too many people too badly; it's no use trying to pretend it isn't there and go on as usual. I can't. I can't even paint decently; my work's simply gone to pot.'

'Sure to,' Nicholas agreed.

'I believe,' said Alix, 'it's jealousy that's demoralising me most. Jealousy of the people who can be in the beastly thing … Oh, I do so want to go and fight … How can you not try to go, Nicky? I can't understand that. Though of course you wouldn't get passed.'

'It's quite easy,' returned Nicholas. 'I don't approve of joining in such things.'

'But I want to go and help to end it … Oh, it's rotten not being able to; simply rotten … Why shouldn't girls? I can't bear the sight of khaki; and I don't know whether it's most because the war's so beastly or because I want to be in it … It's both … Oh bother, why were we born at a time like this, as Kate calls it?'

'We weren't. The late 'eighties and early 'nineties were very different. They probably unfitted us for the Sturm und Drang of the twentieth century. Though, if you come to that, there was plenty of *Sturm und Drang* in our own country at that period, as usual … I suppose Poles have no right to look for peace … O Lord, how good it would be to see Germany and Russia exterminate each other altogether! I believe I'd cheat my way into the army and fight, if I thought I could help in that.'

'I dare say we shall see it, if this war goes on much longer … I've been wondering lately,' went on Alix, 'if there isn't a third way in war time. Not throwing oneself into it and doing jobs for it, in the way that suits lots of people; I simply can't do that. And not going on as usual and pretending it's not there, because that doesn't work. Something *against* war, I want to be doing, I think. Something to fight it, and prevent it coming again … I suppose mother thinks she's doing that.'

'She does,' said Nicholas. 'Undoubtedly. I'm not sure I agree with her, but that's a detail. She thinks she's doing it … Well, I gather she'll be home very soon now.'

'And I suppose Mr West thinks he's doing it, doesn't he – fighting war, I mean, with his Church and things.'

'Yes, West thinks so too. Again, I don't particularly agree with his methods, but that's his aim.'

'You don't particularly agree with any methods, do you?'

'No; I think they're mostly pretty rotten. And in this case I believe, personally, we're up against a hopeless proposition. West calls it the devil, and is bound by his profession to believe it will be eventually overcome. I'm not bound to believe that any evil or lunacy will be overcome; it seems to me at least an open question. Some have been, of course; others have scarcely lessened in the course of these several million years. However, as West remarks, the world, no doubt, is still young. One should give it time. Anyhow, one has to; no other course is open to us, however poor a use we may think it puts the gift to … That's West, I think. Hullo, West; we've been talking about you. We were discussing your incurable optimism.'

2

West looked tired. He shook hands with Alix and sat down by the window. Alix did not feel it mattered that he should see she had been crying, because clergymen, who visit the unfortunate, the ill-bred, the unrestrained, must every day see so many people who have been crying that they would scarcely notice.

'Incurable,' West repeated, and the crisp edge of his voice

was flattened and dulled by fatigue. 'Well, I hope it is. There are moments when one sees a possible cure looming in the distance.'

'I was saying,' said Nicholas, 'that you're bound, by your profession, to believe in the final vanquishing of the devil.'

'I believe I am,' West assented, without joy. 'I believe so.'

He cogitated over it for a moment, and added, 'But the devil's almost too stupid to be vanquished. He's an animal; a great brainless beast, stalking through chaos. He's got a hide like a rhinoceros, and a mind like an escaped idiot: you don't know where to have him. He drags people into his den and sits on them … it's too beastly … He wallows in his native mud, full of appetites and idiot dreams, and his idiot dreams become fact, and people make wars … and get drunk. There are men and women and babies tight all about the streets this evening. Saturday night, you know … Sorry to be depressing,' he added, more in his usual alert manner; 'it's a rotten thing to be in these days … The fog's bad outside.'

Alix rose to go, and West stood up too. For a moment the three stood looking at each other in the fog-blurred, firelit room, dubious, questioning, grave, like three travellers who have lost their way in a strange country and are groping after paths in the dark … Nicholas spoke first.

'That's your bell, isn't it, West? You two could walk together as far as Gray's Inn Road.'

Nicholas lit the gas and settled down to write.

Alix and West went down the stairs and out into Fleet Street, and the city in the fog was as black as wood at night.

3

Alix thought, 'Christians must mind. Clergymen must mind awfully. It's their business that's being spoilt. It's their job to make the world better: they must mind a lot, and they can't fight either,' and saw West's face, tired and preoccupied, in the darkness at her side.

'War Extra. 'Fishul. Bulgarian Advance. Fall of Kragujevatz,' cried a newsboy, as best he could.

'It'll be all up with Serbia presently,' said West. 'Going under fast. A wipe out, like Belgium, I suppose … And we look at it from here and can't do anything to stop it. Pretty rotten, isn't it?' His voice was bitter.

'If we could go out there and try,' said Alix, 'we shouldn't feel so bad, should we?'

He shook his head.

'No: not so bad. War's beastly and abominable to the fighters: but not to be fighting is much more embittering and demoralising, I believe. Probably largely because one has more time to think. To have one's friends in danger, and not to be in danger oneself – it fills one with futile rage. Combatants are to be pitied; but non-combatants are of all men and women the most miserable. Older men, crocks, parsons, women – God help them.'

'Yes,' Alix agreed, on the edge of tears again. Then West seemed to pull himself up from his despondency.

'But really, of course, they've a unique opportunity. They can't be fighting war abroad; but they can be fighting it at home. That's what it's up to us all to do now, I'm firmly convinced, by whatever means we each have at our command. We've all of us some. We've got to use them. The fighting men out there can't; they're tied. Some of them never can again … It's up to us … Good-bye, Miss Sandomir: my way is along there.'

They parted at the corner of Gray's Inn Road. Alix saw him swallowed up in black fog, called by his bell, going to his church to fight war by the means he had at his command.

She got into her bus and went towards Violette, where no one fought anything at all, but where supper waited, and Mrs Frampton was anxious lest she should have got lost in the fog.

Part II

Daphne

CHAPTER 14

Daphne at Violette

1

Daphne Sandomir was in the train between Cambridge and King's Cross. She was always very busy in trains, as, indeed, everywhere else. On this journey she was correcting the proofs of the chapter (Chapter 4, Education of the Children) which she was contributing to a volume by seven authors, shortly to appear, to be entitled alliteratively *Is Permanent Peace Possible?* and to come to the conclusion that it was.

Daphne Sandomir's interest in many things had always been so keen that before the war you could not have picked out one as absorbing her more than a score of others. She had been used to write pamphlets and address meetings on most of them: eurhythmics, for instance, and eugenics, and the economic and constitutional position of women, and sweated industries, and baby creches, and suggestion healing, and health food, and clean milk, and twenty other of the causes good people have at heart.

Then had come the war, an immense and horribly surprising shock, to which her healthy and vigorous mind, not shattered like some, had reacted in new forms of energy.

There were in England no ladies more active through that desperate time than Daphne Sandomir and her sister Eleanor Orme; but their activities were for the most part different. Mrs Orme was secretary of a Red Cross hospital, superintended canteens, patrolled camps, relieved and entertained Belgians and dealt them out clothes, was the soul of Women's Work Committees, made body-belts, respirators and sand-bags, locked up her cellar, bought war loan, and wrote sensible letters to *The Times*, which usually got printed.

Mrs Sandomir also relieved Belgians, got up Repatriation and Reconstruction societies for them, spoke at meetings of the Union of Democratic Control (to which society, as has been before mentioned, she did not belong) and of other societies to which she did belong, held study circles of working people to educate them in the principles making for permanent peace, went with a motor ambulance to pick up wounded in France, tried, but failed, like so many others, to attend the Women's International Congress at the Hague, travelled round the world examining its disposition towards peace, helped to form the SPPP (Society for Promoting Permanent Peace), wrote sensible letters to *The Times*, which sometimes got printed and sometimes not, articles in various periodicals, pamphlets on peace, education and such things, and chapters in joint books.

She had just returned now from her journey round the world, where she had been interviewing a surprising number of the members of the governments of the belligerent and neutral countries and making a study of such of the habits and points of view of their subjects as could be readily investigated by visitors. Immediately, she came from Cambridge, where her home was, and where she had been starting a local branch of the SPPP, and addressing a meeting of the Heretics Society on the Attitude of Neutral Governments towards Mediation without Armistice.

She was a tall, graceful, vigorous person, absurdly young and beautiful, vivid, dark-eyed, clever, and tremendously in earnest about life. She had lately (it seemed lately to herself and all who knew her) gone down from Newnham, where she had done brilliantly in the Economics Tripos and got engaged to Paul Sandomir, an exiled Pole studying the habits and history of the English constitution at Fitzwilliam

Hall. Their married career had been stimulating and storm-tossed. Finally Paul Sandomir had died in a Warsaw prison, worn out with consumption, revolution, and excitement. The extreme energy of the parents had always reacted on the children curiously, discounting enthusiasms, and flavouring their activities with the touch of irony which one often notes in the families of one or more very zealous parents. They greatly esteemed and loved their father and mother. To them Daphne was one of the dearest and most beautiful people in the world, if too stimulating. They felt, on the whole, older than she was, and worldly-wise in comparison.

2

King's Cross. Daphne, taken by surprise, seized her scattered proofs and crammed them into her despatch-box. Gathering her possessions to her, she turned to see Alix at the carriage door.

'Oh – you dear child … A porter, Alix. Do you see one? Yes, will you take them to a taxi, please.' Relieved of them, she turned with her quick, graceful movement and took the smaller Alix in her arms, Physically, mentally, morally, it was certainly Daphne who had the advantage.

They got into the taxi. Daphne said to the porter, 'I think you get eighteen-and-six now, don't you? Are you married?'

'Yes, ma'am.'

'How many children?'

'Nine, ma'am.'

'Oh, I think not. You're too young for that, really you are, you know. Let's say four. Well, here's eightpence. Tell him Spring Hill, Clapton. Thank you so much.'

The taxi sprang up the incline to the street.

'Of course,' said Daphne, frowning over it, 'eighteenand-six is shocking, with these high prices. Goodness only knows when we're going to get it improved. But it's immoral to try and make it up by private subsidies … Is there anything the matter with our driver, child? You seem to be interested in him.'

'I was only trying to discern how many children he's old enough to have,' Alix explained. 'It seems nicer not to have to ask him; it's so embarrassing not being able to believe his answer. I think five is the outside limit, don't you, darling?'

Daphne put on her pince-nez and regarded the driver's back.

'Certainly not. Three, if that. In fact, I doubt if he's married at all. But never mind now. I want to hear about you, child. Nicholas gave me a rather poor account of you when he wrote the other day. He seemed to think this Clapton life has been getting a little on your nerves.'

'Oh, I don't think so. I'm all right.'

Daphne regarded her consideringly.

'Nerves. Yes. You oughtn't to have any at your age, of course. No one need, at any age. You should do eurhythmics. You'd find it changed the whole of life – gave it balance, coherence, rhythm. I find it wonderful. You must certainly begin classes at once.'

'I don't think I've time, mother. I'm going to the art school every day.'

'I think you should make time. I hadn't much time while I was on my travels, if you come to that. But I made some to practise my eurhythmics. I knew how important it was to keep fit and balanced and healthy, and that I should never be much use in influencing all those people I interviewed (so reasonable and delightful they mostly were, Alix, and simply longing for peace – I must tell you all about it) unless I kept my own poise. It's the same for you. You'll never be any use at painting or anything else while you're mentally and physically incoherent and adrift. That's one thing settled

– eurhythmics. And the other is, you must leave this Pansy, or Violet, or whatever it is, at once, of course, and we'll take a flat. What about these Frampton Tucker people? Of course I know they're hopelessly dull and ordinary – I've met Emily Frampton very seldom, but quite often enough. A kind little mediocrity, the widow of a rather common man of business. Laurence Frampton married her, for some incomprehensible reason of his own; people do sometimes. He took her to Oxford with him, and only survived it a year. They lived at Summertown. Her two girls were quite little then. I believe she was quite happy. I met her once when I was staying at Oriel ... she never took *in* Oxford, of course; it was too many miles outside her ken, and she very sensibly hardly attempted to belong or mix. But she rather liked Summertown society, I remember. They lived in a house called Thule, and kept six cats. I suppose she hasn't changed at all, probably.'

'Probably not. She's very nice and kind.'

'Oh – all that.' Daphne waved it aside. 'Of course. But too stupid to be tolerable, even as a background to your day's work, no doubt. I'm sorry I've left you there so long, child. I should have thought of it before, but it was all arranged without me, and I was too busy to send you advice. I don't wonder you look a wreck.'

'I don't,' said Alix. 'And Cousin Emily's not bad. She's always giving me hot milk – gallons of it. And ovaltine, to make me fat, she says. She's awfully kind.'

'Encouraging you to think about your constitution. No wonder you're nervy. What about the girls?'

'Oh ... they're quite good sorts.'

'The younger one is good-looking, isn't she?'

'Yes. Evie is beautiful. And jolly, and popular. Kate goes to church and does parish work, and reads the *Daily Thrill* aloud in the evenings. Evie has young men. Her chief one just now is at the front; he's a Gordon of Gordon's jams.'

'That sink of iniquity! The girl can have no principle. But jam is going to be nationalised very soon, I trust, like many better things. I hope so. It richly deserves it ... Another thing, Alix – you must start health food. I'm going to help Linda Durell to start a Health and Thrift Food Shop, you know. Linda's terribly unbusinesslike, of course. So many people are, if you come to that. And *so* many people don't eat the right things at the right moments. That man Nicky lives with, now, who stayed with us – he never seems to have the faintest notion of healthy feeding. Goes out every morning before breakfast without an apple or a glass of milk. One should *always* begin the day with an apple, Alix – remember that. But parsons are hopeless, of course. Such insane ideas about this world not mattering, as if it wasn't the only one we've got. I've no patience with religious people; can't think why Nicky lives with one of them. Though, mind, I like this Mr West in himself; he's quite sound on most points of importance, and intelligent, too; I've been on Sweated Industries committees with him, and I believe he's doing good work for women's trade unions. Perhaps he'll change his mind about this church business when he's older.'

'I don't believe he will. It seems to mean rather a lot to him, doesn't it? To him it's the way of jogging the world on. As committees are to you. '

'My dear, I detest committees. Most of their members are too stupid and tiresome for words individually, and their collective incompetence is quite unthinkable. But what other way is there in this extraordinarily stick-in-themud world?'

Alix shook her head. Indeed, she didn't know. She felt helpless to give the world any sort of jog out of its mud, by any means whatsoever.

Daphne caught the blank look of her eyes, and suddenly put her strong arm round the thin, small body.

'My poor baby, you must get strong, you know, and happy. No one needs to be ailing or depressed if they'll just say to themselves, "I am going to be well and strong and to stand up to the world. I'm not going to give in to it. I am the master of my body and soul." I said that when our darling died; I kept on saying it, and I came through on it. There was too much to do to give way. There is still. We've got to be strong women, for our own sakes and the world's – especially we who have the brains to be some use if we try. The poor old world needs help so very badly just now, with all the fools there are who hinder and block the way. You and I have both got to help. Alix … There is so much to get done.'

Daphne, holding her close, lightly kissed the thin fingers she held. Alix thought, 'Mother is splendid, of course. But she's bigger than I am, and stronger, and she hardly ever feels ill, and she doesn't know how Paul died and she's not in love with Basil and didn't tell him so. And I believe she's so keen and busy that she doesn't have time to think about the war, except about how to stop it … Perhaps that's the way – to be thinking only how to stop it and prevent another … *Is* that the way?'

Alix became aware, from the clasp of Daphne's hands on hers, their firm, light pressure, full of purpose, that Daphne was willing her to health and happiness, trying, in fact, suggestion. Daphne believed in health suggestion, as well as health food. She belonged to societies for promoting both. She had often in the past made health suggestions to Alix, but Alix had not always taken them. At the present moment Alix, overcome by the contrast between her mother's undying hope and purpose for her and her own inability to justify them, giggled weakly, in the sudden way she had.

'I'm sorry, darling,' she apologised. 'No, I'm not hysterical, only footling. I'm sorry I'm such a rotter and no credit to you and no use to the world. But I'm all right really, you know. I don't need healing a bit.'

Daphne held her from her, scrutinised her critically, and said, 'You're suffering from hyperaesthesia. How many cigarettes are you smoking a day?'

'Nine. No, I'm too young for that, like the porter – let's say three. Oh, I don't know – I don't count really. Quite few. Cousin Emily doesn't really like it much. She and Kate don't smoke at all, and Evie's only just learning. We're not a vicious household; our chief excesses are chocolates and hot milk.'

'Well, my outside rule is five, you know, in peace time, and now it's three. I should advise only two for you. Linda Durell is for starting and selling Health Cigarettes, but I won't have it, I think they are too disgusting. One must draw the line somewhere … Is this Clapton? Who lives in Clapton, by the way? I know the secretary of the Women's Wage Increase Committee does – but who else? Of course people used to, in the nineteenth century. Your greatgrandfather did. And Cowper, I think –or was it Dr Watts? Someone who wrote hymns. Those look like good people's houses there.'

'Yes. Oh, bishops live here, and retired generals, and stockbrokers, and thousands of babies. And the Vinneys. And lots of dreadfully common people, Kate says. They all play tennis in the Park. This is Spring Hill.'

'So I see. And there's Primmerose. Tell him to stop.'

'No, darling, Primmerose is someone else's. It's Violette we want; do remember, mother, because the Primmerose people are common, and we don't like being confused. Here we are.'

3

They got out. Daphne, having decided without discussion the probable size of the chauffeur's family, judicially tipped him and told him to return for her at half-past five. She then entered Violette and met Mrs Frampton in the hall. Mrs Frampton, like Alix and so many others, was much smaller than she was; Daphne had to bend graciously to shake hands. Mrs Frampton was a little shy of the tall, distinguished, clever, beautiful cousin of her clever, distinguished, little-known second husband. Daphne, was, in a manner, a public personage; most people knew her name. She had for long been at once ornamental and useful, a fountain-head of a perpetually vigorous stream of energies, some generally approved, others regarded by many as harmful, that watered England; but Violette, for good or ill, was outside their furthest spraying. Mrs Frampton looked from far off, as she had looked at Professor Frampton, at the brilliant, not-to-be-understood energies of a worker in worlds by her not realised. This makes one shy, even if one believes oneself to be a denizen of a superior world, and Mrs Frampton lacked this consolation. She was a humble person, and knew that Daphne and Professor Frampton had the best of it.

They sat in the drawing-room, where there would soon be tea. Daphne looked round the room with an inward gasp: she really hadn't expected it to be quite so bad as this. The Summertown drawing-room, which she vaguely remembered, had been a little the drawing-room of her cousin Laurence. She took it all in rapidly, and, as if hypnotised, came back to rest on 'Thou seest me' and the watching Eye.

'My poor child,' she thought. 'I must take her away at once. It's a wonder she's not actually had a *crise de nerfs*, with the wretched nervous system she inherits from Paul, and that Eye always watching her ...'

Mrs Frampton meanwhile was amiably talking, nervous but pleased.

'It's been so delightful having dear Alix all these months. So nice for the girls, too. We've made quite a little party of young people, haven't we, Alix? And other young people drop in quite frequently –Alix's brother, of course, which is always so very nice – he's wonderfully clever, isn't he – and that pleasant Mr Doye, who lost his finger; I'm sure we quite miss him now he's gone back to the army again; and friends of my girls, and friends of Alix's. Often we're quite a party. It keeps us all quite cheerful and merry, even in these dreadful days, doesn't it, Alix?'

'Yes, ' said Alix.

'Only this child works so hard at her drawing and painting all day, she doesn't get much time for play. I'm sure they work them too hard at these art schools. She looks quite overdone and poorly, don't you think so, Mrs Sandomir?'

'Oh, she'll be all right directly,' said Daphne, who didn't approve of discussing people's poor health in their presence, thinking it made them worse.

'It's mostly nerves and fancy, I expect, ' she added, giving a light pat to Alix's arm. 'Shouldn't be given away to. I expect you've been spoiling her. '

'No; I haven't– no indeed.' Mrs Frampton was pleased. 'I *have* thought she looked thin and below par often, and I've made her take lots of milk, and that nice ovaltine, and even malt and cod-liver oil, but she wouldn't go on with that. There's a very nice stuff that's being advertised everywhere now –Fattine – and I want her to try that.'

'Oh, Alix was always thin. I don't believe in worrying with medicines. We mustn't make her sorry for herself by talking about her like this … That's Evie, isn't it? *She* doesn't look as if she needed medicine, anyhow. I should like to have her for an advertisement in the windows of my Health Food shop.'

Evie was followed by Kate, Florence, and tea. Daphne thought Kate and the tea-cups both deplorable. Kate had been going round her district with parish magazines. She hadn't succeeded (district visitors never do) in collecting all the pennies for them, and told her mother which person hadn't paid.

'And of course that Mrs Fittle, in Paradise Court, lay low and pretended to be out, as usual. I expect she was –' Kate pursed her lips, which meant drunk. Mrs Frampton nodded intelligently.

'The Clapton people are terribly difficult to deal with.' Kate explained to Daphne. 'Dreadfully ungrateful, too, very often. The clergy and workers may do anything for them, but it's all no more than what's their due, and no thanks, only grumbles. Do you find them like that in Cambridge?' (which was the town in which Daphne, if she had one anywhere, presumably had a district).

'Not a bit,' said Daphne briskly. 'The idea of expecting me to find anything so commonplace,' was her inward comment. 'This girl is the worst of the lot.'

'Kate does a great deal of parish work,' Mrs Frampton explained. 'She's quite busy always, with church things.'

'Yes?' Daphne was vague, hiding how much she disapproved of church things.

'Now I'm afraid I'm used to a rather different sort of service from those Kate attends,' Mrs Frampton continued. 'I'm old-fashioned, I know. Kate's church goes a touch too high for me.'

Something in her visitor's face, a certain blankness, suggested to her that probably Daphne knew no difference between high and low, but condemned both with impartial unfairness. She remembered that Alix hadn't been brought up to go to any sort of church. Alix, being of a later generation, had indeed a fairly open mind on these matters; but Daphne, the product of a more pronounced and condemning age, rejected with emphasis. The Christian religion, as taught in churches, was to her pernicious, retrograde, the hampering relic of a darker age. Some glimmering of this attitude filtered through to Mrs Frampton, and flustered her. She added, 'But of course we can't all think the same way about things, can we? … I hope you enjoyed your trip round the world, Mrs Sandomir.'

'Very much, thank you.'

'You visited the Balkans, didn't you? That must have been very alarming and wild. I'm sure it was wonderfully brave of you to go there, with all this upset, and all the natives so unsettled. I'm afraid I shouldn't have had the courage. '

'The upset,' said Daphne, 'was less advanced than it is now, when I was there. I had a most interesting time …' But not really, in the main, suitable to tell Mrs Frampton about, so she rapidly selected.

'The Bulgarian babies – you never saw anything so pleasant. You'd love them, Mrs Frampton. You should go there some time. And their teeth come through when they're about six weeks old, for some reason. It's just as well, because their ideas about milk and cleanliness are most behindhand. I talked to a sort of mothers' meeting about it, but I don't think they even began to understand. I expect my Bulgarian wasn't idiomatic enough. Oh dear, the dirt of those infants …'

'Fancy! It does seem a wickedness not to keep little babies clean, doesn't it? There's one at a house in this road – Primmerose – and I'm sure it goes to one's heart to see the way it's kept.'

Kate said, fastidiously, 'Those Primmerose people aren't nice in any way, I'm afraid. There are some very regrettable people come settling round here lately – people one can't dream of knowing. It's a great pity.'

'People will settle, won't they,' Daphne said vaguely. 'It's better perhaps than being unsettled, like the Balkan people.' Daphne never punned except in absence of mind, rightly believing the habit to rise from weakness of intellect; but she was thinking now not of Clapton nor of the Balkan people, but of an address she was giving that evening to a meeting of the NUWSS on her recent experiences, and which she had only inadequately prepared. She pulled herself together, however, and became charming, attentive, and intelligent for the rest of tea.

'And what did you think of the United States?' Mrs Frampton inquired. 'Will they come in, do you think, or won't the President let them, whatever occurs? You met the President, didn't you? How did he strike you?'

'Oh, delightful. Like most governments; they're nearly all charming personally, I believe. So much stronger, as a rule, in the heart than in the head. They mean so much good and do much harm, poor dears. A curse seems to dog them. They're the victims of an iniquitous and insane system; and they lack foresight and sound judgment so terribly, for all their good intentions.'

'You would scarcely say the Kaiser had good intentions,' Mrs Frampton suggested dubiously.

Daphne said, 'I don't know him, but I'm told he has all sorts, good and bad, like other mischievous people.'

'We all know, anyhow, where good intentions pave the way to, ' said Kate, more epigrammatic than usual, so that Mrs Frampton said, 'Hush, dear,' and added, 'He'll have to face the consequences of his actions some day, when he's called to give account of his life. Perhaps we oughtn't to forestall his condemnation, poor man.'

Daphne said, 'Indeed, I'm quite sure we ought. Condemnation will be singularly little use at the moment you refer to,' and then, because that moment would be a fruitless, and indeed most unsuitable, topic of conversation between her and Mrs Frampton, she left it, and talked about flats in town, a subject which she and Violette regarded from standpoints very nearly as far sundered as those from which they contemplated the last judgment.

After tea, Mrs Frampton said she and Kate and Evie would now go away and leave Daphne and Alix alone together, which they did.

The door shut behind them, and Daphne passed her long, capable hand over her forehead and shut her eyes for a moment.

'My dear child – what you have been through! It must end at once. So kind, and so unthinkably trying! No wonder – oh well, never mind, you'll soon be all right now … Do they know *anything* about anything that matters? No, quite obviously not.'

'I'd rather they didn't, mother. I don't like the things that matter. I've been quite comfortable.'

'Comfortable! With that Eye! Nonsense, child … The idea of our *having* such relations, even by marriage … Laurence Frampton was really too queer. I've often wondered whether his head wasn't a little going when he did it; he had been peculiar in several ways. Quite suddenly voted conservative – which years was it, now? I think myself life had tired him; people wanted to abolish Greek in Responsions, and so on, and he had some worries in his college, and private money difficulties too, I believe; Oxford people are so extravagant sometimes; so he fell back on a little cushiony wife as one might on to a pillow, and died quietly soon afterwards. Most tragic, really; such a brilliant fellow he was … Now there's my taxi back again. I'm going first to Nicky's, then to dine at the Club with Francie Claverhouse, before addressing the NUWSS. By the way, I'm fearfully out of temper with them – have you been following their policy lately? They've been *criminally* weak on Conscription … We shall have to have a split, as usual … Good-bye, darling. Run and fetch your cousin Emily to say good-bye to me. No, only your cousin Emily; I can't speak to Kate, she's the epitome of all the ages of the drab and narrow feminine. And Evie is immoral, and carries on with Gordon's jam. It isn't right that you should be here. None of them have any principles.'

While she talked, Daphne was collecting her bags, papers and furs, with her quick, graceful decisive movements. Alix watched her, feeling, as she sometimes did in her mother's presence, as if she sucked up all the ozone in the air and left none for her.

They found Mrs Frampton in the hall, full of shy and beaming kindness. Daphne took her hand and looked down on her cordially.

'I must be flying. I'll look in to-morrow, if I may … Good-bye, and thank you so much for being good to the child.'

The narrow Kate and the immoral Evie appeared in the background, and Daphne had to shake hands with them after all before escaping into the taxi.

4

Violette watched her drive away up Spring Hill.

Evie thought how handsome she was, and how well she wore her clothes.

Kate was not quite certain she wasn't a touch fast.

Alix thought, 'How jolly it must be to be like mother, so certain and so strong.'

Mrs Frampton thought, 'She seems so nice and clever, but a little alarming, perhaps,' and said to Alix, 'Your mother seems wonderfully well and busy. I expect she's always quite full of plans and occupations and interests, isn't she?'

'Yes,' said Alix.

CHAPTER 15

Alix at a meeting

1

Daphne took Alix from Violette to stay with her at her club. It was the end of November. Daphne proposed that they should spend a fortnight in town, till the end of the art school term, then go down to their house at Cambridge for the Christmas vacation. She meant to spend this period holding meetings about the county of Cambridgeshire with a view to starting village branches of the Society for Promoting Permanent Peace. Meetings – branches – study circles – this was the machinery behind the ideals. Daphne, at times irrelevant, inconsequent, prejudiced, whimsical, perverse, was an idealist and a businesswoman.

She made Alix come to meetings while they were in town. She saw in Alix the raw material of a member of the SPPP. She said, 'You mustn't be selfish, darling. You are a little selfish, you know, and you're old enough now to leave it off. You try to hide from things, like an ostrich. You try and pretend they don't exist. In point of fact, they do, and you know it. You know it all the time: you can't forget it, so you waste your trouble trying. You must leave that to the Violettes. They can ignore. You can't … Ignoring: that's always been the curse of this world. We shut our eyes to things –poverty, and injustice, and vice, and cruelty, and sweating, and slums, and the tendencies which make war, and we feed ourselves on batter, and so go on from day to day getting a little fatter– and so the evils too go on from day to day getting fatter, till they get so corpulent and heavy that when we do open our eyes at last, because we have to, they can scarcely be moved at all. It's sheer criminal selfishness and laziness and stupidity. Mr West was talking about it the other day. I like that young man; he believes in all the right things. And in so many of the wrong ones as well – I can't imagine why. I told him I couldn't imagine why; and he said he found the same difficulty about me. So there we are. However, what was I saying? Oh yes – laziness, selfishness and stupidity. It's those three we've got to fight. We've got to replace them by hard working, hard living, and hard thinking. And the last must come first. We've got to *think*, and make everyone think … One of the worst things about a war is that so many of the best thinkers are in the middle of it, and can't think, and may never be able to think again. I don't in the least agree with those complacent young men and women who believe that no one over forty either can or will think. "The war has let the old men loose upon the world," I believe is the phrase. Conceited rubbish, of course. They won't talk it when they and their friends are forty-eight, like me. Personally I know just about as many young fools and obscurantists and militarists as elderly ones. Any number of both. It's not a question of age; it's temperament and training. But still, grant that the young men of fighting age form a very large proportion in each nation of the clearest Intellects and the keenest idealists and the best workers for truth, and that they are nearly all now in action, or put out of action. Grant that many of them will never come back, that many others will come back weakened physically and mentally and incapable of the work they might have done before, and some perhaps with their mental vision a little blinded and perverted by what they've had to play a part in for so long. That's the worst tragedy of all, of course, that possible perversion. Better never come back at all.' Daphne's voice shook momentarily, but she went on bravely: 'Paul would have been a fine worker. He was going to be very like his father. Well, Paul's gone under – a sacrifice to the Brute. Thousands of other finely-wrought instruments like Paul have been smashed and lost to the world … It's an irreparable tragedy, of course … But we who are left and who are free have got to do their work as well as our own. And we've got to begin at once. There's no time to be lost.'

Daphne consulted her watch, and added, 'You'd better come to a meeting of the SPPP at Queen's Hall with me after dinner, dearest. It would interest and instruct you. Several people are going to speak, including me.'

'It's all right when you speak,' said Alix. 'But some of them are rather the limit, really, mother.'

'Oh, my dear, of course. The very outside edge: over it. What does it matter? It's causes that count, thank goodness not the people who work for them. When you're my age you'll have learnt to *swallow* people, without getting indigestion. Now we must have dinner at once, and then you shall come and begin to practise impersonal idealism. It *is* so important.'

2

Alix supposed it must be. Meetings are so very mixed, speeches so unequal, people so various.

Lack of clear thinking – that, as Daphne had said, was probably what was wrong with nearly everyone. Perhaps it is the commonest defect, and the most irritating. It makes people talk sentimental rubbish. It makes them lump other people together in masses and groups, setting one group against another, when really people are individual temperaments and brains and souls, and unclassifiable. It makes them say (Alix picked out all these utterances in the Queen's Hall to-night, among many other utterances truer and sounder and more relevant – indeed, indubitably sound, relevant and true) that young men are good and intelligent and pacifist (no, pacifist) and admire Romain Rolland, and elderly men bad, stupid and militarist, and admire Bernhardi. That women are the guardians of life, and therefore mind war more than men do. That democracies are inherently and consistently peaceful enough (stated) and intelligent enough (assumed) to prevent wars from ever occurring if the reins of foreign policy were in their hands. ('Rubbish,' muttered Daphne. 'He's missing the whole point, which is to *make* democracies so, by a long and difficult education. Everyone knows they've not much sense yet.') That the reason why war is objectionable is that the human body is sacred and should be inviolate. What did that mean, precisely, Alix wondered? That women are the chief sufferers from war. A debatable point, anyhow; and what did it matter, and why divide humanity into sexes, further than nature has already done so? That among the newspaper owners and members of the governments of each nation were some so misguided and lacking in financial foresight as to encourage wars because they had some shares in armament industries, and hoped, presumably, to recoup themselves therefrom for the heavy financial losses which they, in common with all other members of the community, must suffer in case of war. 'Fools they must be,' Alix commented, and speculated that these covetous individuals, even granting that they had pinned their hopes entirely on the financial issue, must be feeling pretty badly sold. For their other and nicer shares would be declining; their income-tax was enormous (and they probably had to pay super-tax too, which was even worse); the papers they owned were losing the advertisements they lived by; and their food cost them more. A bad look-out for these covetous ones.

From this the speaker got on to capitalism in general. Well, Alix was entirely with him there.

A new speaker (much better, quite good, in fact) was

speaking of secret ententes, as speakers will at these meetings. The Moroccan crisis … that was rather interesting. The Balance of Power. A rotten theory, but surely, as things were, necessary? Yes, as things were; but not as they were going to be. For there must, in time, be General Disarmament. Disarmament. A fancy some lean to and others hate, no doubt. But most hate it. The question was, would they hate it more after this war, or less? *Si vis bellum, para bellum*; that was the true version of that saying. True, for it had been proved so. Look at the Germans, preparing for war for years; look at all the other nations, also preparing for years. And now they had all got it. That is what armies and fleets lead to. So instead of armies and fleets, let us have International Councils for Arbitration. A Concert for Europe.

A jolly sound notion, thought Alix, but wished the speaker would meet rather more precisely the obvious difficulties in the way of this method of keeping the peace. It certainly was a sound notion: one felt that it could, after much shaping and experiment and failure, be workable, be made something of. There was no earthly reason why not. And certainly the more it was discussed and publicly aired in all the nations, the better for its chances. But people were apt, on this subject, not to be quite practical enough; they often laid stress on the advantages of the principle, rather than on its detailed methods of working. Of course the advantages, if it could be worked, were incontrovertible; surely no one could be found to question them.

And here Alix found a weakness she had vaguely felt before in the standpoint taken by many of these people. Many of them (not nearly all, but many) seemed to imply, 'We, a select few of us called Pacificists, hate war. The rest of you rather like it. We will not allow you to have it. WE will stop it.' As if some of a race stricken with agonising plague had risen up and said to the rest, 'You, most of you, are content to be ill and in anguish and perishing. But WE do not like it. WE insist on stopping it and preventing its recurrence.' An admirable resolution, but ill-worded. What they meant, what they would mean if they thought and spoke accurately, was surely, 'We all loathe this horror – how should anyone not loathe it? We all want to stop it occurring again, and WE have thought of a way which we believe may work. This is it …'

That was sense; that was what was wanted, that anyone who thought they had found a way should use it and expound it to the rest. But oh, it wasn't sense, it was madness, to talk as if people differed in aim and desire, not merely in method. For there was one desire everyone had in these days, beneath, through and above their thousand others. People wanted money, wanted victory, wanted liberty, wanted economic individualism, wanted socialism, wanted each other, wanted love, wanted beauty, wanted virtue, wanted a vote, wanted fame, wanted genius, wanted God, wanted things to drink, even to eat, wanted more wages, wanted less taxes, less work, wanted children, wanted adventure, wanted death, wanted democracy, oligarchy, anarchy, any other archy, wanted new clothes, wanted a new heaven or a new earth or both, wanted the old back again, wanted the moon. They wanted any or all of these things and a thousand more; but through them, above them, beneath them, a quenchless fire of longing, burning, searing and consuming more passionately as the crazy weeks of frustration swung by, they wanted peace … Even some who wanted nothing else in this world or any other just had energy to want peace. There were those so tired and so forlorn and so battered and broken that they could scarcely want at all; they had lost too much. They had almost too utterly lost their health, or their courage, or their limbs, or their hope, or their faith, or their sons, husbands, brothers, lovers and friends, or their minds, to want anything from life except its end; but still, with broken, drifting, numbed desires, they wanted peace …

All the heterogeneous crowd of humanity, so at variance in almost everything else, was just now surely one in the common bond of that great desire. They swayed, that heterogeneous crowd, into Alix's giddy vision; she saw them thus strangely, perhaps unwelcomely, linked, in incongruous fellowship, those who had possibly never before believed themselves to want the same things. The one desire linked, in all the warring nations, socialists and individualistic men of business, capitalists and wageearners, slum landlords and slum dwellers, judges and criminals, soldiers and conscientious objectors, catholics and quakers, atheists and priests, prize-fighters and poets, representatives of societies differing so widely in some ways as the Fellowship of Reconciliation, and the National Service League, the WSPU and the Anti-Suffrage Society, the Union of Democratic Control and the Anti-German League, the German Social and Democratic Party and the Radicals; the staffs of journals as widely sundered by temperament and habit as the *Times* and the *Manchester Guardian*, the *Morning Post* and the *Daily News*, the *Spectator* and the *English Review*, the *Vorwärts* and the *Kreuz Zeitung*, the *Church Times*, the *Freethinker* and the *Record*.

Alix saw humanity as a great mass-meeting, men and women, 'clergymen, lawyers, lords and thieves', hand in hand, lifting together one confused voice, crying for peace, peace, where there was no peace. Where there could not yet be, nor ever had been, peace, because … because of what? That really seemed the question to be solved. Because, one supposed, of some anti-peace elements in every country; in every class, in every interest, nay, in every human being, that somehow subverted and hindered the great desire.

An odd world, certainly, and paradoxical, and curious! tragic. But lit by glimmers of hope …

3

More and more through that evening Alix came to believe that these so-called Pacificists (idiotic name – as if everyone wasn't Pacificist) really had found a way, really had, if not exactly their hands on the ropes, anyhow their feet on a road that might possibly lead somewhere. It was the same rather breathless feeling of possible ways out, or in, that she had about the Church sometimes. Only sometimes; for at other times she happened on people who belonged to the Church who made her feel that there were no roads out, or in, or anywhere, but only dull enclosures, leading nowhere; and she hadn't yet attained to the impersonal idealism Daphne urged on her (so necessary, so difficult a thing) which could swallow people for the sake of the causes they stood for. She attached too much importance to people.

She was glad when a young, keen-faced, humorous woman, with a charming voice, began to speak about Continuous Mediation without Armistice. A fascinating subject, competently handled. A continuous conference of the neutral nations, to convey the ever-changing desires of the belligerents to one another, to inquire into the principles of international justice and permanent peace underlying them, to discuss, to air proposals, to suggest, to promote understanding between belligerents. It couldn't, anyhow, do much harm, and might do much good. It would express the views of impartial observers (are any observers impartial, Alix wondered?) on these vexed questions; it would express through intermediaries the views of the peace-seekers in each warring nation to the peace-makers in the others, now that they were hindered from direct speech together. For so many thousands in the enemy countries are longing for peace; there must be no mistake about that. Of course, thought Alix, impatient again. How should there be any mistake about so obvious a thing? The only difficulty was that each country longed for peace on its own terms; peace, as they would say, with honour; and no country liked its enemies' terms. This continuous mediation business would perhaps draw them nearer together, make them see more nearly eye to eye. It certainly seemed sound.

4

'They're talking sense all right, ' said one young officer to another, behind Alix.

Then Daphne spoke, on the attitude towards war of the common people in the neutral and belligerent nations, on principles of education, and particularly on the training of children in sound international ideals – her special subject.

She told of how in Austria the Women's Committee for Permanent Peace had issued an appeal to parents and teachers urging them to counteract the influences exciting children to race hatred, and train them in respect for their enemies and constructive national service.

A comprehensive subject, treated with breadth, detail, and clarity. The young officers again approved.

Alix thought how fine a person Daphne looked and was: gracious, competent, vivid, dominating, alive. Possessed of some poise, some strength, some inner calm … What was it, exactly, and why? One saw it in some religious people. Perhaps in them and in Daphne it was the same thing: they both had a definite aim; they both knew where they were trying to go, and why. Perhaps that is what makes for strength and calm, thought Alix. Daphne wasn't running away from things, or from life: she was facing them and fighting them.

'She's good, isn't she?' said one of the officers. 'I like hearing Mrs Sandomir. She never talks through her hat. So many of these Pacifist and Militarist people do.'

Alix was glad Daphne had a sense of humour, and didn't rant or sentimentalise. She could talk of the part to be played by women in the construction of permanent peace without calling them the guardians of the race or the custodians of life. She didn't draw distinctions, beyond the necessary ones, between women and men; she took women as human beings, not as life-producing organisms; she took men as human beings, not as destroying-machines. She spoke about propaganda work to be undertaken by the SPPP in the country districts; she suggested methods; she became very practical. Alix listened with interest, for that was what Daphne was going to do in Cambridgeshire in the Christmas vacation. It sounded, as foreshadowed. sensible and useful, though of course you never know, with meetings in the country, till you try, and not always then.

5

Enough, more than enough, no doubt, has been said of a meeting so ordinary as to be familiar in outline to most people. That it was not familiar to Alix, who had hitherto voided both meetings and literature on all subjects connected with the war, is why it is here recorded in some detail. There was some more of it, but it need not be here set down.

When it was over, Daphne and Alix returned to the club. They sat in the writing-room and talked and smoked before going to bed.

'Rather sensible, on the whole, I thought, ' said Alix, lighting Daphne's cigarette. She had more colour than usual, and her eyes were bright and sleepless. Daphne glanced at her sidelong.

'Glad you approved,' she said, 'The SPPP is rather sensible, on the whole: just that … What about joining it, on those grounds? It will only bind you to approve of its general programme, and, when you can, assist in it. And its programme is really purely educational – training people (beginning with ourselves) in the kind of thinking and principles which seem to make for international understanding and peace. You'd better join us. We're fighting war, to the best of our lights, and with the weapons at our command. One can't do more than that in these days, and one can scarcely do less. One mayn't be very successful, and one may be quite off the lines; but one has to keep trying in the best way one personally knows. One can't be indifferent and inert nowadays ... Well?'

Alix leant forward and dropped her cigarette end into the fire.

'Well,' she returned, and thought for a moment, and added, 'I wonder. I'm not really good at joining things, you know.'

'You are not,' Daphne agreed, decisively. 'You sit on edges, criticising the fields on both sides and wondering what good either of them is going to be to you. Such a paltry attitude, my dear! Unpractical, selfish, and sentimental; though I know you think you hate sentimentality. It's quite time you learnt that there's no fighting with whole truths in this life, and all we can do is to seize fragments of truth where we can find them, and use them as best we can. Poor weapons, perhaps, but all we've got. That's how I see it, anyhow ... Well, darling, at least it can't do any *harm* to try and get children and grown-up people taught to get some understanding of international politics and the way to keep the peace, or to look upon arbitration as a possible, practical, and natural substitute for war – can it, now? If it only in the end results in improving ever so slightly the mental attitude of a person here and there, adding ever so little to the political information of a village in each country, it will have done *something*, won't it? And – you never know – it may do quite a lot more than that. You must remember we've got branches in all the belligerent countries now. Free discussion of these things gets them into the air, so to speak; trains people's ways of thought; and thought, collective thought, is such a solid driving-power; it gets things done. Thoughts are alive,' said Daphne, waving her cigarette as she talked, 'frightfully, terrifyingly, amazingly alive. They fly about like good and bad germs; they cause health or disease. They can build empires or slums; they can assault and hurt the soul' (unconsciously in moments of enthusiasm, Daphne sometimes used a prayer-book phrase stored in her memory cells from childhood, for her father had been a bishop), 'or they can save it alive. They can make peace and make war. They made *this* war: they must make the new peace. Thought is *everything*. We've got to make good, sane, intelligent thought, however and where ever we can, all of us … Come and work with me in Cambridgeshire next week and help me to make it, my dear.'

'Well,' said Alix again. 'I might do that. Come and watch you, I mean, and listen. I think I will do that.'

6

It was late. Everyone in the club except them had gone to bed. They went too.

Alix thought, in bed, 'Fighting war. That's what Mr West said we must all be doing. Fighting war. I suppose really it's the only thing non-combatants can do with war, to make it hurt them less … as they can't go …' She wrenched her mind sharply away from that last familiar negation, that old familiar bitterness of frustration. 'I suppose,' she thought, 'it may make even that hurt less …'

On that thought, selfish by habit as usual, a thought not suggested by Daphne, who was not selfish, she fell asleep.

CHAPTER 16

On peace

1

On the tenth of December, Daphne, Alix, and Nicholas went down to Cambridge. Liverpool Street Alix found restful. Liverpool Street, as the jumping-off place for East Anglia, has a soothing power of its own. Stations often have, probably because they indicate ways of escape, never the closed door.

But Cambridge, which they reached all too soon, was not restful. Cambridge city, even out of term time, even during terms such as these, which all the young thinkers are keeping in trenches overseas, is too conscious of the world's complexities and imminent problems and questionable destinies, to be peaceful. Cambridge is the brain of Cambridgeshire, which, having all its more disturbing thinking thus done for it, can itself remain quiet, like a brainless animal.

Daphne's sphere of work did not include Cambridge, which already thought about these things, and heard, gladly and otherwise, Mr Ponsonby on Democratic Control and Lord Bryce on International Relations, and many other people on many other subjects. All she did in Cambridge was to foster and stimulate the life of the already existing branch of the SPPP, and to make it her centre for propaganda in Cambridgeshire.

Nicholas and Alix, having been brought up in Cambridge, did not know Cambridgeshire much. Alix discovered Cambridgeshire, through this quiet, pale December. There are moments in some lives when it is the only shire that will do. Many feel the same about Oxfordshire; more about Shropshire, Sussex, Worcestershire, Hampshire, or the north, or the south-west. The present writer once knew someone who felt it about Warwickshire, but these, probably, are few. Most people may like Warwickshire, to live in or walk in or bicycle in, but will give it no peculiar place as healer or restorer. It is, perhaps, essentially a shire for the prosperous, the whole in body and mind; it has little to give, beyond what it receives. But Cambridgeshire, 'of all England the shire for men who understand', in its quiet, restrained way gives. It is not for the rich, and not for sentimentalists, and not for Americans; but it is for poets and dreamers. To those who leave it and return it has a fresh and sad significance, like the face of a once familiar and understood but half-forgotten friend, whose point of view has become strange. New meanings, old meanings reasserted, rise to challenge them; the code of values inherent in those chalky plains that are the setting of a quiet city seem to emerge in large type. Cambridge is of a quite different spirit. In Cambridge is intelligence, culture, traditionalism, civilisation, some intellectualism, even some imagination, much scholarship, ability, and good sense, above all a high idealism, a limitless fund of generous chivalry, that would be at war with the world's ills, the true crusading spirit, that can never fit in with the commercial.

And round it, strangely, lies Cambridgeshire, quiet, chalky, unknown, full of the equable Anglian peoples and limitless romance; the country of waste fens and flat wet fields and dreamy hints of quiet streams, and grey willows, and level horizons melting into blue distance beyond blue distance, and straight white roads linking ancient village to ancient village, and untold dreams; and probably not one Cambridge person in two hundred understands anything at all about it; they are too civilised, too urban, too far above the animal and the peasant. Here and there some Cambridge poet, or painter, or even archaeologist, has caught the spirit of Cambridgeshire; but mostly Cambridge people are too busy, and too alive, to try. You need to be of a certain vacancy …

But, though they understand so little of it, in times of need it sometimes raises quiet hands of healing to them. Sometimes, again, it doesn't.

2

Alix, wandering over it with Daphne, who held meetings, found it grey, toneless, faintly-hued, wintry, with larks carolling over the chalky downs and brown ploughed fields. That country south of Cambridge seemed to her the truest Cambridgeshire, rather than the level plains of Ely and the fenlands, and rather than the border regions of the north-west, where Royston, among its huddle of strange hills, broods with its hint of a hostile wildness. Royston is rather terrifying, unless you use it for golf, and Daphne had a poor meeting there.

Meetings in Cambridgeshire are often poor, that is the truth (excepting only in election time, when apathy gives place to fierce excitement). Whether they are about National Service, or Votes for Women, or Tariff Reform, or Free Trade, or Welsh Disestablishment, or Recruiting, or Peace – you cannot really rely on them. Cambridgeshire rightly believing that the day for toil was given, for rest the night, does not lightly thwart this dispensation of Providence. And the few borderland hours of twilight or lamplight which providence has set between these two spaces of time, are, there seems little doubt, given us for the purposes of tea, smoking, conversing, and courting. So meetings do not really come in.

But Daphne held them, all the same, and some people came. She usually held them in the village schoolroom.

Sometimes she got the vicar's permission to address the children during school hours, sometimes that of the vicar's wife to speak to the Mothers' Meetings while it met. But she preferred evening meetings, because of her lantern slides, which showed the photographs she had taken on her travels of men, women, and children in the other villages of other countries, thinking, so she said, the same thoughts as these men, women, and children in Cambridgeshire, saying, in their queer other tongues, the same things, playing, very often, with the same toys. (This, of course, was by way of Promoting International Sympathy.)

The women and children liked these meetings and slides. The women, being open-hearted, kindly, impressionable, pacific, saw what Daphne meant, and said, 'To think of it! I expect those mothers, poor things, miss their boys that are fighting, the same as we do ours. Well, it isn't their fault, is it? it's all that wicked Kaiser.'

The children said merely, 'Oo-ah! look at that!'

Then Daphne would go on from that starting-point to expound that it wasn't all, not quite all, that wicked Keyser. That it was, in fact, in varying degrees, not only all governments but all peoples, who had made war possible and so landed themselves at last in this.

This was less popular. The women didn't mind it; they were receptive and open to conviction, and didn't much mind either way, and were prepared to say, 'Well, to be sure, we're none of us very good Christians yet, are we?' For ideas didn't matter to them very much, nor the wrongs and rights of the war, but the fact of the war did. But some man behind, who had made up his mind on this business and knew that black was black and white was white, would sometimes observe, with vigour and decision, 'Pro-Hun.'

'I am not a pro-anyone,' said Daphne, 'nor an antianyone. But I am, in a general way, pro-peace and anti-war, as I am sure we all are in this room.' Then those who believed themselves to differ would shout 'Fight to a finish,' and 'Crush all Germans,' and 'Smash the Hun, *then* you may talk of peace,' and 'Here's some soldiers back here, you hear what *they've* got to say about it,' and other things to the same purpose; and once or twice they sang patriotic songs so loud that the meeting closed in disorder. But at other times they gave Daphne a chance to explain that she meant by peace, peace in general and in future, not a premature end to this particular war. That end, she remarked, must now be left to be decided by others; it was the future they were all concerned with. When once she got through to this point, the room usually began to listen again, and heard, with varying degrees of attention, interest and tolerance, how they could help to make a permanent peace, and even put up good-humouredly with hearing how they had helped, for some centuries, to make war, by encouraging commercialism, capitalism, selfishness, ignorance, and bad habits of thought.

On the whole, and with exceptions, so far as Cambridgeshire listened to Daphne at all, it was receptive and not unkind. The villages, of course, varied, as villages will. In some the squire and the vicar and the other chief people would not allow the meeting at all, rightly thinking it pacificist. In others they allowed it and came, and sat in front, and differed, asking Daphne if she had not heard the recommendation, *Si vis pacem, para bellum*, and remarking that while we are in a war is not the time to talk of peace. 'You might as well say,' said Daphne 'that while we are suffering from a plague is not the time to talk of measures to prevent its recurrence.'

Villages, as has been said, differ. Some, for instance, are more intelligent than others. Great Shelford is rather intelligent, and means well; many of its inhabitants are leisured, and will readily, if advised, form study circles, and read recommended literature. In fact, they did. Quite a promising little nucleus of the SPPP was established there. Sawston, two miles and a half away, is otherwise; so is Whittlesford. Of Linton, Pampisford, Landbeach, Waterbeach, the Chesterfords, and Duxford, it were better, in this connection, not to speak. Frankly, they did not understand or approve the SPPP. They thought it ProGerman.

'That silly word,' said Daphne helplessly, to Nicholas, after a rather exhausting evening at Sawston. (Nicholas's own evening had been restful, for he had spent it at home, reading Russian fairy-stories.) 'What does it *mean*? Do they mean *anything* by it? Do they know what they mean?'

'Oh, they know all right,' returned Nicholas, grinning. 'They mean you have exaggerated sympathies with the Hun.'

'Have I?' Daphne wondered. 'Well, I suppose one tries to have some sympathies with everyone – even with nations which prepare for and start wars and brutally destroy small adjacent nations in the process. But as little, almost as little, with these as it is possible to have … When will people understand that what we're out to do is not to sympathise or to apportion blame, but simply to learn together the science of reconstruction – no, of construction rather, for we've got to make what's never yet been. People do so leave things to chance – mental and spiritual things. When it's a case of reconstructing material things, as we shall have to do in Belgium and France after the war, no one will be allowed to help without proper training; people are training for it already, taking regular courses in the various branches of constructive science. But we seem to think that the nations can build themselves up spiritually without any learning or preparing at all, just because it's not towns and villages and trades and wealth and agriculture that will need building up, but only intelligence and beauty and sanity and mind and morals and manners. The building up has got to be done in the same industrious and practical spirit; you can't leave spiritual things to grow into the right shape for themselves, any more than material ones. You've got to have your constructionists, with their constructive programmes; you can't leave things to luck, sit down and say "Trust in Time, the great mender," or "Wait and see". Time isn't a member of anything: time, unused, is like an aged idiot plodding along a road without signposts into nowhere … We can't each go about our individual businesses grabbing our share of the world without troubling ourselves to get a grasp of the whole and help to shove it along the right track. It's uneducated; it's like the modern Cretan, so different from his early ancestors, who saw life steadily and saw it whole – at least that's what one gathers from his remains.' (Daphne had, just before the war, been in Crete, excavating.)

Nicholas said, 'You over-rate the early Cretan. I've noticed it before. You over-rate him. He wasn't all you think; and anyhow, he had a smaller island to think out; anyone could have got a grasp of Cretan affairs. He was probably really as selfish as – as Alix, or me.'

'I can't imagine,' said Daphne, considering him with disapproval, 'why you don't join the SPPP, Nicky, or some other good educative society, and help me a little.'

'I? I never join anything. I never agree with anybody. I don't want to educate anyone. Why should I? I leave these things to enthusiasts, with faith, like you and West. I've no faith in my own ideas being any better than other people's, so I let them go their ways and I go mine. '

'You won't always do that,' Daphne told him, encouraging him, because she had faith in the spirit of his fathers, which looked despite himself out of his eyes. 'When you're my age …

'I shall then, ' said Nicholas, 'doubtless be suffering from what is, I believe, called by the best people "the more embittered temper and narrower faith of age". You need entertain no further hopes for me then.'

3

During the Hauxton meeting, which was in the schoolroom on the afternoon of new year's eve, Alix sat on the low churchyard wall in faint sunshine and looked over brown fields and heard the larks. Hauxton is quiet, and smells of straw, and has a little grey church with a Norman door. Its road runs east and west, and there are geese on the little green. On this last afternoon of the year it lay quietly asleep in the pale winter sunshine. Whenever the little east wind moved, wisps and handfuls of straw drifted lightly down the road. The larks carolled and twittered exuberantly over bare fields. From time to time a flock of chaffinches rose suddenly from the ricks and flew, a chattering flutter of wings, down the wind. Beyond the fields, cold, faintly-hued horizons brooded. Hauxton looked drowsily to the sunset and the dawn, to the past and future, to the old year and the new.

'The future is dubious,' Daphne had been saying in the schoolroom, before Alix came out. Well, of course futures always are, if you come to that. 'In this dim, dubious future, let us see that we build up one positive thing, which shall not fail us ...' And by that, of course, she meant Peace.

Peace: yes, peace must be, of course, a positive thing. Here, in Hauxton, was peace; a bare, austere, quiet peace, smelling of straw. No one had had to make that peace; it just was. But the world's peace must be made, built up, stone on stone. No, stones were a poor figure. Peace must be alive; a vital, intricate, intense, difficult thing. No negation: not the absence of war. Not the quiet, naturally attained peace of Samuel Miller and Elizabeth his wife, who slept beneath a grey headstone close to the churchyard wall, having drifted into peace after ninety and ninety-five years of living, and having for their engraven comment, 'They shall come to the grave in the fullness of years, like as a shock of corn cometh in in his season.' Not that natural peace of the old and weary at rest; but a young peace, passionate, ardent, intelligent, romantic, like poetry, like art, like religion. Like Christmas, with its peace on earth, goodwill towards men. Like all the passionate, restless idealism that the so quiet-seeming little Norman church stood for …

Alix believed that it stood for the same things that Daphne stood for. It too would say, build up a living peace. It too would say, let each man, woman, and child cast out first from their own souls the forces that make against peace – stupidity (that first), then commercialism, rivalries, hatreds, grabbing, pride, ill-bred vaunting. It too was international, supernational. It too was out for a dream, a wild dream, of unity. It too bade people go and fight to the death to realise the dream. Only it said, 'In my name they shall cast out devils and speak with new tongues', and the SPPP said, 'In the name of humanity'. There was, no doubt, a difference in method. But at the moment Alix had more concern with the likenesses, with the common aim of the fighters rather than with their different flags.

The pale sun dipped lower in the pale west, and was drowned in haze. It was cold. The little wind from the east whispered along the bare hedges. The year would soon be running down into silence, like an old clock.

4

Daphne and the meeting came out of the school. Alix went to meet her. Daphne looked satisfied, as if things had gone well. The few women and many children coming out of the meeting looked good-hearted, and still full of Christmas cheer.

'Such dears,' said Daphne, as they got into the car. (Lest a damaging impression of Daphne be given, it may be mentioned that she always drove her own car herself, and only, in war time, used it for meetings for the public good and for taking out wounded soldiers.) 'So attentive and nice. I left pamphlets; and I'm coming again after the Christmas holiday to speak to the children in school. I told them about German and Austrian babies … The mothers loved it … It's *fun* doing this. People are such dears, directly they stop misunderstanding what one is after. Understanding – clear thinking – it nearly all turns on that; everything does. Oh for more *brains* in this poor old muddle of a world! Educate the children's brains, give them right understanding, and then let evil do its worst against them, they'll have a sure base to fight it from.'

Alix thought of and mentioned the Intelligent Bad, who are surely numerous and prominent in history.

But Daphne said: 'Cleverness isn't right understanding. I mean something different from that. I mean the trained faculty of looking at life and everything in it the right way up. It's difficult, of course.'

Alix thought it was probably impossible, in an odd, upside-down world.

The sun set. The face of Cambridgeshire, the face of the new year, the face of the incoherent world, was dim and inscrutable, a dream lacking interpretation. So many people can provide, according to their several lights, both the dream and the interpretation thereof, but with how little accuracy!

5

The Sandomirs, in their house in Grange Road, saw the new year in. They drank its health, as they did every year. Daphne, though she suddenly could think of nothing but Paul, who would not see the new or any other year, nevertheless drank unflinching to the causes she believed in.

'Here's to the new world we shall make in spite of everything,' she said. 'Here's to construction, sanity, and clear thinking. Here's to goodwill and mutual understanding. Here's to the clearing away of the old messes and the making of the new ones. Here's to Freedom. Here's to Peace.'

'Heaven help you, mother,' Nicholas murmured drowsily into his glass. 'You don't know what you're saying. All your toasts are incompatible, and you don't see it. And what in the name of anything do you mean by Freedom? The old messes I know, and the new ones I can guess at – but what is Freedom? Something, anyhow, which we've never had yet.'

'Something we shall have,' said Daphne.

'You think so? But how improbable! After war, despotism and the strong hand. You don't suppose the firm hand is going to let go, having got us so nicely in its grasp. Rather not. War is the tyrant's opportunity. The Government's beginning to learn what it can do. After all this Defending of the Realm, and cancelling of scraps of paper such as Magna Carta and Habeas Corpus, and ordering the press, and controlling industries and finance and food and drink, and saying, "Let there be darkness" (and there was darkness) – you don't suppose it's going to slip back into *laissez faire*, or open the door to mob rule? The realm will go on being defended long after it's weathered this storm, depend on it. And quite right too. Lots of people will prefer it; they'll be too tired to want to take things into their own hands: they'll only want peace and safety and an ordered life. They'll be too damaged and sick and have lost too much to be anything but apathetic. Peace, possibly (though improbably): but Freedom, no. Anyhow, it's what neither we nor anyone else have ever had, so we shouldn't recognise it if we saw it … There are too many pips in this stuff,' he grumbled. 'Much too many.'

Daphne finished hers and stood up, as midnight struck, with varying voices and views as to the time, from various church clocks in Cambridge city. 'So,' she said, 'that's the end of *that* year. No doubt it is as well … And now I'm going to bed. I've a great deal to do tomorrow.'

She went to bed. She had a great deal to do on all the days of the coming year. But the first thing she did (in common with many others this year) was to cry on the stairs, because it was a year which Paul would never see, Paul having been tipped out by the last year in its crazy career and left behind by the wayside.

6

Nicholas and Alix lay languidly, in fraternal silence, in their chairs. They never went to bed or did anything else with Daphne's prompt decision. At a quarter past twelve Alix said, 'I'm thinking of joining this funny society of mother's.'

Nicholas opened his small blue eyes at her.

'You are? I didn't know you joined things.'

'Nor did I,' said Alix. 'But I'm beginning to believe I do … I think I shall very probably join the Church, too, before long.'

Nicholas opened his eyes much wider, and sat up straight. 'The *Church*? The Church of England, do you mean?'

'I suppose that would be my branch, as I live in England. Just the Christian Church, I mean … Do you think mother'll mind much?'

Nicholas cogitated over this. 'Probably,' he concluded. 'She doesn't like it, you know. She thinks it stands for darkness.'

'That's so funny,' said Alix, 'when really it seems to me to stand for all the things she stands for – and some more, of course.'

'Exactly,' Nicholas agreed. 'It's the "more" she takes exception to.'

'Oh, well,' Alix sighed a little. 'Mother's very largeminded, really. She'll get used to it.'

Nicholas was looking at her curiously, but not unsympathetically.

'Why these new and sudden energies?' he inquired presently. 'If you don't mind my asking?'

'It's what I told you once before,' Alix explained, and the memory of that anguished evening attenuated her clear, indifferent voice, making it smaller and fainter. 'As I can't be fighting in the war, I've got to be fighting against it. Otherwise it's like a ghastly nightmare, swallowing one up. This society of mother's mayn't be doing much, but it's *trying* to fight war; it's working against it in the best ways it can think of. So I shall join it … Christianity, so far as I can understand it, is working against war too; must be, obviously. So I shall join the Church …. That's all.'

'H'm.' Nicholas looked dubious. 'Not quite all, I fancy. There are things to believe, you know. You'll have to believe them – some of them, anyhow.'

'I suppose so. I dare say it's not so very difficult, is it?'

'Very, I believe. I've never tried personally, but so I am told by those who have.'

'Oh well, I don't care. Lots of quite stupid people seem to manage it, so I don't see why I shouldn't. I shall try, anyhow. I think it's worth it,' said Alix with determination.

'Well,' said Nicholas, after a pause, 'I dare say you're right. Right to try things, I mean. I suppose it's more intelligent.'

For a moment the paradox in the faces of both brother and sister was resolved, and idealism wholly dominated cynicism.

'Well,' said Nicholas again, 'here's luck!' He finished his punch. It had, as he had said, too many pips, so that he drank with care and rejections rather than hope.

CHAPTER 17

New Year's Eve

1

On this (surely) most unusual planet, nothing is more noticeable than the widely differing methods its inhabitants have of spending the same day. One person's new year's eve, for instance, will be quite different from another.

Even within the Orme family, they were different. Margot spent the evening at a canteen concert. She took a prominent part in the programme, having a charming, true and well-trained contralto voice. She sang charming songs with it, some of them a little above the taste of the majority of soldiers, but pleasing to the more musical, others not. It was a long and miscellaneous programme, varying from Schubert and Mendelssohn to 'Stammering Sam' and 'Turn the lining inside out till the boys come home,' so everyone was pleased.

2

Dorothy Orme was assisting at a dance at the hospital. (You must do something with soldiers on new year's eve; it is particularly urgent that they should be kept indoors, because of the Scotch.) It was a jolly dance, and both the soldiers and nurses enjoyed it extremely. When twelve struck they joined hands and sang 'Auld Lang Syne,' and everyone hopefully wished everyone else a happy new year. (Only two Jocks had got out and kept their Hogmanay elsewhere and quite elsehow – a creditably small proportion out of forty men.)

Dorothy got home by two, said it had been a topping evening and she was dead tired, and went to bed.

3

At Wood End, Mr and Mrs Orme entertained Belgians. Nine Belgian children, and parents and guardians to correspond. They played games, and danced a little, and fished for presents with a rod and line in a fish-pond in a corner of the dining-room, where Mr Orme lay curled up, secretive and helpful, so that the right things got on to the right hooks.

It was a great success, and ended at ten. Mrs Orme's head ached, and Mr Orme's back.

They had had a great deal to do; they had had Mademoiselle Verstigel to help them, but none of their children, who were all busy elsewhere, and whom, therefore, they did not grudge. They were generous with their children, as well as with their time, energy and money.

4

Betty Orme, who has hitherto been only remotely referred to in these pages, spent the evening driving three nurses and a doctor from Fruges to Lillers. She was a steady, levelheaded child, with a fair placid face looking out from a woollen helmet, and wide blue eyes like Terry's. She acted chauffeur to a field hospital, drove perfectly, repaired her car with speed and efficiency, and was extremely useful. Her nerves, health, and temper were of the best brand; horrors left her unjarred and merely helpful.

The nurse at her side, a garrulous person, said, 'Why, it's new year's eve, isn't it? How funny. I've only just remembered that! … I wonder what they're all doing at home, don't you?'

But Betty was only wondering whether her petrol was going to last out till Lillers.

'I know I'd a lot rather to be out here, wouldn't you?' said the talkative nurse.

'Rather,' said Betty abstractedly.

Even through their helmets and motorcoats and thick gloves they felt the wind very cold, and a few flakes of snow began to drift down from a black sky. 'More snow,' said Betty. 'It really *is* the limit … I wonder if it'll be finer next year.'

5

John Orme was in a trench, not far from Ypres. It was bitterly cold there; snow drifted and lay on his platoon standing to, their feet in freezing mud. They were standing to at that hour of the night (11.30pm) because they had been warned of a possible enemy attack. They had been badly bombarded earlier in the evening, but that was over. There had been four men hit. The stretcher-bearers hadn't come for them yet; they lay, roughly first-aided, in the mud. John, vigilantly strolling up and down, seeing that no one slept (John was a very careful and efficient young officer), passed a moaning boy with his arm blown off and his tunic a red mess, and said gently, 'Hang on a bit longer, Everitt. They won't be long now.' Everitt merely returned, beneath his breath, 'My God, sir! Oh, my God!' He could not hang on at all, by any means whatever. And there were no morphia tablets left in the platoon … John turned away.

Someone said, 'New year'll be in directly, Ginger. How's this for a bright and glad new year?'

John remembered, for the first time, that it was December the 31st. It didn't mean anything more to him than the 30th. After all, it must be some day, even in this timeless and condemned trench.

He didn't believe in this attack, anyhow. It had been a ration party rumour, and ration parties are full of unfulfilled forecastings. But he wished he had a morphia tablet for that poor chap ...

6

Terry Orme was in his dug-out, which was called Funk Snuggery. It was a very noisy night. The enemy seemed to be having a special new year's eve hate. Whizz-bangs, sugar-loaves, beans, all sorts and conditions and shapes of explosive missiles filled the earth and heavens with unlovely clamour. It was disturbing to Terry, who was reading Moussorgsky. (Terry belonged to that small but characteristic class of persons who read themselves to sleep with music. John preferred Mr Jorrocks.) Terry dug his fingers into his ears, and perused his score.

There was another man in Funk Snuggery. The other man looked at his watch, waited three minutes, and said 'Happy new year.' Terry, stopping his ears, did not respond, till he shouted it louder.

Terry looked up, 'What's that?' he inquired. 'Oh, is it? Fancy! Thanks; the same to you ... But I *shan't* be happy this year unless they let me hear myself think. Beastly, isn't it? ... They say after a time it spoils one's ear. Wouldn't that be rotten. Have a stick?'

The stick was of chocolate, and they each sucked one in drowsy silence. It was next year, and still they would not let Terry hear himself think. He put away Moussorgsky with a sigh, and curled up to go to sleep.

7

Hugh Montgomery Gordon was in billets, in a village in Artois. He and a friend went out for a stroll in the evening; they visited an *estaminet*, where they found poor wine but a charming girl. They told her it was new year's eve; she told them it was *la veille du jour de l'an*. They taught her to say 'Happy new year' and other things. She and they all spent a very enjoyable evening.

'Absolutely it, isn't she?' said Hugh Montgomery Gordon languidly to his friend as they walked back to their billets. 'Don't know when I've seen anything jollier. He yawned and went indoors, and spent the rest of the year playing auction.

8

Basil Doye, in camp on the Greek mountains, sat and smoked in a tent assaulted and battered by a searching north-east wind from Bulgaria. He and his platoon had been occupied all day in digging trenches, and spreading wire entanglements which caught and trapped unwary Greek travellers on their own hills. Basil Doye was tired and bored and cold, in body and mind. A second lieutenant who shared the tent was telling him a funny story of a bomb the enemy had dropped on Divisional HQ last night, and of the General and staff, pyjama-clad, rushing about seeking shelter and finding none. … But Basil was still bored and cold.

'O Lord!' said the other subaltern presently, 'the year'll soon be done in. It's going out without having given us a scrap with the Bulgars; how sickening! … Why in anything's name couldn't they have sent us out here *earlier*, if at all?'

'Our government, ' said Basil, abstracted and unoriginal, 'is slow and sure. Slow to move and sure to be too late. That's why. So here we are, sitting on a cold hill in a draught, with nothing doing, nor likely to be.'

To himself he was saying, 'She'd fit on these hills; she'd belong here, more than to Spring Hill. She's a Greek really … that space between the eyes, and the way she steps … like Diana … Oh, strafe it all, what's the good of thinking?' Savagely he flung away his cigarette.

A great gust of wind from Bulgaria flung itself upon the tent and blew it down. Then the sleet came, and the new year.

9

West was in church. The lights were dim, because of Zeppelins. The vicar was preaching, on the past and the future, from the texts, 'They shall wax old, as doth a garment; as a vesture shalt thou lay them aside, and they shall be changed', and 'Behold, I make all things new'.

The year was going to be changed and made new in nineteen minutes and a half. West (and the vicar too, perhaps), though tired and despondent (the week after Christmas is a desperate time for clergymen, because of treats), were holding on to hope with both hands. A desperate time: a desperate end to a desperate year. But clergymen may not, by their rules, become desperate men. They have to hope: they have to believe that as a vesture they shall be changed, and that the new will be better than the old. If they did not succeed in believing this, they would be of all men the most miserable.

West sat in his stall, looking, so the choirboys opposite thought, at them, to see if any among them whispered, or any slept. But he did not see them. He was looking through and beyond them, at the vesture, ragged and soaked with blood, which so indubitably wanted changing. Once his lips moved, and the words they formed were: 'How long, O Lord, how long?' Which might, of course, refer to a number of things:

the war, or the vicar's sermon, or the present year, or, indeed, almost anything.

The sermon ended, and there was silent prayer till twelve o'clock struck. Then, as is the habit on these occasions, they sang hymn 265 (A and M).

10

Violette had a new year's eve party. A quiet party; only the Vinneys to chat and play quiet card games and see the new year in.

At half-past eleven they had done with cards, and were conversing. Kate had gone to church at eleven. Vincent and Sidney Vinney were now in khaki; they had, in view of the coming compulsion scheme, joined the army (territorials) and got commissions. Vincent, being married, had applied for home service only. Sidney, as he had just pointed out to Evie, might get sent anywhere at any moment. But Evie, receiving letters from Hugh Montgomery Gordon at the battle front, and, indeed, from many others, was not to be touched by Sid Vinney.

Evie was talking to young Mrs Vinney about the fashions.

'Those new taffeta skirts at Robinson's are ten yards wide, I should think. You wouldn't believe it, the amount there is to them. And quite a yard off the ground. We shall have to think so much about our feet this next year. Feet – well, more than that, too!'

Mrs Vinney said, 'Well, do you know, I don't think it's right, at a time like this. Not ten yards. I say nothing against six; because we women must try and carry on, and look smart and so on. It would never do for the men to come home and find us skimpy and dowdy and peculiar, like some of those suffragettes … What I say is, it'll be lucky for the girls with neat ankles this year …'

They said a little more like this, till it was time to mix the punch. Then they drank it, and said 'Here's how', and 'A very happy new year to all and many of them', and 'Here's to our next festive gathering', and 'Here's to the ladies', and 'Luck to our soldiers', and other things respectively suitable. Then the Vinneys went home to bed, because Mrs Vinney did not approve of making nights of it at times like these.

Soon after twelve Kate came back from church.

Kate said, 'It's turned so cold outside, I shouldn't wonder if we get snow … Those Primmerose people are spending a terribly loud evening; I heard it all across the common. You'd think people would want to be somewhat quieter on new year's eve, and this year in particular' (with all these sorrows and Zeppelins about, she meant). 'A quiet evening with a few friends is one thing; but it doesn't seem quite fitting to have all that shouting and banjos. And I could smell the drink as I passed, for they had a window open, and it was wafted right out at me. '

'Well now,' said Mrs Frampton, 'just fancy that!'

11

The year of grace 1915 slipped away into darkness, like a broken ship drifting on bitter tides on to a waste shore. The next year began.

Essays and journalism, 1936–1945

1 Marginal Comments

The Spectator, 3 January 1936

1936 is opening, even more noticeably than most years, in an atmosphere of mutual international distastes. One is not surprised to be told that this has been a remarkably home-keeping Christmas; for abroad is just now, for most nations, a somewhat perilous pleasure-ground, and the winter resorts of other days have assumed, for one reason or another, an intimidating, even a menacing, air. Yes; even our adored Balearics … while as for the Italian Riviera … One can still cruise, you say, about the high seas? But doubtfully, warily, looking up at the heavens, looking for all the fire-folk seated in the sky.

To set against these imperfect sympathies, each nation would appear to be taking increasing pleasure in its own qualities and exploits. One boasts itself a democracy, which can write letters to its representatives telling them where they get off, thus changing history; another delights to be a corporate State, obeying orders in unison; another to be a great republic, thinking with resolution and continuity of its own security; one is proud to be marching, Roman civilisation in hand, into uncultured lands; one to be outside European imbroglios; soothing the troubled waters and the raging flames with oil. There is always some cause for national self-love; and for my part I find it a pretty and engaging spectacle, in a world of nations whom there are all too few to love. For this reason I enjoy the broadcast European interchanges, and regret the cancelling last week of that between an Englishman and a Russian. I always like to hear the Briton posing the alien with the time-honoured British question, asked by English tourists abroad for many centuries, 'How do you like having no freedom?' and to hear the foreigner vehemently explaining that he has as much as, or more than, his questioner. I should like to have heard, and hope still to hear, the repartee of the representative of the USSR. 'In Russia we say that it is you capitalist States who have no freedom.' Or, 'Freedom is of no importance. What matters is social welfare.' Or, 'Well, you see, Russians have never had any freedom, so don't miss it.' I should enjoy him on capitalist vice and soviet virtue, and the Englishman on the reverse. It would be, surely, an agreeable entertainment, and to cancel it because inaccuracies, or asperities, or both (in fact, human nature) would keep breaking in was a timid and a tedious act. 'The free range and fair balance of give-and-take argument could not be secured,' the BBC is reported to have said. But who wants it, when we might have instead the free range and unfair lack of balance of human and national vanity, beside which fair argument is but a dull and prosy affair? Give us free human nature to divert us, and we will not ask for fairness. Alice, a dull little prig, was shocked by the unfairness of the 'nice knock-down arguments' used by Humpty-Dumpty and the other beings she encountered; had she been wiser, she would have listened to them with delight. 'How unfair they are both being!' That is what we say when we hear these international back-chats: doubtless we should have said it again had we been permitted to hear the Anglo-Russian dialogue; but should we have turned it off for that? A thousand times no. No one wants people to be fair or balanced about the places they live in; a fine and maniac frenzy should possess them (and does) when they describe their no doubt deplorable homes. For one must remember this: if we do not laud our own places of residence and national habits, these may lack altogether a trumpeter, and become melancholy affairs indeed.

Give us, then, our Anglo-Russian air-chat, for we shall enjoy it greatly.

2 Marginal Comments

The Spectator, 24 January 1936

Perusing the articles in my daily and weekly journals, I read very frequently of shrieks and cries. The other day, having learnt from various newspapers that the air was thus being rent, I paused to consider this phenomenon, so audible to leader-writers, of continual clamour. I had been reading of 'shrieks', 'howls', 'yells', 'shouts', 'yawps', that were, it seemed to the writers, being emitted by 'sanctionists', who desired the application of the League Covenant to aggressing nations. While in journals of another colour, I read that similar loud cries were being uttered by those who disapproved of such hampering of aggressor States. And I perceived that the tones in which these opposed schools of thought uttered their comments sounded peculiarly loud and shrill to those of the other party.

Here, thought I, was a psychological discovery. Do the voices of those with whom we disagree always sound louder than those which utter our own views? Often have I read letters to the Press from those who hold that cyclists should, like other vehicles, carry rear-lights, describing the 'loud shrieks' with which they hear cyclists protest that they will do no such thing; and cyclists riposte with their tale of the 'bellowings' of those who would so inconvenience them. And, through those four noisy years long since, did not we in England read of Germans shrieking their hate, while they in Germany heard of similar loud cries of distaste 'emitted in England and in France'? Little Archbishop Laud, disapproving of the House of Commons, called it 'this noise'; while members of this body professed to hear 'Canterburian howlings'. And so always. As Bishop Berkeley remarked, 'the worst cause produceth the greatest clamour'. The wrong party is also the noisy party. How rarely do we ourselves shriek or howl our views! How frequently do our assailants so! You may overhear fragments of dialogue anywhere which indicate this truth. 'He [she] shouted at me like Mad. But I said to him [her] quite quietly …' 'I didn't say a word. But this I did say, and I said it very quietly … It is rarely; 'I bellowed at him; I howled him down; he answered me quietly'. An onlooker, reporting the dispute, would, I think, represent as the louder speaker him with whom he least agreed. Reading in a novel, 'said Smith, quietly', you may almost safely infer Smith to be in the right; your heart goes out to Smith. There are exceptions; there are occasions in fiction when the bad speak quietly, and very sinister this is; their quietness becomes then abnormal, unnatural, rather terrifying. Quietness should be left to the good; usurped by villains, it curdles the blood.

I leave it to psychologists to explain this peculiar alliance of wrong-headedness and noise; such surface observers as myself can but note it. I have wondered if it extends to those aerial voices which address us on such varied themes. Do those which utter sentiments and opinions which we can approve come to us as still small voices; gently stroking the light air? Do those which deliver themselves of false doctrine thunder raucous in our ears? But this, you will say, can be rectified by the turning of a knob. I suppose that we must tune wrongheaded wireless speakers very low that they may not sound to us like shrieks, whereas those who speak truth will, even if communicated with the utmost capacity in our machines, still sound soft and quiet. 'He said to us very quietly.'

So Truth comes treading soft-foot, murmuring like a dove or a noontide bee, scarce audible but to the instructed ear, while Error, harpy-like, rends the air with her shrieks.

3 Marginal Comments

The Spectator, 6 March 1936

Having watched the other night the pacifying with peace-gas bombs of a truculent humanity in Leicester Square, I was moved to speculate on the possibilities of this gas, should it ever become more widely used. There is no question but that it would be gratifying to possess a private set of peace-bombs for one's own use, to hurl at our unreasonably irritated acquaintances. How agreeable to watch these infuriate beings dropping drowsily to sleep in the midst of their invective against us, waking presently to ingeminate, with Lord Falkland and the Rajah of Bhong, 'Peace! Peace beautiful peace! I think all this bustle is wrong.' Should they dimly call to mind the cause of their former irritation against us, it would be as one remembers some irrational dream. Can they (they would ask themselves) really have been angry over such a trifle? They would beam with obliging and lethargic amity, and one could proceed with one's own invective, only interrupted by an occasional 'Quite, quite! How right you are!'

Such a use of peace-bombs would seem a wholly satisfactory adjunct to human amenities. But, should others attempt thus to pacify ourselves, or should the gentle gas enwrap humankind in general, its benefits might be less uncritically accepted. I was conversing the other evening with a gentleman who remarked on the pleasure to 'be derived from the growing (we agreed that it was growing) ferocity of those literary persons who differ from one another from time to time in the public Press. How greatly (we agreed) we miss it when one or other of these duels, staged so agreeably for our pleasure, ceases (is it the editor who tires, or the combatants?). How delighted we feel when the antagonists reel into yet another ring, there to continue their ardent backchat. We are (this gentleman opined) finding our way back to the good old days of literary rough-house, when writers derided one another in public not merely for their bad writing, but for their humped backs, their blindness, their age, their poverty, their ungenteel pedigrees or professions (such as that of usher or attorney), the irregularity of their domestic lives, the excessive number of the children born to them out of wedlock, and so forth. Poetomachia, the strife of poets, always keen, shows signs of becoming again a hooligan and all-in warfare, in which below the belt is counted a good place for a hit; and this (said the gentleman) is as it should be, and all to the good. Could we pacify these pugnacious beings with a whiff of gas, should we indeed do so? Peace in others is but a dull spectacle. At an ice-hockey match, the spectators deem themselves defrauded if the sticks be not used for at least one good battle, followed by the cooling off of a selection of the combatants in the penalty-box.

And how far less inspiring would have been the open-air Mass celebrated last Sunday in Rome, had pacificatory gas hovered over and bemused the celebration. The soldiery, instead of presenting arms at the Elevation of the Host, might have cast them down instead; the guns fired from the Janiculum and the air squadron droning overhead might have sounded 'incongruously bellicose'; while Signor Mussolini, addressing the populace after the service on 'this great day of vengeance and victory', could scarcely have done so with such triumphant exuberance, with the treacherous fumes. creeping into his lungs.

It is probable that all governments might quite safely be entrusted with any number of peace-bombs; they would gladly fling them. among other nations; but would be very thrifty of their use at home. Still, if we all had some to drop on other people, I suppose everyone would in time be tranquillised and bepeaced.

4 Marginal Comments

The Spectator, 27 March 1936

Continuing my investigations into entertaining human activities, I attended last Sunday evening a 'rally' of British Fascists at the Albert Hall, only to reflect again and as usual, what a piece of work is man, and what an odder piece stills a crowd. The floor of the hall had apparently been reserved for impassioned Fascists, and very obediently these did their stuff. We began with some songs (or hymns, perhaps, is the word) about vested powers, Marxian lies, Moscow-rented agitators, Red Front and the massed ranks of reaction. One line stated that 'the streets are still', which was, at the moment, not noticeably the case. After the songs, THE LEADER ENTERS, said the programme. And enter he did, heralded by a procession of banners, rolling drums and blasting trumpets, and lackeyed by an attendant beam of spotlight (mauve). Between massed ranks of his frenzied approvers, the Leader proceeded up the hall to the platform, wearing an air of exalted uplift which he maintained despite a sudden derisive laugh which broke out from somewhere in the hall. The whole business had a comically histrionic air.

Then (said the programme) THE LEADER SPEAKS. And Speak the Leader did, for two solid hours. It was the old familiar fascery and tushery, such stuff as Blackshirt dreams are made on: how, when We come into power, we shall stop all this talking at Westminster, ally, on highly advantageous terms, with the other Fascist States and with Japan, and break and exile British communists and Jews. At every reference to British Jews, Sir Oswald appeared to experience a considerable and painful excitement; he cried out, he gestured, he pointed. The affair became more and more like a violent revivalist meeting of Holy Rollers, Shakers, or what not. The Fascist part of the audience, answering hysteria with hysteria, responded with frenzied applause. Crowds are like that. If anyone shouts to them with enough repetition, vehemence, and spotlight that any section of persons, such as Jews, Christians, landlords, lawyers, soldiers, pacifists, witches, Germans, French, or Portuguese, are the cause of all their troubles and must be punished, it seems that they will believe and applaud. Thus are set afoot hunts after old women, spies, aliens, Protestants, Roman Catholics, and those who differ from the huntsmen in politics or race. Crowds have the half-ludicrous, half-sinister suggestibility of the pack, who may be sent by the huntsman's word after any quarry. One felt, woe to any Jew who should that night cross the path of that applauding mob. Yet, taken singly, most of them were probably the ordinary, stupid, kindly Briton, who can be persuaded of anything.

Those who had come to see disturbances were rewarded by several somewhat violent ejections. Heckling by political opponents is obviously not part of what We mean to allow. Definitely, We do not believe in free speech. This is one of the great differences between Us and the old effete constitutional parties. At the end of the meeting, the audience were invited to send up questions to be answered. Many did so; but only a few were answered. Like other examination candidates, Sir Oswald apparently selected the easy ones. People near me sent up questions about freedom, British tolerance, and so on: these were overlooked. The reply I liked best, following as it did the diatribe against Jews, was, We believe in complete tolerance of all religious sects.

Certainly an odd meeting. I suggested lately that we might go to it for entertainment. But I was wrong. It was too like a meeting in a mental home for that.

5 Marginal Comments

The Spectator, 1 May 1936

A bishop has come opportunely to the aid of the War Office against pacifist clergy, referring the Minister for War to a passage in one of those Articles of Religion which have, since Edward VI's Privy Council bound them round the neck of the Church of England, hung there with such firm inconvenience. One may imagine the eagerness with which the War Office sent out a messenger to purchase a Prayer Book, with what curiosity the department turned the pages of this unexpected ally until, at its end, they came on these thirty-nine bland affirmations, with their so intriguing headings. Passing by Original Sin, Works done before Justification, Works of Supererogation, Excommunicate Persons, how they are to be avoided, Homilies, Predestination and Election, and many other excellent and wholesome matters, they have arrived, doubtless, by now, at Article 37, Of the Civil Magistrates, and been gratified to read, after an affirmation of the lawfulness of capital punishment, that 'It is lawful for Christian men, at the commandment of the Magistrate, to wear weapons and serve in the wars'. (There seems to be a certain resigned acceptance in the phrase, as of a chronic feature in life; as, in this country, one speaks of 'the rain'.) 'Which seems,' says Bishop Southwell, 'to settle the matter,' and to dispose of the Bishops' Lambeth Resolution on the unchristianity of war. Let us hope that this will help the Minister for War with his recruiting.

It is an interesting miscellany of assorted matters which the Articles 'seem to settle' for the clergy Article 37 itself is boldly monarchical, and asserts, in longer words, the divine rule of kings. Article 33 is firm about excommunicate Persons, who must be taken of the whole multitude of the faithful as

Heathens and Publicans (our forefathers were very sound on tax-collectors) until they be openly reconciled to the Church by penance. Then, the clergy must diligently and distinctly (but we are not told how often) read aloud in Churches the second Book of Homilies. It is to be hoped that these wholesome and forthright Edwardian exhortations are never neglected or curtailed. As to what the clergy must believe, this was laid down by the Reformers of 1552 with some elaboration, and not all Queen Elizabeth's Arminianism could do more than slightly modify their Zwinglian firmness on Predestination, Election and Works before Justification, which 'we doubt not but they have the nature of sin'. Predestination has been held by some interpreters of the Articles to be slightly under a cloud, since, though its consideration 'is full of sweet, pleasant and unspeakable comfort to godly persons', yet 'for curious and carnal persons to have continually before their eyes the sentence of God's Predestination is a most dangerous downfall, whereby the Devil doth thrust them either into desperation, or into wretchlessness of most unclean living'. Still, on the whole Predestination seems to come well out of the Articles, wherein the vain and erring Pelagius faintly raises his voice but once, to be firmly put in his place by those triumphing continental Calvinists who so infected the mild and rational Cranmer with their wild, unearthly fantasies. Bound to these, as also (Article 8) to the Athanasian promise of everlasting fire for those who do not keep whole the Catholic faith, the humanitarian subscriber to the Articles should feel little difficulty about 'the wars'.

Finally (says the royal preface) should any member of either University (dons have always been rightly suspect) affix any new sense to any Article, 'We will see there shall be due Execution upon them'.

In how great quandaries have the world's clergy always found themselves!

6 Marginal Comments

The Spectator, 14 May 1936

The fait accompli: magic phrase! One knew already that faits, once they are accomplis, are apt to be accepted by the world pretty quickly, but surely the speed with which the London Sunday Press accepted the announcement made late on Saturday night in Rome of the annexation of someone else's empire, the deposition of its Emperor, and the assumption for all time of his title by the King of Italy, beat all records of obliging complaisance. There was, of course, no time for editors to deal with the subject; but all London was placarded with recognitions of the new order. 'The new Emperor', 'The Man who was Emperor', 'Rome an Empire again', 'The Duce makes his King Emperor of Abyssinia', 'Italy annexes Abyssinia'— so the headings ran, without one use of the word 'claims', or that other useful word 'alleged', which, it seems, is applied to Italian poison-gas but not to an Italian Empire. One had not realised that the thing was as easy as all that. (By the way, if Signor Mussolini has been wanting an Emperor for fourteen years, why did he not make his King one fourteen years ago? There seems no reason why the King should not have assumed the title of Emperor of Eritrea, or of Italian Somaliland, or, for that matter, of Italy itself. Any sovereign may call himself an Emperor if he likes.)

Signor Mussolini's announcement of the happy event was differently translated in every Sunday paper, in the odd way English correspondents abroad have of always differing about what even the loudest-speaking foreigner has said. Some versions were funnier than others, and some rather inaccurate in parts; but all got the main point, that Abyssinia was annexed, and all seemed to regard the annexation, based though it is on a still only partial *occupatio bellico*, as the real thing, an *occupatio justa*. I have not heard any international annexation expert on the matter, but probably they would decide it to be (quite apart from League considerations) one of the many 'premature annexations' of history, like the Italian proclamation of 1911 announcing the end of Ottoman rule in North Africa when the Turkish Army was still in strong resistance; or Lord Roberts's proclamations of British sovereignty over the Orange Free State and the South African Republic in 1900, with the war still in full cry; proclamations denounced by Lord Bryce at the time as 'monstrous, and opposed to the first principles of international law'.

However, whether premature, fictitious, monstrous, or in order, the annexation of Addis Ababa scents, according to Italian accounts, a flourishing concern. Infant Ethiopians already give the Fascist salute in the streets, the clergy have hastened to make their submission (who knows but they may before long mend their Coptic schism with Rome and recant their Monophysite heresy?), the banks, shops and post office arc functioning 'in a manner truly Roman', and I dare say by now the Addis newspaper is appearing again. In fact, a good time is being had by all, in this prosperous Fascist resort, for which tourists will now require Italian visas, and which is, some Italians suggest, to be renamed Roma Africana. The various foreigners accredited to represent their countries in Addis, such as Ministers, Consuls, spies, and so forth, may for the moment be feeling a little uprooted and uncertain in their position; but one supposes that all these details presently arrange themselves.

Lunching in a small Italian café on Sunday, I heard an exultantly patriotic conversation among a party of Italians, triumphantly concluded with the words, 'C'e un vecchio proverbio inglese, might ees right'. How ultimately, if not immediately, true is this ancient English proverb!

7 Marginal Comments

The Spectator, 16 October 1936

Someone has written to a weekly paper saying that he has a dossier, carefully indexed, of some 700 happenings in the Spanish civil war, and often reads in it, though doing so makes him feel sick. Despite this nausea, he sups full with horrors, drinks deep of atrocious tales, ejaculating, one infers, Horrible, horrible, most horrible! To judge by the rich horror-menu provided by some of our newspapers just now, his must be a common taste. On horror's head horrors accumulate; the Spanish are spoken of in a way which would have delighted their Elizabethan sailor rivals, who called them thrice cursed men and cruel fiends of hell. These English sailors had some justification; their own experience, and that of the poor Indians, of the fierce Spaniard was certainly unfortunate. It was a cruel age, and the English were none too gentle themselves. There are, no doubt, plenty of cruel Spaniards today; no one has ever called them humane; the Iberian stock, infused with centuries of Moorish blood, is not likely to be that. Nor is war. Combine, as now, Spaniards and war, and you get, naturally, a very barbarous barbarity. But the sadistic tortures alleged with such gusto by a certain section of the Press, on the evidence, apparently, of 'refugees' and others; and believed so trustfully by many of their readers, seem to belong to a category of their own; that odd, dark, deformed world where sadistic imagination runs riot.

I say seem to belong; no one can swear that all these stories are not true. Many English on the spot have declared their disbelief in them; they sound intrinsically improbable; and the alleged eye-witnesses whose addresses are published are not given to answering letters. Sometimes these are returned by the Post Office, marked, 'Cannot be traced'. Beyond any inferences that may be drawn from these facts, one cannot go. The case is, for the unbiassed, simply not proved either way. But one may at least plead for a little decent scepticism, a little moderation in abuse. We might well emulate Purchas, who, when compiling his Pilgrimages, apologised for some of the ill tales he had set down about the Dutch, 'as if I sought, like an unseasonable and uncharitable, tale-bearer, to raise discord between neighbours'. There are, of course, he goes on, some ill-behaved Dutch, as some ill-behaved English, but their crimes are personal, not national, and he dislikes national abuse. 'And for this cause I have omitted some odious relations', and altered some 'offensive speeches disgorged by the passionate losers'. 'So with my Prayers for Peace on both sides I commend both to the God of Peace'. Wise and tolerant man, he knew that men are human, many of all races inhumane, but that, for his part, he was not going to inflame national hatreds. The Dutch, the Spaniards, the English, the crafty Portugals, the beastly Cannibals, the boasting Abassins, these all trailed their coats and sought their fortunes round the world, involved too often in fierce and greedy activities; but he admired their ardours and endurances more than he blamed their barbarousness, and he never, we may be sure, compiled lists, with index, of their worst hearsay deeds, or tried to make out that one race was far more atrocious than another. Those who delight to spread these tales of Spain presumably believe or wish them true, and think that we ought to be told what the Spanish are like, so that we may hate them. The same was done, on both sides, during the last European War: the Germans said that we gouged out the eyes of prisoners of war; we said that they made a habit of cutting off the arms of Belgian children and of crucifying Canadians. And so, one supposes, these odious relations will go on, so long as war itself goes on.

8 Marginal Comments

The Spectator, 30 October 1936

I have just been listening to Mr Howard Marshall's broadcast account of his spirited interrogations of the Archbishop of York as to 'What the Church is For'. The Archbishop having told him this, Mr Marshall proceeded to fire at him a number of pointed questions, which were answered with archiepiscopal caution. Should, Mr Marshall wanted to know, the leaders of the Church of England pronounce an opinion on such questions (I quote from memory) as the present social and economic system, obedience to the Sermon on the Mount, Jarrow, rearmament, pacifism, war. I gathered that, on the whole, the Archbishop's replies meant that, from a mixed lot such as the leaders of the Church, where each leader might and did think differently from the next on most matters, no joint pronouncements were possible on specific controversial questions; the Church's job was to endeavour to impart the mind of Christ, leaving to the private judgement of individuals decisions as to what this implied on particular heads.

Concerning war, the Archbishop thought, as Churches have usually thought and said, that Christians might fight in a just war. It was easy (I think he said) to conceive of a just war waged by this country, in which it would be right for Christians to take part. It certainly should be easy, considering all the just wars we have spent the centuries in waging. I hoped that Mr Marshall would ask if the Archbishop could as easily conceive of this country waging an unjust war, in which the established national Church would so far oppose the State as to declare it wrong to join. But he did not ask this. Nor did he ask who was to decide on the justice or injustice of the war in question. The Archbishops' Convocation? The

223

Church Assembly? Individual clergy? Did he think that there would be a chance of any of these uniting in deciding such a question against the State and in discouraging the subjects of the Crown from enlisting to fight in the unjust war? What is an unjust war? Was the war against the Boers unjust? Did the Church discourage it? I forget.

If by any chance Great Britain were to break several covenants, pledges and treaties, and invade, bomb and gas some weaker country in order to annex it, would that be unjust? It was unjust, we said, when Italy did it; but the Church to which the Italian State adheres said otherwise. It would be instructive to watch our own national Church in similar circumstances. But we have done ourselves so well in the past that repletion, principle and common sense join, for the moment, hands in a virtuous ring of mutual support.

I am a little tired of all these 'just' wars that we hear so much about. I would almost rather a war were frankly unjust, so that its aims and its methods might the better accord. All these just quarrels, just defences, just armings, just conquests and annexations and punitive measures — the white and dazzling flame of so much justice seems almost to extinguish the question whether it can be just at all for a government to make its citizens and subjects turn savage weapons of assault on the citizens and subjects of another State because it has fallen out, however justly, with that other. Can the corporateness of the State justly comprise the inciting of millions of individuals to violent physical outrage on millions of other individuals? Do the words 'a just war', so easily uttered by each nation when they prepare to wage one, really, in the eyes of the leaders of Churches, answer adequately these questions? It will be interesting to hear what the representatives of other Churches have to say on this and other matters when Mr Marshall interviews them.

9 Marginal Comments

The Spectator, 29 July 1937

God knows it would be magnificent to be a dictator. To look round a picture gallery and say 'I don't like those ones. Remove them' — this we can all say, but with a peevishness how frail and ineffectual! It is only given to dictators to banish their artistic bugbears with a gesture of the hand, as we others, contemptuously turning a knob, purge the air about us of unpleasing sounds. Even so, we cannot purge the air in which others listen; nor can we order to be sterilised or shut up those who produced the sounds. To have a whole jazz band, crooners and all, not merely silenced but sterilised, or gaoled as criminal imbeciles (better both) — how delightful this would be! To reflect on the baulked longings of the lowbrow, the philistine, all the great vulgar, for their jazz — what a solace for the spiteful highbrow as he listened to his Beethoven and Bach! As to pictures and books, none was ever such a yes-man that he did not consider all libraries and picture-galleries to need his purging; but fortunate is he who can gratify his desires outside his own dwelling. Of such have been emperors, popes and kings, presidents of South American republics, Mexican generals, and modern dictators. A good time, it is clear, has been had by all these arbiters.

It is a fruitful day-dream. If one were arbiter in Great Britain, of what would one not get rid? The industrial towns, the greater part of London, most of the houses along the new arterial roads, all nineteenth-century Gothic churches, practically all Nonconformist chapels, most police stations, and considerable selections from our street statuary — but, if one is to begin on buildings, there is no end; no doubt the forthcoming bombing raids of which we hear so much will settle all that, though with the somewhat dull and heavy-handed indiscrimination characteristic of militarism in action. As to pictures, to imagine oneself wielding the winnowing-fan in the National Gallery, the Tate, the Royal Academy, and other exhibitions, is to feel, for the first time, sympathy with Herr Hitler in his pleasures. One would expel different pictures; but to expel any pictures must be infinitely charming. Turned loose among music and books (or, as some prefer to call them, among numbers and titles) what pleasure to sort and sift, reject and retain! (Are there, by the way, any musical compositions which should not be called numbers? A book, I understand, is always a title. I like these names, and have begun to use them myself.) Anyhow, all jazz and Elgar would go, and most modern British music.

One trouble about arbiters is that few people, even among dictators, are versatile enough. Training and taste being extremely departmental, you will rarely find in the same person good judgement in numbers, titles, and pictures, let alone buildings. There are those with a very pretty literary taste who like vulgar music; and musical highbrows who like vulgar literature; in fact, I have heard the view that really good ears for music and poetry are practically incompatible, though adequate training in either may produce something that serves. It is said that Herr Hitler has good musical taste, though no other.

Since writing this I have walked in Hyde Park and heard a speaker praising General Franco for a good Christian, abusing his Spanish enemies as a red rabble of diabolical scoundrels and thugs (rather oddly, as he also said that he admired the Spanish people) and calling Mr Eden 'a contemptible little cur', for aiming at neutrality in a struggle between Right and Red, God and the Devil. An interesting reversal of the usual abuse of the Foreign Secretary for his supposed Francophilism. But are Hyde Park speakers privileged, or are politicians fair game, or is 'contemptible cur' less slanderous than, say, 'man of straw', which is said to be good for a large sum? However, I suppose soap-box orators know how far they can go.

10 Apeing the Barbarians

First published in *Let us Honour Peace* (London: Cobden-Sanderson, 1937), 9-18.

The human race being, however you look at it, in a pretty ghastly mess, and likely to remain in it for some time to come (perhaps for ever, since it has done so for several million years already), there is little enough room for complacency on the part of the believers in any of the panaceas for its relief. It is improbable that anything will help us much. Still, everyone has his own ideas about this or that pest and the best way of getting rid of it. And, to do us justice, we have, during the years of our existence as recognisable humanity, got rid, not without dust and heat, of a considerable number of pests, and rendered less noxious than they were a considerable number more. That is to say, some of us have; that part of the human race that is considered more civilised than some other parts. I suppose that even the less civilised have also rid themselves of certain pests but probably different pests. There is one stage in the advance towards that insubstantial, undefined condition that we call civilisation when society sets about to rid itself of heretics and witches, another when half of it perceives that it must rid itself of the custom of destroying heretics and witches; yet another when so much opinion is united on this point that the persecution of heretics and witches actually ceases. Civilisation is perpetually in transition between one stage and another; and different parts of the human race are at different stages at the same moment, which makes for awkward time-lags and awkwarder clashes. Some sections of it just now would appear to be in rapid retreat, and to have returned to the violent and heretic-persecuting stage which they, in common with other sections, had begun to leave.

The contemporary scene wears a very odd, unbalanced air; and human beings mingle in it dressed, as it were, in the clothes of all the centuries, speaking vainly to one another in outworn tongues, contemporary tongues, and tongues not as yet quite formed or understood.

Hence, or largely hence, this bewildering muddle. War, the settling or attempting to settle disputes between governments and sections of people by arming one section against another with destructive weapons is, like heretic-burning and ordeal by torture, one of the primitive, age-old barbaric pests, which humanity is, it is hoped, slowly outgrowing as it staggers on its erratic and extremely dilatory way towards some form of adult civilisation. All civilised people today admit that it is a childish and outmoded barbarity, worse than the legal torture of individuals in that it is on a larger scale, more dangerous to the comity of the human race not only in that it is infinitely more destructive, but in that it is sanctioned, in the eyes of many, by custom, so that people who would cry out against the burning to death of one man for committing a crime, condone the burning to death, quite as painfully and quite as deliberately, of hundreds of men, women and children who have committed no crime; they condone it as war, unfortunate but unavoidable. This acceptance makes war a much worse peril to civilised standards than is the beating to death of prisoners in concentration camps, which is loathed and condemned by general world opinion. War too is loathed and condemned by most civilised people. But the snag is that large numbers of people in all countries are very little civilised; they have lagged behind in the crawl; there are governments, and, it would seem, large masses of the governed who do not take this view of war; they even admire and glorify it; they bring up the boys of the nation in military formation, making them march to militant songs, making them chant in chorus, 'Prepare! Prepare! Prepare to attack with weapons of sharp construction!' and so forth. They distribute books encouraging that sanguinary excitement which is the fever contracted by the laity when their imaginations dwell over much on the perils of their country, on the sinister designs (usually thought of as 'encirclement') of other countries, and of the high courage of their own defenders. They suspect (no doubt often rightly) all foreigners; xenophobia rages, with all the usual symptoms, foaming at the mouth, snapping, howling, readiness to bite to death. No nation is immune, nor ever has been, from this unpleasant disease, the worst of which is that it is highly infectious. Once a state of war starts, all the combatant nations get it. But at the present moment it seems to be enjoying a remarkably good run even in countries nominally at peace. And it is the hot-bed from which war springs. That dragon which guarded the well of Ares by devouring all who sought to approach it had acute xenophobia, he hated all foreigners, and when Cadmus, having slain him, sowed his teeth in the ground, on the advice of the experienced Athene, sure enough armed warriors sprang up from each tooth, and there was an army ready-made. The teeth of the foreigner-hating dragon seem just now to be sown all about.

Psychological conditions, then, make for war, and large numbers of people have no kind of objection to it on principle, provided they think it will pay them, either in prestige, land, or some material advantage. And those who do object to it on principle – those whom we are calling, for the moment, the more civilised section of humanity – are up against this snag: the war waged by others, unlike more internal barbarities, threatens their interest, their possessions and their very life. It is not possible to look on at war with detached disgust as a revolting private custom of the barbarians, which they can be left to enjoy. It is a game which involves an opponent, and a game for which any opponent may be selected by the challenger, against his own will. Therefore the more civilised, hating war as they do from every angle, from that of ethics, humanity, expediency, survival-wish, common sense, are impelled, by fear of what may be done to them and their possessions if they are caught unready, to join the barbarian game, to fling themselves with desperate ardour into the competition in piling up weapons of torture and destruction which is bound to end in the guns going off, the bombs dropping, the incendiary gas burning populations to death. Faced with savages who declare continually and publicly that they are proud to be militarist and that prolonged peace is an ideal for cowards and decadents, and that there can only be peace after their own domination of the world by conquest, the civilised lose their nerve and follow a bad example, not in words but in deeds. Much as they loathe war, they arm; they will, they say, fight if necessary, fight if attacked, fight for liberty, democracy, civilisation, culture, peace, nationality, empire, survival: in brief, for their country. Though, as Harry Lauder observes, what's the good of fighting for your country? If you win, they don't give you any of it. No more will they give you much liberty, democracy, civilization, culture or peace, however victorious in a war you may chance to be, because there will be precious little of any of these left to give. Civilised people are aware of this; but they are prepared to face war and all its bestial destructions because they believe that it may be the only way to avert something worse.

It is here that they join issue with the pacifists. They believe, in the first place, that their armed condition may keep the war-mongers at bay; they play for time; dictators may fall, and totalitarian states become chaotic and harmless. They may be right; though many pacifists disagree with them and hold that armed nations are to one another like red rags to bulls, and only irritate, alarm and incite to aggression. Also, no nations can be relied on to become harmless permanently;

and the odds are that, if you keep expensive and explosive things like munitions on tap, they will be used some time against someone. But, in the short run those who arm may be right in believing that attackers may thus for a time be kept off; and this should be fairly faced and considered by pacifists.

Prolonged bluff is, of course, no use; it is always seen through. Those who prepare weapons must be prepared to use them; they will almost certainly have to do so in the end. Prepare for war, and you will eventually get war. Do not prepare for war, and you may get anything else, including extinction, but you cannot well get war. This, says the armer against aggression, is the voice of poltroonery. Would you let Britain's voice in Europe go under, let her empire go, let democracy and liberty be bludgeoned to death by brigands, the small nations be crushed or annexed, the robber powers impose their horrid tyrannies? To which the pacifist answers that as to that he will take a chance. None of this dreadful programme may happen; some of it will pretty surely happen to any nation that engages in a war today. Democracy and liberty, those frail unfortunates, always look pretty foolish after a few weeks of military rule; Fascism sees its chance and lifts its ugly head; neither Britian's voice nor any other in Europe would be saying much that made for edification; in fact, all the European voices would be saying pretty much the same things in the same tones. Propaganda, hate, lies, intolerance, xenophobia, and all other stupid phobias, the fevered excitement of the third-rate mind, silly nationalisms, fear, selfishness, shocking cruelties on all sides which before long cease to shock, savage determination to give as good or as bad as it is received, the loss of all standards of civility, culture and intelligence, terrified animal concentration on survival … these are only some of the things beside which the physical suffering and destruction of war is relatively trivial. A nation at war is a nation dragooned into acceptance of the Fascist state. As Max Plowman has put it, 'Fascism is not a colossus bestriding the continent and threatening to step across the English Channel, but an insidious infection that grows unobserved in the body politic and then suddenly appears under some sharp pressure of circumstance, as a full-grown disease ... Fascism represents the apotheosis of military power: it relies wholly upon the devilry of modern war to decide what is right and good, just and desirable. In order to meet it with equal force you must adopt its ethic ... just as in 1914 those of us who dreamed of "a war to end war"' had to become as completely militaristic as our enemies ... Fighting Fascism by armed means implies becoming Fascist in order to fight Fascism. This is precisely what the peace-intending National Government is now doing and what its unconscious supporters – the Labour Party and Trade Unions – are actively helping it to do. In voting for, or acquiescing in, rearmament, they vote the means of achieving the Totalitarian State.'

It is a specious cry – arm against Fascism and war; it brings in anti-Fascists and anti-militarists, lovers of justice, liberty, democracy, and peace, all bent on this sinister suicide pact, all set to kill the thing they love. Wars to end war only give war a fresh lease of life; sanctioned and accepted once more, unchained and let out for yet another run, thrown yet another of its favourite meals, the encouraged and pampered monster goes growling on its maniac way, the stronger after each orgy for the next. Much practice has developed its savagery into an appalling efficiency; a little more, and there will be a war that will really end war for good and all, together with all other modes of human activity. And the responsibility will lie with everyone of us who consents to its unchaining, for any purpose whatsoever. No giving war a respectable name, or a noble name, or a fine high-faluting name, or even a name that makes it sound sensible and necessary, is going to alter its character as a lunatic civilisation-destroyer; its respectable name is, indeed, an added danger, since it thus entraps the good, and is haloed by their honourable intentions. Leave it to the brigands, and it will appear nakedly for what it is, a senseless herd ferocity, condemned by all decent people; let decent people themselves accept it, and it begins to wear a plausibly sanctimonious air, as if a cannibal orgy were to be attended by bishops and got up to look like a church service. Making hundreds of incendiary bombs a day, as the factories of all countries are just now engaged in doing, should be regarded as a manifestation of a particularly low type of criminal mania; it would seem to call for the attentions of an alienist; were a private person discovered making even a few of these things, the excuse that he thought someone might be about to throw one of them at him and he must have some ready to throw back would get him nowhere but to Broadmoor. Since it is the governments of the world that are thus occupied, and the bombs are turned out by the ton, and their destined targets are whole populations, including children, the affair goes well; if you kill enough people at once, it is no longer murder, it is patriotism, or class war, or the saving of civilisation.

The business of acting like savages because other people do is a mistake that all savages make. It gets civilisation nowhere. The vicious circle wants breaking, by some original, strong, and intelligent power, which cares enough for the long run of civilisation to stake its possessions on the gamble of disarmament, which cares enough for intelligence and humanity to reject utterly and without compromise these barbarous and imbecile methods of controversy. It might lose on the throw; it might lose most of what it had. Or it might not; though I should not care to put much money on that hope myself. But it seems worthwhile that some power should try it. Civilised experiments have not always worked in a savage world, but they have always been worthwhile; they have made landmarks, they have been looked back on later as pioneering achievements, like the first flights in the air. Pioneers do not always survive to see what comes of their experiments; but if no one made them, nothing would come of them. The point about the disarmament experiment is, what is the alternative? War and more war, stupid and cruel destruction, the savage dancing his tribal dance, whooping in his feathers, tomahawk and war-paint, until the jungle swallows him up and the world as we know it crashes in ruins.

It may be said, what is the use of making a rout about disarmament when nothing is more certain than that we shall not at present disarm? Had we not better concentrate entirely on trying to build up the conditions of peace, economic, social, racial and political? Such attempts should be, of course, the pacifist's constant job, as everyone else's. But it is worthwhile, too, to keep on talking about disarmament, if only to keep the idea alive. Once that minority voice dies, something of value is sunk and goes under, and war as an accepted institution scores another point. Until the victims of nationalism, tribalism, racialism, sectarianism, class, creed, and all the other extensions of egoism, become so far civilised that they subordinate themselves to a political, economic and social commonwealth and live a decent adult human life, settling their differences like reasonable beings, it seems worthwhile that all those who feel strongly on the matter should continue to protest against the present intemperate and nerve-ridden unreason which impels civilised and humane persons to ape the distasteful ferocity of the barbarians that we shall all, if we go on like this, extremely soon become.

11 Notes on the way

Time and Tide, 5 October 1940

[In order to preserve the essentially individual character of Notes on the Way we allow those who contribute them an entirely free pen. We must not be taken as being necessarily in agreement with the opinions expressed – Editor, *Time and Tide*]

Where an hour back two houses stood in this small street, there is a jumbled mountain of fallen masonry, rubble, the shattered debris of two crashed homes; beneath it lie jammed those who lived there; some of them call out, crying for rescue, others are dumb. Through the pits and craters in the rubbled mass the smell of gas seeps. Water floods the splintered street; a main has burst; dust liquefies into slimy mud. The demolition squad stumble in darkness about the ruins, sawing, hacking, drilling, heaving; stretcher bearers and ambulance drivers stand and watch. Jerry zooms and drones about the sky, still pitching them down with long whistling whooshes and thundering crashes, while the guns bark like great dogs at his heels. The moonless sky, lanced with long, sliding, crossing shafts, is a-flare with golden oranges that pitch and burst and are lost among the stars. Deep within its home a baby whimpers, and its mother faintly moans '*My baby. Oh, my poor baby. Oh, my baby. Get us out.*' The rescue squad call back. 'All right, my dear. We'll be with you in ten minutes now'. They say it at intervals for ten hours. Water and milk are passed down to those who can be reached. The rescuers work on. They are kind, skilful, patient, brave, thirsty men; they wish that a mobile canteen would turn up with hot tea or cocoa. They are friendly and polite;

one of them mutters obscene oaths at Jerry as he zooms overhead, whooshes through the air, and crashes somewhere near at hand; another nudges him, indicating that a tin hat near him covers a female ambulance driver; he apologises unnecessarily. 'Sorry, mate, didn't see you there.'

Someone is dug out; she is seventy-four, gay and loquacious; she does not cease talking as she is carried to an ambulance and driven to hospital, she is so pleased to be out. Half an hour later her married daughter is extracted; she has a grey, smeared, bruised face; she cries and is sick. 'Oh my back, my legs, my head. Oh, dear God, my children.' She is carried to an ambulance, driven away. 'The children are safe.' she is told. 'They will be out quite soon. You'll see them soon.' But she will not, for they are all dead, two boys of eleven and twelve, two babies of three and one. 'If only,' she moans 'they didn't suffer much …'

Dawn is near. It grows colder. Still Jerry zooms and crashes, still the rescuers dig, saw, heave and console. 'All right, my dear, you'll be out in a jiffy.' There are only two voices to answer now; one exhausted woman's, and a baby's wail. Not much hope now for the others. At dawn the demolition squad, the ambulance drivers and the stretcher bearers are relieved by others; only inside the ruins the personnel remains the same.

'It's this every night now,' says a demolition worker, drinking a mug of cocoa on the pavement before he goes. 'This and fires.'

'There were a few casualties,' says a bland voice next day. 'But little material damage appears to have been done.'

ᴥ

A sample corner of total war. Elsewhere, men are being burnt alive, blinded, shot, drowned, smashed to bits when their planes crash. Civilian war deaths are no worse than those of the young men in the fighting forces; all alike are sentient human beings, dying suddenly or in agony. 'Eighteen of our planes were lost, but eight of the pilots are safe.' And ten not. Do not let us cant about 'women-and-children'. However it may be about children – and I admit that here our feelings outrun reason – it is no worse that women should be killed than men. It is all part of the blind, maniac, primitive, stupid bestiality of war, into which human beings periodically leap, spitting in civilisation's face and putting her to confused rout. The alternative, here and now? No one can see any, except surrendering to the still more blind, maniac, primitive, stupid bestiality of Nazi rule over Europe, which would be to spit at and rout civilization even more earnestly. Not even the most pacific pacifist can see (so far as I can discover) any third way. It is a choice of bestialities: let the foul scene proceed, or let it give place to one fouler, while we abandon Europe to a cruel and malignant enslavement, breaking faith with the conquered countries which look to us for freedom, handing over to their torturers those who have sought safety with us, as did so unprotestingly the Fascist and anti-Semite old French Marshal, canting meanwhile of a regenerated France. A disgusting dilemma, and one which agonizes many pacifists.

But, oddly, some intelligent pacifists do not seem to feel the dilemma. They say that the Nazi 'new order in Europe' would have good points. Odd, because of all people pacifists should surely be the first to hate an order which is based on armed terrorism, which glorifies war, whose leaders proclaim that prolonged peace is ignoble and makes man decadent, that only in war can he rise to his true stature; an order which undermines and attacks one small country after another, enslaving its people; which hates freedom, thought, culture and truth, moulds young minds to its own image, tortures and imprisons racial, political and intellectual dissidents. What can any pacifist find in all this to approve, or even to tolerate? Apparently its discipline, and its unification. It would be better, they say, than the former anarchy of independent states. By 'unification' they seem to mean the subjugation of many nations by one. Obviously such unity would be merely nominal, since most of the conquered nations would be simmering pots boiling over every little while, cauldrons of anger, murder and hate. To impose even the most tolerant, easy and democratic foreign rule on the European nations in our present stage of international development would seem impracticable; to impose the Nazi rule, with its authoritarian theories of enslavement and a ruling race, its gross in humanity, is to invite disaster. So even the rather damned peace of unification we should not get for long.

But people seem genuinely to differ about Nazi rule and Nazi practices. I have met pacifists who say they are no worse than our own; this seems to me an uninformed and unobjective view. Without wanting to make a case, or to whitewash this or any other country at war or at peace (and officially we are far too smug and self-complacent) I feel that one should try to observe the ordinary rules of evidence. But it would seem that the Nazi régime has a queer attraction for some quite un-Nazi kinds of mind; if it had not, presumably it would not have got about Europe as it has; those who can tolerate it, or some of its aspects, and those (perhaps prejudiced) whom it sickens altogether, speak to one another across a gulf which carries away and drowns their words; it is no use either side getting vexed and shouting.

ᕙ

Is it any more use getting vexed about our self-praise? I doubt it. Probably we must endure for the duration hearing about our crusade, about the fight of Christianity against Paganism. This does seem a pretty hopeless confusion of terms, for it misuses both words. We are not fighting Nazi Germany on account of Christianity, but to stop her aggression in Europe. Her ally, Italy, is an officially and predominantly Christian country. So is her unofficial ally, Spain. In France, it is the clerical, Christian elements which have led the surrender and are leading the co-operation with Germany, the Fascist, anti-Semite, anti-British campaign, and the persecution of the pro-British secularists of the Third Republic. Among our own unofficial allies are Christian America and Moslem Turkey. The religious situation is altogether too mixed to be summed up as it often is; the cleavage is political, national, social, not religious.

Another riddle: why do so many religious speakers exhort us to 'return to God'? At what period of our murky, selfish, magnificent human history did men walk on close terms with God? Perusing its barbaric pages, one sees much the same state of things always and everywhere; that is, there was some godliness, more ungodliness. Of course if 'returning to God' means going more to church, the speakers have a case. Does it mean only this? I believe not, for they often go on to mention modern worldliness, modern pleasure-seeking, modern wrong values. But we have certainly more social conscience today than we had, bad as conditions still are. As to pleasure-seeking. I imagine that most human beings in all ages have chased after the flying skirts of pleasure, even if they have not always caught up with her much; and no doubt most human values have always been pretty wrong. I wish our religious leaders would exhort us instead to begin to try to discover what God is, and drop the theory that we once knew. Is it perhaps the Eden complex that still haunts man's nostalgic soul?

We have found two new hobbies during the past month – we have become cave-fanciers and ruin-gogglers. The troglodytes will tell one another which are the best underground haunts, which the warmest, the deepest, the most sociable, the smelliest, at what hour you should queue up to secure the best pitches. The ruin-tasters make a daily tour of last night's damage; they are fastidious and choosey; unlike some ruin-hunters, they value ruins not for their antiquity but for their extreme novelty. 'That's old stuff; last Wednesday,' they will say, disdainfully passing by a jumbled mass that was a block of flats, where now, suspended in chaos, a bath hangs upright high above the street, pathetic banner of tottering civilisation among barbarous ruins. 'There's a good one in my street,' we say, proud of our own monuments. 'Makes you think, doesn't it,' we say. But just what it makes us think, I am not sure. Or if that is really the word for one's reaction to these ruined homes. There is some sore feeling round about Baker Street (and no doubt elsewhere) when its night's smashes (and we get good ones in Marylebone) are included by the News Bulletins in 'some damage to a north-west suburb'. This nettles our bomb-vanity.

'A good book for the shelter'. This is what is asked for now in libraries. I have only been in a shelter once, and then I was entertained by conversation, so I don't know how a shelter book should differ from a book above ground. But, above ground or below, if you want a new book which is a delightful extension of an old one, read *Jane Fairfax*, by Naomi Royde Smith. You will find Emma there, and all her friends and foes, as well as many characters out of the other Austens, and it is beautifully done, a perfect period pastiche. How would Emma herself have behaved in a shelter? Arranged everyone's life, no doubt, been the life and plague of the party, while sly and lovely Jane sat mute and thought the more. But read this book.

Finally, two linguistic queries. Who first put about the odd pronunciation *sireen*? and why and when? Was it used before the war? And when did the BBC and the more educated newspapers (the less educated have done it for some years) begin using regularly the American *store* for the old English *shop*? Shop has been the English word for these places of sale since before Chaucer. The Oxford Dictionary gives 'store' as 'US and colonial'. It has (in this sense) no antiquity. Perhaps taking it over is part of the American alliance, like the destroyers. I hope we have given America a word in return. And are we in future to have store-lifters, to go storing, to talk store, and are we now a nation of store-keepers?

12 Consolations of the War

The Listener, 16 January 1941

In this horrid business of war, the brightest spots can only be rather melancholy consolations. It is, of course, an extremely horrid business: a grotesquely barbarous, uncivilised, inhumane and crazy way of life to have had forced on us by a set of gangsters who are making us use their own weapons and practise their own horrid incivilities – as if we were jungle savages like themselves instead of twentieth-century men and women who had hoped war to be for ever outlawed. That is the worst outrage that the gangsters have perpetrated on us – forcing us to adopt their own shockingly bad manners. For war, of course, is as revolting an example of bad manners as can well be imagined. We do not think it is a grand life: as a member of the House of Commons remarked lately, we think it is a perfectly beastly life, only to be endured because the things we are fighting against are still more beastly. So its consolations are rather small stars in a pretty murky night.

Well, then, as to these consolations. You begin each day by waking up alive (so far) and a little surprised sometimes to be so. Each extra day, I mean, is not a matter of course, but a gift we had not necessarily counted on having. Your windows and crockery may have got smashed in the night, bits of your walls and ceilings may have fallen down, your house or apartment may be in varying stages of dilapidation or even ruin, but you are indubitably alive.

If you do wake alive, you may enjoy – when you go out – observing the fresh ruins, if any, and if ruins are to your taste. Of course no one wants ruins, but it is no use pretending that those made last night are not interesting next day. I sometimes think how greatly our eighteenth-century

243

ancestors would have enjoyed them. They paid architects to build picturesque ruins in their parks and gardens; we have hordes of ruin-makers who nightly do it free. We stroll out, then, and see the sights; here is a jumbled pile which was a house, and dangling poised at its very top, high above the street, is a large bath and broken lavatory basin and seat. There – round the next corner, not so far away from my own flat – is the ruin of a house with a little Austin car poised on its summit, blown up there from its garage by blast. The demolition workers fetch it down and stand it in the street, a little battered and thick in grey dust, in which someone inscribes the legend: 'For Sale. Good Condition. One Owner Only'. I've been told that there is to be seen somewhere a trolley-bus which has climbed on to the top of a house, but I cannot find anyone who has actually seen this.

From such bizarre spectacles one must get what interest one can, among the tragedies of smashed homes and broken glories of architecture. Some hopeful souls imagine to themselves the nobler, seemlier buildings which will one day, so they hope, take the place of the destroyed. This cannot always be done, of course; not when we lose our medieval Guildhall, our Wren churches, and (worse) those all too few churches which survived a much earlier fire in 1666 – churches such as St Giles', Cripplegate, where Milton is commemorated, and the lovely All Hallows by the Tower. There is no pleasure to be derived from the destruction of All Hallows, unless you are so malicious as to feel a little relief that the corner of its interior which was modernised and sentimentalised to commemorate the last war has perished with the rest. Ruin is indiscriminate and stupid; it falls on beautiful and ugly, noble and mean, with the most impartial injustice. On the whole, these ruins depress; you have to look a long time and with great determination for their brighter spots.

For aesthetic pleasure, you must wait until dark. London nights, once garish, have become beautiful; black, with tiny lights like glow-worms faintly piercing the blackness – and on a clear night the stars. Or, on a moony night, magically black and silver, an ivory city sharp with shadows and deep lanes of night. And always the long lances of light that sweep the skies, crossing, seeking, probing. Suddenly the quiet is shattered by a long howling as of wolves on the trail; again and again the uncanny wail rises and drops; it ceases, and after a minute or two comes that deep drone of bombing planes; flashes begin, and crashes; the sky is aflare with golden fruits that burst and are lost in the stars. Sometimes the heavens blaze red, in east, west, or centre – or everywhere at once. Buildings are outlined against fire. Here a water-main has burst, and a great lake floods a street below a mountain of ruins; a gas-main, too, has burst, and flames leap roaring to the sky, mirrored in the water. Oh, what a scene! as Horace Walpole said of the fall of the Bastille. Above it, the enemy zooms malevolently, pitching them down with loud whistling whooshes and thundering crashes, while the guns bark like great dogs at his heels. And I say nothing for this horrid scene, except that, aesthetically, it has a kind of lurid and infernal beauty. And that, if your job calls you out to it, as mine sometimes does, you do at least get an eyeful, and see something you don't see as a rule in the London streets.

Another thing you get is a sense of friendly companionship. The men and women working together among fire and bombs – firemen, ambulance drivers, rescue squads, wardens – they have a new comradeship, which overrides class and sex. The words 'mate' and 'chum' are grown common forms of address. That is pleasant; we don't in normal times, in this rather stiff and shy country, get enough of it; it's more like the western states of America, with their companionable 'brother' and 'sister'. This greater friendliness extends beyond the air-raid workers to people in general; you meet it in the streets, in trains, 'buses and shops: and (I am told by those who frequent them) you meet it in shelters, too. Perhaps especially there.

Shelters we must count among the major consolations of war. They are quite a new pleasure, and are among the town amenities most missed by evacuees to the country. They have taken the place of the cinema as an essential of the good life. I know of one woman – by profession she is a charwoman – who goes to her favourite shelter (I'm told that they differ greatly as cinemas do) every evening at seven o'clock. She stays there until eleven, when, bombs or no bombs, she goes home to bed. Evening travellers by the underground trains may see the shelterers in the subway stations, dossing down for the night on rugs and pillows and wooden bunks, with canteen workers selling tea and chocolate. Often they have concerts and other entertainments, and sometimes distinguished persons to visit them … but I don't think this can be very wholesome, for it seems to start them being a little smug, and shouting 'We can take it!' – which is an irritating cry, since it is hard to see what else any of us can do but take it, whether above ground or below. Still, if it cheers them up … Anyhow, shelter life has, I think, come to stay; even in the peace (if any), this odd, communal, troglodyte life led nightly by so many Londoners will, I prophesy, go on; it must save so much trouble.

Being saved trouble is always a major pleasure, of course; and wartime saves us trouble in more than one way. Clothes, for example. It doesn't matter now much what anyone wears; women can go about London in slacks; silk stockings are definitely off, and to wear warm woollen ones and thick brogues or boots in town as well as country is a pleasure that formerly only the strong-minded allowed themselves, but that now even the shy may safely adopt. Evening clothes, too, are seldom seen. The typical Englishman is said to derive pleasure from dressing in a stiff shirt for his dinner each night when living alone in a jungle; he may enjoy this piquant contrast between his surroundings and his clothes, but you can take it from me that he and his sisters enjoy more never dressing for dinner in wartime London. It saves trouble, money, time, and gives us a lazy, go-as-you-please feeling that I find most agreeable. I only wish I could think that the fashion would outlast the war, and not give place to some terrific reaction into formal smartness.

Then, coming back to aesthetic pleasures, the pageant of life is enormously enriched by the presence of so many foreigners in our midst. So far as civilian foreigners go, many of them were promptly interned last summer, as you know, some quite unjustly. But slowly – far too slowly – that injustice is being put right. In any case, the uniforms of Polish soldiers mingle with those of Czechs, Norwegians, Dutch and Free French; women from the Central European countries with handkerchiefs tied about their heads embellish the streets. And not only foreigners. Driving in the country, you are continually hailed by the rich accents of young men in battle-dress from Alberta or Montreal, who seldom know where they are and always want to go somewhere else. They are, as a rule, enormously charming.

I will end with a consolation not aesthetic but psychological; the gratifying feeling that we have the sympathy of the best people: that is to say, the best nations, and the better people of the temporarily less good nations. We haven't had it in all our wars, and rightly. We have by no means always had the sympathy and goodwill of the American people; and the fact that we have it now gives us an enormous amount of support and satisfaction. Sympathy and mutual trust have been cemented by a common hatred of this horrid business of Nazism. We have grown into a relationship of which President

Roosevelt can say: 'There was no treaty, no written agreement – but there was a feeling, which has proved correct, that as neighbours we could settle our disputes peacefully. There will be no bottleneck in our determination to aid Britain'.

When I cast my mind back to the earlier history of our relationship, and its stormy beginning, I cannot help recalling Patrick Henry's words of defiance flung at us across the Atlantic in 1775: ... 'Is life so dear or peace so sweet as to be purchased at the price of chains and slavery? Forbid it, Almighty God. Give me liberty or give me death'.

I think Patrick Henry would now be on our side, and would use those words with a different reference. Among the consolations of war, this community of purpose and ideals with the kind of people with whom community is worth having, ranks high. I think really I should have mentioned it first.

13 Looking in on Lisbon

The Spectator, 1 July 1943

It is probably presumptuous for someone who has only spent two recent months in Portugal, and only part of that time in Lisbon, to attempt even the most superficial comments on Lisbon life. All, naturally, that I can do is to set down a few notes from the point of view of a passer-by who was allowed to loiter for a brief space in this enchanting city. There has been plenty written about Lisbon lately; Europeans have grown Lisbon-minded; a western oasis in the frightening desert (like Switzerland, but accessible to many to whom Switzerland is a moated fortress, impregnable, enemy-barred, without approach), Portugal shines like a mirage to those still fettered in the wilderness; to these it must wear the improbable air of the golden gates. When and if at last the gates open for them, it still seems improbable, a dream: they do not quite know that they are there; bewilderment, exhaustion and relief must disqualify them as detached observers of the scene around them. For the rest of us, the visitors, the travellers in transit, the residents at work, the scene is admirable drama, in which tragic and comic strands are nicely interwoven, and people, great and small, from all (nearly all) the nations, arc unceasingly shuttled in and out.

This applies, of course, mainly to Lisbon, the port of transit. Lisbon is rather like a parish, in that everyone knows who is in it at the moment, what they are doing and why, and probably when they will leave it. If they happen to be English, their comings and goings are recorded in that admirable weekly journal the *Anglo-Portuguese News*, and often if they happen to be Portuguese. Should they happen, as they extremely often do, to be German, Italian or Japanese, they may, for all I know, be mentioned in one of the journals sympathetic with their aims which are also sold in Lisbon. Anyhow, one way and another, and quite apart from the Press, it is difficult not to know, at any given moment, who is in Lisbon; even the spies, like other professional men and women, are known about, though not, through etiquette, mentioned in print. This publicity, this sounding-board quality of Lisbon, makes the Lisbonese deride the idea that the Nazis shot down a British Airways passenger plane because they hoped it might contain Mr Churchill. The arrivals and takings-off of the British Airways' planes are invested with complete publicity. Unless those who shot down that plane were acting on their own initiative, and out of mere wantonness, they had instructions to get Leslie Howard, a most effective anti-Axis film propagandist who had just had a great success in Portugal and Spain.

This agreeable compactness of Lisbon society must have made the outbreak of war a very awkward social solecism. Diplomats, Embassy staffs and other residents who had been dining, lunching and cocktailing with one another, meeting and talking at clubs, cafés and gatherings (though, it seems likely, with decreasing enthusiasm and ease as the European chasm yawned ever wider) now found themselves rudely severed, with echoing straits between them thrown. At first, I was told, reserved and chilly bows were the mode when late friends turned enemies encountered one another in the street; then, as war asserted itself, one would hurry round a corner or into a shop to escape meeting; later, when the affair had, so to speak, frozen solid, most people did not even trouble to do this; enemies looked past one another with nonchalant impassivity; though I have been out with people who still turned aside when a German CD car swept up to the kerb and began to disembark German CD. I suppose it was a little awkward to meet the enemy when the enemy was with neutral and mutual friends. Did one take off one's hat to an enemy lady in these circumstances? I imagine that one did. But no doubt diplomatic training and Portuguese tact were equal to such social emergencies.

The giving of parties in war-time is naturally badly hampered by all the people who must not meet. I do not know if any mischievous or careless hosts ever ignored the war and threw unmeetables together; I imagine not; the Portuguese do not do things like that. But there are lesser complications. One was told of a distinguished Portuguese who was preparing his rooms for a reception he was giving, and who usually, having rather a taste for the European dictators (or for some of them; he had no portrait of M. Stalin), kept their photographs on his table. A courteous and careful man, he said to the friend with him, 'The English are coming; we must put away Adolf and Benito. And some of the French, so we won't have the old Marechal. But Francisco can stay: I have no Spanish tonight.'

Though it may seem absurd that civilised beings in a neutral land cannot continue personal acquaintanceship while their countries are at one another's throats, there is, in practice, some sense in it, apart from the suspicion that they might be dropping unguarded words. I discovered myself that such acquaintanceship had its difficulties. On the day after the call at Lisbon of a number of repatriated British and Italian wounded prisoners, I talked at Estoril to a Portuguese countess, Italian by birth, passionately Italian in affections. She spoke of the Italian prisoners: they had been brutally ill-treated by us, she said. 'In England?' I asked. 'Surely impossible.' She shrugged her shoulders. 'By the Australian soldiers, when they were captured. Those great brutal Australians, they hurt them, they knocked them about in the most frightful manner. It was terrible.' Terrible, I echoed, for I expect it was, and anyhow I did not wish to make an international incident of it over tea. I feel sure that, in a rough-house between an

Australian and an Italian, my sympathies would be with the Italian. 'And,' she went on, bitterly, 'the English wounded prisoners were so well treated in Italy, sent to the mountains for their health, given everything.' I said I was sure they had been; and added that I was sure also that the Italians had been well treated in England; we liked them so much, I said. I think I made no impression, and that she was convinced that her fellow-countrymen had been ill-treated both by Australians in the field and by English in England. In the bitter gaze of that patriotic Italian eye I saw myself engrossed into an Australian soldier, huge, brutal, a kicker and puncher of small wounded Italians. It was then that I began to see reason in the convention by which enemies do not converse …

But some patriots overdo this aloofness. Among the cosmopolitan and ever-shifting crowd at my small hotel there were at one time a few Japanese. (I think that before they came the Chinese from France, several families with the most attractive ivory children and trousered nurses, had departed.) An Englishman who arrived just before I left Lisbon found that his table at lunch was near that of a Japanese. He told me that he had gone straight to the bureau and informed it that either he or 'that yellow monkey' must be shifted, for he was not going to eat within view of him. I said, 'There may be other Japanese here.' He said no, there were not; he had demanded the list of visitors and the nationalities of all of them; there was only the one yellow monkey, and he wasn't going to see him while he ate.

Such heated patriotism must make life difficult, not only for the patriots but for their Portuguese hosts. Indeed, these have in many ways a delicate task, steering through all the hostile sensibilities: all their finesse, sympathy and good manners are required; fortunately they have plenty. So too have some of our countrymen in Portugal, who have acquired through habit that cosmopolitan outlook on foreigners, even enemy foreigners, which is too instinctive to be called tact, too casually tolerant to be called sympathy, which is part of the easy heritage of those who rub up every day against other races, other traditions, other tongues, other ways and are used to friendly acceptance of both sides. This habit of sophisticated acceptance, which tacitly persists even among estranged enemy nationals, is part of the unconscious good manners which, together with their friendly hospitality to strangers, makes both the English and the Portuguese in Portugal charming to be among.

14 A Happy Neutral

The Spectator, 9 July 1943

You cannot go about Portugal without being aware that the sympathies of most Portuguese are with the British in the present struggle. With the British: not necessarily with Britain's allies. Russia is on the whole regarded with suspicion, fear and disapproval, an attitude dictated by the Government and Press. The United States is remote, and there is a tendency to regard it as an arrogant rival of Brazil. Great Britain, with all its faults and mistakes and past mutual irritations, is still the Oldest Ally (as any beggar will diplomatically tell you), and is tolerated, though with reservations. There is no doubt about the majority-feeling in the crowd that lines up to read the news placarded in the Avenida of an evening. There is no doubt about the admiration for the British airmen who occasionally descend on the country and are removed for internment with every symptom of affectionate esteem. There was no doubt about the anger among Lisboans at the bombing of the British Airways plane with Leslie Howard, whom they had greatly liked, and other English on board. And there was no doubt about the general reaction to a large portrait of the Führer which for a time was displayed in a German propaganda window: the Portuguese are practiced and deft spitters; the portrait had to be removed and the window washed.

Not that the many Germans in Lisbon are (so far as I heard) unpopular; they run a lively propaganda, spend a lot of money, and have many friends, particularly among the richer classes. There is said by some Portuguese to be a deep social cleavage in this matter, as in Spain, but I think it cannot be very pronounced. One also heard that the pro-German

Portuguese were pro-Spanish too; natural enough, seeing the hold the Nazis have on Spain, and the ardent Nazism of the Spanish Press. If the pro-Spanish Portuguese are the only pro-Germans, that limits pro-Germanism in Portugal pretty strictly, for Spain is not generally popular, the Portuguese have suffered too much at her hands, and the cry of Iberia Unida must be alarming to a nervous people, however brotherly and well meant its intention.

I met at Sintra a vivid and vehement Condessa; a handsome, youngish woman, remarkable among her countrywomen for being long-limbed and going about in slacks, with her fine dark head Eton-cropped. (Portuguese middle-class women are apt to be very feminine; plump and small, they trip about on high heels, wear their black hair in waved masses, and are shocked at women in trousers – this was one of the complaints made of them by the cosmopolitan Italian countess at Estoril, who herself wore slacks to annoy them. The peasant women, on the other hand, are often, like the peasant men, magnificent creatures, free-stepping, handsome, upright, coiling their splendid hair in low Greek knots, striding along with incredible loads on their heads. They are still, as apparently they always were, much handsomer than the rich. Why this seems always to be so in the Latin countries and the reverse in Nordic countries is one of the ethnological mysteries. But this is by the way.)

My Sintra Condessa said (she was brought up partly in England and spoke English fluently), 'I am almost the only pro-Ally woman in my miserable class. I do British propaganda all the time, oh, how angry it makes them! My own children come home with Nazi ideas and bring their young pro-Nazi friends. Those horrible Nazis, I say to them, why do you admire them? They don't know why, it is just that it is the fashion among their class and they are snobs. They have Spanish friends, too, who come into my house and praise Hitler to my face. They tell me the democracies are decadent and finished, and that Fascism will rule Europe. I would like to spank them all, them and their little Führers and Duces and Caudillos. What is the matter with our class? The poor people don't talk that nonsense. *They* don't like dictatorships. If those damned Nazis should ever march against us, my class will run to embrace them, while I march at the head of my tenants, an army of pitchforks."

I confess that I should not care to meet the Condessa armed with a pitchfork with her tenantry marching behind her over the mountains of Sintra. The rest of her spirited conversation, and there was plenty more, must be treated as off the record. As to her views on her own class, I know too little of that to endorse or deny them, but I think she was unfair. None of those I met seemed pro-Nazi, but rather Anglophile. From the Condessa's words, and those of some other Portuguese, one envisaged, behind the high walls of those delicious quintas whose fragrance stole sweetly into the senses as one passed, bevies of arrogant Fascist condes and condessas, applauding the fine exploits of Hitler in Europe while they lolled beneath their vines and fig-trees beside their blue-tiled swimming-pools, growing plump on ortolans, sweets and crystallised fruits and on the sweat of their oppressed tenantry.

'Ce sont retraités de paresseux qui vivaient, comme on dit, de la sueur du peuple, genre d'alimentation peu ragoûtant, mais qui nous a donné, somme tout, presque tout ce qu'il y a d'admirable sur la terre …'

So someone has written about the Portuguese aristocrats in their quintas, and I confess that, in spite of their perverse alleged affection for the ill-conditioned and barbarous foe, I have a stirring of envious sympathy for them. But no: I fear that they are not like this now; I believe they are a hard-working, hard-taxed, amiable squirearchy, no doubt with prejudices and limitations, and usually without broad views on European affairs, but not pro-Nazi. I cannot believe in these clear-cut divisions according to class, anyhow in Portugal.

Back in Lisbon, walking down those steep, narrow and ancient ways towards the great green river bearing on its breast the ships from the seas of all the world, I meet again the beggar woman who whines to me with outstretched hand of the old, old alliance (what is it that she says to the Germans? I never discovered), and the little newsboys scampering bare-legged along the hot pebbles of the pavement, offering me *The Times*, the *Daily Express*, breaking off to press *Das Reich* and the Spanish *Arriba* on a fair, horn-rimmed young Teuton. (Do the newsboys ever blunder? Their instinct seems unerring.)

In the main, I should guess that the Portuguese, a sensible and peace-loving people, think less of favouring either side in the catastrophic disturbance that cleaves the world than of preserving their own invaluable neutrality and peace. As we know we are lucky to be an island, they know they are lucky to lie on Europe's western edge, instead of being a Balkan or a Baltic State, and now a State no more. Pleasure in this fact communicates itself through the clear and sunlit air of Lisbon, seeming to heighten the gay, pale colours of the city, to blare in the merry noises of the streets and in the deep, triumphant cries of the women who swing along bearing mountains of golden oranges or crates of cackling fowls on their heads. Portugal is gloriously neutral; that is its gift from the gods and to Europe; a gift never, one hopes, to be snatched away.

15 The BBC and War Moods: I and II

The Spectator, 20 January 1944 and 27 January 1944

Faced with a potentially receptive public that oscillates between hope (rather than fear) of the catastrophic, greedy cashing-in on circumstance and apathetic acquiescence, a public drugged with the disordered yet complacent view of a world slipping into disintegration, an uncertain mind that welcomes the crystallisation into firm outlines of its own hazy values, that does not know what nourishment it wants, but will feed on any scraps fed to it – faced with all this, radio has limitless opportunity. A kind of idle, restless attentiveness is bred towards the kaleidoscopic panorama that jigs behind that bland clock-face; fragments of its pattern click with some pattern already within our brains; they enlarge, mould, correct it; or merely fit easily in; or they are dismissed and rejected, finding no connecting contacts.

This is so with music, which can, like nothing else (except philosophy and religion), order the mind's crazy, incoherent chaos into a pattern. But what pattern? That formed by the jigging of jazz, dance bands, sentimental singing, the lumbering windy cinema organ, ending with a smirking and treacly 'Keep smiling', endorsing the view that life is a tale told by a vulgar idiot — roughly, it may be called, the simian view? The BBC believes, apparently rightly, that that is the majority view; but, though the demand has probably grown with war conditions and war mentality, the supply has not, I believe, grown; this is not the pattern it is sought to impose on us.

Then there is the sentimental mood interpreted by charming

tunes, usually familiar; this pattern is received by the senses and emotions. At the other pole, there is harsh and bold cacophony, austere, diligent, abstract, almost fleshless; this is a pattern we are being encouraged more frequently to receive; it does not, I think, fit with war moods, which are, when not tensed for action, labour and endurance, relaxed to tired, pleasure-craving, sensuous simplicity, and not experimental. And last, there is the pattern formed by the highest and sublimest arrangement of notes, rich in passion, beauty, intellect, spirit. It is held that a larger public is being won for this. It is possible. The little-trained can grasp it, or bits of it, while remaining deaf to or jarred by Svendsen, Bax, Walton, and symphonic tone-poems. The present tragedy, the present heroism, connect with the one, not with the other; the present lunacy is saned by it. Much in war connects also with the simian drivel, much else with the familiar tunes. One way or another, the pattern of music somewhere fits the mood.

The assault on the mind with words seems more calculated to mould, to lay a form on, uncertain thought and feeling. Here war moods are definitely assumed, played on, or played up. The war dramas, for instance, about one or another European country. Sometimes the country is personified, speaks, Hardy-like, with a voice; usually only its inhabitants speak. Music screams; there is a note of hysteria, loud noises off, as of trains, explosions, mines going up, patriots being shot. The people are all patriots, guerilla-minded, noble of speech and deed; they are all underground; no one seems to live and work on the earth's surface. They do not sit and talk about money, their animals, crops, love, funerals; they have an air perpetually keyed up for the hour of liberation. In the intervals between wrecking-activities and firing-squads, bursts of shrill music express them. We find them disembodied and remote; they are not people in the round, with faces and voices and qualities; these persecuted romantics function in limbo, divorced from life; they are noble, tormented shades, so little real that they hardly exact pity.

There are some intelligent and sensitive minds working on these 'national day' programmes, and a few have been admirable; notably one on France, with French music and poetry; it avoided all the snags, and achieved beauty. And there was once a very lovely talk on cruising among Greek islands, spoken beautifully by a Greek woman; the nostalgia was acute, Greece shimmered vivid before us; it was worth a dozen patriotic dramas, for it had corporeal detail and no propaganda aim; Greece was islands and sea, and spoke no word; countries should never speak; but never. These programmes, assuring us that Frenchmen, Greeks, Czechs, Norwegians, Poles, are fighting the good fight, omit in doing so to make them Frenchmen, Greeks, Czechs, Norwegians and Poles; they are merely embodiments of an aim. Do they think to rouse our sympathy for these puppet patriots? As to our foes in these dramas, their brutality is as inevitable as the broken English in which they converse among themselves, and as unimpressive. Unimpressive not because war moods do not include hate, but because they are puppet enemies. There are always minds to receive the pattern of hate, and to reject it. More, I think, to reject it. Noel Coward's famous song was disliked, probably, by the majority.

Hate is not often emitted by the BBC; more derision, placid sarcasm, and moral disapproval. There are pauses, inflections of voice, even in the news, that convey these. Compassion is not encouraged, except for ourselves and our Allies; enemies killed, hurt, or homeless from our bombing get none. I should guess the BBC tone in this matter (which has improved in the last months) to be just about as civilised as the majority view among listeners, more so than one minority, less so than another. The tone is 'serve them right; they began it'; one never hears, as one hears from so many of the public, 'poor things', or 'it's tough on the children'; nor does one hear the crude exultations of others. Bombed Germans are not put to us as people, but as pawns in the war effort; that is part of Government policy.

The war effort, constantly to the fore, damages many programmes. It often spoils landscapes. 'Come, I will show you Quebec,' our guide said one evening. To be shown Quebec, that ancient French city climbing up from the St Lawrence, steep and narrow-streeted, to the citadel, the great river sweeping ice-green at its feet, its harbour ship-laden, its old squares full of cafés, markets, churches, and the French tongue of Louis Quatorze — that would be something. But what a Quebec that BBC guide showed us! One heard not bells, nor French chatter, nor street cries, but shrieking engine-whistles, hooting factory-sirens, creaking cranes, the clatter of machinery — it might have been Leeds. 'Very like England,' the tourists kept saying. But Quebec is not in the least like England. There were comments on the traffic and the factories; Quebec was shown in terms of 'the war effort'. Quebec itself eluded its guides; perhaps they were not trying, perhaps they did not care for Quebec, only for Quebec in relation to the war.

It reminded me of a conversation long ago with the wife of the Soviet Ambassador. 'You should go,' she said to me, 'to Russia. You would enjoy it.' 'Yes,' said I, 'I should indeed.' And saw snowy steppes running towards dark forests, my jingling sleigh whirled along behind white horses, the flowery meadows and rich orchards of the Crimea, the golden domes of Kiev, the awful outline of the Kremlin … 'Yes,' I said, and kindled, 'I should enjoy seeing Russia.' 'You would like,' said the Ambassador's wife, with kindly firmness, and she kindled too, 'our schools, our hospitals, our factories, our prisons, our creches, our youth hostels, our public lavatories.' 'But no,' I corrected her. 'I don't like schools, hospitals, factories, prisons, creches, youth hostels, or public lavatories, even in England. I want to see the wild horses on the steppes, the Volga …' 'Our factories,' murmured the Ambassador's wife, 'our lavatories …' It was like an incantation. Her eyes shone with visions of that Russia that she desired me, that I did not desire, to see. We parted: all the Russias stretched enormously between us.

Similarly these showmen of Quebec and elsewhere. They believe — or determine — that news of factories falls like music on our ears, meeting a mood and a need. In an incalculable world, who shall say that they are always wrong? They may have received, through the delicate tentacles they put out, some encouragement in their strange view. To most of us, however, there is a dull, metallic unreality about these war-conditioned places.

But not all their places are thus marred. They can tell good and beautiful travellers' tales, of coral reefs, mountains, deserts, islands, beaches; they should tell more.

How does the BBC meet our craving for romance? Partly by descriptions of lovely and remote places such as the Barrier Reef or Rocky Mountains or Burma jungle; partly by stories of battle and adventure. Indeed, often the bare news is enough. The BBC admirably sends out envoys by sea, land, and air; they accompany bombers to Germany, go to sea in submarines, hover over the Atlantic looking for U-boats; march into the desert with the armies and bring back stories exciting in themselves and sometimes brilliantly told. I have heard few talks of finer colour and texture than the account last July by Commander Anthony Kimmins of the invasion of Sicily; it had tension, suspense, and all the quiet beauty of the dark dawn sea carrying the great Armada on to the ancient beaches of Europe. Almost all detailed accounts of the war overseas are welcomed; they are usually good, sometimes very good, and, even when not so, are what people want to hear. Several kinds of need meet here: the desire for news about our war and those fighting it, the liking for a good story, and the heroical-romantic mood that craves adventure. This last can be appeased by tales other than of this war; it was appeased one night by Colonel Walter Elliott (who has a good voice for it) in a brilliant and refreshingly irrelevant postscript about a Border battle.

From high adventure we are summoned too often to something the BBC calls 'planning for the future'. It is all very sensible, very drab, concerned with houses, building, social insurance, pensions, etc. Often the young and simple ('Youth') are organised in discussion meetings; they sound touchingly half-baked and callow, and are expressing themselves, even though led. The BBC has creditably avoided pandering to the soft-headed confusion of mind which believes that this war is being waged against Germany to end poverty, to improve housing, education, social legislation, or other domestic conditions in Great Britain, rather than to defeat Germany in her project of conquering Europe. But post-war, as distinct from war, aims are encouraged; and Sir William Beveridge, J B Priestley and others outline hopes for the future which have a comforting solidity, slices of pie in a sky not celestially remote. Criticism sometimes comes from those who prefer the pie to be kept on the top shelf of the larder and not taken down; in the eternal battle between Progress and Status Quo the BBC is successful in getting peppered from both sides. But Progress wins, hands down; one never hears a Status Quo talk or discussion. Interest in the pie is being well and intelligently fostered.

But it is an island pie. Those more interested in the inter-national skies are, except for the news, ill catered for. Here the BBC compares poorly with the Press. There are far too few talks about the European countries, except talks of the 'Behind-the-prison-bars' type. The general curiosity about what will happen in these countries after the bars are down is studiously unsatisfied. We are kept in the dark about the international problems, frontier problems, internal social, political, ethnographical problems, which will confront a liberated world. There are many speakers, both English and foreign, who could not solve, but might illuminate, these delicate and enthralling problems without indelicacy; that they do not do so must be policy. A misguided policy, for, as Mr Vernon Bartlett observes, in his interesting post-war diary of that name, tomorrow always comes. Information is what we want; information about political trends, forces and factions, international relationships, the latest developments in the shifting uneasy drama of Europe, news about the whole bloody chaos, as it has been well called. Lack of intelligent discussion of these things leads to dull and ignorant inertia, and will later, when the news all breaks, lead to cynicism. A series of talks about Europe should be arranged in some of the time now allotted to Urban District Councils, housing, the war effort; education in world affairs is as important as in national affairs; incidentally, it is immeasurably more exciting. Lack of it is, I think, the most serious lack in the BBC today, at one of the most important and fateful hours of history. There seems to be no adequate reason for it.

There might well be a Brains Trust to answer questions about Europe. For this kind of entertainment has caught the public fancy more, perhaps, than any other. It is not consistently amusing, but it is amusing often enough to raise weekly expectations. Some of its *habitués* know so much more than we do, and are so ready with admirable answers, that we listen awed. We get to know their merits and foibles, and should be disappointed if they did not do their tricks – if Dr Joad, for instance, should omit his tirade against women, or Commander Campbell his adventures among South Sea Islanders, or if Commander Gould or Dr Huxley should be caught out on a question. The standard of expectation has now been raised, for lately one of the Trust gave rein to his emotions and verbally assaulted another, and we all enjoy a scene, when safely removed from us by distance. The selection of questions is not always good; it seems waste of time in what should be a conversation piece and a flow of ideas to ask how gas is produced from coal, which any encyclopaedia can tell us. But the Brains Trust model is a good one. There is one Brains Trust which many of us would like to assemble and fire questions at – the seven governors of the BBC. Let me commend this suggestion to their attention. There is nothing that listeners would like better than to hear their questions dealt with and discussed among this authoritative council.

We have strange moods, and the BBC believes them even stranger than I do. It holds that we want ventriloquists, and news about war savings told at immense length, and other fantastic items. It also knows that we want almost infinite Variety, which age cannot wither nor custom stale, plays, stories, a very little poetry very late at night, when it is presumed that we shall be so drowsy as not to notice it, and fifteen minutes once a week about books. This last is a good feature (if feature is the word). The speakers have all been interesting, unpretentious and attractively interested in their subject. Perhaps Raymond Mortimer and V S Pritchett have the best broadcasting voices, with V Sackville-West and Cyril Connolly as good runners-up. (There are others, perhaps equally good, whom I have not heard.) This talk is on the Forces programme. A suggestion has lately been made by someone that all the rubbish, and only the rubbish, should be put on the Forces, leaving the Home programme free or better things. This would be hard on the minority listeners in canteens, hospitals, messes and elsewhere where the Forces programme is left continuously on; it would mean that they never heard anything but rubbish; as it is, the Forces has some lapses into intelligence, and the minority in a community can hear, from time to time, some real music or a talk, which is only fair. There is no doubt that listening conduces to selfishness, or such a suggestion could not have been made by a listener who has himself unhindered access to the better programme.

There is much else I should like to say, and no more space. But let me not end without a word of praise for the straightforward, unpretentious pieces of information handed out just after, or during, the midday meal, about how best to deal with goats, pigeons, rabbits, bees, pigs, crops and dung. These speakers have a thoroughness and earnest zest that endear: in a reeling world here, one feels, is sanity. Mr Middleton has the same quality; so to do many of the speakers in 'Country Magazine', as, for instance, the old countryman who said he didn't care for tractors on his land so well as horses, because tractors didn't make manure.

16 Notes on the Way

Time and Tide, 8 December 1945

'In the present débâcle of morality,' said the business man ...
I forget how he finished the sentence, but of course he was
right. His tone was matter-of-fact, as of one referring to an
accepted assumption, on which we had all to base the conduct
of our affairs and build for them such protection as we could.

Débâcle is right. The breaking up of the ice, the unbarring
of the gates, the rushing forth of the uninhibited, cruel,
predatory lusts of man, usually a little restrained by the age-
old grip of communal living, which weakens and fails in
confusion and crisis.

Observe the present scene; enquire of the police. Thieves
there have always been; today their number is astronomically
multiplied; the situation is quite out of hand. Black marketing,
loot stolen by occupying armies from the citizens whom
they have liberated or conquered, brought to London, Paris,
Moscow, New York, Amsterdam, to be sold at staggering
prices to fences, who resell them at prices more gratifying
still; it is the new piracy, and the pirates, the soldiers of
three continents, settle down affluently as loot-kings. Many
are deserters of long standing, who, finding military life a
burden too heavy to be sustained, flitted from it and crept
underground, men without those papers, those essential
scraps of cardboard, that at once reassure us as to our
identity and enable us to nourish and support it; lacking such
reassurance and comfort, these men without status, thinking
that they had to live, took up crime.

The plague has spread to civilians, and no possessions are safe. Shops – even bookshops – are watched by defeatist detectives, who, though they arrest hundreds of thieves a week, fail to arrest thousands more. Put down anything, literally anything (except bread, which is, in this country, too redundant even for thieves) for a moment in a public place, and it is gone. Books are stolen from the most respectable libraries, whose members were guaranteed honest by the householders who proposed them for membership; perhaps they were so once; perhaps the householders were too. But not now. People one had thought honestly reared (perhaps they were, perhaps their rearers knew no such stress as ours) will relate how they have bought clothing coupons somewhere, stuck them into their own books and used them; one would suppose a nervous and an anxious business. Others, or the same, boast openly how they have illegally come by petrol, made false income tax returns, any piece of crookery. Rich and poor are alike robbed; during the bombing some of the rescue and demolition workers pocketed what they could find of the scattered possessions of those who had lost nearly everything; 'they oughtn't,' said sardonic policemen, 'to be allowed those big pockets in their dungarees.'

The troops who guard the continent – and not only the Russian troops, though these are universally reported the most ruthless and efficient – despoil the helpless whom they encounter, and visit in plunder gangs the homes from which they have been expelled. Europe has, they say, become a nest of gangsters; many are ex-slave workers, many ex-partisans. The maquis training, so excellent for killing the enemy and wrecking his machinery, is proving also excellent for killing and robbing fellow-citizens, less good for leading a citizen's life oneself; the ex-guerrilla approaches such a life cumbered with too many identity cards, ration books and tommy-guns;

he knows his way too well about the farms and hen-roosts of
the countryside, and is what is called quick on the draw.

It is, of course, not only honesty and orderliness which
have receded; cruelty has immeasurably increased in these six
dreadful years. From the hideous torturings and massacres
on the continent, the reports of which sicken, then stun
and daze and perhaps harden, the minds of those who hear
and read them, cruelty slides down the scale, through the
car drivers who knock down their victims and speed away,
not waiting to discover if they have killed their man or can
still help him, down to the shabby, selfish callousness of
those who prefer that others should starve rather than that
their own fats or sugar should be cut. Racial and political
partisanship and hate have intensified into craziness; those of
opposed constitutional views snarl at each other like furious
cats, laying the general chaos of Europe at the door of their
particular foes. Left-wingers accuse Poles (I forget why
left-wingers dislike Poles; probably because Moscow does);
right-wingers blame Russians abroad and Jewish refugees
in Britain (I forget why right-wingers dislike Russians and
Jewish refugees); the Churches put it all down to the decline
in church-going; eschatologists to the final assault of the devil
on this world before its end; ordinary people just to the war.

But, differ as we may about its causes, everyone is agreed
about the fact, which is that morality is in a bad way. One
cannot deny. It is in a much worse way than it was in 1939;
or in 1913; or 1900, or … I am not sure how much further
back than the present century we can go. Some way, perhaps;
certainly during the last half of the nineteenth century there
was less active cruelty in most of Europe; people were more
shocked at torture, massacre, persecution; when Bulgars

were massacred in immense numbers by Turks, there were loud cries of indignation. There was less mass violence than today, though Britain was usually full of refugees, fled from the horrors of their native lands. But, if less violence, there was also less humanitarianism, less care for and expenditure on social welfare, more content that the poor should live in penury while the rich feasted, less provision for the old and sick. And that was in the age of the great humanitarian idealists.

Step back further down the dark and fearful corridors of human history; pause for a moment to hear the abolitionists describe the filthy horrors of the slave trade, the lashing to death of black workers for white planters in Jamaica; note the indifference of the average Briton, of those in high places in Church and State. A hundred years later similar atrocities in the Congo and Brazil roused this country to horror; we were more humane by a century. We were moving on, climbing a little up, the human conscience was developing. Or anyhow in this country. No longer did English prisoners rot in damp and rat-run dungeons, no longer were men and women flogged at the whipping-post watched by absorbed crowds, hanged for small thefts, transported, put as infants to work in mills and mines.

Travel back further, into the bawdy brutalities, the pillories, gibbets, chained lunatics, hunted beggars, huge meals, starvation, riots and bloody repressions of the Georges; into the cruel persecutions of the high-minded and enchanting seventeenth century, when, in the name of religion men tortured one another to death, when the most savage war in history wasted Europe for thirty years, when the modern Japanese order 'Kill cruelly' was observed by all penal codes as a matter of course, when old women were burned alive for witches and children of nine hanged for thieves, when people crowded round pillories to throw rotten eggs at the branded and mutilated victims, flocked to see painful executions, and howled execration if the victim died too soon. The sixteenth century was still more formidable, the fifteenth more so again. Read the Paston letters for the wild barbarity of English country life, with neighbouring squires breaking into one another's houses, murdering the owners, carrying off the ladies and the loot. And so back into the Middle Ages, with their brutalities, witch-burnings, Jew-torturings, cruelly ingenious punishments, and beyond into the devout and barbarous simplicities that engulfed the pride of Rome.

Human history is so enchanting, human thought weaved over it such a golden mesh of beauty and excitement, man has been in his higher manifestation so noble, so brilliant and so courageous, that the whole effect is that of a poem, whose rhythm and sweep and lovely incidental felicities carry us away. The cruelties, the stupidities, the horrors, the squalor, tend to be submerged in that entrancing and many-faceted stream. But it is well, when we complain of the immorality of today, to look more exactly into our past. War upheaves, blasts, turns up the earth, and its more revolting denizens (among human beings and in each human being) wriggle out from their lairs and take the field. This last war, the greatest in history, has done just this. Larger and more destructive in scope, it was not in detail so barbarous as many others. The classic example is the Thirty Years War. That its barbarities did not shock the public conscience so deeply as the barbarities of today is the measure of the advance of conscience and civilisation. Of this its most recent historian has written 'Bloodshed, rape, robbery, torture, and famine were less revolting to a people whose ordinary life was encompassed by them in milder forms. Robbery with violence was common enough in peace-time, torture was inflicted at most criminal trials, and prolonged executions were performed before great audiences ...' In short, society was, in all lands, a more than half savage affair, justice, liberty, humanity, often a mockery; war did not make all that difference.

As to the cruelties of war, only the doings of the Japanese in this war can compare with those of, say, the Napoleonic wars, when Spanish and Portuguese peasants used to crucify captured French soldiers on barn doors; or with the sacking of cities in the Thirty Years War or with the Black Prince's butchering of the citizens of Limoges, or indeed the general conduct of the English armies in France throughout the Hundred Years War, whose track was marked everywhere by pillage, rape, murder, and the burning of crops. As to French atrociousness one remembers the ghastly incidents of the Jacquerie of 1358, of the Huguenot persecutions, of the Revolution. 'I agree with you at shuddering at the cruelty of the horrid French', wrote Lady Bessborough to her little boys at Harrow in 1793. But there were the no less horrid Germans, Spanish, Russians, even British; in fact, it was a horrid world.

The Nazis are commonly said to have beaten all records in their behaviour to Jews. But Christian behaviour to Jews has nearly always, until comparatively lately, been dreadful. In medieval Europe they were periodically massacred by thousands; the Inquisition of the fifteenth and sixteenth centuries made them their especial concern; their money was dragged from them by the rack, their faith and race punished by fire. Even under Hitler, they were better off.

Morality has had a bad set-back, it is too true. It has slid back a little down the road towards the jungle of barbarism whence humanity has slowly climbed. But it is still some way above the level of even quite recent centuries, and there is no call for pessimism.

Miss Anstruther's Letters

First published in *London Calling*, ed. Storm Jameson
(London: Harper, 1942)

Miss Anstruther, whose life had been cut in two on the night
of May 10th, 1941, so that she now felt herself a ghost, without
attachments or habitation, neither of which she any longer
desired, sat alone in the bed-sitting-room she had taken, a
small room, littered with the grimy, broken and useless
objects which she had salvaged from the burnt-out ruins of
that wild night when high explosives and incendiaries had
rained on London and the water had run short: it was now a
gaunt and roofless tomb, a pile of ashes and rubble and burnt,
smashed beams. Where the floors of twelve flats had been
there was empty space. Miss Anstruther had for the first few
days climbed up to what had been her flat, on what had been
the third floor, swarming up pendent fragments of beams
and broken girders, searching and scrabbling among ashes
and rubble, but not finding what she sought, only here a pot,
there a pan, sheltered from destruction by an overhanging
slant of ceiling. Her marmalade for May had been there, and
a little sugar and tea; the demolition men got the sugar and
tea, but did not care for marmalade, so Miss Anstruther got
that. She did not know what else went into those bulging
dungaree pockets, and did not really care, for she knew it
would not be the thing she sought, for which even demolition
men would have no use; the flames, which take everything,
useless or not, had taken these, taken them and destroyed
them like a ravaging mouse or an idiot child.

After a few days the police had stopped Miss Anstruther
from climbing up to her flat any more, since the building was

scheduled as dangerous. She did not much mind; she knew by then that what she looked for was gone for good. It was not among the massed debris on the basement floor, where piles of burnt, soaked and blackened fragments had fallen through four floors to lie in indistinguishable anonymity together. The tenant of the basement flat spent her days there, sorting and burrowing among the chaotic mass that had invaded her home from the dwellings of her co-tenants above. There were masses of paper, charred and black and damp, which had been books. Sometimes the basement tenant would call out to Miss Anstruther, 'Here's a book. That'll be yours, Miss Anstruther'; for it was believed in Mortimer House that most of the books contained in it were Miss Anstruther's, Miss Anstruther being somewhat of a bookworm. But none of the books were any use now, merely drifts of burnt pages. Most of the pages were loose and scattered about the rubbish-heaps; Miss Anstruther picked up one here and there and made out some words. 'Yes', she would agree. 'Yes, that was one of mine.' The basement tenant, digging bravely away for her motoring trophies, said 'Is it one you wrote?' 'I don't think so', said Miss Anstruther. 'I don't think I can have …' She did not really know what she might not have written, in that burnt-out past when she had sat and written this and that on the third floor, looking out on green gardens; but she did not think it could have been this, which was a page from Urquhart's translation of Rabelais. 'Have you lost *all* your own?' the basement tenant asked, thinking about her motoring cups, and how she must get at them before the demolition men did, for they were silver. 'Everything', Miss Anstruther answered. 'Everything. They don't matter.' 'I hope you had no precious manuscripts', said the kind tenant. 'Books you were writing and that.' 'Yes', said Miss Anstruther, digging about among the rubble heaps. 'Oh yes. They're gone. They don't matter …'

She went on digging till twilight came. She was grimed from head to foot; her only clothes were ruined; she stood knee-deep in drifts of burnt rubbish that had been carpets, beds, curtains, furniture, pictures, and books; the smoke that smouldered up from them made her cry and cough. What she looked for was not there; it was ashes, it was no more. She had not rescued it while she could, she had forgotten it, and now it was ashes. All but one torn, burnt corner of notepaper, which she picked up out of a battered saucepan belonging to the basement tenant. It was niggled over with close small writing, the only words left of the thousands of words in that hand that she looked for. She put it in her note-case and went on looking till dark; then she went back to her bed-sitting-room, which she filled each night with dirt and sorrow and a few blackened cups.

She knew at last that it was no use to look any more, so she went to bed and lay open-eyed through the short summer nights. She hoped each night that there would be another raid, which should save her the trouble of going on living. But it seemed that the Luftwaffe had, for the moment, done; each morning came, the day broke, and like a revenant, Miss Anstruther still haunted her ruins, where now the demolition men were at work, digging and sorting and pocketing as they worked.

'I watch them close', said a policeman standing by. 'I always hope I'll catch them at it. But they sneak into dark corners and stuff their pockets before you can look round.'

'They didn't ought', said the widow of the publican who had kept the little smashed pub on the corner, 'they didn't ought to let them have those big pockets, it's not right. Poor people like us, who've lost all we had, to have what's left taken off us by *them* … it's not right.'

The policeman agreed that it was not right, but they were that crafty, he couldn't catch them at it.

Each night, as Miss Anstruther lay awake in her strange, littered, unhomely room, she lived again the blazing night that had cut her life in two. It had begun like other nights, with the wailing siren followed by the crashing guns, the rushing hiss of incendiaries over London, and the whining, howling, pitching of bombs out of the sky on to the fire-lit city. A wild, blazing hell of a night. Miss Anstruther, whom bombs made restless, had gone once or twice to the street door to look at the glowing furnace of London and exchange comments with the caretaker on the ground floor and with the two basement tenants, then she had sat on the stairs, listening to the demon noise. Crashes shook Mortimer House, which was tall and slim and Edwardian, and swayed like a reed in the wind to near bombing. Miss Anstruther understood that this was a good sign, a sign that Mortimer House, unlike the characters ascribed to clients by fortune-tellers, would bend but not break. So she was quite surprised and shocked when, after a series of close-at-hand screams and crashes, the fourth exploded, a giant earthquake, against Mortimer House, and sent its whole front crashing down. Miss Anstruther, dazed and bruised from the hurtle of bricks and plaster flung at her head, and choked with dust, hurried down the stairs, which were still there. The wall on the street was a pile of smoking, rumbling rubble, the Gothic respectability of Mortimer House one with Nineveh and Tyre and with the little public across the street. The ground-floor flats, the hall and the street outside, were scrambled and beaten into a common devastation of smashed masonry and dust. The little caretaker was tugging at his large wife, who was struck unconscious and jammed to the knees in bricks. The basement tenant, who had rushed up with her stirrup pump, began to tug too, so did Miss Anstruther. Policemen pushed in through the mess, rescue men and a warden followed, all was in train for rescue, as Miss Anstruther had so often seen it in her ambulance-driving.

'What about the flats above?' they called. 'Anyone in them?'

Only two of the flats above had been occupied, Miss Anstruther's at the back. Mrs Cavendish's at the front. The rescuers rushed upstairs to investigate the fate of Mrs Cavendish.

'Why the devil', enquired the police, 'wasn't everyone downstairs?' But the caretaker's wife, who had been downstairs, was unconscious and jammed, while Miss Anstruther, who had been upstairs, was neither.

They hauled out the caretaker's wife, and carried her to a waiting ambulance.

'Everyone out of the building!' shouted the police. 'Everyone out!'

Miss Anstruther asked why.

The police said there were to be no bloody whys, everyone out, the bloody gas pipe's burst and they're throwing down fire, the whole thing may go up in a bonfire before you can turn round.

A bonfire! Miss Anstruther thought, if that's so I must go up and save some things. She rushed up the stairs, while the rescue men were in Mrs Cavendish's flat. Inside her own blasted and twisted door, her flat lay waiting for death. God, muttered Miss Anstruther, what shall I save? She caught up a suitcase, and furiously piled books into it – Herodotus, *Mathematical Magick*, some of the twenty volumes of *Purchas his Pilgrimes*, the eight little volumes of Walpole's letters, *Trivia*, *Curiosities of Literature*, the six volumes of Boswell, then, as the suitcase would not shut, she turned out Boswell and substituted a china cow, a tiny walnut shell with tiny Mexicans behind glass, a box with a mechanical bird that jumped out and sang, and a fountain pen. No use bothering with the big books or the pictures. Slinging the suitcase across her back, she caught up her portable wireless set and her typewriter, loped downstairs, placed her salvage on the piled wreckage at what had been her street door, and started up the stairs again. As she reached the first floor, there was a burst and a hissing, a huge *pst–pst*, and a rush of flame leaped over Mortimer House as the burst gas caught and sprang to heaven, another fiery rose bursting into bloom to join that pandemonic red garden of night. Two rescue men, carrying Mrs Cavendish downstairs, met Miss Anstruther and pushed her back.

'Clear out. Can't get up there again, it'll go up any minute.'

It was at this moment that Miss Anstruther remembered the thing she wanted most, the thing she had forgotten while she gathered up things she wanted less.

She cried, 'I must go up again. I must get something out. There's time.'

'Not a bloody second', one of them shouted at her, and pushed her back.

She fought him. 'Let me go, oh let me go. I tell you I'm going up once more.'

On the landing above, a wall of flame leaped crackling to the ceiling.

'Go up be damned. Want to go through that?'

They pulled her down with them to the ground floor. She ran out into the street, shouting for a ladder. Oh God, where are the fire engines? A hundred fires, the water given out in some places, engines helpless. Everywhere buildings burning, museums, churches, hospitals, great shops, houses, blocks of flats, north, south, east, west and centre. Such a raid never was. Miss Anstruther heeded none of it: with hell blazing and crashing round her, all she thought was, I must get my letters. Oh, dear God, my letters. She pushed again into the inferno, but again she was dragged back. 'No one to go in there,' said the police, for all human life was by now extricated. No one to go in, and Miss Anstruther's flat left to be consumed in the spreading storm of fire, which was to leave no wrack behind. Everything was doomed – furniture, books, pictures, china, clothes, manuscripts, silver, everything: all she had thought of was the desk crammed with letters that should have been the first thing she saved. What had she saved instead? Her wireless, her typewriter, a suitcase full of books; looking round, she saw that all three had gone from where she had put them down. Perhaps they were in the safe keeping of the police, more likely in the wholly unsafe keeping of some rescue-squad man or private looter. Miss Anstruther cared little. She sat down on the wreckage of the road, sick and shaking, wholly bereft.

The bombers departed, their job well done. Dawn came, dim and ashy, in a pall of smoke. The little burial garden was like a garden in a Vesuvian village, grey in its ash coat. The air choked with fine drifts of cinders, Mortimer House still burned, for no one had put it out. A grimy warden with a note-book asked Miss Anstruther, have you anywhere to go?

'No', she said, 'I shall stay here.'

'Better to go to a rest centre,' said the warden, wearily doing his job, not caring where anyone went, wondering what had happened in North Ealing, where he lived.

Miss Anstruther stayed, watching the red ruin smouldering low. Some time, she thought, it will be cool enough to go into.

There followed the haunted, desperate days of search which found nothing. Since silver and furniture had been wholly consumed, what hope for letters? There was no charred sliver of the old locked rosewood desk which had held them. The burning words were burnt, the lines, running small and close and neat down the page, difficult to decipher, with the o's and

279

a's never closed at the top, had run into a flaming void and would never be deciphered more. Miss Anstruther tried to recall them, as she sat in the alien room; shutting her eyes, she tried to see again the phrases that, once you had made them out, lit the page like stars. There had been many hundreds of letters, spread over twenty-two years. Last year their writer had died; the letters were all that Miss Anstruther had left of him; she had not yet re-read them; she had been waiting till she could do so without the devastation of unendurable weeping. They had lain there, a solace waiting for her when she could take it. Had she taken it, she could have recalled them better now. As it was, her memory held disjointed phrases, could not piece them together. Light of my eyes. You are the sun and the moon and the stars to me. When I think of you life becomes music, poetry, beauty, and I am more than myself. It is what lovers have found in all the ages, and no one has ever found before. The sun flickering through the beeches on your hair. And so on. As each phrase came back to her, it jabbed at her heart like a twisting bayonet. He would run over a list of places they had seen together, in the secret stolen travels of twenty years. The balcony where they dined at the Foix inn, leaning over the green river, eating trout just caught in it. The little wild strawberries at Andorra la Vieja, the mountain pass that ran down to it from Ax, the winding road down into Seo d'Urgel and Spain. Lerida, Zaragoza, little mountain towns in the Pyrenees, Jaca, Saint Jean Pied-du-Port, the little harbour at Collioure, with its painted boats, morning coffee out of red cups at Villefranche, tramping about France in a hot July; truffles in the *place* at Perigueux, the stream that rushed steeply down the village street at Florac, the frogs croaking in the hills about it, the gorges of the Tarn, Rodez with its spacious *place* and plane trees, the little walled town of Cordes with the inn courtyard a jumble of sculptures, altar-pieces from churches, and ornaments from chateaux; Lisieux, with ancient crazy-floored inn, huge four-poster, and preposterous little saint (before the grandiose white temple in her honour had arisen on the hill outside the town), villages in the Haute-Savoie, jumbled among mountain rocks over brawling streams, the motor bus over the Alps down into Susa and Italy. Walking over the Amberley downs, along the Dorset coast from Corfe to Lyme on two hot May days, with a night at Chideock between, sauntering in Buckinghamshire beech-woods, boating off Bucklers Hard, climbing Dunkery Beacon to Porlock, driving on a June afternoon over Kirkdale pass … Baedecker starred places because we ought to see them, he wrote, I star them because we saw them together, and those stars light them up for ever … Of this kind had been many of the letters that had been for the last year all Miss Anstruther had left, except memory, of two-and-twenty years. There had been other letters about books, books he was reading, books she was writing; others about plans, politics, health, the weather, himself, herself, anything. I could have saved them, she kept thinking; I had the chance; but I saved a typewriter and a wireless set and some books and a walnut shell and a china cow, and even they are gone. So she would cry and cry, till tears blunted at last for the time the sharp edge of grief, leaving only a dull lassitude, an end of being. Sometimes she would take out and look at the charred corner of paper which was now all she had of her love; all that was legible of it was a line and a half of close small writing, the o's and the a's open at the top. It had been written twenty-one years ago, and it said, 'leave it at that. I know now that you don't care twopence; if you did you would'… The words, each time she looked at them, seemed to darken and obliterate a little more of the twenty years that had followed them, the years of the letters and the starred places and all they had had together. You don't care twopence, he seemed to say still; if you had cared twopence, you would have saved my letters, not your wireless and your typewriter and you china cow, least of all those little walnut Mexicans, which you know I never liked. Leave it at that.

Oh, if instead of those words she had found light of my eyes, or I think of the balcony at Foix, she thought she could have gone on living. As it is, thought Miss Anstruther, as it is I can't. Oh my darling, I did care twopence, I did.

Later, she took another flat. Life assembled itself about her again; kind friends gave her books; she bought another typewriter, another wireless set, and ruined herself with getting necessary furniture, for which she would get no financial help until after the war. She noticed little of all this that she did, and saw no real reason for doing any of it. She was alone with a past devoured by fire and a charred scrap of paper which said you don't care twopence, and then a blank, a great interruption, an end. She had failed in caring once, twenty years ago, and failed again now, and the twenty years between were a drift of grey ashes that once were fire, and she a drifting ghost too. She had to leave it at that.

Notes on the text

BY KATE MACDONALD

Non-Combatants and Others

Chapter 1

VAD: Volunteer Aid Detachment, in which untrained women volunteered for unskilled hospital jobs to release the trained nurses for more complex tasks. They wore a particularly nice uniform.

Belgians: there were many Belgian refugees in Britain, who had come over after the fall of Belgium at the beginning of the war.

special constable: volunteer member of civil defence and organisation.

frowsty: they are people who enjoy fresh air in all seasons, keep the windows open and their small fire is unlikely to make them sleepy with excessive warmth or smoke.

Antwerp: the port of Antwerp was bombed heavily by the German invasion.

Chesterton: possibly G K Chesterton, the noted literary figure, who had a large and imposing figure.

body belt: a wide, easily-knitted tube that keeps the torso warm, rather like a vest without sleeves or shoulders.

Zepps: Zeppelins, inflatable rigid airships that carried bombs.

'Mais elle est boiteuse, la pauvre petite': (Fr) 'But she is lame, the poor little girl'.

difficile: (Fr) difficult, socially awkward.

Hill 60: site of a protracted battle near Ypres in April and May 1915.

Hartmanns-weilerkopf: Hartmannsweiler Kopf / Hartmannswiller Kop, a large hill overlooking the Rhine Valley in the Vosges Mountains, site of extensive fighting throughout 1915.

Sedd el Bahr: Turkish village on the Gallipoli peninsula, where many British troops landed during the Gallipoli campaign in 1915.

Leon Gambetta: the *Léon Gambetta* was a French armoured cruiser that was sunk south of the Italian coast by an Austro-Hungarian submarine in April 1915.

It was headed obscurely: R + men + tears = Armentières. Soldiers were banned from mentioning their whereabouts in letters in case the enemy read them; their officers censored the letters.

strafed: shelled, shot at with high intensity fire.

stand to: army command for men to get into formation and stand at attention, awaiting orders.

made into a French landlord: his body is now occupying a piece of French land.

Blighty: seriously wounded soldiers were sent back to Blighty (Britain), whereas the slighter wounds could be dealt with in France, and the men sent back to the front quickly. A 'Blighty wound' was a guarantee of at least a couple of months away from the war, if not longer, but could of course also mean death.

peri: periscope, widely available from the Army and Navy Stores and other suppliers catering for soldiers' extra supplies.

perdu: (Fr) lost, hidden.

your enemies: Alix's father was Polish, and had died in a Russian prison.

Chapter 2

Minnie: the British Army slang name for the shell from the German Minnenwerfer trench mortar.

tussore, shantung: types of silk dress fabric.

dug-outs: shelters and huts hollowed out from the sides of the trenches, reinforced with wooden beams, doors and walls. They were slightly more bombproof than being in the open.

six courses: it's difficult to know whether Macaulay wants us to think that John is being cheerfully and distractingly facetious, or simply lying out of desperation to keep his ignorant family's conversation away from the things he cannot discuss at a civilised dinner table, and which fill his sleeping mind.

Friends: Quakers, who are more formally called Members of the Religious Society of Friends. They were active in peace work.

Union of Democratic Control: a British organisation with pacifist leanings that lobbied for less military involvement in government decisions.

Newnham: one of the University of Cambridge's women's colleges.

Royal Free: the Royal Free Hospital, Hampstead, north London.

Trinity Hall: another Cambridge college.

'Peace, peace, where there is no peace': Jeremiah 6.14, which correctly reads 'Peace, peace, when there is no peace'.

Clive Bell: prominent art critic and member of the Bloomsbury Group.

Laocoon: Laocoon was a Trojan priest from Greek mythology who was attacked with his two sons by giant serpents. His name is a metaphor for being in an impossible and deadly tangle.

Chapter 4

Marcus Stone: prominent Victorian painter, well-known for his large realist paintings on sentimental and emotional subjects.

Landseer: Sir Edwin Landseer is most famous for his imposing paintings and sculptures of wildlife, particularly Scottish stags and the stone lions in Trafalgar Square.

Evening Thrill: an invented cheap evening newspaper.

Mrs Blankley: an invented generic 'lady novelist', probably intended to represent a productive class of Victorian romantic novelists.

little here below: a quotation from Oliver Goldsmith's *The Vicar of Wakefield*.

commence breakfast: Kate uses this fussy and consciously genteel phrase, aspiring to sound correct, to show that she is concerned what people will think of her.

Continuous Mediation without Armistice: later to be called the Wisconsin Plan, this was a method of mediation devised by the American peace activist Julia Grace Wales in 1914, and supported by the International Congress of Women. President Wilson was in favour of this approach until the sinking of the *Lusitania* in 1915, and the Plan would lose all momentum by the time the USA entered the war in 1917.

sal volatile: smelling salts, whose strong ammonia smell encouraged the lungs to work harder to get more oxygen into the blood.

Daily Message: an invented cheap daily newspaper.

feuilleton: a serialised story, often illustrated by cheap reused engravings, that was a staple feature in cheap daily and weekly newspapers of the period.

tongue: ox tongue was a standard cold cut of meat, here used for Sunday when cooking was not done for religious reasons, or to let the servants have time off.

Home Chat: a very popular women's magazine that supplied dress-making patterns to its readers.

Chapter 5

the Great Man: Lord Kitchener's full-face portrait was a ubiquitous feature in recruiting posters for the war.

ABC: a chain of inexpensive tea-rooms.

hospital blues: soldiers under treatment or convalescing in hospital wore a special blue uniform with red facings.

flip-flapping, wiggle-waggling, and joywheeling: references to the names of amusement rides at the Earl's Court entertainment grounds, which would be replaced in the 1930s.

Golders Green Garden City: this is probably Hampstead Garden Suburb, located east of Golders Green, founded in 1906 and notable for its open spaces and gardens for each house.

Cambridge Magazine: a new (and would be short-lived) intellectual magazine (1912-22) commenting on politics and the war.

futurists: movement of artists who advocated the breaking down of civilisation to destroy its ills and rebuild from a clean beginning.

my before-breakfast proceedings: West means his spiritual exercises, also conducted in the evening.

ASC: Army Service Corps, responsible for supplying serving units with transport, barracks and other supplies.

UDC: Union of Democratic Control (see above).

Chapter 6

Octavia Wills: Octavia Hill (whom Miss Simon means) was a Victorian social reformer, one of the founders of the National Trust, and created many large housing developments.

Christabel and Co: Christabel Pankhurst, her mother Emmeline and sister Sylvia, were prominent campaigners for votes for women, sometimes with militant action.

''The poor ye shall have always with you': Mark 14.7, which should read, 'For you have the poor with you always, and whenever you wish you may do them good'. Miss Simon's instincts are correct.

Chapter 7

iodo-form: a disinfectant.

super: superintendent, the senior nurse present.

capeline bandage: a bandage covering the head or rounded end of an amputation like a cap.

Bei uns geht's immer so: (Ger) 'It's always the same with us!'

in die Nacht Quartier: (Ger) 'In the night quarter'.

'Heil'ge Nacht, Heil'ge Nacht': (Ger) 'Holy Night, Holy Night'.

'Mein Bi-er und Wei-ein fri-isch und klar: he is singing 'Der Wirtin Töchterlein', an early nineteenth-century German ballad about the landlady's daughter.

Chapter 8

Cox's: a private bank.

Cook's tour: Thomas Cook's was the first and the most well-known British tour company.

driving a motor ambulance: the closest women could get to serving on the front line in the war was to drive ambulances or motor-cycles as messengers.

Miss Tucker: Basil hasn't realised or is too distracted to have noticed that Kate Tucker is the elder of the sisters, and so she is, in correct etiquette, Miss Tucker. Evie would be Miss Evie Tucker to denote her junior status.

brawn: a jellied preserve of the meat from a boiled pig's head.

Lord Derby: the Earl of Derby, Secretary of State for War, and instigator of the Derby Scheme which strongly encouraged men to join up by requiring them to make a public declaration of their willingness to serve.

Chapter 9

DCM: Distinguished Conduct Medal, awarded for gallantry in the field.

foot-warmer: a flat metal container for hot water, covered with carpet, on which cold passengers could put their feet.

jingoism: excessive, aggressive and ostentatious displays of patriotism.

Hymn of Hate: an aggressively nationalistic German patriotic poem by Ernst Lissauer, published in 1914 in Germany and in the USA (then a neutral state) and distributed to the troops of the Crown Prince of Bavaria.

Deptford riots: anti-German demonstrations of violence in Deptford, south-east London, in October 1914.

five bob: five shillings in the pound, a tax rate of about 25%.

Defence of the Realm Act: this was enacted in 1914 with a number of subsequent revisions to censor and control publications during wartime that might be prejudicial to the morale of the troops.

Old Moore: *Old Moore's Almanac* was an annual ready reference guide that carried lists of predictions for the future.

Chapter 10

Faber: Frederick William Faber, nineteenth-century Catholic priest and noted English hymn-writer.

Dr Watts: Isaac Watts was an eighteenth-century Congregationalist and prolific writer of hymns popular in the non-conformist tradition.

Girls' Friendly Society: nineteenth-century Christian organisation for the welfare of working-class girls.

Associate: a rather prissy way of describing a 'follower' or boyfriend.

Hymns A and M: Hymns Ancient and Modern, the standard hymnal for the Anglican church.

'Tis only your estrangèd faces: from the poem 'In No Strange Land' by Francis Thompson.

'I will not cease': lines from William Blake's 1804 poem 'Jerusalem', which became popular in Britain in 1916, in an anthology edited by Poet Laureate Robert Bridges, which post-dates the action of the novel. Its use as a hymn is the likely reason for its use here, as well as for the Radical tendencies of this preacher.

about a pilgrim: John Bunyan's seventeenth-century hymn 'He who would true valour see'.

mustard leaf: a prepared poultice of mustard-seed powder inside a protective dressing, applied for chest infections and aches and pains.

Dommage: (Fr) 'What a pity'.

Chapter 11

cocaine: cocaine was a standard ingredient in painkillers at this period; Alix may have used a liquid version applied by a dropper, like oil of cloves.

fancies: small decorated cakes iced in bright colours.

Hall man: Trinity Hall, Cambridge.

sweated girls: women workers paid a pittance for long hours and hard, often dangerous work.

Chapter 12

Buszard's: long-established bakery and confectioner's on London's Oxford Street.

the Board: the Medical Board that determined whether a soldier was fit to go back to his duties or not.

Peacock Pie: 1913 collection of poetry for children by Walter de la Mare.

turning knife: small curved knife used for trimming vegetables.

Chapter 13

Sturm und Drang: (Ger) 'storm and stress', from the eighteenth-century German Romantic movement in literature, art and music, used to label moments of high emotional drama.

Chapter 14

Economics Tripos: a three-part (equivalent to three years) course in Economics at the University of Cambridge.

Fitzwilliam Hall: the early incarnation of the present-day Fitzwilliam College, founded in the nineteenth century as a base for male students who could not afford to become members of a college to study at Cambridge.

here's eightpence: Daphne is calculating how much she should give the porter as a tip, based on his weekly wage and number of dependent children.

eurhythmics: method of teaching music through movement, and often used in this period to cover all kinds of physical exercise with an aesthetic element.

Summertown: formerly a village north of Oxford, now within Oxford itself. Well-to-do tradesmen built large villas there in the nineteenth century, and for that reason, and the relaxation of the rule that forbade Oxford dons to marry, was considered in the twentieth century to be a less desirable address for *haute* Oxford society than, say, living in college or in a country house. Nancy Mitford and John Betjeman would both be rude about north Oxford in their critiques of Oxford society.

ovaltine: a patent malt extract drink made with hot milk, sometimes also chocolate, advertised as an encouragement to sleep.

hyperaesthesia: a condition of feeling overstimulated in the senses.

Cowper: celebrated Romantic poet.

knew no difference between high and low: at this period the liturgical differences between the Protestant non-conformist churches and chapels (low) and the Established Church of England and its variants heading towards Catholicism (high), were expressed outwardly in church architecture and what the officiating minister wore, and usually correlated to class strata as well. For Daphne to pay no attention to these fundamental divisions in British society makes her very unusual, and also intellectually haughty for dismissing matters by which a great many of her fellow British citizens organised their lives.

to abolish Greek in Responsions: to allow new students at Oxford to not meet a basic standard in Greek, that is, opening up the university to students who had gone to state schools where Greek was not taught.

Chapter 15

Queen's Hall: a large concert hall and auditorium in central London.

Romain Rolland: French dramatist and novelist who won the 1915 Nobel Prize for Literature.

Bernhardi: Prussian military historian and theorist, advocating an aggressive approach that ignored treaties.

pretty badly sold: as in sold down the river, or cheated.

Si vis bellum, para bellum: the correct Latin phrase is *Si vis pacem, para bellum,* 'If you would have peace, prepare for war', meaning that the best conditions for peace are those in place when war can be waged, but is not.

Fellowship of Reconciliation: international and national religious movements advocating peace.

National Service League: a pro-militarism group founded in 1902 to pressure the government into instituting national service and redress Britain's apparent inadequate preparations for war.

WSPU: the Women's Social and Political union, the leading militant suffragette movement campaigning for women's right to the vote.

Anti-Suffrage Society: the British movement that rejected the need for women to have the vote, arguing that women were better placed to influence politics through men.

Union of Democratic Control: see above.

Anti-German League: a group that lobbied for the removal of Germans from British civil society and positions of authority; its secretary would be tried for fraud in 1917.

Chapter 16

Mr Ponsonby: Member of Parliament who opposed Britain's entry into the war, and was an early member of the Union for Democratic Control.

Lord Bryce: distinguished academic and diplomat, author of the 1915 Bryce Report which became an influential source of much anti-German propaganda and atrocity stories, many of which were widely republished, before it was found that many were also unfounded.

'of all England the shire for men who understand': from Rupert Brooke's 1912 poem 'The Old Vicarage, Grantchester'. Macaulay and Brooke had been friends before the war.

Great Shelford: Cambridgeshire village and Macaulay's home from her early teens.

Russian fairy-stories: Arthur Ransome published his collection of Russian fairy stories, *Old Peter's Russian Tales*, in 1916. Perhaps Nicholas had received an early review copy.

Chapter 17

from Fruges to Lillers: a journey of 37 miles east towards the front line south of Ypres.

Moussorgsky: Mussorgsky was a nineteenth-century Russian Romantic composer, whose works include the opera *Boris Gudonov* and the piano suite *Pictures at an Exhibition*.

Essays and journalism, 1936–1945

1 Marginal Comments, 3 January 1936

Alice: from *Alice in Wonderland*, a story frequently used as a metaphor for politics.

2 Marginal Comments, 24 January 1936

Archbishop Laud: Archbishop of Canterbury during the reign of Charles I, who was executed during the Civil War.

Bishop Berkeley: eighteenth-century Irish philosopher who developed a theory of immaterialism, which argued that physical substance only existed in the mind.

those aerial voices: radio broadcasts.

3 Marginal Comments, 6 March 1936

Peace! Peace beautiful peace: from the Methodist hymn by Warren D Cornell.

Rajah of Bhong: a character in the musical comedy *A Country Girl* (1902).

vengeance and victory: this was written during the Second Italo-Ethiopian War, by which Italy annexed large parts of East Africa.

4 Marginal Comments, 27 March 1936

the Leader: Sir Oswald Mosley, leader of the British Union of Fascists.

Holy Rollers, Shakers: North American sects whose adherents succumb to violent physical movement during their devotions.

5 Marginal Comments, 1 May 1936

Pelagius: a fifth-century theologian who supported free will in religion.

6 Marginal Comments, 14 May 1936

occupatio bellico: ownership through military occupation, normally temporary.

occupatio justa: ownership through the law.

League: the League of Nations.

Monophysite: the theological position that after the Incarnation, Jesus Christ was either human, or a mixture of divine and human, or divine, which is in opposition to the view held by the Church of England, for example, that Christ was simultaneously human and divine.

'C'e un vecchio proverbio inglese, might ees right': (Ital) 'There is an old English proverb, might is right.' Macaulay spent her childhood years in Italy.

7 Marginal Comments, 16 October 1936

Purchas: seventeenth-century English clergyman who collected and published travellers' tales.

Abassins: archaic name for Abyssinians, from the region now called Ethiopia.

8 Marginal Comments, 30 October 1936

Howard Marshall: a journalist and BBC radio broadcaster, he would become famous for his sports commentaries.

Jarrow: the Jarrow March took place in October 1936, as an organised protest against unemployment and poverty in the north of England.

9 Marginal Comments, 29 July 1937

Mr Eden: Anthony Eden was the Foreign Secretary.

Hyde Park: Speakers' Corner in Hyde Park in London is the traditional place to hear speeches of protest.

10 Apeing the Barbarians, 1937

Harry Lauder: popular Scottish comedian and singer.

Max Plowman: British writer and pacifist, founder of the Adelphi Centre which ran on communal lines and hosted an influential summer school in 1936.

11 Notes on the way, 5 October 1940

Naomi Royde-Smith: Macaulay shared a flat with Royde-Smith during the First World War.

13 Looking in on Lisbon, 1 July 1943

Leslie Howard: English actor and producer, who died when his BOAC plane was shot down by the German air force on 1 June 1943 on its way from Lisbon to Britain.

CD car: a member of the Corps Diplomatique, who had diplomatic privileges.

Adolf, Benito, Francisco: Hitler, Mussolini, Franco.

14 A Happy Neutral, 9 July 1943

Iberia Unida: a united Iberia, that is, the uniting of Spain and Portugal into one state.

Führers and Duces and Caudillos: the political titles of Hitler, Mussolini and Franco.

quinta: country estate and vineyard.

'Ce sont retraités de paresseux qui vivaient, comme on dit, de la sueur du peuple, genre d'alimentation peu ragoûtant, mais qui nous a donné, somme tout, presque tout ce qu'il y a d'admirable sur la terre': (Fr) 'They were the retreats of the lazy who lived, as they say, on the sweat of the people, an unpleasant kind of food, but which gave us, after all, almost everything there is admirable on earth.'

15 The BBC and War Moods, January 1944

Svendsen: Johann Svendsen, a nineteenth-century Norwegian composer and musician.

Bax: Sir Arnold Bax, modern English composer and author.

Walton: Sir William Walton, English composer most famous for his collaboration with Dame Edith Sitwell on *Façade*.

Noel Coward's famous song: his satirical song 'Don't let's be beastly to the Germans' (1943) did not translate well on radio without his visual comedy performance, and after complaints the BBC banned the song from its broadcasts.

Anthony Kimmins: Kimmins was a naval officer in the First World War, then became an actor and director. He rejoined the Navy in the Second World War, and his account of the invasion of Sicily from 22 July 1943 was recorded as a British Pathé newsreel.

Beveridge: William Beveridge was a Liberal politician and social reformer. His 1942 report *Social Insurance and Allied Services* (also known as the Beveridge Report) laid the foundations for the modern British welfare state.

J B Priestley: novelist, essayist and broadcaster with a talent for conveying the opinion of the reasonable and friendly Englishman.

Brains Trust: a popular and long-running BBC radio programme in which noted experts and public figures answered questions sent in by the public.

Mr Middleton: C H Middleton was one of the earliest radio gardening experts.

16 Notes on the Way, 8 December 1945

maquis: the French Resistance.

Paston letters: a collection of fifteenth-century letters between members of the Norfolk Paston family.

Miss Anstruther's Letters

the little public: the little public house, the pub.

stirrup pump: a hand-operated pump to pump out water from a flooded basement.

More Handheld Press titles

Discover more of our books about pacifism,
and more of our books by Rose Macaulay

A Quaker Conscientious Objector

Wilfrid Littleboy's Prison Letters, 1917–1919

Edited by Rebecca Wynter and Pink Dandelion

In 1914 Wilfrid Littleboy (1885-1986) was a Quaker living in Birmingham in the English Midlands. By the end of the First World War, he had served time in Wormwood Scrubs and in Dorchester Prison in the west of England. Published for the first time, this private collection of his prison letters tells how this middle-class accountant came to be incarcerated for his pacifist beliefs. The letters follow Wilfrid's decision as an absolutist conscientious objector to go voluntarily to prison in 1917 rather than join the armed forces. He served his prison sentences cheerfully, with an abiding faith in his choice, and an increased awareness of working-class politics.

Prefaced by an extensive introduction by two Quaker historians, Wilfrid's letters bring to life the realities of conscience, military discipline, and early twentieth-century prisons through his reading, reflection and his work. The letters are uplifting and engaging, vividly telling the story of hope through faith, books and nature, alongside the daily endurance of prison conditions in wartime Britain.

Wilfrid Littleboy went on to hold national Quaker leadership roles in the UK. His experience as a CO helped sustain in British law the right to conscientiously object to war.

paperback £15.99
ISBN 978-1-912766-27-7

The Conscientious Objector's Wife

Letters Between Frank and Lucy Sunderland, 1916–1919

Edited by Kate Macdonald

Frank and Lucy Sunderland, English pacifists and fervent supporters of Labour politics and the Garden City movement, were separated in 1916 when Frank was given his prison sentence for being a conscientious objector. They wrote to each other from November 1916 until April 1919, while Frank was incarcerated at Wandsworth and Bedford prisons. Lucy looked after their three children in Letchworth, and earned enough to keep the family afloat by keeping hens, collecting insurance premiums and taking in sewing.

   This unique collection of letters from a private family archive is important as a working-class record of wartime experience. These letters show how their shared ideology of a socialist pacifism upheld the couple in separation, planning for a better future in a more equal society for all. The letters give contemporary evidence of events on the Letchworth Home Front: spotting airships, food rationing, hearing the London air-raids, the arrival of 'Spanish flu' in 1918, and the sufferings of the European civilian populations immediately after the war.

hardback £19.99
ISBN 978-1-9998813-6-8

What Not

A Prophetic Comedy

by Rose Macaulay

Rose Macaulay

What Not

A Prophetic Comedy

What Not is Rose Macaulay's speculative novel of post-First World War eugenics and newspaper manipulation that influenced Aldous Huxley's *Brave New World*.

Published in 1918, *What Not* was hastily withdrawn due to a number of potentially libellous pages, and was reissued in 1919, but had lost its momentum. Now republished for the first time with the suppressed pages reinstated, *What Not* is a lost classic of feminist protest at social engineering, and rage at media manipulation.

Kitty Grammont and Nicholas Chester are in love. Kitty is certified as an A for breeding purposes, but politically ambitious Chester has been uncertificated, and may not marry. Kitty wields power as a senior civil servant in the Ministry of Brains, which makes these classifications, but does not have the freedom to marry who she wants. The popular press, determined to smash the brutal regime of the Ministry of Brains, has found out about Kitty and Chester, and scents an opportunity for a scandalous exposure.

The Introduction is by Sarah Lonsdale, senior lecturer in journalism at City University London.

'Her writing is stirring, funny, uniquely imaginative. This book should not be forgotten again' — *The Guardian*

'*What Not* is a forgotten gem in a prolific career' — *The Times*

paperback £12.99
ISBN 978-1-912766-03-1

Rose Macaulay
Potterism
A Tragi-Farcical Tract
A novel in which truth battles slander.

Potterism
A Tragi-Farcical Tract
by Rose Macaulay

Rose Macaulay's 1920 satire on British journalism and the newspaper industry is about the Potter newspaper empire, and the ways in which journalists struggled to balance the truth and what would sell, during the First World War and into the 1920s. When Jane and Johnny Potter are at Oxford they learn to despise their father's popular newspapers, though they still end up working for the family business. But Jane is greedy, and wants more than society will let her have.

Mrs Potter is a well-known romantic novelist, whose cheap novelettes appear in the shop-girls' magazines. She has become unable to distinguish fact from fiction, and her success gives her an unhealthy estimation of her own influence. Arthur Gideon resists the fake news and gushing sentiment peddled by the Potter press, but an unexpected tragedy binds him even closer to their influence.

The Introduction is by Sarah Lonsdale, senior lecturer in journalism at City University London.

paperback £12.99
ISBN 978-1-912766-33-8